ONCE BURNED,

TWICE SPY

Book 13 of the NEVER SAY SPY series

Diane Henders

Since You Asked...

People frequently ask if my protagonist, Aydan Kelly, is really me.

Yeah, you got me. These novels are an autobiography of my secret life as a government agent, working with highly-classified computer technology... Oh, wait, what's that? You want the *truth*? Um, you do realize fiction writers get paid to lie, don't you?

...well, shit, that's not nearly as much fun. It's also a long story.

I swore I'd never write fiction. "Too personal," I said. "People read novels and automatically assume the author is talking about him/herself."

Well, apparently I lied about the fiction-writing part. One day a story sprang into my head and wouldn't leave. The only way to get it out was to write it down. So I did.

But when I wrote that first book, I never intended to show it to anyone, so I created a character that looked like me just to thumb my nose at the stereotype. I've always had a defective sense of humour, and this time it turned around and bit me in the ass.

Because after I'd written the third novel, I realized I actually wanted other people to read my books. And when I went back to change my main character to *not* look like me, my beta readers wouldn't let me. They rose up against me and said, "No! Aydan is a tall woman with long red hair and brown eyes. End of discussion!"

Jeez, no wonder readers get the idea that authors write about themselves. So no, I'm not Aydan Kelly. I just look like her.

Oh, and the town of Silverside and all secret technologies

are products of my imagination. If I'm abducted by grim-faced men wearing dark glasses, or if I die in an unexplained fiery car crash, you'll know I accidentally came a little too close to the truth.

I hope you enjoy the book!

For Phill

Thank you for being my technical advisor and the most tolerant husband ever. Much love!

To my beta readers/editors, especially Carol H., Judy B., and Phill B., with gratitude: Many thanks for all your time and effort in catching my spelling and grammar errors, telling me when I screwed up the plot or the characters' motivations, and generally keeping me honest.

To Cassie at Crowe Photography: Thank you for coming all the way up here from Victoria! Your flexibility and expertise made the photo shoot easy, even for a camera-hater like me.

To everyone else, respectfully:

Canadian English is an unholy hybrid of British and American English, so I apologize if spellings in this book look odd to you. But if you find typos, please send an email to errors@dianehenders.com. Mistakes drive me nuts, and I'm sorry if any slipped through. Please let me know what the error is, and on which page. I'll make sure it gets fixed as soon as possible. Thanks!

CHAPTER 1

My heart was already thumping too fast when I sidestepped into the dark alley with my Glock at the ready.

My head wasn't in the game. Good way to get myself killed. Focus, dammit...

A clank from behind a garbage dumpster was my only warning before a shadowy figure lunged out.

Man with an assault rifle.

A blaze of adrenaline made me pull my shot just a fraction, but my bullet still hit his chest. He dropped.

Pulse jackhammering, I crept forward to press my back against the wall of the building. What was around that corner? If I poked my head out, would somebody shoot it off?

I eased down into a crouch.

Slow breath.

In.

Out for the count of three.

A quick peek...

A vicious crack made me jerk backward as a bullet struck the building where my head would have been if I'd been standing.

I scuttled back the way I'd come, past the blank gaze of the dead man beside the dumpster.

Dammit, why had I gotten myself into this?

A flash of movement to my left.

I pivoted, my pistol jerking up and my trigger finger already tightening.

"*Shit!*" The word left me in a breathless squeak as I snatched my finger out of the trigger guard. A young girl stared at me wide-eyed from only a few yards away, her face a pale oval in the murk.

Hands shaking, I was turning away when I glimpsed her reaching upward.

Toward the trigger rigged to her explosive vest...

My bullet caught her between the eyes, slapping her to the pavement an instant before she would have blown us both to oblivion.

Horror gripped my throat, but I had no time to indulge it. A bearded turban-clad man charged out of the darkness yelling, his face contorted as he brandished a long black object.

My sights snapped to his chest.

An instant later I sucked in a hard breath and swung my weapon aside to let the innocent commuter race past me, still waving his black umbrella and shouting at a departing bus.

Another bullet ricocheted nearby with a malevolent whine. I slammed my back against the nearest building, my blood pressure ratcheting up to near-stroke levels.

Enough.

"Let's end this!" I yelled, my voice raw with tension.

"Already?" The response was taunting, and my temper ignited like a hissing fuse.

I managed not to let it explode into bellowed obscenities. "Yeah," I snapped. "I'm done."

The lights came on and I holstered my Glock before the

range director could see how much my hands were trembling. Sliding my acoustic earmuffs down around my neck, I pulled out my earplugs and pocketed them as I made for the door of the simulator.

Braced for insults, I stepped out.

The dour-faced man eyed me with a sardonic twist to his mouth. "Don't tell me the great Aydan Kelly lost her nerve."

I gave him a level look. "No, I just remembered I've got a meeting at one and I need to get ready."

As if I could forget Stemp's damn meeting. That's why I couldn't focus in the first place.

Disbelief dripped from the range director's tone. "Yeah, sure. A meeting. That's why you chickened out after two minutes." His lips curled in a smile that was probably supposed to look like friendly teasing but didn't quite make it past a sneer. "You almost shot that non-combatant, too. Better be careful. Hate to see you lose your title as the oldest female agent to pass requalification."

Usually I could let his bullshit roll off my back, but today...

My teeth came together with an audible click as I battled the urge to smash my elbow into his grin. Or at least remind him that my forty-eight-year-old muscle and fitness could kick his paunchy fiftyish ass any day...

I did neither.

"Have I *ever* shot a non-combatant?" I growled.

His unpleasant smile widened. "You mean, besides the three you killed last year?"

"That was the first time I'd ever been in the simulator," I grated. "I haven't killed a single non-combatant since. And I've had a one hundred percent kill rate for hostiles; and a zero percent kill rate for myself. And I do this at least twice a month, usually more. Who else has that kind of record?"

"John Kane." His grin was cocky now that I'd risen to his bait.

"He's not an agent anymore," I snapped.

The range director's smile slipped a bit, but he rallied immediately. "Greg Holt."

To hell with this pissing contest.

I eased my jaw muscles and gave him my nicest smile. "Being compared to top agents like Kane and Holt is a huge compliment. Thanks, that makes my day!"

I used his moment of stunned silence to flee.

At the top of the stairs I took a slow breath to prepare for imminent claustrophobia, then activated the retinal scan to leave the secured area. When the heavy door of the exit chamber closed behind me with a subdued thump, I stepped hurriedly forward to trigger the next scan. Then I closed my eyes and counted down the long thirty seconds before the next door opened to freedom.

There was plenty of air in the chamber. I wouldn't suffocate.

Much.

Only a few more seconds. Breathe...

When the chamber released me at last I scurried out into the lobby of Sirius Dynamics, mentally congratulating myself on making it through the chamber without hyperventilating. Take that, claustrophobia.

Still, though, maybe I'd just step outside for a few minutes. To check messages on my cell phone.

Right.

I tossed my security fob to the guard in his bulletproof

glass wicket and made a beeline for the door.

When I stepped outside, a stinging faceful of wind-driven snow scoured away my claustrophobia in an instant. I spat an expletive and huddled into the dubious shelter of the doorway to take out my cell phone, my fingers already chilling in the bitter cold.

The display showed three new messages from my best friend, and I groaned. Bridezilla was on the rampage again. But at least listening to Nichele's wedding chatter would keep me from thinking about my upcoming meeting.

What if I was getting assigned to a new mission?

"I spent the past month preparing, dammit," I growled into the blustering wind. "I'm ready!"

And I had been certain of that, until I got the meeting request and all my doubts and fears came rushing back...

Don't think about it.

I touched the Play icon.

"Hey, girl!" Nichele's perky voice lilted out of the speaker. "This is your daily nag! Have you picked out your dress yet? I'm buying a tie for Dave's best man, and I want it to match your dress. Oh, and you won't believe what I caught the caterer planning! And the florist; oh-em-gee, Aydan, it's like the guy's got some kind of mental *block!* Wait 'til you hear..." I tuned out the rest of her wedding woes until she concluded, "...call me ASAP, 'kay?"

The other two messages contained more cheerful nagging about the damn dress. Shivering, I punched the speed dial for her number and wrapped my free arm around myself in an attempt to conserve some body heat.

Nichele picked up with a triumphant crow on the second ring. "Aydan! Finally! I thought you'd fallen off the face of the earth, girl! Or gotten lost in this blizzard. The news says there have been over two hundred accidents in Calgary since six this morning. Is it snowing up there in Silverside, too?"

"Snowing to b-beat shit," I agreed, my teeth beginning to chatter. "And m-minus twenty and windy as all hell. I'm f-freezing my ass off."

As I spoke the words Clyde Webb bounded up the steps, his skinny six-foot-two camouflaged by a puffy hooded parka and a striped scarf that muffled him nose to chin. I mouthed 'Hi Spider' and gave him as cheery a wave as I could muster with a half-frozen hand.

He shot a watery-eyed frown at my coatless condition, then shucked off his jacket and dropped it over my shoulders despite my headshake. Countering my mute protest, he gave me a firm nod and a pat on the arm before whisking through the doors of Sirius.

I huddled gratefully into his warm parka and returned my attention to Nichele.

"...so Mitch, the best man..." she was saying. "...would you believe, the only suit and tie he had was the one he wore to his high school graduation thirty years ago? Truckers! So I already bought him a suit but we have to get your dress soon, girl, so I can buy him a matching tie! You remember the wedding's in *three days*, right? You know most brides have all this stuff settled *months* before their weddings, right?"

I drew a deep breath. "Yeah, I know, Nichele. I'm sorry, I've been totally slammed at work lately."

"Well, why don't you just wear the dress I picked out for you a couple of summers ago?" she persisted. "It looks awesome on you, and that gorgeous green will totally work with my Christmas theme."

"Um... that dress died in a tragic hairspray accident," I mumbled. Before she could demand details, I added hurriedly, "I promise if the roads aren't closed tonight, I'll come down and we can go shopping."

I winced as the words left my mouth. A two-hour drive in the winter darkness was no picnic at the best of times, and in a howling blizzard it was damn near suicidal. And I'd still have to drive back in the middle of the night to be at work the next morning.

Unless my meeting catapulted me into even more immediate mortal danger...

I shivered despite the warmth of Spider's parka and sneaked a glance at my wristwatch. Fifteen minutes to go.

"Thanks, Aydan! I knew I could count on you! Oh, hang on..." Nichele's voice faded and the phone relayed a low-pitched mumble. A moment later she was back on the line. "Dave says to stay off the road," she reported. "You know how he is about anybody who's not a professional driver." Another mumble in the background prompted her to add, "He says he'll bobtail up in his highway tractor and get you as soon as you're done at work, and then he'll take you home to Silverside when we're done shopping. Just tell him what time you want him there."

My heart warmed. How lucky I was to have Dave perpetually poised to rescue me with his big truck, even if it meant driving for hours through a blizzard in pitch darkness just for the sake of a stupid dress.

I didn't voice my opinion about the dress.

"Tell him thanks," I said instead. "But I don't know yet what my afternoon's going to be like. I've got a meeting in a few minutes, and I'll know more after that. I'll call you as soon as I can..." I crossed my fingers, hoping social calls would still be on my priority list later. "...and you can leave your Bridezilla updates on my voicemail in the meantime."

"Smartass! I'm only forgiving you because we've been best friends since we were five."

"And because you know you actually *are* Bridezilla," I teased.

"Bite me." I could hear the smile in her voice. "But hey, while I'm being Bridezilla anyway, who are you bringing as your date?" In a suggestive sing-song she added, "I've saved a spot for Hot John. A nice big spot for his nice big-"

"Don't go there!" I interrupted. "I, um... I'll probably..."

There was no way I'd ask Kane. That would give him entirely the wrong idea. And Hellhound? My lips curved into an evil grin at the thought of Arnie's discomfort if anyone even uttered the word 'wedding'. It would be fun to tease him about it, but I wasn't mean enough to actually invite him.

"...I'll be on my own," I finished firmly.

"Oh, Aydan! Go on, just ask Hot John. I'll save a spot for him just in case."

Knowing the futility of arguing, I said, "Okay. I have to go now. Talk to you later."

"See you soon, girl. Stay warm! Ciao!"

I ducked back into Sirius with a breath of relief.

Spider was standing beside the security wicket, wiping moisture from his cheeks.

"What's wrong, Spider?" I eyed him with concern.

"Nothing; I was just walking into that wind and the snow stung my eyes." He smiled as I handed him back his parka and added, "What were you doing out there in only your jeans and sweatshirt? You looked half-frozen."

"I was. Thanks for your jacket. You're such a good friend!" I gave him a smile and stepped up to the security wicket to sign in again. "I'd been down in the dungeon," I added over my shoulder. "I just needed a breath of fresh air."

"Oh." He nodded sympathetic comprehension as I joined him again, fob in hand. "Well, it doesn't get any fresher than that."

"No kidding. My face feels like it's been sandblasted. Who needs Botox and skin peels? All I have to do is stand in that blizzard for a few minutes and my wrinkles will be long gone."

"You don't have wrinkles," he protested. Pink rose in his cheeks as the obvious lie hung in the air between us. "Well, maybe a few little ones..." he amended, reddening. "...but I still can't believe you're the same age as my mom."

Jeez, was everybody conspiring to remind me of my age today?

Some of that thought must have shown on my face. Spider backpedalled, blushing harder. "Anyway, you always look great, and you're amazing at your job, and that's what really matters!"

"Thanks, Spider." I gave him a one-armed hug and let him off the hook with a subject change as we turned toward the stairs. "Do you know what our meeting is about?"

He shot a wary glance at a pair of civilians waiting in the lobby. "Yes."

We climbed the stairs in silence and my heart rate accelerated well beyond the demands of the modest exertion.

When we reached the top, I tried again. "Am I getting a new mission?" My voice cracked on the last word and I swallowed.

Spider hurried down the hallway, avoiding my gaze and evading my question. "Aren't you looking forward to another mission? I figured you'd be bored after a month of doing decryptions day and night and having constant headaches from the network."

I trotted beside him. "I was... am, I mean. Sort of. But..."

He paused, looking down at me worriedly. "Are you okay? Aren't you mission-ready?"

"Well, yeah, of course... but..." I glanced up and down the empty hallway and lowered my voice. "Don't tell anybody, but... I just... That last mission with Holt... it shook me. I thought I was better than that, you know?"

Spider frowned. "What do you mean? Your mission was successful. The terrorist attack never happened so that was a big win; and it wasn't your fault that your informant switched sides and killed your arms buyer. Any mission where none of the good guys die is a successful one."

"I know, but..." I sighed. "Holt's so... I just..."

Screw it. Now wasn't the time for a heart-to-heart.

I shrugged and finished, "Nothing I did on that mission went right. Just bad luck, I guess."

I didn't utter the words that pounded inside my brain.

I had screwed everything up and Holt had to rescue me.

I wasn't good enough.

"And I bet Holt kept needling you about it every chance he got. He's a jerk," Spider said hotly. "You're a 'way better agent than him, and a 'way better person. Don't let him get you down."

I sighed again and turned to trudge toward the meeting room. "Thanks, Spider. I just hope I don't get him for a partner again."

"Not this time." He gestured me ahead of him to the doorway.

I stepped forward only to halt at the sight of the two forbidding figures seated at the meeting table. My mouth dropped open and I blurted the first thought that flashed into my mind.

"Oh shit, who do we have to kill?"

CHAPTER 2

Hellhound's chair creaked as he stood, his homely face creasing in a grin that flashed white teeth through his beard. "Hey, darlin'." He opened muscular tattooed arms, and my own face split in a wide smile as I stepped into his hug.

"Arnie! It's so good to see you!" I cuddled close and hugged him in return.

Successfully resisting the mischievous urge to slide my hands lower and give him a more personal squeeze, I stepped back. Better not go there in public. Given the slightest encouragement he'd melt my mind with his legendary kisses despite the presence of the other two.

Or because of it. He did love to stir the pot.

My lips twitched with wicked amusement, and I brought my inappropriate thoughts to heel by continuing, "But you're scaring me. Are you here in... um... an official capacity?"

"Yep. But don't worry, darlin', I'm a weapons specialist today. We ain't killin' anybody. 'Least, not as far's I know." He turned to the other man at the table. "Chow, ya ain't plannin' to knock off some poor schmuck at the conference, are ya?"

Dr. Chow scowled with half his face. The other half

remained immobile as usual, the fire-ravaged scar tissue and prosthetic eye a horrifying reminder of his former military service.

"Maybe," he growled. "Depends on who pisses me off." He shot a sour look at Hellhound's bulky arm still draped around my shoulders. "I can tell you right now, if you pull any lovey-dovey shit in front of me I'll kill you both."

"Oh, come on, Reggie," I wheedled. "Don't be jealous. You know you'll always be my favourite Head of Weapons Research."

The undamaged side of his mouth turned up and he shot an evil glance at Hellhound as he replied, "I know. Admit it, Kelly, you just can't get enough of my left nut."

I clasped my hands in an expression of rapture and breathed, "Your nuts are all I ever think about."

Spider turned beet red and Hellhound let out a bellow of laughter just as Director Charles Stemp strode into the room and closed the door behind him.

One of his eyebrows lifted a fraction at the sight of Reggie's and Hellhound's unwholesome grins, and I hurriedly advised, "Don't ask."

Stemp returned his usual expressionless gaze. "I had no intention of doing so," he replied without inflection. "Let's begin."

Hellhound dropped into his chair again, making it squeak in protest. I hurried around the table to take a seat next to Reggie, with my back to the wall. Spider slid in across from me, his blush fading but curiosity sparkling in the gaze he bounced between Hellhound, Reggie, and me.

"Agent Kelly," Stemp said to me. "Apologies for the short notice, but we require an agent to accompany Dr. Chow and his team to Calgary for a conference today and tomorrow."

My heart sank. Damn. I'd have to make that shitty drive after all.

"I told you I wanted her in the first place," Reggie interrupted. "And the U.S. had already requested her, so it was pretty much a sure thing. You could have told her last week."

Stemp betrayed no emotion, his voice as dispassionate as ever. "Noted. However, my objections to using Kelly still stand. I'm wary of such specific interest from the other countries..."

"Count*ries*?" Reggie emphasized the plural. "Who else requested her?"

"The United Kingdom," Stemp replied. "I don't like it; and what's more, her cover as Arlene Widdenback the arms dealer is still active and I don't want anyone to make that connection with you."

"Nobody's going to recognize me," Reggie countered. "And the other countries are our allies, remember?"

"Your reasoning is fresh in my mind, as is our status with Five Eyes," Stemp replied crisply.

My pulse ticked up. Five Eyes? Was Ian Rand behind the U.K.'s request for my presence? But surely an individual MI6 agent wouldn't have that much pull...

My stomach dropped. Shit. He'd broken his promise and reported me to his chain of command. Fear chilled my blood. Had he betrayed Moonbeam and Karma and Skidmark, too?

"So, um..." My voice came out slightly hoarse. "Do they... did the U.K. and U.S. give any reason why they wanted me, specifically? They shouldn't even know I'm an agent, should they?"

"The United States knows," Stemp replied. "Your clearances were registered with the Department of Homeland Security when you passed through their airports on your missions; although I had hoped they wouldn't disseminate that information throughout all their intelligence agencies."

"But I've never been to the U.K., so they wouldn't have any record of me unless Agent Rand told them. He promised he wouldn't, but..." I trailed off.

Ian hadn't actually promised me that. Moonbeam and Karma and Skidmark had assured me of his word, but I couldn't reveal their deep cover even to Charles Stemp, the Director of Clandestine Operations. And I especially couldn't reveal it to Charles Stemp, their son.

"The United Kingdom's request did not originate from Agent Rand's intel," Stemp said. "Nora Taylor, their head of Weapons Research, merely asked to meet with you while she was here."

I frowned. "I don't know any Nora Taylor."

"She said as much. But she knows of you." Stemp's gaze sharpened. "She is Dr. Sam Kraus's widow and the sole beneficiary of his estate."

Spider's eyes widened. "Sam was married? And Ms. Taylor owns the civilian research branch of Sirius Dynamics now?"

"She would, if it hadn't been seized as the proceeds of crime after Kraus's arrest," Stemp replied. "However, she has not been informed of that. As far as she knows the estate is currently tied up with probate red tape, and she has been working with us to unravel the complexities of the holdings. She wants to meet with Agent Kelly to reminisce about Kraus."

My bullshit-detectors sprang to quivering attention. "How did she get my name? Why would she know I knew Sam?"

"When Kraus was fleeing his murderous compatriots after..." Stemp glanced at Hellhound and Reggie, obviously filtering out classified information. "...your trip to Georgia, he called his wife to tell her he feared for his life and that he might have to go into hiding for an unspecified period of time. He told her you were helping him."

Conflicted memories twisted my guts and wrung my heart. I had helped Sam, all right. Straight into Stemp's custody, and subsequently into a death that probably wasn't from natural causes.

"Does she know we arrested Sam?"

"No; as far as she knows he vanished after that last phone call and was subsequently discovered dead a couple of months later. Kraus never mentioned a spouse to us, and since Ms. Taylor is a British citizen and their marriage took place in the United Kingdom, we didn't discover their relationship until after Kraus's estate went to probate. At that time we chose not to provide any details other than his death from a heart attack."

"Do you think she knows anything about Sam's... other activities?" I asked.

"When we realized Ms. Taylor was a high-level manager in MI5 with a correspondingly high security clearance, we chose not to inform her of any details while MI5 conducted a confidential internal investigation on our behalf. They cleared her of any suspicion, and she has since been promoted to their Head of Weapons Research."

"And do you think they did a thorough investigation?" I asked.

Stemp lifted a shoulder in one of his infinitesimal shrugs. "We have no choice but to provisionally accept their findings. But if she was involved in Kraus's illegal operations she would certainly have a vested interest in finding out how much you know."

I gulped. "And she's involved in Sirius's civilian operations now. How... isn't that a giant security breach waiting to happen?"

"The management company that Kraus engaged years ago to run the civilian branch is continuing as before, so Ms. Taylor is not directly involved. Of necessity, the chain of command informed her of our intelligence operations here, but she has no jurisdiction or clearances. Our status is secure."

"Well, that must be a relief to the chain of command," Reggie drawled. "Business as usual; and Taylor has a huge security clearance. They must be absolutely creaming themselves."

Stemp's tone remained as clinical as ever; but I knew him well enough to identify the annoyance simmering under that cool façade. "Yes, the chain of command prefers to foster cordial relations with Ms. Taylor for the time being; and they see this as an opportunity to please both her and the United States. On the strength of Ms. Taylor's security clearance, they divulged Kelly's agent status to her and ordered me to assign Kelly to this conference, despite my advice to the contrary."

Stemp transferred his attention back to me. "Dr. Chow and his team will be presenting our ultrasound weapon prototypes in a conference with the other Five Eyes countries at the Calgary facility tomorrow. There is also a meet-and-greet this evening at twenty-one hundred hours. You and Helmand will provide security. You will also make yourself available for conversations with Ms. Taylor, and, if possible, determine whether she was aware of Kraus's activities. Webb will coordinate your operation from here."

Stemp fixed Reggie and Hellhound in his flat reptilian gaze. "Kelly is in charge. You will obey her orders immediately, without question, and to the letter."

I gulped as the magnitude of the mission dawned on me.

Oh, God, investigating Nora Taylor would have been more than enough for me to handle. But I was also going to be solely responsible for safeguarding a classified death ray and Canada's most brilliant weapon developers. If they fell into enemy hands...

My mind skittered with fear. Stemp's reservations about this mission had reawakened all my insecurities. He would have preferred to assign a top agent like Holt; not Aydan Kelly, former bookkeeper...

I straightened my spine. Shut up. I could do this. And anyway, Stemp hadn't said he was worried about my abilities; only about my identity.

Focus on what you can control.

"How many people on your team?" I asked Reggie. My voice came out sounding calmer and more professional than I felt.

"Just Melinda, Murray, and me."

Plus Hellhound and myself made five. Plus our assorted

luggage and deadly weapons.

"So we'll need two vehicles," I said. "Um... why don't we just fly down? Can't we use one of the military helicopters?"

"See, that's what I said!" Reggie seconded with a triumphant glance at Stemp. "Kelly's in charge, right? If she thinks we should fly..."

"That would be the optimum solution," Stemp agreed. "And I already pitched it to the chain of command. However, they say they can't justify the expense."

"But..." I began, then shut up. It was pointless to argue that they'd authorized helicopters for me before. I wasn't their unique and precious decryption asset anymore; I was an agent with so much dangerous classified knowledge that it was a miracle they still allowed me outside the secured facility at all.

Claustrophobia shortened my breath. Don't think about being locked up. Just do the job.

"Okay," I said instead. "I don't want to take my own car, though. No point in attracting anybody who might be watching for Arlene Widdenback. Arnie, did you drive here?"

"Yeah, I've got the Forester."

"Reggie, your car has hand controls, doesn't it?" I asked.

"Yes," he said, belligerence edging the word. "So what?"

"So if we take your car it means you have to drive, because I've never used hand controls before and I don't want to take a chance using unfamiliar controls in poor road conditions," I said in the most matter-of-fact tone I could muster.

"I've already requisitioned a Hummer from the motor pool," Stemp said. "Kelly will drive."

Reggie's face hardened, but he said nothing.

"Webb will arrange your hotel reservations," Stemp went on. "I suggest you leave as soon as possible. This storm is weakening and the roads have been plowed; however the forecast indicates that another front may hit later this evening."

I barely managed to contain my sigh. "Okay. I'll need to pick up some things from my house on the way by, but we can leave whenever everybody's ready."

"Melinda and Murray can be ready with the weapons in half an hour," Reggie said. "But it'll take me a couple of hours to powder my nose."

He spoke the last sentence with bitterness, and I eyed him uncertainly. If it was a joke, nobody seemed to be laughing.

I abandoned speculation as Hellhound spoke. "Okay, that'll gimme time to grab some lunch an' gear up at Stores. Meet in the lobby at fifteen-thirty?"

"Make it fifteen hundred," Reggie corrected. "I'll rush it a bit. No big deal if I have to finish up in the car. I'm not driving." Bitterness still darkened his tone.

"Sounds good," Hellhound agreed easily. "It'll be better if we can drive mostly in daylight. It'll be damn near pitch dark by the time we get there anyway, with this cloud cover."

Stemp nodded and stood. "Very well. Check-ins every hour on the hour while you're in transit. Dismissed." He strode out.

Spider turned to us. "I'll book your hotel and email you the reservation information. Four adjoining rooms? Or..." A flush rose on his cheeks as he glanced at Arnie and me. "...three...?"

"Three," Hellhound said. "I ain't stayin' at the hotel. I'm gonna stay at the secured facility an' guard the weapons."

I briefly considered pointing out that the bunker of Calgary's facility was probably one of the safest places in the country, but Arnie knew damn well how secure it was. If he said he needed to guard the weapons, it wasn't my place to argue.

"Okay," Spider began, but I interrupted.

"Um, Spider... can we make it two adjoining rooms?" I glanced at Reggie. "If Reggie doesn't mind bunking with me?"

Spider blushed scarlet as his gaze pingponged between Reggie, Arnie, and me.

I hastened to explain, "If I'm responsible for protecting everybody and something goes wrong, I don't want to have to decide which room to run to first. Get a suite with a separate bedroom if you can, and Reggie can have the bedroom. Murray and Melinda can have the adjoining room and I'll-"

"I want a separate room," Reggie interrupted.

"But..."

"I. Want. A. Separate. Room," he repeated slowly and clearly, his voice rock-hard. "If you have to decide which way to run, run to Murray and Melinda first."

"But, Reggie, you're the Head of-"

"I don't give a shit!" he snapped. "Three adjoining rooms, Webb." He rose and limped toward the door.

Worry rose, and I blurted, "Reggie, are you okay? Did you hurt your leg?"

He turned, his good eye raking me as his hand clenched. "Got a little abrasion on one of my *stumps*." The word came out with vicious emphasis. "I'm fine." He limped out, his shoulders rigid. Even the scar-twisted forefinger and thumb on his pincer-hand were curled as though to form a fist despite his missing fingers.

"Hell, that guy's as sweet an' cuddly as a fuckin' alligator," Hellhound observed. He grinned at me. "An' he's fuckin' crazy. No guy in his right mind would turn down a chance to hit the sheets with ya, darlin'."

"I wasn't offering that," I protested. "I just think it'd be easier to protect everybody if they're closer together. Ideally we'd all be in the same room." I shuddered. "Except that Murray and Melinda would probably use it as an opportunity to show off their kinky sex life, and that's more than I want to know."

Hellhound laughed. "Don't worry, Chow can take care a' himself. That asshole's ornery enough to stop bullets in midair. Come on, let's gear up at Stores an' then grab somethin' to eat."

"I had lunch already, so you're on your own after we leave Stores. I need some time to strategize."

"Awright, let's roll, darlin'."

At Stores we collected a pair of two-way radios for backup communication while we were on the road, and after a moment of thought I requested bulletproof vests for myself and my three boffins.

"Shouldn't you wear one, too?" I asked Hellhound.

"Got mine in the Forester. I'll be wearin' it when I pick up my cargo, an' keepin' it on 'til we're in the bunker."

My heart sank. I had been hoping he'd chuckle and tease me about being overly cautious.

Dammit, now I was really worried.

Hellhound clipped his radio to his jeans pocket and

added, "I'm headin' for the Greenhorn. Sure ya don't wanna come?" Before I could reply, he leaned down to rasp softly in my ear. "Or we could go to your place for dessert, an' ya know you'll get to come."

His sexy gravelly voice sent shivers down my spine. The shivers magically warmed as they travelled south, and I sucked in a breath.

Hellhound drew back far enough to smile down at me, his eyes heating up, and I realized that my indrawn breath had sounded suspiciously like a hungry little moan.

Not surprising, since that's exactly what it had been.

I followed it up with a small self-pitying whimper. "God, Arnie, I want to. So much that it actually hurts..."

He grinned and his voice coasted down into a deep rough rumble like a big-block engine with a radical cam. "I can make it all better, darlin'."

Every nerve in my body sprang to tingling attention, and this time there was no question that I'd moaned.

"I can't." I leaned into him for just a moment, but pulled away before the heat of his hard body could ignite mine. "I have to stay here and plan. This trip was a complete surprise and I want to make sure I'm ready."

Hellhound nodded. "No problem, ya can take a rain check." His voice deepened to that sexy growl again. "An' the longer ya wait to collect it, the better it's gonna be when ya do."

I swallowed hard, fighting the temptation to abandon Reggie and his crew to their fate.

Duty won, by a shamefully small margin.

"So I'd like to split the team between your vehicle and mine," I said, trying to sound professional. "That way we'll limit our liability if we're attacked."

Hellhound straightened, his teasing smile vanishing behind the stony façade I'd named 'The Killer'. "No can do. I ain't qualified to transport personnel."

"Not *qualified*?" I stared up at him, open-mouthed. "Are you kidding me? With your combat experience? Arnie, I'd put my life in your hands without hesitation, any day, any time."

A spasm flickered across his face and was gone. "I know, darlin'," he said quietly. "An' that scares the shit outta me. I don't want that kinda responsibility. I move weapons; an' I kill people. That's all I do." He stared at his feet, and his next words were so soft he likely didn't expect me to hear them. "That's all I am."

CHAPTER 3

My heart twisted. "Arnie..." I began.

He flung up a hand. "Hell, darlin', I didn't mean that the way it came out. I just meant I ain't cleared to transport anythin' but weapons. Ya gotta be an agent to transport personnel." He shrugged and added, "Unless they're dead. Then I can take 'em."

"Let's hope it doesn't come to that."

"Hope not." He leaned down to drop a kiss on my lips. "See ya later."

He strode off down the hall and I followed him with my gaze, half of me enjoying the play of his hard muscles and my other half worrying about the scars on his gentle heart.

I spent the next two hours coming up with every disastrous scenario I could imagine and planning my responses, but I had an uncomfortable feeling that my imagination had only scratched the surface.

We'd be dangerously exposed on our trip to Calgary. Travelling across open prairie, confined by snowbanks to a highway with dubious traction, there would be no place to run or hide if we were attacked. An enemy had only to force us off the road and our vehicles would be immobilized. After that it was only a question of who had the most firepower.

The thought of being pinned down in a snowbank in the middle of a blizzard made me shudder.

Three o'clock came far too soon. Feeling woefully unprepared, I stopped in at Stores again on my way to the lobby and requisitioned a few more goodies, including a duffel bag containing a P90 submachine gun and more rounds of ammo than I hoped to ever use in my lifetime.

That thought wasn't as reassuring as it might have been, considering that my lifetime could be rudely terminated in only a few short hours.

I sighed, put on my bulletproof vest, and zipped my parka over it. Then I slung the heavy arms bag over one shoulder and the second duffel containing our bulletproof vests over the other, and plodded down to the lobby.

Murray and Melinda were waiting beside a small mountain of suitcases. They had spiffed up for the occasion; Murray in sharply-creased dark dress pants and a white shirt with a maroon bow tie, and Melinda in black slacks, high-heeled leather boots, and a gray cashmere sweater.

Obviously they were all set to go. Unlike me. I directed a brief burst of annoyance at Stemp. He could have at least given me a heads-up yesterday.

But he was such a stickler for 'need-to-know'; and really, I couldn't blame him. He was just doing his job. Jerk.

Crossing to the security wicket to turn in my fob, I surveyed the lobby. A couple of well-dressed women were seated in the reception chairs and a handsome business-suited Asian man stood near the door. Probably civilians. I adjusted the machine-gun bag on my shoulder, trying to look casual. Nothing to see here, folks.

There was no sign of Reggie, though his high-tech wheelchair lurked behind Murray and Melinda's luggage. Dammit. I really didn't want to hang around waiting for him.

As I crossed the lobby Hellhound stuck his head in the door, looking even more imposing than usual in his giant black parka. I had borrowed that parka on another memorable occasion; and despite my five-foot-ten height and hundred and sixty pounds, two of me would have fit comfortably inside. Today it strained across his shoulders, filled to capacity with his powerful bulk and bulletproof vest.

"All set, darlin'?" he inquired.

"Yeah, everybody's here except R-" I broke off as the Asian businessman limped toward us.

Limped.

...Holy shit.

"*Reggie?*" I demanded, gaping at his unmarred face. No sign of the scars. The smooth skin of his left cheek, jaw, and forehead matched his right side perfectly. Even his lips had been repaired. His shiny black hair now covered his entire scalp, and he had a normal left ear instead of the featureless hole I'd seen only two hours earlier. I sneaked a glance at his pincer-hand. Four perfectly-formed fingers and a thumb. If not for the immobility of his prosthetic eye, I wouldn't have believed it was him.

"Let's get this shit-show on the road," he grated.

Okay, that was the Reggie I knew.

Hellhound nodded and withdrew.

Pulling my attention away from Reggie's transformation with an effort, I gathered my wits and addressed the group. "Stemp got us a Hummer from the motor pool..."

I tried not to let my disappointment show. When Stemp had said 'Hummer', I had hoped for the badass H1 Alpha. The H2 we'd been assigned was nothing more than a glorified truck. A heavy-duty truck with aggressive tires and powerful four-wheel drive; but still. Not an H1.

I suppressed a sigh and finished, "...and it's idling outside. They delivered it about ten minutes ago, so we're probably down half a tank of gas by now."

Murray snickered and Melinda shook her head. "Those gas-guzzlers are an environmentalist's nightmare."

"Ordinarily I'd agree," I said. "But today I'm pretty happy to have one."

She sniffed but nodded and donned her parka before hoisting a suitcase in each hand. Murray grabbed a couple, too, and Reggie lifted the remaining two into his wheelchair and wheeled it toward the door. I brought up the rear with my concealed armament.

Outside, the bitter wind made my eyes water but at least it wasn't snowing anymore. Swirling ribbons of drifting snow chased each other down the street.

I clicked the lock release on the Hummer's key fob and slung my two duffels inside. "Load up," I said to the others. "And suit up. There are bulletproof vests in the red duffel. I'll be right back; I just have to get my winter emergency gear from my car."

My poor car. I'd have to leave it freezing in the parking lot for the next twenty-four hours. Good thing Sirius had block heater plugins, or it likely wouldn't even start by the time I got back to it tomorrow.

I jogged across the street, shivering. The snow squeaked under my boots, an audible signal of the cold.

As if I needed a reminder. I shivered some more.

When I returned with my backpack and sleeping bag, Hellhound was placing the last suitcase in the rear cargo bay of the Hummer. Murray and Melinda had already retreated to the warmth of the back seat, and Reggie stood with a proprietary hand on his folded wheelchair.

"Last thing to load, just like I promised," Hellhound said as he reached for it.

Reggie relinquished it reluctantly. "Be careful," he snapped. "That thing's expensive."

Hellhound nodded and tucked the chair expertly into a gap he'd left between the suitcases.

I leaned close to them to mutter, "Have you loaded the weapons yet?"

"Yeah, they're already in the Forester." Hellhound matched my quiet tone. "Took 'em out through the bowlin' alley right before I came in to get ya."

That explained his hasty withdrawal from the lobby. He wouldn't leave his vehicle unsupervised with classified weapons inside.

"And you're armed?" I asked.

He nodded. "Got my sidearm. Didn't bring my snipin' gear. Don't figure we'll need any long-range stuff."

"Okay, good. I've got a P90 in case we need some firepower." I turned to Reggie. "It's in the blue duffel I loaded in the back seat. If we get into a tight spot, can you do the shooting while I drive?"

He nodded, brightening as though he hoped it might actually happen.

Trying not to think too much about that, I went on, "I have to stop off at my farm and grab my overnight stuff, and then we're good to go."

Hellhound nodded. "I'll follow ya there." He shot a scowl at the snow hissing across the pavement. "It was a shitty drive up here this mornin', an' this ground drift's gonna make it even worse. Are ya okay takin' the lead? The Hummer's higher than my Forester an' ya might get better visibility."

"No problem. So we're heading to the secured facility first?"

"Nah, ya might as well go straight to the hotel," he disagreed. "I'll split off when we get to the city limits-"

"No," Reggie interrupted. "We'll all go to the secured facility so I can make sure the weapons are locked down. I have to maintain the chain of custody. We can go to the hotel afterward and grab supper, and then go back for the stupid-ass meet-and-greet."

Hellhound hesitated. "Awright," he agreed after a moment. "See ya at your place, then, darlin'. Drive safe."

"You, too." I reached up to give him a quick kiss.

"Get a room," Reggie growled, and stalked off.

With sudden concern, I watched him limp to the passenger door of the Hummer. Would he have difficulty clambering into the tall vehicle wearing his prosthetic legs?

My worry was unfounded. Grabbing the handle above the door, he stepped up and swung into the seat, his powerful upper body making the move look effortless.

Hellhound was right. Reggie could take care of himself.

"Chain a' custody, my ass," Hellhound muttered. "I took over the fuckin' chain a' custody when I picked up the weapons from the lab. He's got some serious control issues."

I sighed. "Yeah, but I don't think it's personal. It's not that he doesn't trust you; it's more that he doesn't trust anybody."

"'Cept you," Hellhound pointed out. "He requested ya special for this."

"Yeah..." I darted a suspicious look toward the passenger seat. "I don't know if that's trust, though. He's probably got some agenda. Remember, this is Reggie we're talking about."

Hellhound grunted agreement, his lips curling wryly. As I turned away he laid a light hand on my sleeve, sobering. "Hey, Aydan... that look Chow gave me when he made that crack about his nuts... ya got somethin' goin' on with him? I'll back off if-"

"No," I interrupted. "There's nothing going on with Reggie. We're friends and we were just joking around. And *especially* no to you backing off because you think I'm getting involved with somebody else. If I ever want you to back off, I'll tell you."

"Yeah, I know, darlin'; I didn't mean that. I meant... are ya sure *he* knows you're just jokin' around? If he's gonna be a problem on this trip, I can play it cool."

"No, there won't be a problem. Reggie can be prickly and I know you don't like him, but he's actually okay."

Hellhound shrugged. "I don't give a shit about him one way or the other. I just don't want any fuckups on this op. 'Specially not from any personal shit."

"No, we'll be fine." I shivered, only partly due to the

cold. "At least I hope so."

"Okay, darlin'. Let's mount up an' do a radio check an' then hit the road for your place." He dropped a kiss on my lips and strode away.

From sheer force of habit I made a circuit around the Hummer with my bug detector, finding only the tracking unit that was standard equipment on all motor pool vehicles. Good to go.

I drew a breath of relief as I slid into the warmth of the driver's seat. Reggie stared straight ahead while I completed the radio check. Murray and Melinda were exchanging whispers in the back seat, so I put the Hummer in gear without comment and headed for the highway.

The snowdrifts had already begun to finger across the westbound lane despite the efforts of the snowplow, and when we turned north onto the gravel road to my farm I was glad of the Hummer's weight and bulk as we churned along the snowy track.

When we neared my lane, my heart sank.

"Shit," I muttered.

"What?" Reggie snapped.

I heaved a sigh. "The best damn neighbour in the world, that's what. Dammit."

CHAPTER 4

A plume of white marked the progress of Tom's snowblower as he cleared out my lane. When our little cavalcade arrived, he continued down the lane to the turnaround in front of my house, then stopped and got down from his tractor to stride toward the Hummer.

Even his heavy snowmobile suit couldn't conceal his broad shoulders and the easy gait that somehow managed to look challenging as he approached the unfamiliar vehicle.

I powered down the window when he was still a few paces away, and his snow-powdered eyebrows shot up. Then his face split in a grin, crinkling irresistible laugh lines around his sky-blue eyes. "Aydan! You bought a Hummer?"

"No." I reeled off the lie I'd hurriedly manufactured during the short drive down my lane. "This is Reggie's vehicle." I hooked a thumb at the passenger seat. "The four of us have to go down to Calgary for work this afternoon, but somebody..." I made a teasing nod toward Reggie. "...had drinks with lunch before he found out we had to drive this afternoon. He doesn't drink and drive, so I get to play with the Hummer."

"Oh." Tom eyed Reggie's unsmiling face. "Well... that's

good, I guess..."

I was pretty sure he was calculating the number of drinks that would leave a guy still impaired three hours later, but fortunately he didn't go there.

"That's a long drive in this weather," he said instead. "I hope you're staying over when you get there."

"Yep, that's why we're here. I'm just grabbing my overnight stuff."

"Okay, I won't keep you, then. Drive safely."

"Thanks, Tom. And thanks for clearing out my driveway."

I powered up the window and reached for the door handle, only to be stopped by Reggie's grumble. "So I'm a fucking lush now?"

"Yeah," I said cheerfully. "But at least you're a responsible lush. Hang tight, I'll be right back."

Kicking through the snow that had accumulated on my front steps, I let myself in. Warmth and silence wrapped around me like a comforting blanket, and I fought the urge to lock myself inside and hide from the world.

Suck it up.

I lifted my grab-and-go bag out of the closet and went back outside before I could change my mind.

When I slid into the driver's seat Melinda leaned forward, wide-eyed. "That was the fastest packing job I've ever seen."

"I'd love to take credit for it," I replied as I put the Hummer in gear. "But I always have a bag packed."

"Of course," Murray put in warmly. "A top agent is always prepared."

I gave him a quick smile in the rear-view mirror and

didn't admit that I'd only gotten around to creating my grab-and-go bags and secret caches a month ago, after my humiliating partnership with Holt The Magnificent.

But I was ready for anything now.

Really, I was.

I'd just keep telling myself that....

I shelved my worries and concentrated on driving, which was more than enough to occupy my mind. When we turned west on the highway the crosswind buffeted us, requiring constant steering corrections. The never-ending rush of snow across our path created the disorienting illusion that the Hummer was veering sideways.

Wise to the tricks of ground drift, I concentrated on the highway lines instead but accumulating snowdrifts obscured most of them. In places the swirling snow blew high enough to obscure our view, and I slowed to allow a margin of safety in case I wasn't the only idiot forging through the storm.

Behind me, Hellhound's Forester showed only as a pair of faint glows in the whiteness, and I knew he was giving me as much space as possible without losing sight of my taillights. From his lower vantage point he probably couldn't see anything else.

Reggie sat silently in the passenger seat, staring straight ahead. I wasn't sure whether he was pissed off at me for some reason or only anxious about the road conditions and/or my driving skills. Or hell, maybe he was sleeping. The immobile left side of his face gave away nothing.

A few soft sounds from the back seat drew my attention, but when I glanced in the rear-view mirror and saw Murray and Melinda huddled together under a blanket I decided that watching the ground drift was preferable to observing their private show.

As the trip dragged on, Reggie called Stemp for our
scheduled checkins but otherwise said nothing. Darkness
closed in early, and the reflection of our headlights on the
airborne snow reduced the visibility even more.

Giving silent thanks for the Hummer's powerful low-
level fog lamps, I kept driving at half-speed, my neck and
shoulders throbbing with tension and my eyes sandpaper-
dry from staring into the white tunnel created by our lights.

"You doing okay?"

The sound of Reggie's voice after his long silence startled
me so much that I twitched the steering wheel. The Hummer
bobbled uneasily. Shit, the roads were getting icier as we
neared Calgary.

I checked my rear-view mirror. Hellhound's headlights
remained faint but steady behind me.

"Kelly! You getting road hypnosis?" Reggie demanded.
"Talk to me."

"I'm fine. Just concentrating." I sighed and eased one
aching finger at a time on the steering wheel. "It really
would've been nice to have a helicopter ride."

"No kidding. Are we there yet?"

The ubiquitous question made my lips creak into a tired
smile despite myself. "I figure we're about twenty minutes
out."

"Fuck, we've been on the road damn near three hours
already."

"Yeah, but slow and steady wins the-"

Behind us, Hellhound's headlights jerked, then vanished in a puff of white.

"Shit!" I feathered the brakes and the Hummer twisted under us. *"Shit-shit-shit!"* My voice cut off abruptly, strangled by adrenaline as I steered into the skid.

Easy, not too much...

The tires grabbed again, yanking the vehicle in the opposite direction.

My reflexes corrected before my conscious mind could register the change, twitching the steering wheel left, then right again as we lost traction once more.

The Hummer straightened, but not enough. We drifted toward the shoulder. The right front tire grabbed again, but the left side was still sliding, *shit-shit-shit...*

A wrenching jerk.

A blinding eruption of white.

Then blessed stillness.

"Everybody okay?" I barked.

Three tentative voices replied 'yes'.

Reggie released the handle above the door and flexed his hand as though easing the muscles. "Nice driving."

Adrenaline-fuelled rage flared into my veins, but before I could explode he went on, "We're on the right side of the road, not too far into the ditch, and we didn't even blow the airbags. Helmand should be able to get us out."

Thank God I hadn't bitten his head off. That had been a compliment, not a gibe.

I drew a deep shaky breath. "I'm afraid not." My voice came out thin and tight. "That's why I braked in the first place. We lost him back there. Reggie..." I hauled the blue duffel bag forward and extracted the P90. "Take this. I'm pretty sure we're only dealing with black ice here, but..."

He nodded, already checking the weapon with practiced movements.

With a shaking hand I reached for my cell phone. It rang as I pulled it out of my waist pouch, and I drew a breath of relief at the sight of Hellhound's number on the call display. Thank God.

I hit Talk. "Hi Arnie, I saw you spin out. Are you okay?"

"Yeah. Planted pretty good, though. Can ya come pull me out with the Hummer?"

"Um. Maybe. We're in the ditch, too. I'm just going to go out and see how bad it is."

"'Kay, darlin', I'll stand by."

Clutching my phone, I slid out of the driver's seat and sank up to my knees in a snowbank. After floundering in a circuit around the vehicle, I spoke into the phone again. "We're half off the road and facing the wrong direction, but we might be able to get out on our own."

"Awright, give it a try. I'm shovellin' now, but I'm prob'ly gonna need a tow. Call me back an' lemme know how it goes."

Back in the driver's seat, I shifted into four-wheel low and crossed my fingers. Come on, Hummer, don't fail me now.

But just as I'd feared, the legendary Hummer performance didn't extend to the H2. The wheels spun and the heavy vehicle settled deeper into its snowy grave.

I sighed. "Shit. That would've been too easy. Guess I'll get out and start digging."

"I'll help," Murray volunteered immediately.

I frowned at his slacks and smart topcoat. "Do you have winter clothes?"

"These are winter clothes." He pulled on a pair of fine leather gloves as he spoke, then reached for the door handle.

"Whoa," I snapped. "No hat, no scarf, thin boots; and in those dress pants you might as well be naked from the waist down. It's minus forty-five with the windchill out here. At best, you'll freeze your hands, feet, and dick in two minutes or less. At worst, you'll die of hypothermia. You stay put. We don't need any casualties."

He opened his mouth as if to argue, but Melinda clutched his hand and gave him an imploring look. "Murray, honey, Aydan knows best; she's a professional, remember?"

Murray subsided reluctantly, and I made a mental note to thank Melinda later.

"I've got my winter gear," Reggie said.

I hesitated, trying to think of a tactful way to tell him that I'd had enough trouble slogging through the snow on two good legs. Reggie was strong enough and stubborn enough to try it with his prosthetics, but it likely wouldn't end well.

"No, I need you manning the weapon," I said. "You're the only one who can do it. Melinda and Murray don't have military training."

I wasn't actually sure whether that was true; but they didn't protest so I must have guessed correctly.

Reggie sat back with a nod, and I added yet another note to my mental Spy Manual: Always know everybody's capabilities in advance.

Out in the bitter cold again, I hurried around to the rear to unload my emergency kit and put on my ski pants, heavy parka, and giant Sorel boots.

After only a few minutes of work, sweat prickled my back despite the icy wind that stung my face. I shed my heavy parka and went to work again wearing only my lighter winter jacket. Sweat-soaked clothes could be deadly, sucking away precious body heat. Better to stay cooler now.

Twenty minutes later, I leaned on my shovel panting and sweating despite my precautions. Dammit, this didn't look hopeful. And not a single vehicle had passed us in either direction on the usually-busy highway.

Shit.

I pressed the speed dial for Hellhound's cell phone and he picked up on the first ring. "Hey darlin', how's it goin'?"

"I've cleared as much snow as I can but we're hung over the ditch embankment at a culvert. The front tires will be pretty much useless and the back ones aren't going to get much traction, either. I'm going to lay out my traction mats and hope for the best. How about you?"

His tone was wry. "Still shovellin'."

I sighed. "Okay, I'll call you back in a few minutes."

When I got back into the Hummer and eased my foot onto the accelerator, the tires spun just as I'd feared. I tried turning the steering wheel hard left and then hard right, hoping to capture a shred of traction, but it didn't help.

"Shit." My expletive came out in a hiss of tension. "We might as well start calling tow trucks. They'll probably take hours to get here."

"I already did, while you were shovelling," Melinda said. "Apparently there's a bad accident between Calgary and Airdrie and the road is closed. With all the accidents in Calgary plus the big pileup on the highway, there are no tow trucks available. I tried all the smaller towns, too, but they won't come all the way out here. We're too close to Calgary."

"Dammit!" I drew a deep breath. "Thanks for checking, Melinda."

Fear trickled down my backbone, but I shook it off. Stay calm. We were uninjured, and the vehicle provided warmth and shelter. We'd be okay.

I punched the speed dial for Hellhound's cell.

He didn't answer.

CHAPTER 5

When Hellhound's voicemail picked up I disconnected, staring at my phone while worry rose like a cold tide. I grabbed the radio handset. "Sirius Alpha Hotel One, this is Sirius Alpha Kilo One, over."

I waited.

No answer.

"Dammit," I muttered, then tried again, fear tightening my chest. "Sirius Alpha Hotel One, Sirius Alpha Hotel One, this is Sirius Alpha Kilo One. Acknowledge, over."

Nothing but the hiss of radio static.

"Fuck!" I slammed my fist on the steering wheel, then dropped the Hummer back into gear. Forward, reverse, forward, reverse. A bit more gas each time. The vehicle rocked dangerously, tires whining.

"Come *on*, you fucking piece of shit!" I grated.

"Aydan..."

Murray's touch on my shoulder made me corkscrew around to face him. "WHAT?"

He blanched at the sight of my expression. "Uh... should we get out and push?"

I got my temper under control, biting off words as if I

could grind them to powder between my teeth. "Wouldn't help. This fucking tank weighs over three tons and we're high-centred. There's no way we can shift it."

I punched my speed dial one more time.

Voicemail.

I gripped the two-way radio like an enemy's throat and mashed the Transmit button again. "Sirius Alpha Hotel One, Sirius Alpha Hotel One, Sirius Alpha Hotel One, this is Sirius Alpha Kilo One, *acknowledge!* Over!"

Still nothing but staticky silence.

"Fuck this," I muttered, then raised my voice to address my companions. "Okay, I'm going to go and check on him. Stay here and wait for me to come back." I repeated myself a little louder, making sure they understood. "Everybody stays with this vehicle, no matter what. Is that clear?"

As I spoke, I extracted my Glock from its concealed holster and tucked it into my parka pocket, then shrugged on my reflective safety vest.

Murray and Melinda clutched each other. "Wh-What if you don't come back?" Melinda quavered.

"Just *stay put*," I repeated. "You have winter gear and blankets, and even if it takes until tomorrow morning, you'll be okay until a tow truck gets here. Run the engine for a few minutes every now and then, just enough to keep from freezing. Huddle together to keep warm if you run out of gas. If anybody starts shooting at you, return fire, but *stay with the vehicle!* You're more likely to die from exposure than from a bullet. Got it?"

"Got it," Reggie said, his voice calm and level. "Just get your ass back here in one piece."

Hood up and scarf wrapped around my face so only my

eyes were exposed, I stepped out into the darkness again. My powerful flashlight reflected only swirling white so I pointed it downward, feeling utterly alone. Stumbling along on trembling legs, I followed the edge of the pavement, stopping occasionally to kick through the drifted snow that nearly obscured the white painted line.

My sweaty clothes were already chilling and I moved a little faster to generate more body heat. Why hadn't I changed into dry clothes before I left? Stupid.

But I hadn't wanted to waste any time. What had happened to Arnie?

I fought the mental image of a deadly ambush, his body lying cold and motionless while the inexorable snow consumed his lifeblood.

I shook my head vigorously to dislodge the thought. He couldn't have been ambushed; he'd just hit some black ice. He was fine.

Oh, God, he *had* to be fine.

But how far back was he?

And in the snowy darkness with our tire tracks already drifting full, would I walk right past the Forester buried in the ditch?

My flashlight penetrated only a few feet into the profound darkness and I fought the eerie conviction that I was enclosed in a small white bubble on a never-ending treadmill, plodding interminably without ever moving forward.

Fear rose like an icy tide. I could easily die out here alone in the storm. Hypnotized by drifting snow, slowly succumbing to disorientation and the sleepy deceptive warmth of hypothermia...

Stay focused.

I checked my watch. I had been floundering over snowdrifts in my heavy boots for ten minutes, but it felt like a lot longer. Horrible certainty filled me, weakening my knees and making my breath catch in a sob.

If I didn't find Arnie in the next ten minutes, I would have to turn back. I wasn't near the limits of my endurance yet, but I would be by the time I slogged all the way back to the Hummer. Nobody could last long in these conditions.

And despite the agonizing pull of my heart toward Arnie, my duty was to the three brilliant scientists I'd left unguarded behind me.

Tears freezing on my scarf, I pushed on.

Long minutes later I spotted an orange hazard triangle at the edge of the road, its base already buried in snow. A few paces later a taillight blazed to life ahead of me.

My heart leaped.

Was he warm and safe inside?

As I hurried forward my momentary flare of hope faded. The taillights weren't on; they were only reflecting my flashlight.

The Forester was dark and silent. Snow powdered its surface, accumulating in the contours of the bodywork. The only sounds were the wail of the desolate wind through the Forester's grille and the sibilance of drifting snow.

Heart thumping, I slithered through the drifts toward the driver's door.

Something moved under my feet.

An involuntary shriek escaped me as I leaped to the side, my flashlight snapping around to lock onto its target.

A bulky black-clad body lay facedown beside the

Forester.

A searing rush of adrenaline paralyzed my heart.

"*Arnie!*" I dove to my knees beside him, frantically clawing the snow away from his face. "*Arnie, ohmigod...*"

"Hey, darlin'." His voice was a weak breathless shadow of his usual rasp. "Glad to see ya."

"What happened?" Cold terror filled me as I took in his position, his left arm pinned under the Forester and his right trapped beneath him.

"Was shovellin' underneath." He drew a short breath. "Truck settled." Another short breath. "Pinned my arms."

I gulped down hysteria and forced myself to inhale deeply and exhale slowly. "Okay, I'll get you out."

"Get my right first." A shudder shook his body. "Can't feel it."

I wedged my flashlight in a snowbank and threw myself at his shoulder, scraping and digging with both hands. "But... your left is under the truck..."

"Yeah." Another short breath. "Can still feel it, though."

"Hang on, Arnie, I'll get you out." Common sense finally filtered through my panic. "Where's your shovel?"

"Under the truck."

"Fuck." I redoubled my efforts, kneeling beside him and flinging snow between my legs like a demented dog.

A few minutes later I had cleared a hollow under his shoulder and chest.

"Can you pull it out now?" I demanded.

His body heaved upward, twisting and jerking, then fell again. "Can't." He panted a couple of breaths. "Can't move it. Can't even feel it."

His right arm. Those brilliant musician's fingers...

I gulped back tears and used all my will to hold my voice steady. "Take your weight off it a bit if you can. I'll pull it out for you."

He heaved and twisted again, and I clamped onto his parka sleeve with both hands and yanked. His arm flopped out, horrifyingly limp. Nausea closed my throat at the sight of his bare right hand, vulnerable skin exposed to the vicious cold.

My voice came out in a thin quaver. "Weren't you wearing mittens?"

"Musta come off when ya pulled my arm out. There's another pair in the Forester."

"Where?"

"Rear hatch."

"I'll be right back," I promised, and lurched to my feet to stumble around to the rear of the vehicle.

A moment later I was pulling the mitten over his cold motionless hand, the skin white in the flashlight's beam.

Oh God. If his hand had frozen, he'd never play the guitar again. A memory-flash of Reggie's scarred pincer-hand made bile rise in my throat. Not Arnie's beautiful, talented fingers. Not that.

Somehow I managed to sound firm and confident. "Okay, I'm going to tuck your arm under your side to keep it warm, and then I'll start digging your left arm out. How..." My voice wavered and I fought it back under control. "How does it feel?"

"Fine. Warm, right next to the exhaust. Lucky I had my parka an' mitts on, or I'd 'a gotten burned. There ain't much weight on it, but my sleeve's caught on somethin' an' I couldn't move enough to rip it. If I coulda used my other hand, I'd 'a gotten out no problem."

Despite his dispassionate words, I could hear a ghost of horror in his voice.

I could only imagine what he must be feeling right now. Losing his hand would end both his military career and his music.

Could he survive the loss?

Would he even want to?

I shuddered and dug.

CHAPTER 6

"Try it now," I panted a few minutes later.

Hellhound heaved upward accompanied by the sound of tearing fabric. Rolling free of the snow-covered vehicle with a grunt, he stumbled to his feet and pushed me ahead of him.

"Get in," he rasped.

Panting, I scrambled into the driver's seat of the Forester and across the console as he slid in behind me and slammed the door.

With his right arm hanging limp in his lap, he reached left-handed for the keys dangling from the ignition. The engine fired immediately and he cranked the heat up to maximum and then turned on the dome light, bathing us in blessed light and an illusion of safety.

"Oh God, Arnie!" Heedless of the console bruising my ribs, I flung my arms around him and buried my face in his icy parka.

"It's okay, darlin'. Everythin's okay now." His left arm came around me and I burrowed closer. Despite his confident words, I could feel his hand quivering on my back.

I hugged him tighter, imagining the terror of being pinned alone in the frigid night, waiting to die.

What if I had turned back only a few yards short of him? My breathing went choppy at the thought.

"Shhh, now darlin'," he soothed. "We're gonna get outta this just fine, don't worry."

Trembling, I drew back and pulled off his balaclava. My throat clenched at the sight of the white patch below his left eye and I yanked off my mitten to press my palm against his face. "You've got frostbite."

"Yeah, I figured. Couldn't keep my face outta the wind. Lucky I had my ski mask on an' my hood up or it woulda been worse." He gave me a wink. "But hell, it ain't like it's gonna make me any uglier."

"You will never be ugly to me." I swallowed hard as I lifted his right hand from his lap. "How... how is it?"

"Gettin' some prickles in my arm now. Circulation's comin' back." His arm twitched and he hissed out a breath. "Can't move it yet, though." He hesitated. "Better take a look at the hand."

Bracing myself for the ghastly sight of waxy frozen flesh, I gently slid off his mitten.

"How bad is it?" Arnie's voice was firm and level, but he stared rigidly through the windshield, not looking.

"It's..." A sunrise of relief bloomed in my chest. "I... I think it's okay."

"...Okay...?" He looked down tentatively.

I stroked the undamaged skin, turning his hand to examine it from all angles. "Yeah. Not even any frostbite on your fingertips. It must have stayed warm in your mitten, underneath you."

He let out a breath, collapsing in the seat as though all his bones had turned to jelly. "Fuck me." Eyes closed, he breathed evenly for a few seconds. "Fuck," he repeated softly. "I figured for sure... all that time without circulation..." He gulped and drew an uneven breath. "Fuck." He fell silent.

My throat closed and tears prickled the back of my eyes as I hugged his hand to me and offered up a fervent prayer of thanksgiving to any god that might be listening.

When I thought I could trust my voice, I said, "The way you were lying with your arm jammed under your chest, your bulletproof vest would have dug right into your armpit. It must have squished some nerves but not actually cut off the circulation."

"Yeah." His arm twitched in my grasp again. "Hope it ain't permanent," he muttered.

"I'm sure it'll be better in a few minutes," I lied. I wasn't sure at all, but there was no way in hell I'd tell him that. "It's just asleep. It'll take a while to come back."

"Guess so," he agreed without conviction. He drew a breath and let it out slowly. "Thanks for comin' to get me, darlin'."

I cupped his dear homely cheek, the roughness of his beard tickling my palm. "I'll always come to get you."

We looked deep into each other's eyes.

My heart skipped a beat.

I broke the moment with a lascivious smile and an eyebrow-waggle. "I'll always come for you, too," I added, hoping the double entendre would be enough to stave off his commitment-phobia. And mine.

Arnie grinned. "That's what I wanna hear, darlin'."

I squeezed his hand before remembering that he probably couldn't feel it, then returned it to his lap. "I'd better call Reggie."

Reggie answered on the first ring. "What's your status?"

"Both of us are safe and warm," I said, ignoring my own shivering. "How about you?"

"Same. What's your plan?"

"Um..." I booted my brain back into gear. "I know our original plan was to keep..."

I almost said 'the weapons in a different vehicle' before remembering we weren't on a secured line.

"...separate vehicles," I continued. "But..." I shot Hellhound a look. "Arnie, can you walk about half a mile?"

"Yeah. Nothin' wrong with my legs."

Oh, God, please don't let anything be wrong with his arm, either...

"We're coming to you," I told Reggie. "Arnie and I can't dig the Forester out, and I don't want our group separated." A violent shiver shook me, my sweat-soaked clothes clammy against my skin.

"Okay. Call me when you're leaving."

"Will do."

When I disconnected, Hellhound frowned at me. "When did ya eat last, darlin'?"

"Too long ago." My shivering intensified.

He twisted to lift a sodden ringlet off my forehead left-handed. "An' you're soakin' wet. We ain't goin' anywhere 'til you're dry an' fed." He jerked his chin at the back seat. "I got dry clothes an' MREs."

My overstressed brain didn't immediately identify the military acronym, and Hellhound grinned at my blank look and elaborated. "Meals, Ready to Eat. The Three Lies: They ain't meals, they ain't ready, an' they sure as hell ain't edible."

My laugh came out jerky with my shivering. "At this point I'm not going to do a gourmet critique."

"I'll get 'em." He got out and went around to the rear door, returning in a few moments with a neatly-folded T-shirt and sweatshirt and a small cardboard box.

While I shivered through a clothing change, he tore open the cardboard box one-handed with the help of his teeth. The box disgorged a foil pouch and a plastic envelope, which he assembled with a bit of water before leaning it upright against the console.

Glorious comprehension flared. The meal had a chemical heater. Thank God.

I picked up the box and hugged it to me.

Hellhound chuckled. "Careful, you'll suck all the heat outta it an' your rations'll be cold."

"I'll take that chance." I embraced the warm box fervently.

In short order I was gobbling the hot spaghetti. When it was all gone I fell back in the seat. "God, I needed that!" I shot an accusing glance at Hellhound. "That wasn't nearly as bad as you said."

He grimaced. "Try eatin' it for two months straight."

"Okay, that would make me puke," I agreed. "But it wasn't bad for a one-off."

"Helps to be starvin'." He gave me a searching look. "How ya doin'?"

"Better." The spaghetti nestled in my belly, radiating warm strength. I blew out a long breath, letting it chase the icy tension from my limbs. "How's your arm?"

He managed to lift it several inches before it fell back

into his lap. "Buzzin' like a sonuvabitch. Like when ya hit your funny bone. Feels like my fingers are gonna explode."

"That's probably good," I said with all the fake confidence I could muster. "At least you can feel your hand now, right?"

"Yeah." He changed the subject. "So, can ya make it back to the Hummer?"

The thought of abandoning our bright warm oasis for the dark and deadly cold made me shudder.

"Yes," I said firmly. "We'll have to carry the weapons. How are they packed?"

"Coupla duffels." Hellhound gave me a half-smile. "Lucky they're portable. Last time we had a fuckin' crate that took up the whole damn cargo bay an' weighed about three hundred pounds."

My ears perked up. "So is this conference an annual thing?"

"Usually, but this is a special meetin'." He shrugged. "When that terrorist threat came through last month, Stemp hadta tell Five Eyes we had the ultrasound death ray since it was all over the fuckin' media. He was some pissed when he found out it was a fuckin' hoax an' he'd spilled the intel for nothin'."

"I can imagine."

And I could. 'Pissed' would be an understatement. Not that Stemp would reveal any emotion, but I knew him well enough to guess.

Hellhound chuckled. "Yeah. But he's such a hardass bastard, he ain't givin' up somethin' for nothin'. We're showin' 'em our death ray, but they gotta pony up their latest tech, too. It oughta be an interestin' conference."

Queasy fear twisted my stomach at the thought of five countries' deadliest weapons together in one place.

I swallowed hard. "Um... yeah, I guess 'interesting' is one word for it." I pulled up my damp parka hood and wound my wet scarf around my face. "Well, let's do it. I'll call Reggie and let him know we're leaving."

Trudging back through the storm, I shifted Hellhound's duffel bag on my shoulder and shone my flashlight at the sky. "Shit. It's snowing again."

Hellhound grunted. "Must be that next storm Stemp was talkin' about." He stopped, rolling his shoulders. "Hey, darlin', can ya pull my second duffel up a bit? My arm still ain't workin' right."

"I can take another bag," I volunteered.

"Nah. Ya got enough to carry." He let out a breath as I moved the strap of one of the heavy bags higher on his shoulder. "An' anyhow, weapons are my responsibility. I gotta maintain the chain a' custody."

"Nobody would ever know if I carried it for a few minutes," I argued as we moved forward again, but I was secretly glad he'd shouldered the largest burdens. His duffel bag wasn't heavy, but my muscles were quivering from cold, adrenaline, and the effort of shifting several hundred pounds of snow.

God, if I could only rest. Just for few minutes...

I stumbled over a drift and fell to my knees.

"Ya okay, darlin'?" Hellhound asked when I didn't get up immediately.

"Yeah." I pushed myself to my feet, shivering again. "J-just about d-done for, though." For some reason that prospect didn't worry me. I could just lie down in this nice soft snowbank and sleep forever...

"Keep movin', darlin'." He nudged me forward. "We gotta be almost there by now. Remember, hypothermia makes ya sleepy an' it fucks with your mind. Keep fightin'."

"Right." As I trudged forward again my cell phone rang, and I fumbled it out of my waist pouch with numb fingers. At the sight of the call display I groaned. "Shit, it's Nichele."

I was about to decline the call when Hellhound snapped, "Answer it!" I frowned confusion at him, but he gestured vigorously at the phone. "Hurry up, answer it! An' keep walkin'."

Too exhausted to think for myself, I obeyed. "Hi, Nichele."

"Hey, girl, what's new? Since you didn't call me this afternoon, I'm assuming you're still at home...?"

"Oh. Uh..." Searching for a response, I blinked into the driving snow; but my instant-bullshit superpower seemed to have deserted me.

"Aydan? Are you still there? Hello?"

"Uh. Y-yeah, I'm still h-here. Um..." It was no use. My brain wouldn't work, and all I had was the truth. "Actually, I ended up h-having to go to a b-business thing in C-Calgary with a b-bunch of people from w-work."

"You're in Calgary? That's awesome, girl! Can you ditch the boring business stuff and come shopping?"

"Um, n-no. I'm actually n-not in Calgary yet. I'm s-stuck on the r-road."

She sucked in a breath. "Omigod, Aydan, you're *outside?* In this horrible blizzard?" The phone crackled, and Dave's deep voice overlaid Nichele's.

"What happened? Are you okay?"

"F-fine. J-just hit some b-black ice and slid off the r-road."

"Where are you? I'll come and get you."

"Thanks, D-Dave, but I've got t-two vehicles in the d-ditch, four other p-people, and a whole b-bunch of luggage and c-crap. We'll just hunker d-down and w-wait it out..."

"No. Big storm's blowing in tonight. You don't want to be out there. Is your car still driveable?"

"Um... yeah, I th-think so... but I'm not d-driving my c-car. I've got a H-Hummer. And Arnie's F-Forester is in the d-ditch, too."

"Oh." Dave's response was guarded, and I knew he was processing that information and concluding that this wasn't an ordinary business trip. "No problem," he added, fortunately managing a tone that wouldn't make Nichele too curious for her own good. "My truck can pull anything out. Where are you?"

"No, D-Dave, I don't w-want you to-"

"Time's a-wasting," he interrupted. "Tell me where you are, or I'll just head for Silverside and hope I find you."

"But the r-road is c-closed. N-nobody's driven by us, and w-we've been here for n-nearly an hour."

"No problem. Me and my truck have made it through worse, and I know all the back roads. Tell me where you are."

I blew out a breath of mingled frustration and relief. "We're s-southbound on Highway N-nine, somewhere s-south of Highway Five-Sixty-Six."

"I'll find you. Leaving now."

He disconnected and Nichele took over again, badgering me with worried questions that took every ounce of my remaining brainpower to answer or deflect.

Time slowed as I trudged on, fatigue dragging at my body. Having asked 'are you okay' in every possible variation, Nichele switched to Bridezilla mode. I zoned out under the flood of wedding details, hauling my attention back to the conversation and mumbling semi-coherent answers only when she asked a direct question.

My feet were clumsy weights at the ends of my legs, and I abandoned the attempt to walk in a straight line. Over and over Arnie nudged me gently back on course.

At least I'd stopped shivering. I drew a breath of relief as warmth crept into my limbs. My eyelids drooped, but Nichele was still talking. Her words blurred together and my answers shortened to mumbles.

Finally the Hummer's taillights glowed faintly through the snow. Thank God. Safe at last.

"Haffa go, N'chele," I slurred.

"Okay, be careful. Stay warm..."

I mumbled, "Mmhm... Mmhm..." to her final admonishments until she hung up at last.

Made it.

Eyes dropping shut, I sank down into the soft welcoming snow.

CHAPTER 7

"No way, darlin'. Get up." An insistent hand clamped under my armpit, pulling painfully.

I struggled feebly against it. "Jus' rest f'r a minnit..."

"KELLY! ON YOUR FEET! MOVE IT!"

Hellhound's full-throated bellow and yank on my arm squeezed out a tiny trickle of adrenaline. I stumbled to my feet.

"Wha'?" I moaned. "Was jus' res'n'..."

"Can't rest yet, darlin'. Get in the Hummer. Just a few more steps. Come on."

"...'Kay." I plodded forward to the driver's door. Pulling open the door took the last of my strength, and I made it into the driver's seat only with the aid of a vigorous boost from Hellhound's knee. He closed the door behind me, and a moment later a flurry of snowflakes and a slam indicated that he was safely in the back seat.

I went limp, every exhausted muscle giving up simultaneously.

"Kelly?"

I ignored Reggie's questioning voice.

Rest.

Sleep...

"Kelly! Hey! Talk to me!" Somebody shook my shoulder. Reggie again. Why wouldn't he just piss off?

"She's hypothermic." Hellhound's disembodied voice floated from the back seat. "Get that wet gear off her an' give her a hot drink."

"We don't have anything hot."

"There're MREs in that black duffel she's holdin'. Grab the FRH outta one of 'em."

More acronyms. My mind ground to a halt.

The duffel bag jerked, accompanied by Reggie's close-range cursing. "Can't get it... Useless fucking hand..."

"Let me," Murray's voice chimed in.

After considerable jostling and a period of time I didn't register, the fog began to clear from my mind.

"Keep drinking," Reggie urged.

I obediently took another swallow, hot liquid burning my tongue. Violent shivers seized me.

"Good, she's finally shivering," Reggie said.

"About time," Hellhound agreed with satisfaction.

"Y-you d-don't n-need to s-sound s-so g-goddamn h-h-happy about it!" I snapped. "I'm f-freezing m-my f-fucking ass off h-here!"

"Yeah, Kelly, we *do* get to sound goddamn happy about it," Reggie countered. "That means you're warming up. You were too damn cold to shiver before."

As if my brain had finally thawed enough to work again, I grasped their meaning at last. "Oh. R-right. H-hypothermia." I gulped some more hot liquid, a repulsive too-sweet fruity thing. "G-God, wh-what is this sh-shit?"

"Just another treat from your MRE," Hellhound said

cheerfully. "Drink up, darlin'."

"G-good Lord, it's d-disgusting." I shuddered in between my shivers, but kept swigging.

At last my trembling eased to a constant fine vibration. I gulped the last of the hot drink and fell back in the seat. "Damn, that was close. Thanks for keeping me going, Arnie."

"No problem. Glad you're back with us, darlin'."

"And thanks for making me answer Nichele's call. It never would have occurred to me to get Dave to come and rescue us."

Hellhound grunted. "Hell, I never thought of it, either. I just knew ya needed to keep talkin' if ya were gonna make it, an' if anybody can keep ya talkin', it's Nichele."

I laughed. "You've got that right..." I jerked upright. "Headlights!"

A glow brightened the whiteness, slowly widening and separating into twin points of approaching light.

"Reggie," I snapped. "Get ready to fire just in case. The rest of you, stay low. That should be our ride, but I'm going to go and check it out."

"Not by yourself, ya ain't," Hellhound growled.

"Okay, let's go." I threw my hood up and muffled my face in my wet scarf again.

The headlights had halted by the time we stepped out of the Hummer into the biting wind. Shivers seized me instantly, long hard paroxysms that twisted my stomach and rattled my bones.

The headlights were surrounded by dozens of yellow lights that outlined the shape of a highway tractor, and a muffled figure swung down from the cab and stumped toward us with Dave's familiar stiff gait.

I drew a breath of relief and eased my grip on my Glock. "Dave! You found us!"

"'Course." He gave me a quick hug, patting my back, then pulled away. "You're shivering. You should get in where it's warm."

"Yeah, that's what I keep tellin' her," Hellhound agreed. "Go on an' sit in the Hummer, darlin'. Dave an' I'll do this."

I was shivering so hard that my revolting fruit drink was threatening to reappear in a spectacular fashion, so I nodded and hurried back to the Hummer.

Reggie lowered the P90 as I slipped into the driver's seat. "All good?" he inquired.

"Y-yep."

"Do I need to hide this?" He hefted the weapon.

"D-Dave w-won't ask questions. B-better k-keep it handy until we're b-back on the road. J-just in case."

He nodded and laid the gun in his lap before reaching into Hellhound's duffel with his good hand. "Here, have another hot drink." He passed me another foil pouch and envelope and scowled, the prosthetic half of his face disturbingly serene beside the angry expression on his right. "I'd do it for you, but this fucking hand is even more fucking useless than what I've got under it." He made a disgusted gesture with his cosmetically-enhanced left hand.

"C-can't you m-move it at all?" I asked cautiously as I tore open the heat pack.

"I can move it a bit, but it's no damn good for anything." He demonstrated, moving the forefinger and thumb together and then apart. The other fingers remained immobile. "I can't grip worth shit. I might as well not have a hand at all when I'm wearing this fucking thing."

"Th-that sucks..." I hesitated.

Should I change the subject? He'd be furious if he thought I was trying to pussyfoot around him, but if I said the wrong thing he'd bite my head off.

I chickened out. Maybe I could throw somebody else under the bus.

"S-so whose idea was the d-disguise?" I asked.

"Stemp's, who else? Fucking asshat. When he showed up with this fucking... *face*..." Reggie spat the word with disgust as he gestured at his head. "...right after I hired on, I told him if he had such a problem looking at my fucking *deformity*, I'd quit right then and save him the trauma." He bared his teeth. "He handed me some bullshit line about how he thought I might want to avoid attention sometimes. Yeah, right. Stemp, the fucking Sensitive Guy. As if."

My heart squeezed at the thought of Stemp labouring over his tools and molds to get Reggie's face just right, only to have his efforts angrily rejected.

"He p-probably meant well," I ventured. "I c-can see where you'd b-be mad if you thought h-he was implying your own f-face wasn't good enough, b-but..."

"Meant well, my baked ass," Reggie spat. "You know what he's like. You're the one that's always getting reprimanded for calling him a dickhead. And didn't I hear a rumour about you jamming a gun under his chin and threatening to blow his head off?"

I winced. Neither Kane nor Stemp would have disclosed that. Holt must have let it slip, dammit. What else had he blabbed about me?

"Well, yeah, b-but there were extenuating c-circumstances," I explained. "I don't h-hate Stemp. He's just... s-sometimes he's not so g-good with human interaction. I d-doubt if he m-meant to insult you."

"Sure he did. He insults people all the time just to rattle their cages. To see if he can find some leverage to manipulate them."

"T-true," I agreed reluctantly. "It's his j-job to be a d-dickhead sometimes, b-but I don't th-think he enjoys that p-part of it. He's b-basically a good g-guy."

"Bullshit." Reggie slouched back, crossing his arms. "He makes me wear this getup to conferences 'so nobody will recognize me', he says. More like he thinks that if I don't wear it people will be so creeped out by my freak-face that they won't be able to concentrate on my presentation. Asshole."

I pressed my lips together to keep from pointing out that it sounded more like Reggie's attitude problem than Stemp's, and busied myself ripping open the pouch of hot liquid. An involuntary shudder shook me as I swallowed the first mouthful of sickly sweetness. "G-God." I shuddered again. "It'll be a m-miracle if I c-can keep this down."

"Just shut up and swallow."

I cocked an eyebrow at him. "Said the typical man."

He snickered, and I relaxed at the return of his usual sardonic humour.

The driver's door opened and Hellhound poked his masked-and-hooded head in along with a blast of icy air. "We're hooked up, an' Dave's gonna start pullin'. Roll your window down so I can give ya steerin' directions."

I complied, and a few minutes later the Hummer was on the highway again, windows closed and heat blasting.

"Well, that was anticlimactic," Melinda remarked, and I

could hear the smile in her voice.

"It felt pretty climactic to me," Murray murmured, just loudly enough to be audible.

"Ignore them," Reggie advised me. "Don't even look back there unless you want to know what they've been doing under that blanket all this time."

"Don't want to know," I agreed.

A tap at my window provided a welcome distraction, and I powered it down to greet Hellhound again.

"We're gonna go get the Forester now," he said. "I'll take the duffels back with me. If we can't get my truck out, I'll bring everythin' back an' we can all go together, but I'd rather go with the original plan if we can."

"Sounds good," I agreed. "Good luck."

Forty minutes later Hellhound's Forester was back on the road. After another check-in call to Stemp, we moved off. Dave's highway tractor pushed through the drifts ahead of us while I hugged his taillights, unable to see anything else in the whiteout. Behind me, Hellhound's headlights were barely visible even though I knew he was only a couple of car-lengths back. The wind shrieked and tore at the Hummer, and my arms ached with the effort of holding it on the road despite its power steering.

Reggie glanced at his wristwatch. "At least we missed the fucking meet-and-greet."

"Maybe not," Murray spoke up hopefully. "I'm sure it'll go on for a few hours. The Brits will be getting their second wind because of the seven-hour time difference, and the Aussies and Kiwis will party no matter how jet-lagged they are."

I groaned. "Can't we just skip it?"

"No chance," Reggie said sourly. "We have to drop off the weapons at the secured facility, so we'll be walking right through their stupid party."

"Well, I'm looking forward to it," Melinda said. "It'll be nice to interact with our colleagues in a less formal setting."

Murray murmured agreement.

"It's a fucking waste of our time," Reggie snarled. "This isn't a fucking social club, it's a top-level national security meeting. Damn Nora Taylor. Good old Howie Coleman would've bitten his own tongue off before he'd make small talk. But no, put a woman in charge and all of a sudden we're having tea and making pinky-friends."

Prying a hand momentarily off the steering wheel, I gave him a backhanded smack on the shoulder. "Nice attitude, asshole. And you were whining about Stemp being a dick?"

He rubbed his shoulder, the good side of his mouth curling into a smirk. "You know I'm only rattling your chain."

"Coleman was a curmudgeonly old fossil, and you're his younger evil clone," Melinda said without heat. "It's no wonder you liked him, but nobody else did. Nora Taylor is a much-needed change, and I'm looking forward to meeting her. And the meet-and-greet wasn't entirely her idea, anyway. I heard that Brad Wilson was all over it, too."

"I don't trust that fake-tanned asshole any farther than I can throw him," Reggie groused. "He's a fucking politician, not a scientist. Doesn't have two brain cells to rub together. I can't believe the U.S. made him their fucking Director of Weapons Research. Idiots." He shot me a look. "And it can't be a coincidence that the research directors of both the U.K. and the U.S. want a meet-and-greet for the first time ever, and that they both asked for you to be there."

I had thought I'd used up my worry quota for the day, but apparently not. Anxiety clutched at my throat. "This meet-and-greet isn't business as usual?"

"No. They've got some agenda, I guarantee it. Better watch your back."

CHAPTER 8

By the time Calgary's streetlights stained the night sickly orange, I was vibrating with tension and fatigue. The Hummer's tires slewed through the heavy snow, following Dave's highway tractor into a gas station.

Hellhound's Forester navigated the corner with even less finesse, drifting sideways and flinging up a white flurry before straightening at the last moment to slide to a halt.

Dave swung down from the cab and slogged back toward the Hummer while Hellhound converged from the rear. I rolled down the window as they arrived.

"Where to?" Dave inquired.

"Thanks for rescuing us, Dave, but we'll take it from here," I said. "You need to go home. Nichele will be worried."

"Talked to her already," he countered. "She's fine. Tell me where you want to go and I'll break trail." He shot a disgusted look at the snowy streets. "Plows are taking their time as usual."

"Actually, we need to go it alone from here," I said. I gave him a shrug and a significant eyebrow raise. "You know."

His face lit with avid interest. "Oh. Secret location?"

"Yeah."

"'Kay. I'll tell Nichele you're tied up in business meetings. Stay safe. And Aydan..." He leaned in the window, his faded blue eyes serious. "You call me if you need help. With... anything. Okay?"

I patted his mittened hand. "I will. Thanks, Dave."

"No problem. Anytime. You know that, right?"

"I know. Thanks."

"'Kay." He gave Reggie an awkward nod before straightening to glare at Hellhound. "You watch out for her, you hear?"

Fortunately Arnie didn't take offense. "I will. Thanks for gettin' us here. That was some heavy-duty drivin'."

Dave frowned as though trying to figure out where an insult might be lurking in the compliment. After a moment he grunted, "You're welcome," and turned to stump rapidly back to his truck.

Hellhound took his place leaning into my open window. "Lead on, darlin'. I'll watch our six."

"Thanks. See you there." I craned my neck to give him a kiss, ignoring Reggie's disgusted snort beside me.

When I had churned the Hummer back onto the street, I raised my voice to address my passengers. "Everybody keep your eyes open. I'm ninety-nine percent sure nobody's following us through this shit, but watch for anything unusual just in case."

Murmurs of assent came from the back seat, and Reggie snorted again. "You mean 'unusual', as in somebody actually being dumb enough to be on the road tonight?"

"Yeah, something like that."

I concentrated on driving, wishing the other drivers would all just go the hell home. Ahead, an SUV described a graceful one-eighty before sliding in slow motion into the side of a half-ton. I eased the wheel over and drove around them.

"Wait, we just witnessed an accident," Melinda protested from the back seat. "We have to stop."

"I didn't see it," I growled. "Reggie, did you see anything?"

"Nope."

"Didn't think so." I kept driving. Behind me, Hellhound did the same.

"But..." Melinda began.

"We're carrying classified weapons to a national security summit," Reggie said. "Trust me, we didn't see anything."

"But what if-"

"No," Reggie and I chorused.

"Sorry," I added.

She sighed and subsided.

After a few minutes of silence, Reggie spoke again. "So what's the story with Dave?"

"I got backed into a corner on an op and he saved my ass, but in the process he figured out that I'm not exactly the civilian bookkeeper I'm pretending to be. I've never given him any details and he doesn't expect me to; but he loves to help and he'll keep his mouth shut. And Stemp cleared him, so it's all good."

"But his wife is a friend of yours and she doesn't know anything?"

"His fiancée; and she's my best friend. And no, she doesn't know anything."

"That must get complicated."

"Oh, hell yeah. But Dave covers for me. It's good to have friends."

"Hm." Reggie crossed his arms and sank his chin on his chest.

The rest of our trip was completed in silence. When we wallowed around the corner into the underground parkade nearly an hour later, I drew a breath of profound relief at the feel of dry pavement under our tires.

Reggie ducked involuntarily as we drove under the height restriction sign. "That was close."

"Yeah, it'd just make my night if I jammed this thing in the parkade," I agreed. "But I checked the height spec as soon as I found out we were getting a Hummer." Navigating through the public part of the parkade, I steered onto the down-ramp. "I think this is the first time I've ever been glad to be going down into the bowels of the earth," I added. "I hate these basement parkades."

"You really should do something about that claustrophobia," Reggie chided.

"Yeah, and while I'm at it I'll just will myself a couple of inches taller and bulletproof."

"Any taller and you'll have to duck when you go through doors," Reggie disagreed. "Better just stick with 'bulletproof.'"

"Smartass." I stopped in front of the heavy steel garage door marked "Executive Parking Only - Private" and powered down the window to present my face for the retinal scan.

The scanner chirped its acceptance and the door rolled up. I drew a long breath and drove forward. Behind us, the door clanged down with the deadly finality of a steel trap, and I reminded myself to breathe while I wound down the narrow ramp into the concrete depths.

I could get out. I wasn't trapped.

Breathe...

I pulled into a parking space on the bottom level and got out, trying not to think about the tons of concrete hanging over my head. My knees threatened to give way and I clung to the Hummer's door until they deigned to hold my weight.

Suck it up. Super-spy Jane Bond would breeze through hypothermia and a blizzard and a concrete coffin and still be ready to take on a dozen enemies. How pathetic would I be if I fell flat on my ass from fear and exhaustion?

Hellhound's Forester cruised down the ramp and parked a couple of slots away, and it was all I could do not to stagger over and fall into his arms. Instead, I tottered around to the back of the Hummer to peel off my still-damp ski pants and swap my heavy Sorels for lighter hiking boots while my passengers disembarked.

A glance at my wristwatch doubled the weight of my fatigue, and I sagged against the vehicle. "God, it's eleven-thirty. Eight and a half hours to make a two-hour drive." A jaw-cracking yawn seized me, stinging my dry eyes with involuntary tears.

"At least the damn party should be over," Reggie muttered. "Come on, let's deliver these weapons and call it a night. God knows how long it'll take to get to the hotel in this shitty weather."

The thought of getting back in the Hummer and braving

the snow again was almost enough to bring real tears to my eyes. Suppressing the urge to curl into fetal position and stay that way until spring, I blew out a sigh and followed him to the Forester.

Hellhound was already standing at the rear hatch, stretching his shoulders and rolling his neck.

"How's your arm?" I asked.

"'Bout ninety percent." He raised both arms over his head, the right lagging only slightly behind the left. "Still buzzin' like a motherfucker, but it's gettin' better."

"Good," Reggie snapped. "Then grab those duffels and let's pack in this shit-show for the night."

"Sounds good to me," Hellhound agreed, effortlessly shouldering the three duffels and lifting out his guitar case.

I heaved an envious sigh. He would be safely indoors for the next twelve hours, maybe more. I still had to go out in the storm tonight, and then again the next morning to come back for the conference.

Maybe they had extra beds here...?

That optimistic thought carried me through the next security checkpoint behind Reggie and Hellhound, and into the depths of the facility.

As we opened the final door, the sound of music and chatter made my heart plummet.

"Jesus Christ!" Reggie snarled. "What the fuck is the *matter* with these people?"

"Clear the way!" Melinda sang out. "Party animals coming through!" She and Murray shouldered past us, ducking into the coatroom only long enough to shed their coats before hurrying ahead.

Hellhound brightened. "Sounds like they're set up in the

bullpen, an' I got a perfect sightline from there to the weapons lockup. Come on, let's stow this shit an' join the party." He gave me a suggestive grin and hefted his guitar. "Gotta make sure my fingers're still workin' right. Might need 'em later."

"Too much information," Reggie griped.

Hellhound pitched his parka into the corner of the coatroom and strode out carrying the weapons duffels and his guitar, while Reggie and I dawdled over removing our outerwear and carefully hanging it up.

When that complicated task was complete and we couldn't stall any longer, we exchange a glance and a simultaneous sigh and trailed reluctantly toward the bullpen.

Just before we abandoned the shelter of the corridor, Reggie's limp vanished and the right side of his face smoothed into an expression as impassive as the mask on his left. Imagining the pain of his abraded skin grinding against his prosthesis for the whole godawful length of this interminable day, I straightened my posture despite the ache in my back and shoulders. If he could do it, I could, too.

A few people glanced over and offered Reggie guarded nods when we entered, but one short cute blonde beelined over to grip his arm with a megawatt smile. In a perky Aussie accent she chirped, "Reggie! So stoked to see you again, love! Ready for a bit of the amber fluid?" She tilted her beer glass in his direction.

No answering smile lit Reggie's face, but I had no time to observe the rest of their interaction. My attention locked onto the broad-shouldered, devastatingly handsome man who was advancing on me with a smile of his own.

"Storm Cloud Dancer," he murmured for my ears only.

He captured my hand between his own, his green eyes sparkling with flirtatious mischief. "Smashing to see you."

A smile lifted the corners of my mouth despite my exhaustion, and I turned my head enough to prevent the security cameras from reading my lips. "Hi, Ian." I kept my voice as quiet as his. "Or do you prefer Orion Moonjava these days?"

He gave a theatrical wince and raised his glass to conceal his mouth as he spoke again. "It's Ian. Please. Orion Moonjava was not the most unpleasant role I've ever played, but it was definitely the most embarrassing."

"Oh, I don't know; I thought you made a pretty good hippy," I countered. "Especially after you dropped that fake Canadian accent. I like your real one better."

"Ah." His smile widened. "I've been told that Canadian women find a British accent quite the aphrodisiac. Perhaps I'll have a better chance with you this time, especially now that we can enjoy the trappings of civilization."

"Like room service... and hot showers... and king-sized beds?" I prompted with a slow smile, watching the sparks flare in his gorgeous eyes. Then I laughed and added, "Give it up. You just want to get me into bed so you can get your fifty bucks back from Skidmark."

His jaw dropped. "He told you about our bet? That old reprobate; I knew I shouldn't trust him."

"Yeah, speaking of that..." A couple of people detached themselves from the crowd to head our way, and I dropped my voice to a rapid whisper. "Did you mention me to Five Eyes?"

"No, of course not. As far as they know you were never there, and you and I have just met."

"But..." I began, but he raised his voice to party-conversation levels and talked over me.

"...and with such lovely red hair, I knew you must have some Irish in the mix somewhere." He turned to greet the tanned thirtyish man and elderly woman who had approached. "This is Aydan Kelly," he informed them. He threw one of his dazzling smiles my way, still holding my hand. "Irish-Canadian, as I correctly guessed." He turned back to me. "Aydan, may I present Nora Taylor, the U.K.'s Director of Weapons Research, and Brad Wilson, her counterpart from the United States."

Despite Reggie's dire warnings and my own suspicions, my defences shattered at the sight of Nora Taylor's smiling eyes and softly wrinkled features. My heart gave a painful tug. Only a few days ago I had marked my mother's birthday with bittersweet remembrance. If she hadn't died thirty years ago, she might look like Nora now...

I swallowed hard and squashed the emotion back into its usual compartment. Too tired. Keep your head in the game.

"Nice to meet you," I said, extracting my hand from Ian's to offer a handshake first to Nora, then Brad. The two people who had specifically requested my presence.

Well, let's just stir the pot and see what surfaces.

I gave them a smile and added, "You have me at a bit of a disadvantage. Since you both requested me, you must know more about me than I know about you."

Nora and Brad exchanged a startled glance.

"I didn't realize you knew Agent Kelly," Brad said to Nora, faint accusation colouring his words.

"I don't," Nora replied with a smile that looked forced. "But after Ian's descriptions of her exploits, I certainly wanted to meet her."

What the hell? Ian had just finished saying he hadn't reported me. I skewered him with my gaze. We had barely exchanged a dozen words and he'd lied to me already, the bastard.

And why hadn't Nora admitted the true reason she wanted to talk to me?

Maybe they were both lying...

Ian hastened to explain, "I read the report your Director provided during the terrorist crisis last month. He was quite stingy with the details but it certainly sounded like an interesting story. I requested this assignment hoping I'd get to meet you and hear about it in person."

What the hell? Surely Stemp wouldn't have identified me in his reports. And why would Ian go to so much trouble to see me? Either he was truly desperate to win his bet with Skidmark, or he had some other agenda.

And I was pretty sure he didn't need fifty bucks that badly.

I gave him a thin smile. "I'd love to talk shop, but... classified. Sorry."

"What was your interest in Agent Kelly?" Nora asked Brad.

"Oh, the same report, of course," he said smoothly. "It's always so much more informative to hear a first-hand account."

There was so much bullshit floating around us, the air was turning brown. I added my own shovelful.

"Well, it was very nice to meet you," I lied. "But it's been an exhausting day and I'm going to go and grab a drink. Excuse me."

I left them standing there eyeing each other with thinly-veiled suspicion.

CHAPTER 9

Weaving through the crowd, I reflexively catalogued the scene. About thirty people stood chatting in small groups, drinks in hands. Nora was the oldest, and the little blonde who had greeted Reggie was probably the youngest; although with Botox and fillers and God-knew-what other cosmetic procedures, it was hard to tell.

About two-thirds of the partygoers wouldn't pose a threat to anything but a lab rat. No pocket protectors or lab coats were in evidence, but the soft physiques and slightly rounded shoulders of the scientists were easy to identify. Reggie was the exception, his powerful shoulders filling his suit jacket and his posture military-straight.

The little blonde scientist was still chattering away at him with an animated smile. Despite the drink in his hand, Reggie didn't seem to be relaxing. He stood with his reconstructed left side turned away from his companion, but even the right side of his face was immobile enough to be a mask. He nodded occasionally while she talked, but he wasn't speaking.

The remainder of the crowd looked dangerously athletic. Hellhound was by far the biggest and scariest; but they all carried themselves as though ready for instant action. Their gazes scanned the crowd constantly despite their casual poses.

As I collected a glass of ginger ale from the bar, Ian strolled up. "Well, that was interesting," he said with his engaging smile. "I didn't expect her to throw me to the wolves like that."

I kept a polite expression on my face. "Well, if you hadn't lied to me in the first place, there wouldn't have been any wolves. *Orion.*"

"Honestly, I didn't breathe a word." His accent sharpened to a knife-edge and his flirtatious sparkle vanished, revealing the hard-eyed agent behind the playboy façade. "I promised Moonbeam and Karma and Skidmark that their secret was safe with me, and that promise extends to you, too. I will literally protect your secret with my life. I did *not* blow your cover. Nora's the one who-"

"Kelly!" Reggie's irritable voice interrupted. When I turned to him, his expression was as impassive as ever despite the belligerence in his tone. "Get lost, Rand," he gritted, barely moving his lips. "I need to talk to my agent. In private." The solid jolt of alcohol on his breath surprised me. We'd been here less than half an hour. Had he been hammering back shots when I wasn't looking?

"Lovely to see you again, too, Reggie," Ian replied with a gracious smile. "Charming as ever, I see."

"Fuck off." Reggie hooked his hand into my elbow and drew me away.

"See you later, Aydan," Ian called after us.

I threw a vague smile over my shoulder at him before focusing on Reggie. "What's wrong?"

"Nothing. Rand gets up my ass, that's all."

"He wasn't anywhere near your ass," I protested. "You're the one that barged into our conversation."

"Yeah, you can thank me later." When I frowned, he added, "The guy's a horndog. He's screwed nearly everybody in this room; most of them twice. You're just fresh meat to him."

I faked enlightenment. "Oh, so that's what you meant when you said he got up your ass. You were being literal."

Reggie snorted. "I wouldn't let him anywhere near my ass. I like women, thanks; but he's not fussy. I wouldn't be surprised if he's done half the guys here, too."

"Maybe," I equivocated. "He does seem like the kind of guy who'd screw anything that moved."

"Or bleated." Reggie's lips twisted in his wicked one-sided smirk.

I snickered, then sobered. "Okay; so besides charging over here to defend my virtue, what's up?"

"Nothing. Just needed to get away from Little Mary Sunshine."

He shot a sour look at the blonde, who unfortunately chose that moment to surface from a conversation with her companions and glance our way. She gave him another sparkling smile and a little finger-wave.

Without acknowledging the gesture, he gripped my arm again and turned us away from her.

"What's the problem?" I asked. "She's cute, she seems to like you..." I nudged him companionably. "God knows why; you're such a cranky sonuvabitch. But you just finished saying you like women, so... where's the problem?"

"She's so fucking perky it makes my teeth ache. And she

never fucking shuts up."

"Maybe because you never say anything," I teased.

"Drop it, Kelly," he growled.

"Okay, don't get your knickers in a twist. I'll save you from the cute little girl." I surveyed the crowd again. "Actually, maybe you can help me out. How many of these people do you know? Can you give me a briefing?"

Relief flickered in his face before his deadpan expression closed down again. "Yeah. Let's sit. My fucking stump is killing me," he muttered, barely moving his lips.

We retreated to a couple of chairs in the corner and Reggie sank into one with a hiss of exhaled breath.

"Did you push too hard with your training again?" I asked, eyeing his stony expression with concern. "I know you want to be ready for the Paralympics, but if you injure yourself you won't be able to go at all."

He shrugged. "When you're pushing for top performance, shit happens sometimes. I've still got nearly eight months. It'll be fine."

"But shouldn't you let it heal? You've probably been making it worse by being on it all day. I can go and get your chair-"

"No!"

I twitched at the vehemence of his response, and he lowered his voice and ground out, "Thanks, though." The words strained out grudgingly between his teeth.

I kept my tone light. "No problem." I changed the subject. "So who are the players here?"

He relaxed. "Well, you met Horndog Rand, and I saw you talking to Brad Weasel earlier..."

"That would be Brad Wilson?" I inquired.

"Isn't that what I said?" He gave me an innocent look, spoiled by the evil twinkle in his eye. "And I'm assuming the woman with him was Nora Taylor, my opposite number from the UK. I haven't met her yet. Little Mary Sunshine over there is Katie Gardner, Australia's top weapons researcher. Brilliant mind. Absolutely fucking brilliant."

His gaze wandered to where Katie stood in animated conversation with a small knot of people. When she glanced our way again his gaze flicked back to me. "Too bad she's so damn annoying. That long drink of water next to her is the Aussie weapons director. Knows his stuff, but he plays the Crocodile Dundee shtick to the hilt. Irritating as all hell..."

Names blurred together in my tired mind as he went on identifying people and positions, adding mostly-disparaging comments about their personalities.

As I had surmised, the soft-bodied people were scientists, and the scary-fit ones were the agents assigned to protect them. Hellhound's weapons-specialist counterparts looked less frightening than he did; but despite his battle-scarred features and the angry redness of the frostbite on his face he was gathering a rapt audience. Someone had turned off the canned music, and Arnie's nimble fingers danced over the guitar strings while his rough sexy voice alternately teased and entreated in a seductive blues number.

God, I could listen to him all day long. And all night, too. Good blues was almost as sensuous as good sex, and he was brilliant at both...

"Hey." Reggie's voice and elbow-nudge roused me from my reverie. "Stay with me here. Those are the agents from the States." He nodded toward two suit-clad men at the fringe of the party who were eyeing the crowd and each other with equal suspicion. "They're new this year," Reggie said. "The dark guy on the left is Dirk from the FBI. The fish-belly-white guy is Grandin. CIA. Those are the only names they gave, so I don't know whether they're first names, last names, or aliases. Katie says they haven't said two words to anybody all night." The right side of his lips curled in a sardonic smile. "All the other countries send an agent to watch out for their scientists, but I'm pretty sure the U.S. sends the FBI and CIA to watch each other."

Across the room, Katie glanced our way again. The smile vanished from Reggie's face as if it had never existed. "Need to piss," he muttered, and stood. His jaw muscles rippled, and I winced in sympathy for the raw pain I was certain he was concealing. His face remained expressionless, and he strode away without limping.

I tracked his progress to the men's room and saw no sign of alcoholic impairment. Maybe he smelled boozy because somebody had spilled a drink on him? But I hadn't noticed any wet spots on his clothes...

"Hi," a cheery voice greeted me from the approximate vicinity of my chest.

I looked down into Little Mary Sunshine's bright smile.

"Hi, Mary," I said without thinking, then bit my tongue too late. "Sorry, you're not Mary," I added. "I was, um... thinking of somebody else."

"No worries!" She stuck out her hand. "I'm Katie Gardner. Oz." She eyed my blank expression and translated, "Australia." Her accent rendered it 'Straya', and I smiled.

"Nice to meet you." I shook her hand. "I'm Aydan Kelly. Canada."

"You must be an agent." Her gaze travelled over my

jeans and Hellhound's giant sweatshirt.

Suddenly conscious of my dishevelled appearance among the well-dressed group, I eased a step backward in case the reek of stale panic and sweat was wafting her way. "Um, sorry. We went off the road on the way here and I had to shovel..." I made a vague gesture at my clothes, realizing as I did that I'd torn a nail sometime during the evening's misadventures and the end of my finger was smeared with dried blood.

Why hadn't I thought to freshen up before joining the party? And Ian had hugged me, poor man. It was a miracle he hadn't keeled over from the smell. I passed a hand over my hair, trying not to wince at the feel of the sweat-induced frizz.

"Sorry," I repeated.

She laughed. "You Canadians really do apologize for everything, don't you?"

"Um, yeah. I guess so." I gave her a grin. "Sorry."

Her laughter pealed out again. "No wonder Reggie likes you."

"Reggie doesn't like anybody," I said reflexively.

"Nah, he deffo likes you," she insisted. "I've never seen him smile before, but he smiled at you. Well, half, anyway." She huffed a little sigh and studied the beer in her glass. "More than he ever gave me. Is he... or... are you..." She raised a cautious blue-eyed gaze to mine.

"We aren't," I said. "And he's not gay, if that's what you're asking."

"Bonzer!" Based on Katie's satisfied expression, I deduced that meant 'good'. She went on to inquire matter-of-factly, "He's blind in his left eye isn't he?"

I hesitated. The fixed stare of his prosthetic eye wasn't hard to miss if anyone observed him closely. But should I confirm or deny?

"And I think he's deaf on his left, too," she went on thoughtfully. "He always turns his right side to me when I'm talking."

Dammit, why couldn't she just be a cute dumb little bimbo?

"Hm," I said, knowing Reggie would be furious if he found out we had discussed him.

"And he doesn't have much mobility in his left hand. I've been wondering if he's had a stroke, but that doesn't add up. He moves too powerfully and his muscular development is symmetrical." She grinned, visibly switching from the analytical scientist to the gregarious party girl. "And believe me, I noticed his muscular development. What a spunk! Wouldn't I love to have a naughty with him!"

"Hm," I repeated, hoping she'd just keep talking and save me from answering.

"You're not going to talk about him, are you?" she asked as though reading my mind.

Dammit.

"Well..." I shrugged. "Confidentiality. Sorry."

"No worries. But..." Her smile dimmed and her forlorn face turned up to me again. "Maybe... he just doesn't like me?"

My heart squeezed. "No, I don't think it's that. He just isn't very comfortable with other people."

"He's shy?" Hope lit her face. "Ace! Then I'll bail him up and have another burl."

"Uh..." I began, hoping for a translation.

"Cheers, love!"

She bounced away, leaving me wondering exactly what she'd just threatened to do to Reggie.

When he reappeared beside me, looking wary, I said, "Katie likes you."

"Oh, for chrissake!" he snarled. "What is this, junior high? Get me the fuck out of here before I develop zits and an overbite all over again!"

I couldn't help recoiling a step from his venom. "Jeez, I thought you'd be happy. She's cute, blonde, and female. That'd do it for most guys." I inclined my chin toward the opposite side of the room, where Katie stood bantering with several men who were giving her puppy-dog eyes, clearly wishing they could roll over and let her rub their tummies. Or rub something.

"I'm not most guys," Reggie growled. "Let's blow this fucking popsicle stand."

I smothered a yawn that made my eyes water. Nora had kept her distance since our introduction, so apparently she didn't want to talk where we could be observed. And I was too damn exhausted to hang around until the party wound down.

Fuck it. We could have our conversation tomorrow.

"Good plan," I agreed. "Let's corral the party animals."

That proved as difficult as I'd anticipated. Reggie grew increasingly cantankerous while Murray and Melinda argued and cajoled in an attempt to stay longer.

At last my patience frayed. "I'm sorry," I said firmly. "But Reggie and I are done for, and I won't separate the group."

Melinda began, "But Helmand's staying...", and I held up

a quelling hand and talked over her.

"I checked, and there aren't any beds here at the facility. If Arnie gets any sleep tonight it'll be in a chair beside the weapons lockup. I'm not planning to join him, so neither are you. Put on your coats. We're leaving now."

Murray capitulated to my show of authority immediately, with a flush and a glint in his eyes that made me glad I wasn't privy to his fantasy life. Melinda bowed to the inevitable with reasonably good grace.

Five minutes later I waved goodbye to Hellhound from the door and blew him a kiss. Smiling, he captured it from the air without missing a beat in his song.

Ian hurried up as I was turning away. "I'm sorry we didn't get to talk more," he said, ignoring Reggie's hostile glower beside me. "Maybe tomorrow?"

"Maybe," I agreed, not wanting to stretch Reggie's nonexistent patience any farther. "See you."

I ignored Reggie's muttered griping while we made our way back to the Hummer. With everyone safely installed in the vehicle, we wound our way back up the concrete ramp and I drew a breath of relief as we left its confines at last.

My relief was short-lived when we plunged back out into the blizzard, but at that hour traffic was sparse and the plows were hard at work. With cautious driving the Hummer performed faultlessly, and only ten minutes later we pulled under the portico of our hotel.

Murray volunteered to register and pick up our parking pass and cardkeys, and after a moment's consideration I agreed. The service desk was clearly visible in the bright lobby. I'd have a good sightline to him, and I could protect Reggie and Melinda in the more vulnerable vehicle at the same time.

Alternating surveillance of the Hummer's mirrors and Murray's progress in the lobby, I had used up the last of my adrenaline by the time he returned unscathed. I gripped the steering wheel to conceal the trembling of my hands and navigated into the parking garage.

After parking in our assigned slot I dragged myself out of the Hummer and around to the back, where I lifted out Reggie's wheelchair and unfolded it.

"Sit," I commanded.

"Fuck off." He glared at me across the chair.

Glaring back at him, I quoted Stemp's words. "Kelly is in charge. You will obey her orders immediately, without question, and to the letter. So. Sit. The fuck. *Down*."

"You're such a fucking bee-yotch."

But he sat. A small groan escaped him as he sank into the chair, and I quietly savored the knowledge that pulling rank had been the right thing to do.

"Here you go," I said, piling his bags onto his lap. He said nothing, and I slung my backpack over my shoulders and moved behind him to the handles of the wheelchair.

"I can manage," he growled, then added in a slightly less combative tone, "I need the upper-body workout. I haven't done anything today."

"Okay," I agreed.

He dug his fingernails into the fake skin around his left wrist, working methodically to release it on all sides, then peeled the prosthetic hand off and vigorously scratched the back and palm of his pincer-hand. "Thank Christ," he muttered. "That's been driving me nuts all day." He plopped the disembodied hand unceremoniously on his lap behind his suitcases and wheeled away at his usual breakneck speed.

Herding Melinda and Murray on ahead, I plodded behind. Somehow I managed to stay vertical until they were all safely installed in our adjoining rooms with instructions to open their doors to nobody but me, and to be ready for breakfast at eight-fifteen the next morning.

Then I stumbled into my own room and fell face-down onto the bed.

A sound woke me.

Before my body was even capable of moving, my brain had hurtled through its database of stored sounds and disgorged the translation and location:

The sickening thud of a body hitting the floor.

Reggie's room.

CHAPTER 10

A massive jolt of adrenaline rocketed me up from the hotel bed. I twisted in midair and hit the carpet running.

Wrenching my own door open, I landed in front of Reggie's in a single bound. The duplicate cardkeys to all the rooms were still clutched in my fist from when I'd fallen asleep, thank God.

I jabbed the first one into the slot.

Luck was with me. Green light.

I lunged through the door, Glock at the ready.

Gun. Aimed at me.

My body reacted almost before my eyes delivered the message. I sprang sideways into the bathroom, raking a glance around it as I landed in a crouch.

Empty.

I snapped around to face the door, my Glock hovering indecisively.

The voice attached to the gun growled, "Get th' fug outta here right fuggen now, or I'll blow y'r fuggen head off."

"Reggie," I said cautiously, "What's going on?"

"Get th' fug outta here, Kelly," he grated. "Or I shwear I'll cap y'r fuggen ash."

"Well, I have to come out of the bathroom to leave your room," I explained, my voice wavering slightly under the hammering of my heart. "And I haven't quite mastered that 'bulletproof' trick yet. So maybe... you could just put the gun down? Please?"

"Ah, for fuckshakesh." The slurred words were delivered on a weary breath, followed by the soft thud of his weapon hitting the carpet.

I eased as little as possible of my head and one eye out the door. Wearing only boxer shorts, Reggie sprawled facedown on the carpet, the gun inches away from his inert right hand. His empty-eyed half-face mask observed with macabre serenity from a stand on the table, but there was no sign of anyone else.

Sidestepping out the bathroom door, I pressed my back against the wall for an instant before pivoting around the corner gun-first.

Still nobody.

Reggie didn't move.

In a couple of quick strides I checked behind and under the bed.

We were alone.

After scooping up Reggie's gun and stuffing it in the back of my jeans, I holstered my own weapon and knelt beside him. My heartbeat shook my entire body and my fingertips tingled from the adrenaline overdose.

Two empty forty-ounce liquor bottles lay on the bed and the air was heavy with the stench of alcohol. Reggie was making strangled snoring sounds, and I carefully turned his head so he could breathe more easily.

"Thanksh," he muttered. Then, "If I move, will you shoot

me?"

"You can move." As he squirmed slowly into a more comfortable position, I added, "I heard you fall. Are you hurt?"

"No." He heaved his torso up on powerful arms and blinked blearily at me. My throat constricted at the roadmap of suffering etched on his body. The left side of his muscular chest and arm was a shiny patchwork of burn scars. Other brutal scars tore across his thighs, back, and abdomen. The precise tracks of a surgeon's scalpel intersected them, somehow seeming crueller than the original damage.

Then I spotted the angry abrasion oozing blood and serum on the stump of his right leg. "Holy shit, that looks bad," I croaked.

"Yeah, I'm a real fuggen prize," he slurred caustically. "Tha's why I wanted my own room. Didn' want you to hafta look at..." His chin jerked down, indicating his devastated body. The good side of his mouth curled into a bitter grimace. "Bet you really wanna have my baby now."

"No, dipshit, we already had that conversation," I said with fake indignation. "I was talking about the abrasion on your leg."

"Oh." He flopped facedown again. "Can't feel it now," he mumbled into the carpet.

"Can I help you up?"

He snorted. "Dunno; can you?"

"If you'll tell me what's the best way to do it."

"Fuckit. Jush leeme here. Gimme a blanket an' I'll be fine."

I sat back on my heels and regarded him for a moment, willing my pulse back to normal. His nice business suit was crumpled on the floor beside his detached prosthetic legs. His wheelchair stood beside the bed.

"Did you get out of bed and miss the chair?" I asked.

"Yeah. Fuggen bedshpread shlid out from under me." He rolled onto his back with a long sigh. Propping his truncated legs against the bed in an attitude of lordly ease, he waved a regal hand. "Well, c'mon, Florence Fuggen Night'ngale..." He hiccupped loudly, then continued, "...get me back in m' chair. Gotta pish."

"You *are* pissed."

He blinked up at me with the owlish dignity only achievable by the completely plastered. "'Am... am...'" he began, then let out another hiccup that turned into a bark of bitter laughter. "H'lo, 'am... am Reggie an' I'm analk...hic...holic." He bobbed his head as though accepting applause. "Thang ya verra mush."

"Come on, idiot," I said. "Put your arms around my neck."

"Putcher... hic... arms 'roun' me baby..." he warbled tunelessly, but he did reach up and lock his arms around me as directed.

I hauled him up to perch unsteadily on the edge of the bed, and from there we managed a perilous transfer to his wheelchair. He fell into it with a grunt.

"Thanksh, Kelly," he said with a gesture that was probably supposed to be grandiose but in fact nearly struck me in the nose. "You can go now," he enunciated carefully.

"Not quite yet." I seized the handles of the wheelchair and steered him to the bathroom.

"Gonna watch me whiz?" He lolled his head back, leering at me upside down.

"Sure." I manoeuvred the chair over beside the tub. "Come on, you're going to sit on the edge of the tub for a minute."

"'Kay," he said, far more agreeably than if he'd been sober.

After another shaky transfer, I wheeled the chair out of harm's way. Then before he could react, I dropped to my knees and spun, shoving my weight at him while I supported his back with one arm and clutched his head to my shoulder with the other.

As I had hoped, he overbalanced neatly into the bathtub while I protected his head from the impact. A spate of violent profanity erupted from his mouth, rapidly strangled when I transferred my grip to his hair, wrenched his head back, and stuck my finger down his throat.

It wasn't subtle, but it did the job.

When he had finally finished retching, he glared up at me from the reeking vomit-puddled tub.

"Wha' th' fug-" he began, only to unleash another volley of swearing when I yanked the shower curtain shut and turned on the shower.

"Go ahead and piss in the tub," I said. "Then wash. Yourself and the tub." I slapped the tube of shower gel onto the edge of the tub.

He swore some more, but a few seconds later the sound of splashing and the herbal scent of shower gel signalled his obedience; although maybe he skipped the pissing part. I didn't observe too closely.

After a few minutes the shower turned off and he pushed the curtain back, clean and looking more like his usual crotchety self.

I tossed him a towel. "Here. I'll get you some dry shorts."

He plied the towel in silence, and I retreated to rifle through his suitcase.

When I returned he was kneeling on the bathmat with the towel wrapped around his waist and his soggy shorts draped over the side of the tub. Wordlessly, he reached out a hand and I gave him the dry underwear. Leaning on the tub for balance, he pulled the shorts on and then discarded the towel.

"Bring my chair," he growled. When I wheeled it closer, he instructed, "Face it this way. Set th' brakes."

I did as he instructed, then stepped forward to help him.

"Back off," he snapped, and turned his back on me and the chair.

Hovering uncertainly, I watched his muscles ripple as he rolled his shoulders, then placed both hands flat on the floor.

A moment later his legs rose ceiling-ward as he unfolded into an unsteady handstand.

"Fuck!" I yelped. "Cut it out, you'll kill yourself!"

"Shut up." He wobbled, and I lunged forward to steady him.

"Get down," I barked. "You're shit-faced. Now is not the time-"

"Get... the fug... outta my way... or I'll kick you... in th' fuggen head!"

"Fine, asshole!" I let go and stepped back. "When you break your back on the bathtub, I'll-"

His arms flexed, then exploded into a powerful upward thrust as he jackknifed his legs downward. The perfect handspring landed him seated and smirking in his chair.

"What... the..." I gaped at him.

"Not bad f'r a fuggen drunk cripple, eh?"

"Fucking drunk idiot, you mean. You could have broken your neck!"

"Been doing it f'r years. Never missed yet." He spun the chair and wheeled out the door. When I followed he halted in the vestibule, blocking the way to his room. "Time f'r you t'go now. Buh-bye."

"Wrong," I snapped, and tried to push past him.

With a lightning-fast spin of the chair he blocked me, then spun again in another successful block as I tried to go around the other way.

"Buh-bye," he repeated, grinning.

"Hello," I countered. I sat down in his lap, bracing a hand on each of his shoulders and twisting to drape my legs over the arm of his chair.

For a frozen moment he stared at me from close range, his mouth hanging open. Then I pushed off and slid over the wheelchair arm to land in his room. Striding over to the armchair, I sank into it and scowled at him.

He groaned. "Christ, you crushed my fuggen nuts."

"Nut," I corrected irritably. "Your left is prosthetic, remember?"

"Whatever. Wha' d'you want from me? Why won't you go 'way?"

"I want to know why..." I drew a deep breath, trying to keep my temper. "...the sweet *fuck*..." My voice was rising in spite of my efforts. "...you pulled *a fucking gun on me*!" All my unspent adrenaline surged out in a roar of rage. "YOU FUCKING PRICK!"

"Oh." His voice was small. "F'rgot 'bout that. Shorry."

"You're too fucking right you're a sorry bastard," I snarled. "Now tell me, *what the fuck was that?*"

"Sh... Sorry," he repeated. "I was a bit waish... wasted."

"No shit. You still are. And you still haven't answered my question."

"You shcared the shit outta me. I was pished." As I opened my mouth to yell at him again, he added, "Pished off, I mean. Sh... scared. Angry. Y'know."

I closed my mouth. I did know. It was exactly what I was feeling.

He sighed and wheeled over to the bed. "Lookit it my way. I'm lyin' here waishted outta my fuggen mind; I get up to take a leak an' the fuggen bedspread dumps me onna floor; an' two sheconds later my door flies open an' I'm looking down a fuggen gun barrel. So yeah, I was fuggen pished off."

"And you just happened to have a firearm on you at the time," I prompted cynically.

He stared at me. "Well, hell yeah. Alla time. What, you don' shleep with your gun?"

I blinked. "Well, yeah, of course, but..."

He made a 'duh' gesture and transferred himself onto the bed, where he stacked a couple of pillows against the headboard and flopped back with a yawn. "Sho... So... can I have my gun back?" When I hesitated, he added, "Please?"

"Maybe. If you explain why the hell you thought it would be a good idea to suck back two forty-pounders of hard liquor tonight."

"Didn't," he muttered sulkily. "They were half empty when I lifted 'em from the bar. Hardly a decent drink in either of 'em. I wasn't anywhere near alk'hol poisoning. You didn't need to make me puke."

"You stole them?" I sank my aching head into my hands. "Why?"

"'Cause I'm a fuggen alk'holic. 'S what I do."

"Every night?" I studied him with concern. "You need help."

"Got help," he growled. "Thish's my first time off the wagon in..." He heaved a defeated sigh. "Three years, five months, an' forty-two days. Fuck."

My heart clenched. "Oh, Reggie, I'm sorry. What happened? What can I do to help?"

"Nothing. Jush leave me 'lone an' lemme sober up." His lips twisted in a bitter parody of a smile as he gestured at the empty bottles. "Party's over."

"But after all that time sober, why would you..." I trailed off, suddenly making the connection. "Oh, shit. You like Katie, too, but you won't respond to her because you think she'd freak out if she saw your real-"

He interrupted with a bark of harsh laughter. "Chrisht, Kelly, give up the fuggen romantic-tragedy bullshit. I had a shitty day, okay? My stump hurts like a bitch, I watched one of my friends..." He glared at me. "...damn near die in a fuggen blizzard, an' I really fuggen hate making sh... small talk. And then there was booze. Once an alk'holic, always a fuggen alk'holic."

I stared at him, debating whether to push the issue. He stared back, defiant.

I backed down first. "So that abrasion on your leg looks pretty bad."

"My *stump*," he corrected. "That's what it's called. Stop trying to be all fuggen tactful."

"Whatever. It's bad."

"Yeah." He directed an unfocused scowl at the ugly wound. "Fugged it up worse when I fell on it. Fuggen shlippery bedspread."

"Do you have bandages? Antibiotic cream?"

"In my suitcase."

I rose and headed for his suitcase. "I'll get it for-"

"Back off, Florence Fuggen Night'ngale. I'll take care of it." He gave me another defiant glare.

Fatigue descended on me like a leaden blanket and I smothered a yawn. "Would you like some company while you sober up?"

"No."

"Is there somebody you can call? An AA sponsor?"

"Didn't do AA. All that shit about God." He snorted. "If there's a God, he's a fuggen sh... sadishtic bashtard."

"But-" I began.

He flung out a hand. "Don't fuggen start."

"I was just going to say-"

"Say goodnight."

Eyeing his implacable face, I blew out an exhausted sigh. "Fine. Goodnight."

I laid his gun beside him on the bed and left.

CHAPTER 11

An irritating sound buzzed at the edges of my consciousness.

Groaning, I pulled the blanket over my head and clung to sleep. Then my damn brain identified the sound as my cell phone vibrating, and booted me into wakefulness. Eyes closed, I fumbled my phone off the nightstand and accepted the call.

"H'lo?" I croaked.

"Good morning." John Kane's warm baritone tickled my ear, and I sighed. Happy dreams...

"Aydan?" His voice quickened with concern. "I'm sorry, did I wake you?"

I groaned. "Wha' time izzit?"

"It's seven-thirty. I'm sorry, you're usually up early and I thought..."

"Seven-thirty? Shit!" I jerked upright, squinting at the clock. "Don't be sorry; I owe you one. I got to bed around three o'clock last night and forgot to set my alarm."

"Do you need to leave right away?"

"No." I fell back with a sigh of relief. "Your timing is perfect. I've got about five minutes before I need to get in the shower. So how are you?"

"I'm fine." I could hear his wry smile as he added, "I don't suppose you were lucky enough to be up 'til all hours because you wanted to be."

A montage of the previous day replayed in my brain and I shuddered. "Oh, hell no."

Caution crept into his voice. "Are you working?"

"Yeah." I didn't elaborate. Couldn't, since he wasn't an agent anymore. I sighed. "So what's up?"

"I was just calling to see if that invitation to come over and work on your car was still standing."

"What, don't tell me you're finally going to have a day with no hockey games or school concerts or family crises," I teased.

"I'm sorry it hasn't worked out for the past month," he said. "It's certainly been frustrating, but this time it may pan out. It's up to you."

"Me? Since when do I have any influence on Daniel's hockey schedule or Alicia's passive-aggressive head games?"

"Well..." He hesitated. "Would... it be all right if I brought Daniel with me?"

"Um..."

"Alicia suggested it," Kane added. "So she likely won't sabotage it this time."

Yeah, right. She had already sabotaged it. She knew damn well I wouldn't deprive Kane and Daniel of precious father-son time; and a wide-eyed six-year-old chaperone would ensure there were no private exchanges between Kane and me.

Instead of voicing that thought I said, "Okay. Um... when were you thinking of coming?"

"Sunday afternoon, if it's all right. If..." he hesitated again. "...you think it's safe? For Daniel?"

I took stock. Today's conference seemed pretty straightforward. We'd finish up and go home; and as far as I knew I had no new missions coming up. I'd be home from the wedding by Sunday afternoon. And nobody had tried to kill me for at least a month...

I suppressed a sigh at the ever-widening gulf between Kane's safe new family life and my violent and dangerous world. "I don't foresee any problems, but we can touch base Sunday morning and confirm."

"That would be great." His voice deepened. "It will be good to see you again. I've missed you."

I shivered at the caress of that velvet voice and my belly warmed.

Bad belly. Stop that.

My admonition had no effect, and my perfidious memory joined the mutiny with a red-hot image of a magnificently naked Kane smiling up at me from rumpled sheets.

Dammit, cut it out. We're going to get to know each other as friends this time. Build trust slowly...

Another X-rated memory blazed into my mind, and my throat went dry.

"It'll be good to see you, too," I croaked. "I have to go now. Thanks again for calling. 'Bye."

I disconnected and squeezed my eyes shut, thumping my forehead with the heels of both hands. Get it out of my head.

Shit, maybe it was best if Daniel came along. If I could keep my hands off Kane long enough to think straight, I'd know I was only torturing us both by holding onto our relationship. Fatherhood was his top priority now; and there was no room for a child in my life.

The thought of being even partially responsible for a child made claustrophobic terror clutch my throat. And if that child, plus a husband, were in my home all day, every day, depending on me, needing me...

Panic quickened my breath and I thumped my forehead again.

Stop it. That wouldn't happen unless I allowed it. And Kane wouldn't try to manipulate me into it.

Probably not, anyway...

"Shut the fuck up!" I growled aloud. "I've already dealt with that shit. Focus on the mission, idiot."

Which brought up another dilemma. Should I go next door and rouse Reggie from his well-deserved hangover so he had enough time to dress and have breakfast?

Or should I just let him wallow until...

Shit. He needed two hours to get his face on. And we were supposed to be at the secured facility by nine-thirty. He'd be late for sure.

I rolled out of bed and yanked on my jeans and sweatshirt.

Standing in front of Reggie's door, I tapped lightly.

No reply.

Shit.

I knocked again, louder this time.

Still no reply.

I swore and plied the cardkey, fervently hoping that he didn't take a potshot at me when I woke him from a dead sleep.

When I eased the door open, light from inside the room raised my hopes. Maybe he was already up.

Or maybe he'd passed out with all the lights blazing last night.

"Reggie?" I called softly. "It's Aydan. Are you up?"

"Get lost!"

The irritable growl wasn't accompanied by a bullet, so I slipped inside and let the door swing shut behind me.

"Christ, Kelly, what part of 'get lost' didn't you grasp?" Reggie snarled. He directed a glare at me from his wheelchair in front of the bathroom mirror. The scarred half of his face was already covered by the mask but the edges hung loose, looking disturbingly like flayed skin.

"Are you done gawking yet?" he ground out. "What the fuck do you want?"

"Sorry," I said reflexively. "It's just... that mask is kinda gross."

"Look who's talking. You look like shit."

I flipped him the bird. "And whose fault is that, asshole?"

He jabbed up a stiff middle finger in return. "I never asked you to come barging in here last night and wreck a perfectly good bender." He turned back to the mirror and continued smoothing the mask into place. "So did you just pop in to piss me off this morning, or do you actually have a reason to be here?"

"I was checking to make sure you'd gotten up in time to get your face on."

"Yep."

I stared at him.

Waiting for a thank you. Or an apology. Or hell, who knew what? Maybe just a dismissive 'fuck you'.

He ignored me.

Fine.

As I turned to leave, his voice stopped me.

"Sorry."

When I turned back to him he met my gaze squarely and added, "I let you down." His gaze wavered and dropped to his lap. "I let both of us down. I'll do better."

"You didn't let me down," I said quietly. "You were there when I needed you, keeping Melinda and Murray calm and coordinating communications and manning the P90. I'm sorry for putting you in that position. I didn't realize what it would do to you."

"Not your fault. A shitty day is just an excuse for an alcoholic. I was weak." His gaze drifted back to his reflection in the mirror. "I thought maybe I could handle it by now..." he added as if to himself.

I wasn't sure whether he was talking about his addiction to alcohol or his attraction to Katie, so I went with a general question. Blunt enough that he wouldn't accuse me of tact again.

"Did you start drinking after you lost your legs?"

He snapped back to the present with a glare. "I didn't *lose* my legs, I got them blown off by a fucking IED. Christ, I hate that expression, 'lost your legs'. Like I fucking laid them down somewhere and just can't remember where I put them."

I threw up my hands. "All right, fine, you prickly alcoholic bastard! Have you always been a fucking lush, or did you start after you got blown up and burned?"

He leaned back in his chair, the good side of his lips quirking up. "No, I wasn't always a lush. I got addicted to opioid painkillers when I was in the hospital. When I finally got out and healed up enough that the docs didn't want to prescribe them for me anymore, I needed something else to take the edge off. Alcohol was easy to get." He grimaced. "I kicked the narcotics and got addicted to booze instead."

"And then kicked that, too," I countered. "For three years, five months..."

"...and forty-two days," he finished. "And here I am back at Day One."

"I'm sorry. That sucks."

"It is what it is. I'll beat it in the end."

"I know you will." I grinned at him. "You're too fucking ornery not to."

He gave me his wicked half-grin in return. "You're pretty damn ornery yourself." He sobered. "Seriously, though, thanks. For..." He hesitated as if choosing his words carefully. "...watching out for me." Before I could respond, he added, "Now get the hell out of my room so I can get this fucking face on."

Smiling, I reminded him, "Breakfast in my room in half an hour."

"Can we make it my room?" He gestured at his wheelchair. "It'll give me a few more minutes off my legs."

"You're going to wear your legs today?" I frowned. "You shouldn't-"

"I'm going to," he interrupted. "So shut the hell up."

I gave him a 'you're-nuts-but-I'm-not-going-to-argue' shrug and withdrew.

When I got back to my own room, a glance in the mirror confirmed that Reggie was right. I did look like shit.

The previous evening's sweaty ringlets had morphed into a rat's nest of tangles overnight, and puffy bluish bags shadowed my eyes. Hellhound's giant sweatshirt drooped off one shoulder and sagged lopsidedly halfway to my knees, adding the final touch to my bag-lady fashion statement.

Growling profanities, I yanked a brush through my hair, then ordered room service for four before retreating to the shower.

When the food cart arrived half an hour later, I waited until the hotel employee had vanished down the hall before tapping on Reggie's door.

He called, "Who's there?"

"It's Aydan, with breakfast."

"Let yourself in."

I did so, pushing the cart ahead of me.

"Damn hotels," Reggie groused. "They call themselves wheelchair accessible and then they put the fucking peephole at standing height."

I blinked at the door. "Shit, that's true. You can't see out of it from a chair."

"Of course it's true; I couldn't make up shit that stupid." He wheeled cautiously over to the cart. "God, those eggs turn my stomach."

"I got you some tomato juice." I handed him the glass. "I thought it might help your hangover. Drink up; I'm going to go and get Murray and Melinda."

"Thanks. Oh, and..." He handed me a slip of paper. "...here's my private cell phone number. Next time call me instead of busting in with guns blazing. And when you come back with Murray and Melinda, just let yourself in." He gave me his lopsided grin. "After all, why start being all polite and knocking now?"

"Good point." I tossed him a salute and went to collect the others.

We made short work of breakfast, and my nervous vigilance during the trek down to the Hummer proved unnecessary. I drove a circuitous route through the congested morning traffic to shake any potential followers, but there were none. Our arrival at the secured facility was equally uneventful.

Too bad I couldn't convince my racing pulse of that.

As I got out of the Hummer in the parking garage I drew a surreptitious deep breath and let it out slowly. We were perfectly safe in here. Nobody had followed us. The tons of concrete and steel above wouldn't come crashing down to imprison us in a hellish tomb devoid of light and air...

Shut up.

I shouldered my duffel bag full of gear and motioned the others ahead of me through the first security checkpoint.

The bullpen was no longer a place of music and chatter. The other delegates had already arrived, and rows of chairs were filled with solemn scientists. The agents and weapons specialists stood around the perimeter of the room, their gazes tracking every movement.

Reggie's shoulders relaxed at the sight of the businesslike atmosphere, and he strode to the front of the room with no trace of a limp. Murray and Melinda hurried behind him to sit near the front.

Taking my cue from the other agents, I put on my best 'don't mess with me' expression and selected a piece of wall to lean against. Hellhound gave me a smile from beside the door to the weapons lockup, but that was the extent of our interaction. No kisses blown this morning.

Ian Rand flashed me a come-hither smile, too, but he didn't abandon his section of wall on the other side of the room. Nora Taylor and Brad Wilson shot me sidelong glances, and the FBI and CIA guys eyed me suspiciously as well.

My shoulders stiffened, and I willed myself to relax. Look casual, dammit. Be super-cool Jane Bond.

I eyeballed each of them in turn, and as my gaze fell on Nora and Brad they glanced away, feigning interest in their respective smartphones.

What the hell were they up to?

The FBI agent broke eye contact the instant I looked at him, and transferred his mistrustful frown to the CIA guy beside him instead. Fish-belly-white Grandin. He looked like trouble to me.

Grandin met my eyes with an arrogant stare, and my built-in asshole-detector pinged.

I gave him a smile, curling my upper lip to show a few extra teeth. He stared back with expressionless shark-grey eyes, as though I was chum leaking blood into his waters.

Okay, asshole. Challenge accepted.

Reggie chose that moment to speak into the microphone at the podium, and Grandin and I simultaneously abandoned our staring match to look toward the front of the room.

"Good morning," Reggie began gravely. As he had done the night before, he spoke without any facial expression, barely moving his lips; and I realized that he was concealing the difference between the normal expression of his right side and the immobile mask on his left.

"Let's get right to it," he went on. "As you all know by now, the terrorist threat last month was a hoax, and it was strictly coincidental that the would-be terrorist's weapon of choice mimicked our classified technology.   But..."   He offered the audience a small ironic bow.   "...since you all insisted on seeing the actual devices..."

He nodded to Hellhound, who bent to activate the retinal scan on the weapons lockup door. The lock released with a click, but as he opened the door a voice shattered the silence in the room.

"Hold it right there!"

CHAPTER 12

Everyone twitched. A burst of adrenaline drove my hand toward my holster while my gaze raked the assembly for the threat.

All the other agents did the same... except fish-belly-white Grandin.

A collective breath of relief wafted through the room when we realized it was Grandin who had spoken. A sardonic smile twisted the corner of his mouth as he repeated, "Hold it right there, buddy. You don't go in unescorted when there's classified technology belonging to the United States in there."

Hellhound eyed him steadily, the personality I had nicknamed The Killer draining all the expression from his battle-scarred face. Without any perceptible movement, his brawny presence seemed to expand to fill the room.

"Ya wanna *escort* me, then, Grandin?" he inquired quietly.

Menace lurked in the innocuous words, and a chilly shiver trickled down my backbone.

"Sure." Grandin gave him a cocky grin and strode forward.

Just before he reached the door, Hellhound let it swing shut. The lock engaged with an uncompromising click.

Grandin glared, but Hellhound remained poker-faced as he stepped aside and assumed parade rest beside the door. "Protocol," he said neutrally. "Ya hafta clear the retinal scan to go in. No exceptions."

Grandin gave him another dirty look and stepped past Hellhound's monumental bulk to the scanner, intentionally jostling him on the way by.

I added another note to my imaginary files: Grandin had a bad case of Small-Dick Syndrome.

The lock clicked anticlimactically open, and Grandin shot Hellhound a triumphant look before taking up a challenging crossed-arm stance in the doorway, holding the door open with his body so that Hellhound had to go past him to access the weapons.

His arrogant symbolism wasn't lost on me. I mentally boosted his Asshole Index a couple more points.

Hellhound stepped through the door without touching him and Grandin's smug expression slipped, as though he had been hoping for a confrontation.

When Hellhound emerged carrying his two duffel bags, he stopped outside the door and pointedly waited for Grandin to step aside and let the door close. Then he strode to the front of the room and laid the bags on the table beside Reggie.

"Thank you," Reggie said with considerably more graciousness than he usually displayed. "Please lay out the weapons."

I spared a moment of surprise at his unwarranted good manners before cynically realizing that he was only concealing the fact that he couldn't manage the zippers easily with his prosthetic hand.

Still expressionless, Hellhound complied before fading back a couple of steps. He took up parade rest again, his hulking form providing an ominous backdrop to Reggie's presentation.

"So," Reggie said. "Here we have two weapons. This..." He picked up the bottle-shaped one first. "...is the lethal version Agent Kelly captured last year; and the one that we believed to be part of the terrorist threat last month."

A few heads turned briefly my way. Nora Taylor and Brad Wilson eyed me a little longer, but their attention swivelled guiltily back to Reggie when I met their gazes.

"As you know, ultrasound is used in many applications from healthcare to industrial testing," Reggie went on, his polished delivery an amusing contrast to his usual expletive-laden conversation. "But ultrasound's fundamental characteristics cause its waves to diverge and disperse rapidly, which severely limits its effective range..."

I studied the silent audience while he delivered his presentation. Nobody moved. All gazes were riveted to the front of the room. Katie's eyes were alight, her lips parted as though viewing some extraordinary work of art. I was pretty sure she wasn't admiring the weapon.

Looking everywhere except at the area where Katie sat, Reggie concluded, "...Beyond eight metres, the tissue damage decreases on an exponential curve so the effects may or may not be lethal between eight and nine metres. At nine metres, or twenty-nine and a half feet, no tissue damage was observed in any of our tests."

He placed the weapon back on the table and the room

erupted in a babble of questions. Most of them seemed to be variations on 'how did you test it' and 'how did you get it', and Reggie held up a quelling hand.

"We lab-tested the effective range by using pig carcasses to simulate adult humans and then evaluating the subsequent tissue damage. Our only documentation of its use on human subjects comes from Agent Kelly." He turned to me. "Aydan, would you please describe its effects?"

Frozen in the stare of thirty-some pairs of eyes, I mentally cursed Reggie. That's why he had requested me, the bastard. Dammit, I *knew* he had some agenda.

"Come on, Kelly," Grandin prompted. "Cat got your tongue?"

I sneezed into the crook of my elbow. The sneeze came out sounding a lot like 'asshole', and Hellhound snickered.

"'Scuse me," I said with a fake smile. "As Reggie said, its effects were instantaneous." My throat constricted at the memory of a handsome young man collapsing like a puppet whose strings had been cut. "It was as fast as pointing a finger," I added hoarsely. "No warning, no sound, no escape. Just... smiling and talking one instant, and the next instant dead. Before his body even hit the floor." I swallowed, the sound clearly audible in the silence that had swelled into the room.

Then Grandin spoke up again. "So how and when did you get it?"

I gave him a level look. "Classified."

A few more people asked variations of the same questions, but I provided no more details and they soon gave up. Reggie fielded some more technical questions before stepping back from the table.

Taking that as his cue, Hellhound stowed the weapons in their duffels again and carried them back to the weapons lockup.

Grandin forestalled him by stepping up to the retinal scan. When the door opened for him, he immediately closed it again before stepping aside to allow Hellhound access to the scanner.

Hellhound took his turn and opened the door, holding it for Grandin without expression.

A few moments later they both emerged empty-handed, and Hellhound took up parade rest beside the door again while Grandin meandered away, looking just a little too casual.

Reggie had been addressing the last of the questions while I watched the little exchange at the weapons lockup, and I tuned back into his words as he finished, "...and I'll turn the floor over to Brad Wilson from the United States."

Reggie strode back to take a seat in the audience as Wilson stepped up. While the audience turned their attention to the front of the room Reggie sank into his chair with a grimace of pain, quickly hidden.

Wilson flashed a mouthful of too-white teeth in a shit-eating grin that made me glance around the room in case there was a gallery of television reporters that I had somehow failed to notice.

"Thank you," Wilson said, projecting his voice like an orator addressing a crowd of thousands. "I can't tell you how honoured I am to be here today, leading the world with cutting-edge technology along with our closest allies..."

His grandiose words faded from my attention as Grandin sidled over to stand beside me, still looking nonchalant.

I turned to give him a flat stare.

He ignored me, focusing on Wilson as though they were the only two people in the room.

What the hell was he up to?

I held my ground and kept my expression neutral despite the squirmy desire to move away. Grandin was the kind of guy who encroached on my personal space from the other side of the room. Arms-length was far too close.

Wilson was still oozing pompous hyperbole, and I skimmed another glance across the crowd. Most faces wore the blank mask of boredom disguised as polite interest, but Nora Taylor was watching me again. So was Dirk, the FBI agent.

As soon as I looked at each of them, they transferred their gazes; Nora's returning to Wilson at the front of the room and Dirk's flitting to Grandin beside me.

Dammit, this was really starting to creep me out.

Wilson was still flapping his gums, but it sounded as though he was winding down at last. "...so without further ado..." He beamed another media-worthy grin at the audience. "...I'll transfer you to the very capable hands of the best weapons research team in the *world!* Let's give them a hand!" His blinding smile could probably be seen from outer space, and he raised his hands high to clap like a groupie at a rock concert.

According to the briefing Reggie had given me the previous evening, Wilson's superlatives were an exaggeration and consequently an insult to the other countries' teams; but nevertheless a smattering of courteous applause welcomed the two U.S. scientists as they approached the front.

"For those who don't already know me, I'm Dr. Joseph

Mitchell," the taller scientist said in a twangy Midwest accent. "And this is Dr. Jason Pino." He indicated his short roly-poly companion. "Unlike Dr. Chow's anti-personnel focus, we've been concentrating on infrastructure. Cripple an enemy's weapons and infrastructure, and they're done. The rest is just mop-up."

As if to emphasize his words, Pino mopped his sweaty brow with a white handkerchief. As he returned it to his pocket he furtively wiped his palms on it, too.

Grandin made a slight movement beside me and my attention snapped to him, but his gaze was focused on the scientists.

Uneasiness prickled the back of my neck as I looked toward the front again, keeping Grandin in my peripheral vision as much as possible. They were up to something; I just knew it.

But what?

My fingers itched to draw my Glock, and I drew a slow breath. In. Out.

These are our allies. Settle down.

"We've arranged a little demo for you," the taller scientist went on. "Costas, if you would bring it, please...?"

I knew from Reggie's briefing that Costas was Hellhound's Weapons Specialist counterpart from the U.S. Even though Grandin had been the one to challenge Hellhound earlier, apparently only Costas was entrusted with handling their weapons.

Costas detached himself from the wall, a tall man with salt-and-pepper hair and café-au-lait skin. As he approached the door to the weapons lockup, he motioned graciously to Hellhound, who bent for the retinal scan again. Costas repeated the process, and Hellhound held the door for him.

With a 'thank you', Costas ducked into the room and returned a moment later bearing a glass cube that looked like a small aquarium. He carried it gingerly to the front and placed it on the table with exaggerated care, as though it might explode if it was jolted.

Along with everyone else, I strained my eyes to identify the aquarium's contents. It looked like a couple of pieces of ordinary construction rebar propped across some low supports. There was also a small glass vial balanced on a fragile-looking tripod.

The Midwest scientist smiled, obviously relishing the attentiveness of his audience. "We've developed bacteria..." he began, but the rest of his sentence was lost in a sudden stir and swell of voices from the crowd.

I studied my team for a clue to the uproar. Reggie was expressionless as always but his shoulders had tensed and his good hand had clenched into a fist. Murray and Melinda looked horrified.

"Hold up!" Katie's clear Aussie accent cut through the babble as she bounced to her feet, frowning. "The UN's Convention on Biological Weapons is very clear about prohibition of the development, production and stockpiling of bacteriological weapons. What you're doing is-"

"Completely acceptable," Mitchell interrupted, reclaiming the attention of the agitated crowd. "This is a common bacterium that lives everywhere in nature. It's completely harmless to humans, birds, fish, mammals; any living thing. You could bathe in the petri dish; heck, you could drink it or snort it into your mucous membranes and you wouldn't get so much as an upset stomach or a sniffle.

This is not a biological weapon as defined by the BWC."

Katie sank back into her chair, still frowning.

"As I said before," Mitchell went on, "We're focusing on infrastructure.   And we've engineered this particular bacterium..." He patted the glass cube smugly. "...to excrete a substance that alters the electron charge in metallic molecules. That means we can reduce any metal or metallic alloy, whether interstitial or substitutional, to its constituent elements at the molecular level."   His smile widened as hubbub rose again, and he pitched his voice louder to be heard.   "The process takes mere seconds, and the bacteria are virtually unstoppable until the molecular deconstruction process is complete. Watch."

He activated a lever on the side of the glass box, and the vial inside toppled off its tripod and shattered.

All babble instantly ceased. The silence was so profound that I could hear my own breath whistling through my nostrils. Beside me, Grandin scribbled feverishly in a small notebook he'd withdrawn from his pocket.

A minute later the rebar inside the glass cube collapsed into a heap of gray powder.

"*Are you insane?*" Melinda's voice snapped out like a whip. "If that containment vessel is breached, your bacteria will consume all the rebar in this building! And the next building, and the next, until nothing is left of this city but rubble!"

CHAPTER 13

My breath stopped.

All those tons of concrete overhead. No rebar to support it.

We'd be crushed.

Claustrophobic panic seized my throat. Trapped-trapped-*have-to-get-out-NOW*...

"That wouldn't happen unless we applied it directly to the rebar in an exposed location, where it could travel throughout the building's structure," Mitchell said. "It can't be deployed by an airborne vector."

I ventured a shallow breath, all my attention riveted on his words. Words of reassurance that I desperately needed to hear...

"It doesn't need to be airborne to be a threat!" Melinda snapped. "Look around you! How many metals do you see? *Everything* is a potential vector if your bacteria escape! The light fixture above you. The electrical plugin under the table has metallic components. Its wires are interconnected throughout the building. Wiring, steel studs, metal handrails, bolts; who knows what might touch the rebar? It would only need one access point to destroy the whole building!"

My head swam and I realized I was hyperventilating. Focusing all my will, I slowed my breathing.

In... two... three... four.

Out... two... three... four.

Slow like ocean waves...

"That would be extremely unlikely," Mitchell argued. "The bacteria would have to be physically applied to the plug-in, and even so, electrical components are always isolated from steel structure. And even if this containment vessel broke right now, the bacteria's lifespan is measured in minutes once any available metallic bonds have been consumed. In the time we've taken to argue about it, everything inside this containment vessel has become completely inert..."

Something jabbed my arm and I let out an involuntary yelp and twitched violently.

A small object skittered across the floor toward the front of the room. An instant later heavy smoke belched from it.

"*Shit!*" My expletive rang out in the momentary silence.

Don't waste breath.

I sucked in a lungful of rapidly diminishing clean air and dove toward my scientists. Flinging my duffel bag onto the nearest chair, I ransacked it. "Here!" I shoved self-adhesive breathing masks at Melinda, Murray, and Reggie, then slapped one over my own nose and mouth.

Reggie's useless left hand fumbled with the mask, and I snatched it out of his grasp and peeled off the backing for him. As Reggie grabbed the mask and stuck it on his face, Hellhound loomed up out of the smoke, coughing.

A self-adhesive mask wouldn't seal over his beard and

moustache, dammit. I snatched a pair of nasal filters out of my bag and thrust them at him. "Up your nose!" I barked.

He obeyed with alacrity, pressing his lips together to force himself to breathe through the filters.

God, what if he couldn't get enough air? His nose had been broken so many times...

The sprinkler system deployed, drenching us in icy water. Coughing and cries of fear filled the air, interspersed with sharp commands from the agents as bodies milled through the smoke, stumbling and bumping into us.

Move.

With my Glock drawn even though I couldn't see more than a foot in front of me, I herded my group through the murk toward where I thought the door should be. My breathing mask plastered itself against my nose and mouth with every rapid inhalation, intensifying my panicky trapped sensation.

Just as we reached the door, a deep rumbling galvanized my already pounding heart.

Was that the sound of concrete collapsing?

I was shoving my team forward when I realized the smoke was thinning. The rumble came from powerful concealed fans sucking out the contaminated air.

"The door's locked!" Murray's voice rose in fear as he grappled with the door handle.

"It's just the emergency lockdown," Hellhound said loudly, his powerful voice rising over the frightened babble around us. "Standard protocol, nothin' to worry about. Security'll be here in a minute to sort it out. Everybody stay calm."

I sucked in a deep shaky breath and forced my voice as

loud and steady as I could manage. "Arnie's right; don't worry. We're fine in here. All areas in the building have a separate fire suppression system and their own air supply."

Knowing about the safety features of the building didn't make me feel any better. We were still trapped in here. And if I didn't get this mask off my face soon I was going to hyperventilate and pass out...

"*It's gone!*" A frantic cry in a Midwest twang accelerated my heart rate to near-coronary levels all over again. "*Somebody stole my bacteria!*"

Everyone whirled to stare through the last wisps of smoke. The lid of the glass containment vessel lay on the table, and only a few smudges of grey powder remained inside.

Suddenly I didn't hate my breathing mask quite so much.

Dirk and Grandin glared around the room, gripping their pistols. Grandin's knuckles whitened on his gun as he caught sight of the Glock in my hand.

Ian's hand hovered over his holster as his gaze flicked between us, and the Aussie and Kiwi agents looked twitchy, too.

Shit, this could go bad really fast.

Keeping my Glock pointed at the floor, I spoke in my loudest, most authoritative voice. "Okay, everybody calm down." I slowly tucked my gun back into my waist holster. No sudden moves. "Let's all put our weapons away. There's no immediate threat here, and security will sort this out in a few minutes. Just stay calm."

I shot a hard look at Dirk and Grandin. Dirk reluctantly holstered his weapon. Grandin just glared, his gun not quite pointing at me, but not exactly pointing at the floor, either.

"Yeah, you'd really like us to be sitting ducks, wouldn't you?" he snapped. "You're the one who threw the smoke bomb."

"Bullshit!" Hellhound barked at the same time as I retorted, "I did not!" I raised my voice above the murmuring that surrounded us and added, "It won't take long to figure this out. This whole area is under constant surveillance from all angles. As soon as security gets here we'll play back the records and find out what happened. And we're locked in, so nobody's going to escape until we figure this out." I glared back at Grandin. "Holster your weapon."

He made no move to comply. "Take off your mask," he countered. "Unless..." His eyes narrowed. "...maybe your bomb wasn't just smoke. Maybe you poisoned us all."

"For chrissake!" I snatched off the mask, half relieved at being able to breathe freely; half afraid of what I might be inhaling. "I didn't throw the fucking smoke bomb, and you *really* need to settle down and holster your weapon. We're all allies here..."

I trailed off. One of our supposed allies had thrown that smoke bomb. Shit.

"Oh, don't be so childish, Grandin." Nora Taylor's voice dripped contempt. "Put your weapon away. You're a hazard to yourself and everyone around you."

She had barely finished speaking when the public address system crackled to life. "Occupants of area C-45, this is security. Lay down your weapons, kneel, and place both hands on your heads. Remain in that position until instructed to do otherwise."

"It's a conspiracy!" Grandin shouted. "You smug

bastards are stealing our technology right from under our noses!"

Hellhound and I exchanged a glance. Then I knelt, laid my gun down in front of me, and put both hands on my head. He did the same. Murray and Melinda and Reggie were next, and soon everyone in the room was kneeling with their hands on their heads except Grandin. Even Dirk capitulated.

"This is your last warning," the loudspeaker blared. "Lay down your weapons, kneel and place both hands on your heads. Failure to comply will be considered an act of aggression and will be met with deadly force."

"In case you need to hear it in one syllable words, Grandin..." Ian said dryly from his kneeling position a few yards away, "...Drop it or they'll shoot you."

To my relief, Grandin obeyed at last, muttering imprecations.

"Just to be clear, Mitchell," Melinda said as the door clicked open. "You're *absolutely certain* that your bacteria were inert by the time the containment vessel was opened, right?"

"Yes," he replied, but his voice quavered.

A dozen body-armoured men marched into the room, their faces mostly obscured by breathing masks. The fans sucked a powerful gust of air through the door along with them, and the last man slammed the door shut behind him. I heard the lock re-engage with a definitive clunk.

"Everybody will need to go through a scan so we can find out who took the metallic powder," Reggie said loudly, without removing his hands from his head. "That rebar would have been broken down into its elements; iron and whatever other metals were in the alloy. It'll show up on a standard ferrous-metal scan."

"What about our classified technology in the lockup?" Nora asked as the armed men fanned rapidly through the room.

"The weapons lockup fails closed during a security event," one of the men replied as he strode by her. "Nobody can get into it until we're at normal security levels. Even an authorized retinal scan won't open it now." He stopped in front of me. "Please stand slowly. Turn and put both hands on the wall, feet apart. If you make any sudden moves, I'm authorized to use deadly force."

The muzzle of his P90 looked very large so close to my face. My mouth went dry.

"Um... What's going on?" I croaked as I rose slowly, hands still on my head.

"We saw you throw the smoke bomb," he said. "Turn around and face the wall."

"I didn't..." I began.

"Found it and bagged it, sir!" At the front of the room, one of the men held up a clear plastic bag containing the small object I'd seen earlier.

"I didn't throw it," I protested. The guard's gun muzzle rose, and I turned and faced the wall as ordered, knees trembling. "It might have looked like that on camera, but my arm twitched because something jabbed it."

"Oh, sure," Grandin gibed. "Your arm twitched. And you just happened to have breathing masks for your whole team."

"I had masks because I wanted to be ready for any kind of attack on the way here," I argued as the guard searched me, his hands probing thoroughly but impersonally. "I had a bunch of other gear, too. And I *know* I got jabbed by something. Check my right arm near the shoulder. I bet there's a mark. It still smarts."

The guard extracted my trank pistol from my ankle holster and Grandin eased closer, his gaze sharpening.

"Back off," I snapped. "That's classified."

The guard whisked the weapon behind his back, away from Grandin's line of sight. Another guard hurried over with an opaque black plastic bag, and the trank pistol went safely into it.

"Check my right arm," I insisted. "And if that smoke bomb came from my vicinity, check Grandin, too. He was standing right beside me."

My guard, apparently the commanding officer, jerked his chin at one of his subordinates and another guard advanced on Grandin.

Grandin protested loudly, but his words turned to gibberish in my ears as my guard stepped back a couple of paces and raised his weapon to point at my chest.

Hell. I really preferred to be on the other end of guns. The deadly abyss of the muzzle made my heart quiver and cower down behind the dubious shelter of my ribs.

"Please remove your sweatshirt," the guard said. "Slowly. No sudden moves."

With shaking hands, I eased the garment over my head and turned my right shoulder toward him. I raised my T-shirt sleeve and craned my neck, but the sore spot was at the back of my shoulder. I probed with a cautious fingertip, and my throat constricted when my finger came back bearing a small smear of blood. I hadn't had time to think about it earlier, but now...

Fear turned my blood to ice.

I had been injected with something.

But what?

CHAPTER 14

The guard took an abrupt step backward. "Dammit!" He keyed his headset and barked, "Quarantine area C-45!"

The exhaust fans roared louder and my ears popped with the pressure change.

"Do you have any more of those handy breathing masks?" Ian inquired lightly, but his voice was tight.

I swallowed hard. "No. But you can have mine if you want." I nodded toward the crumpled mask lying on the floor. "For all the good it'll do now."

His lips tightened, but he nodded and turned to the commander. "We'll need to see the security footage."

"I don't have access to it at the moment," the commander replied. "After we secure the area we'll provide it."

At least he wasn't pointing his gun right at me anymore, but he still held it at the ready. Behind his clear face shield, his gaze took in every movement in the room.

"May we please get up now?" Nora inquired. "This is quite uncomfortable." Her voice was calm but her soft wrinkled features were strained as she knelt on the hard concrete floor, her arms trembling with the effort of holding her hands on top of her head.

"I'm sorry, ma'am, not yet." The commander jerked his chin at me. "On your knees, hands on your head. If you try anything, I'll shoot."

I obeyed, my hands trembling almost as much as Nora's.

Grandin was still loudly protesting, and the commander raised his voice. "Ladies and gentlemen, may I have your attention please!"

Grandin kept complaining. "...a violation of my rights of diplomatic immunity and an act of aggression against the United States..."

"MAY I HAVE EVERYONE'S ATTENTION, PLEASE!" Either the commander had a promising career ahead of him as a hog-caller, or there was a bullhorn built into his headset. His shout effortlessly overrode Grandin's voice and made me flinch.

"We apologize for the inconvenience," the commander went on at a more comfortable volume in the ensuing silence. "We'll do our best to resolve this unfortunate situation as soon as possible, and your cooperation will streamline the process. For your own safety, we will be searching everyone and temporarily confiscating all personal items including weapons-"

Grandin bellowed, "I'm carrying diplomatic archival material! You have to safeguard it! I demand my rights! THIS IS AN ACT OF WAR!"

The commander's weapon swung up and the lungful of air that Grandin had sucked in for his next yell escaped in a loud hiccup.

"Shut. Up." The commander's words were quiet but very sincere.

Grandin shut.

"As I was saying…" the commander continued, "…we will inventory each item that we remove from your possession, and when you are satisfied that the inventory list is complete and accurate we will ask you to sign the inventory and you will receive a copy of it. If you are carrying any classified items or diplomatic archival material…"

He shot Grandin a chilly look. "…please notify us and we will provide opaque sealable bags, in which you will place the items with your own hands. All items will be grouped and labelled with their owner's name, and stored in that corner under armed guard."

The commander nodded toward the front of the room. "For security verification, this process will take place in full view of everyone. Once itemized and moved to the storage area, the stockpiles will not be touched by anyone, including our security personnel, for any reason. Your collective supervision is an important part of this process. If at any time you see or suspect tampering by anyone, including our security personnel, please call out immediately to draw everyone's attention. As soon as your physical search is completed we'll question everyone and process each of you through the ferrous-metal scanner, after which you'll be allowed to move around freely inside this room until the situation is resolved. Thank you."

He addressed his troops. "Process them out. Start with Ms. Taylor."

She gave him a smile of gratitude, but I lost interest in her when the commander turned back to frown at me.

"Get up," he commanded.

I stood, sucking in a breath as my knees wobbled.

"Please move slowly to the scanner and step between the stanchions." His tone was level. So was his weapon.

I obeyed, moving cautiously. Please God, don't let me trip over my own feet. It might be the last thing I ever did.

Heart pounding, I stepped between the two panels that bracketed the door and stood still while one of the other armed men activated the scan. The commander kept his weapon trained in the vicinity of my feet, his eyes and hands steady. He wouldn't shoot me by accident, but he sure as hell wouldn't hesitate to shoot me if I gave him cause.

My hands were cold and numb locked on top of my head. My breathing was shallow and too rapid, and clammy sweat chilled my body.

Claustrophobic fear?

Or some deadly poison infiltrating my bloodstream?

Don't think about it. Just breathe.

Nice and slow and deep...

"A small metallic object in her left front pocket," the tech announced.

"There's a rivet in my jeans-" I began.

"Like a small needle," the tech interrupted.

The commander's P90 snapped up to point at the centre of my chest. "Empty your left front pocket," he snapped.

"But you just searched me..."

"Do it now!"

I eased my left hand down from my head, flexing my fingers in an attempt to get some feeling back into them.

"Don't try anything!"

"I'm not; I just can't feel my fingers..."

Taking in his tense expression, I gave up on the explanation and cautiously probed my pocket. Just inside the top, my fingertips encountered a small unfamiliar shape.

I swallowed hard, my throat constricting with fear. "I think..." My voice wavered and I cleared my throat. "I think I found the dart," I croaked. "I felt somebody bump into me in the smoke, but I didn't realize..."

The commander was already barking orders into his headset, and a moment later one of the armed men appeared with tweezers and an evidence bag. I glimpsed something that looked like one of our classified tranquilizer darts before he whisked it away.

"Hands on your head again. This way, please, Agent Kelly," the commander said without inflection, indicating the back corner of the room.

"Hey, where're ya takin' her?" Hellhound's voice boomed out, making everyone turn to stare. Still on his knees with his hands on his head, he scowled at the commander. "This's my 'collective supervision'," he growled. "Where the hell are ya takin' her?"

"Over to the corner of the room," the commander replied. "Not out of anyone's sight."

"Awright." Hellhound fell silent, but his gaze tracked the commander's every move.

"*Not* all right!" Grandin snapped. "We have a right to hear all conversations. For all we know, all of you are colluding to get our-"

"For Christ's sake, give it up!" Reggie barked. "If we were going to steal your goddamn tech you'd never have a clue we were doing it. We're not dumb enough to put on a fucking shit-show like this, and Kelly sure as hell wouldn't throw a smoke bomb when she knows damn well the whole place is under surveillance."

Katie's mouth dropped open and her eyes lit up. Apparently she was seeing the real Reggie for the first time, and she liked what she saw even more than his restrained scientist persona. Despite my increasing discomfort, my heart warmed with hope for Reggie.

"Never mind, Dr. Chow; he makes a good point," the commander replied calmly. "Agent Kelly, I have some questions for you. Please come to the centre of the room and answer loudly enough so everyone can hear."

Heart hammering, I moved to the spot he pointed out. I couldn't seem to control my breathing, and I couldn't feel my hands anymore. My shoulders tingled and ached.

"May I lower my hands now?" I asked breathlessly.

"No. Describe exactly what happened."

"I was standing there..." I nodded toward the section of wall I'd formerly occupied. "Watching Dr. Mitchell's presentation. It was..." I drew in a breath and tried to let it out slowly, but it whooshed out and sucked in again despite my best efforts. "...everybody was upset by it." I panted a couple more breaths. "He and Melinda... were arguing..."

I gulped more thin air. Maybe the exhaust fans were malfunctioning. Not enough oxygen in the room...

"Go on," the commander prompted.

"Um..." I tried to wiggle my fingers, but I couldn't feel them. My shoulders were numb now, too. "I was just... standing there... watching... and then... something jabbed me. I saw the smoke bomb... flying across the room. Grabbed the masks."

I had to stop and pant again. My head felt as though it was floating off my shoulders. My arms were floating, too.

"Grandin was beside me..." I sucked more of the

inadequate air. "He was writing..." Inspiration seeped into my oxygen-deprived brain. "His pen..."

My panting accelerated. Air. I needed air.

"...must've been... dart gun..."

The edges of the room darkened.

"Gonna sit now," I announced, and the floor rushed up to meet me.

A short jumble of sound and sensation resolved into strong arms holding me, exuding the comforting scent of leather that always clung to Arnie's clothes.

"Okay, darlin', you're gonna be okay," he murmured. "Just take it nice an' easy. You're gonna be okay."

Another warm hand cupped my belly. "Breathe into my hand," Reggie's voice urged. "You're hyperventilating. Come on, belly breathe. Nice and slow. In... two... three... four..."

Fighting off the urge to just lie there until all the bullshit went away, I opened my eyes and dragged myself into sitting position.

"Whoa, hang on there." Arnie's bulk warmed my back. "Don't try an' get up yet, darlin'. We dunno what's in your system."

Another surge of fear shook me, but the dizziness seemed to have abated and I could feel my hands again. They were ice-cold, and I shivered and tucked them into my sweaty armpits.

My team crouched around me, looking worried. The commander held his ground beside me with his weapon at the ready; but everybody else was eyeing me as though I was Typhoid Mary.

Hell, maybe I was.

"His pen," I repeated firmly. "Get Grandin's pen. I bet

that's how he shot me."

"She's crazy!" Grandin snapped. "Her smoke bomb must have fried her brain. She obviously injected herself as a ruse."

I lurched upright. "I didn't *have* a smoke bomb! If it came from where we were standing, you must have thrown it yourself."

"Enough." The commander turned to Hellhound and Reggie. "Move away from her. Agent Kelly, you'll need to be searched again." He addressed his team with a nod at Hellhound and Reggie. "Search these two as well, immediately."

"Fuck, she was gonna pass out. We were just keepin' her from smashin' her face on the floor!" Hellhound protested. "We didn't slip her anythin'."

The commander ignored him. "Up against the wall again," he said to me. "You know the drill."

I rocked forward on unsteady legs and propped my hands against the wall while he searched me again. He was clinical and quick, but I was getting goddamn tired of having his hands on my body.

The warmth of anger sustained me long enough to totter back to the scanner, but by the time the scan was complete I was breathing hard and fighting dizziness once more.

"Let her sit down or she's gonna hit the deck again," Hellhound snapped as his captor herded him toward the vacated scanner.

The commander relented. "Sit with your back against the wall. Hands flat on the floor. Don't move."

I sank gratefully to the floor and the dizziness abated enough for me to pay attention to the proceedings again.

Grandin's search had been completed and the young guard had offered him the written list of his belongings for approval. As he took it, the commander spoke.

"So where's this pen Agent Kelly mentioned?"

Something flickered across Grandin's face too quickly to identify before he assumed an outraged expression. "Your man stole it from me!" He jabbed a finger at the list. "See? There's my notebook on the list, but he didn't record the pen!"

The young guard flushed. "There was no pen, sir."

"There was! How the heck would I have written in my notebook if I didn't have a pen?" Grandin demanded. "Kelly even saw it! You people can't even be trusted to take a simple inventory. What else are you stealing from us?"

Comprehension dawned. That sneaky bastard.

"He ditched it somewhere," I said. "He shot me, threw the smoke bomb, and while the room was full of smoke he ditched the dart gun. Check the garbage containers."

"This is an outrage! You're trying to frame me!" Grandin segued into another loud-mouthed conspiracy theory, but I tuned out his voice and watched his body language. He looked... smug. This was exactly what he wanted.

Was it a distraction to draw attention away from someone else's activities?

I zeroed in on Dirk, but he was being processed under the watchful gaze of one of the armed men and wasn't in a position to do anything but cooperate.

Brad Wilson?

He wasn't doing anything, either. But he looked just as satisfied as Grandin.

When he noticed me watching him he hurriedly converted his expression to a worried frown.

Okay, assholes. You think you're getting away with something, but it's all being recorded. And when I get a look at that footage, I'll figure out what you're up to...

My heart sank.

What good were the recordings? If the footage had been altered to make it look as though I'd thrown the smoke bomb, we had a huge security breach...

A wave of nausea made me groan aloud.

CHAPTER 15

Released from the scanner, Hellhound was beside me in an instant.

"How ya doin', darlin'?" He smoothed the hair away from my damp forehead.

"Comes 'n' goes..." I mumbled. "Sleepy. Dizzy. Sick..." I blinked heavily as the room twisted on its axis.

"Move away from her." The commander was back.

"Fuck off," Arnie growled. "Go ahead an' shoot me if ya want, but stop pissin' around. Get a fuckin' medic in here."

The commander apparently decided not to press the point. "Medics are already outside," he said. "It takes time to set up the positive-pressure quarantine bubble outside the door. They'll be inside any minute now."

"'Bout fuckin' time," Arnie snapped.

I slumped against him, my vision wavering in and out of focus. "You shouldn' be here," I slurred, fighting for coherence. "What 'f I'm contagious?"

"Then it's already too late to worry about it," he said calmly. "I ain't goin' anywhere, darlin'."

"Back off!" A hostile hiss dragged my attention over to where Reggie was being searched.

One of the guards had both hands around Reggie's leg, exploring the socket of his prosthesis through his pants.

"Get your fucking hands off me," Reggie snarled.

"I'm sorry, sir, but-"

"Back the fuck *off!*"

The commander strode over. "Is there a problem here?"

"Sir, I've found something strapped to his legs but he won't let me-"

As though realizing that everyone's attention was now focused on him, Reggie drew himself up to his full height and cast a withering glare over the crowd.

"Fine," he enunciated clearly, with such bitter venom that my stomach twisted. "Yes, I have something strapped to my legs. Prosthetics. I'm a double amputee." He jerked one pant leg up to reveal his prosthesis and scowled at the young guard, whose face glowed crimson even through the shield of his helmet. "Have a good gawp, all of you," Reggie ground out. "Go ahead, feast your eyes, motherfuckers."

"Oh, Reggie!" Katie's eyes brimmed with sympathy.

"Save your fucking tears for somebody who gives a shit," Reggie snarled, and turned his back on her.

Everyone developed a sudden fascination with the floor or ceiling. Katie stood open-mouthed, a hand to her scarlet cheek as though he had slapped her.

I tried to say, 'Don't be such a dick, Reggie', but my unwieldy tongue only delivered a mumble that sounded like 'doan-be-sujja-dig'.

"What, darlin'?" Hellhound inquired, bending close. "What'd ya say?"

"Dig."

He frowned and I squeezed my eyes shut and tried again,

concentrating fiercely. "Heeza dig. Rejji. Fuggen dum dig."

Arnie's worried frown deepened. "What? Aydan, I dunno what you're tryin' to say."

"What colour was the pen?" It was the commander again.

I squinted up at him. He seemed to be dancing the hokey-pokey. Moving forward and then backward. Forward and back, without even moving his legs.

That was cool. How did he do that? I squinted harder.

"Can you hear me?" he demanded. "What colour was Grandin's pen?" He lurched forward again. This time I was sure I saw his right foot move in.

He had a sense of humour after all!

I giggled and sang, "Putcher-ryfoo'-inya-putcher-ryfoo'-ou'... Do-thokee-pokee-an'..."

I couldn't remember how the rest of it went.

"Do-thokee-pokee," I repeated, frowning. "An'... an'... sumthin..."

"Aydan?" Arnie was doing the hokey-pokey now, too. It wasn't as funny when he did it.

"Aydan, come on, stay with me, darlin'." He patted my cheek with a gentle hand. "We need to know what colour Grandin's pen was."

Why didn't they just check the camera footage?

I tried to ask, but the words were too complicated.

"Blah, blah," I said instead.

"What?" Arnie's face swooped in, weirdly distorted. His nose took up his whole face. It was a hideous nose, but I loved it anyway. I tried to pat his nose but my hand wouldn't move.

"Aydan, what'd ya say? Did ya say it was black?"

"Blah," I repeated.

"I think she's sayin' it was black."

"Black? Like the one we found in your waist pouch?" the commander asked.

"She stole it! She stole my pen and falsely accused me!" Grandin's voice came from a long distance away, so I didn't mind a bit.

But the commander had demanded something...

The words did an amusing jig in my head. "'Mander 'manded," I said, then giggled and tried to tug on Arnie's sleeve. I couldn't find my hands, so I burbled, "'Mander 'manded. 'Sfunny, Arnie."

"I'm here, darlin'. What're ya tryin' to say? What colour was the pen?"

I focused as hard as I could. His nose was enormous. Under it, his moustache bristled with thousands of hairs. I stared, transfixed. So many hairs. Dark ones and bright ones. Like a waterfall of black and silver...

"...Siller."

"Are ya sayin' it was silver, darlin'? Not black?"

"Siller..." I repeated faintly. The word wouldn't stay. I tried to hold onto it but my hands were gone.

"For heaven's sake, she needs medical attention. She's losing consciousness! She could be dying!" Despite the frantic note in her voice, Nora's cultured British accent trickled over me like soothing balm.

Bomb.

No.

"I didn' doot," I protested.

"Hurry!" Nora called from above the Milky Way.

"Thanks, Mom," I mumbled, and sank into warm and

fuzzy darkness.

I rose slowly through blackness, hovering just beneath its surface to admire the silvery ripples of light playing above. Languid and smooth, they twisted and broke apart only to re-form and begin their sensuous dance over and over.

Bubbles of speech rose past me, garbled blobs that bloomed into random words as they broke the surface of the darkness.

Sleek slippery words all curvy around their edges, slithering like silken snakes...

Warm round words, comfortably bulgy and smelling of cinnamon and safety...

Hard dangerous words...

Bomb.

My eyes snapped open.   "Wa-theldee-gimme?" I demanded.

Arnie leaned over me, but his head fell off. I cried out in horror as it bounced off my stomach and fell to the floor, where it rolled away into a corner and lay smiling up at me.

But a moment later it was back on his shoulders as he leaned lower, then lower still. All I could see was his face, swelling bigger and bigger.

His head was going to explode.

Like a bomb...

"NO!" I tried to fend him off but my arms wouldn't move.

More words bubbled past me.

Hallucination. I clung to that one despite its spiky edges.

Hallucination. That's what this was.

Hal.

Lou.

The spikes hurt.

"Stop," I begged.

Sin.

A.

Shun.

The syllables stabbed like daggers into my mind. Hal. Lou. Sin. A. Shun. Hal. Lou. Sin...

"Stop!" I cried again.

Arnie's nose plunged down and attacked me. Nostrils like a two-car garage. Twin black caverns spouting hirsute waterfalls...

I screamed.

Over and over...

After a measureless time the hallucinations subsided. Arnie leaned down again, and this time his head stayed on and his words made sense.

"Hey, Aydan. How ya doin'?"

"Wa-theldee-gimme?"

"Sorry, darlin', I dunno what you're sayin'. Keep tryin'; I'll get it."

I squeezed my eyes shut as a silvery ripple disrupted my vision, turning Arnie's face into a bright mylar balloon.

"Wha'..." I enunciated carefully. "...th'ell... d'he... give... me?"

"Doc said it was ketamine. Street drug. Ya mighta heard it called Vitamin K. It fucks with your memory an' gives ya hallucinations, an' it knocks ya out."

"Mem... loss?" I squeezed my eyes tighter. My mind felt slippery. Thoughts flickered past like quick shiny minnows, and I gripped one with all my concentration. "How... long?"

"Ya been down for about an hour. It's comin' outta your system now, an' the doc says you'll prob'ly be okay in another hour or so."

I let out a breath of relief, then tried another tack. "Gran'n?"

"Ya mean, did Grandin drug ya? Or are ya askin', did he throw the smoke bomb?"

Too complicated.

I mumbled, "Uh...?"

Arnie answered anyway. "I been sittin' with ya the whole time so I ain't seen the video, but Chow said there was somethin' weird about it. We'll look at it together soon's you're feelin' better."

"Medal?"

"What, darlin'?"

I opened my eyes to stare up at him, hoping he could read my mind. Or what was left of it.

"Medal," I repeated. I thought very hard. "Batee...ria," I added triumphantly.

"Oh, Mitchell's bacteria an' the metal powder, right. They didn't find it on anybody."

"Whathfug?"

"I dunno what the fuck, darlin'. Everybody got scanned. Nobody had it on them. Not even up their ass or anythin'. That scanner'd detect even the smallest bit a' metal, no matter where it was."

I sighed and closed my eyes again.

CHAPTER 16

The next time I opened my eyes I could process my surroundings better. I lay on a gurney in the corner of the bullpen, and Hellhound sat beside me, holding my hand. An IV line snaked down from a pole into my other hand, and a heart monitor emitted a steady beeping. A few feet away, one of the armed guards stood stiffly, his weapon at the ready and his gaze trained on me.

Everyone else was clustered on the opposite side of the room, wearing surgical masks and gloves. The tense muttering of many voices formed a backdrop of sound, but I couldn't make out any words.

"Hey, darlin'," Hellhound said with a smile. "How ya doin'?"

"Better." I ventured a slow stretch, wiggling my fingers and toes. "I can feel my arms and legs, and my brain isn't trying to swim away. But... why aren't you wearing a mask and gloves? What if-"

"Hell, I been beside ya right from the start, so if I'm gonna catch somethin' from ya, I've already caught it. 'Sides, a mask won't seal over my beard, an' I ain't shavin' it off."

I reached up and threaded my fingers through his beard

to tickle his chin. "But you're hiding such a great jaw under there."

He grinned. "Thanks, darlin', but ya know I don't shave the facial fungus in winter. An' you'd miss it if I did."

He leaned down to kiss me lightly, and the tickle of his beard and moustache made me smile.

"Mmm, good point," I agreed.

"Christ, I told you before! None of that mushy shit!" Reggie's grouchy tone was belied by the humour in his eye as he limped over. "You gonna live, Kelly?"

"I think so." My belly chilled. "Unless I've been shot up with some slow-acting poison or disease. Do... do they know yet?"

A frustrated breath hissed out of the valve in his mask. "Nobody's talking to us. All they'll say is that we're quarantined."

I swallowed an unwieldy lump of fear. "Oh. That's, um... not so good."

"Stemp's on the way," Reggie added. "He's coming in a military helicopter instead of driving, the fucking bastard. But at least he's bringing a team, and when he gets here we'll start getting some answers."

"What happened?" I asked. "I remember the jab in my arm and the smoke bomb and trying to get out..." I frowned. Slippery memories. "...and then..." They waited, frowning, too. "Um... the smoke cleared..." I jerked upright. "Shit, did they find that bacteria?"

"No." Reggie shrugged. "And they're not going to. There's no way to detect bacteria short of swabbing everything in here and culturing the swabs. They've done that, but it'll take a couple of days for the results. They haven't found the metallic powder, either, even though they brought in handheld scanners and searched the whole room. All they found were the smudges in the bottom of the containment vessel and a light dusting on the table and floor. Not enough to account for all that rebar."

"But..." I knotted my fists in my hair. "That's not possible. Nobody left the room. They couldn't have gotten it out..." My stomach dropped. "...or did they? Did somebody leave while the room was full of smoke?"

"No. The security footage from the corridor outside shows the door never opened."

I flopped back on the pillow. "Then where the hell..."

Staring up at the ceiling, my attention caught on the exhaust fan grilles. Behind them, the big fans still rumbled away. My heart stopped.

"Ohmigod." My voice came out in a thin quaver. "C-Could it have gotten... sucked into the exhaust fans?"

Both men's eyes widened.

"Shit!" Reggie snarled, and pivoted to shout at the guard. "Check the exhaust grilles above the table for metal powder!" The man stared open-mouthed behind his face shield, and Reggie shouted, "*Wake up, fuckhead! The grilles! Check the fucking grilles!*"

The commander strode over, his weapon at the ready. "What's the problem here?"

"Check the exhaust fan grilles, dammit! The metal powder might have been sucked through them!"

The commander snapped an order into his headset and one of the guards snatched up a handheld scanner and rushed toward the front of the room.

"Where do those fans vent *to*?" I demanded, my heart

pounding. "If that bacteria was still active when it was sucked up..."

The commander shook his head. "All the exhaust fans have HEPA filters. Every room has complete biological containment. Bacteria and viruses can't escape."

Reggie sank into a chair on the other side of my gurney with a wince as his leg bent, but his voice was as steady as ever. "Chill, Kelly. The bacteria had to be inert by the time the containment was breached. If it hadn't been, the whole HVAC system would have caved in by now. Remember, you've been out of it for a couple of hours."

"Oh." I let out a trembling breath. "Right. I forgot."

The guard returned, scanner dangling from his hand. "Nothing. I even opened the plastic grille and swabbed the duct, and there was no ferrous metal."

"Then where the hell is it?" I demanded.

The commander and his guard gave me identical frustrated shrugs and turned away.

"Wait!"

The commander turned back at my command. Through the clear face shield of his breathing mask, I read the expression of a man barely containing his irritation. "Yes?"

"Did you find the dart? Or needle, or whatever injected me?"

"Yes." He scowled.

I tried to sit up, but the room made a tricky spin. Hellhound's hand landed on my shoulder and I fell back, my heart pounding. "Where did you find it? What was in it?"

The commander's scowl deepened. "Why don't you tell us?" He whirled and stomped away.

"Wha...? What the hell is his problem?" I sputtered.

Hellhound frowned. "Don't ya remember? They found the dart in your pocket."

"*What?*" I bolted upright only to fall back on the pillow again when a wave of dizziness turned my gurney into a ship tossing on rough seas. Complete with seagulls...

I groaned and squeezed my eyes shut. When I reopened them, the gurney was stationary again and the seagulls were gone. Thank God.

"Yeah, the dart was in your pocket," Hellhound said gently. "Ya musta forgot 'cause a' the drugs. Don't worry, we'll figure out what's goin' on. Dickwad over there..." He nodded across the room at the commander. "...he's a bit of an asshat, but he's makin' the best of a shitty job so I'm cuttin' him some slack."

"You figure he's okay?" I eyed the commander's retreating back.

"Yeah. He's done everythin' by the book, an' it ain't easy with all a' Five Eyes here. If it was just Canadians he'd have more control, but he's gotta cut a fine line between keepin' everybody safe an' dealin' with dickheads like Grandin an' his fuckin' diplomatic immunity."

"Right, I forgot about that, too." I massaged my temples. "Dammit, what else am I forgetting? How much of my memory will I lose?"

"Ya shouldn't lose any of it, 'cept for the part where you were actually drugged." Hellhound eyed me worriedly. "Ya better talk to the doc about it."

Reggie had been staring into space while we talked, and he returned to the conversation with a slap to my pillow that made me jump.

"Fuck!" he snapped. "They faked it! Those fuckers! I

need Murray and Melinda!" He launched to his feet and wobbled with a harsh hiss of breath as his injured leg took his weight. Then he righted himself and strode across the room to where Murray and Melinda were huddled together. A few moments later they were all pulling up chairs around my gurney.

"Is this a council of war?" Ian's tone was light as he approached our group, but there was an undertone of suspicion in his voice.

Reggie shot him a scowl, but said nothing.

"Nope," I lied. "It's just a social chat. Pull up a chair and join us."

"You're not going to scream at me again, are you?" he inquired warily.

"Um... no..." I frowned. "What do you mean, 'again'?"

"You don't remember?"

"No..."

Shit, was he trying to give me some kind of secret message? If so, I hadn't a clue what it was.

Hellhound took in my expression and squeezed my hand. "Maybe ya don't remember. Ya were hallucinatin' then."

"I came to see how you were, and you screamed at me," Ian confirmed. "You said something that sounded like 'don't tell'." The warning in his gaze came through clearly.

Shit. My chain of command knew about my part in Ian's op, but if Nora began to suspect we'd known each other before last night...

I ransacked my aching brain for a cover story.

"Dunno why ya think she was sayin' 'don't tell'," Hellhound demurred. "I couldn't figure out what the hell she was tryin' to say. Mosta the time she was just screamin'."

I sent a mental 'thank you' his way and resisted the urge to give his hand a grateful squeeze just in case anybody was watching us closely.

"Well..." Ian's jocular tone held a faint edge. "No offense intended, old chap, but any woman in her right mind would scream if she opened her eyes and saw your face above her."

"Huh. Good point," Hellhound agreed mildly, and my heart twisted for him.

"I was screaming because I hallucinated that Arnie had been decapitated," I snapped at Ian, my mouth running off while my mind scrambled for some plausible justification for why I might have said 'don't tell'. "And look who's talking about scaring women, jerk!"

Ian's perfectly-groomed eyebrows rose over his striking green eyes while I struggled to find some part of his appearance to insult. There was nothing, of course. He was flat-out gorgeous.

"Are you sure I wasn't screaming 'dental'?" I snarled. "'Cause all your bright-white capped teeth are enough to scare anybody." It was a pathetic insult, especially since his mouth was currently concealed by his mask; but it was all I had.

Ian seized the opportunity. His chin rose and his brows drew together. "They're natural," he said, his accent sounding impossibly haughty. "But if that's all the thanks I get for being concerned about you, then fine." He strode away without a backward glance.

"Told you he was a prick," Reggie growled.

"No kidding," I agreed, hiding my relief. If anyone questioned Ian or me now, we had our story straight.

But what else had I blabbed while I was under the influence?

I shelved that uncomfortable question for future worrying when Reggie motioned the others closer.

As they leaned together over my bed, Reggie muttered, "Murray and Melinda, check my logic on this. They've got to have faked that demo. No gas could break molecular bonds that quickly and completely. And even if there was a gas that could do it, the vial wasn't a pressure vessel so it was too small relative to the air volume in the containment unit. It couldn't have held enough for a useful concentration. What do you think?"

After a moment of silence, Melinda said slowly, "I don't know. Mitchell didn't claim the vial contained gas; he said it contained bacteria that would excrete a gas, or possibly a liquid; he didn't specify. A vial that size could contain trillions upon trillions of bacteria, and they could move very quickly over the surface of that rebar." She hesitated. "But my gut feeling is the same as yours, though I'd need to see their research before I could form an opinion."

"I bet they were faking it," I agreed. "Did you see how nervous Dr. Pino was?"

Reggie shrugged. "He's always nervous. The guy's a twitchy sweaty little chipmunk."

Murray gave him a disapproving look. "He has hyperhidrosis, and it's aggravated by social anxiety." After a glance at my blank face, he elaborated, "Hyperhidrosis is a medical condition characterized by excessive sweating."

"The poor guy," I said. "That has to suck. He was drenched by the end of the presentation."

"Yeah," Reggie agreed with malicious satisfaction. "It

looked like he'd pissed himself."

"Don't be such a dick, Reggie," I said absently.

"Pino's a dick, so why shouldn't I be?" he replied. "Pino the penis."

"Reggie!" I smacked him on the arm.

"Seriously, the guy's a douchebag," Reggie insisted. "Ten years ago he got caught stealing work from undergraduates and publishing their research under his own name. I can't believe he ever got a security clearance." He snorted. "Maybe he stole that, too."

Murray frowned. "He did seem more anxious than usual. And I'm suspicious of their presentation, too; but molecular bonding isn't my area of expertise." He glanced over his shoulder. "We should ask Katie. She's the best-"

"No!"

Reggie's loud objection made us all stare.

Melinda's eyes narrowed. "Yes, Reggie. Not only is she brilliant, but you also owe her an apology. A public one." With a searing look at Reggie, she called across the room. "Katie, could you come over here, please? Reggie has something he needs to say to you."

I cringed, wishing I could pull the sheet over my head and block out the upcoming scene. Reggie would tear poor Katie apart.

Katie planted her hands on her hips, her eyes flashing. "Is that so? What do you want to say, *Reggie?*" Her clear voice lilted above the other conversations in the room, and everyone fell silent.

Thirty-some pairs of eyes focused on Reggie.

He gave Melinda a look that was clearly intended to make her combust and fall in ashes at his feet; but Melinda remained impervious, her eyes glinting with the gleeful evil only the best of friends can channel.

"Come on, Reggie," she prompted in dulcet tones. "Speak up."

"You're dead meat," Reggie grated under his breath. "I'm going to..."

"Come on, then, you mongrel," Katie taunted. "I'm waiting."

I flinched. Oh, Katie. You don't realize that Reggie's capable of stripping the skin from your body with mere words, leaving all your tender nerves exposed...

Reggie drew himself up, exuding black rage. "Katie," he said in a tone that made me shiver. He raised his voice so everyone in the room could hear. "I owe you an apology for what I said earlier. I was being an asshole."

Murray nudged Melinda and muttered, "Who is that guy, and why is he wearing Reggie's face?" Melinda snuffled, obviously smothering giggles behind her mask.

Oblivious to their commentary, Katie stared back at Reggie. "Bloody oath you were," she agreed, her small form straight and unyielding.

"I'm sorry," he said, his posture just as stiff as hers, but his tone sincere.

I fought back a smile. Right there: That's why we were friends. Reggie might be an abrasive cantankerous son of a bitch, but he was also brave as hell, fair-minded, and brutally honest.

Katie relented immediately, her eyes softening. "Aw, no worries, love."

"Thank you," Reggie said formally. "Would you join us, please? We need your expertise."

She stiffened. "Oh, that's it, is it? You only apologized because you want my mind."

Reggie's eye widened. A slow flush climbed his neck, emphasizing the division where his own reddening skin ended and his prosthetic mask began.

The room was so silent I could hear my own pulse thumping in my ears. Thirty gazes bounced back and forth between Reggie's discomfiture and Katie's indignation.

At last Reggie spoke.

"No," he said clearly. "I want you for much more than your mind. I want to run my hands all over your hot little body. I want to go down on you until you come so hard you see stars. And I want to make love to you until the only name you remember is mine."

CHAPTER 17

The room had been quiet before but now it was absolutely soundless, everyone standing paralyzed.

I gaped up at Reggie. Oh, God. There was that brutal honesty again; with the worst possible timing.

Melinda choked.

Murray mumbled, "Jeez, Reggie, sexual harassment much?"

An explosive snort of laughter came from Hellhound's direction.

Katie stood frozen in place, eyes wide and cheeks crimson.

"Oh..." she said faintly. "I... I..." She swallowed. "I was... hoping... you might like my sense of humour."

Reggie turned as red as Katie. "I, um... I do," he croaked, looking utterly wretched. Then he squared his shoulders again, his face hardening. "So if you're done with the joke, get your fucking sense of humour over here," he snapped.

A dangerous pause made me squeeze my eyes shut and clench the sheet in my fist.

Then Katie's laughter pealed out, shattering the silence. "Aw, Reggie, you're funny when you get all blokey."

I opened my eyes again with a breath of relief as she strolled over.

"What's up, then?" she inquired.

She slid into the chair that Reggie pulled out for her, but despite her easy movements, she didn't make eye contact with him. When his sleeve brushed her shoulder she flinched infinitesimally, and Reggie looked as though he'd taken a punch to the stomach.

"We need your professional opinion," Murray said as though their awkward exchange had never occurred. He lowered his voice and everyone leaned in. "Katie, Reggie thinks that the bacteria demo might have been faked. What do you think?"

"Ha." She relaxed and glanced over at Reggie, her smiling eyes crinkling above her mask. "Glad I'm not the only one."

He relaxed, too. "So, can you think of any bacterial excretions that might affect metal like that?"

"No. I just can't see metallic bonding being dismantled that quickly and completely. Especially when the s and p electrons are delocalized the way they are in alloyed metals..." She shrugged. "Non-directional bonds just don't break like that no matter what chemical you apply to them, and I can't imagine how any substance could alter an electron's charge. You can reduce an alloy to its elements in multiple steps using chemicals combined with physical processing, but to go from solid metal to powder within seconds? It seems really unlikely."

As Reggie sat back with a nod, she added, "But I'd have to evaluate their research before I'd accuse them. Just because I can't imagine how it would work, it doesn't mean it's impossible. I wouldn't have believed your ultrasound weapon would work, either, if I hadn't just seen it." Her eyes crinkled mischievously again. "Maybe you were faking it, too."

"Smartass," Reggie growled.

She winked at him, but sobered fast. "But why would they fake their presentation? It's a right risky move, and their reputations are on the line." She hesitated, then added, "Well, Mitchell's is. Pino doesn't have much of a rep to lose."

"I don't know why." Reggie frowned at me. "But I'm willing to bet it's connected to the attack on Aydan."

A stir at the doorway made us all glance over. A slim figure garbed in an isolation suit and breathing mask slipped through the door and the commander intercepted it. After a brief exchange, they both strode over to my gurney.

As the figure approached, my heart lifted at the sight of blue eyes bracketed by the beginnings of crows-feet.

"Dr. Roth!" I gave her a smile. "Am I ever glad to see you!"

She smiled back. "We have to stop meeting like this." Switching to professional mode, she checked the monitor and IV, then pulled up a chair. "I need to ask Aydan some questions," she told the group. "This will only take a few minutes."

The commander stepped closer and toggled a button on his headset. A small red light glowed, and I guessed that it was a camera. My conversation with Dr. Roth would be recorded.

I swallowed hard.

Everyone except Hellhound got up and wandered away, but he remained seated beside me. Dr. Roth eyed our clasped hands with the hint of a smile hovering at the corner of her mouth.

"So, Aydan," she said. "Tell me everything you remember."

"I was standing there watching Dr. Mitchell's and Dr. Pino's presentation," I began. "They had, um..."

Classified technology.

"...some really scary stuff," I generalized, and went on, "I was... um..."

Dammit, I didn't want to admit I had been half-paralyzed by claustrophobia. As far as the Department's psych team knew, I was over that.

"I was really riveted," I said lamely. "Which was stupid of me, because I wasn't paying enough attention to everybody else. Then I got jabbed in the arm and at the same time a smoke bomb flew out. I'm pretty sure Grandin threw it, because he was standing right beside me and it came from our direction. After that..."

I frowned. My mind felt distant and blurry, flickering like a bad video.

"Um... I had my duffel bag I got filter masks on everybody..."

Smoke. Confusion.

"I, um... I guess... we headed for the door...?" I turned to Arnie, who nodded encouragingly. "But we couldn't get out."

I was sure about that part, because if I'd gotten out that door I'd damn well still be running.

"And then... Mitchell yelled out that his bacteria were gone..." I frowned and thumped my forehead. "Come on, brain, get with the program."

It was no use. I let out a breath of frustration. "I don't

remember much after that. Just flashes of stuff. Reggie being a dick. People... dancing...?" I shook my head. "I was probably hallucinating."

Hellhound chuckled. "So that's what ya were sayin'. 'Ya put your right foot in, ya put your right foot out, ya do the hokey-pokey'. Ya were laughin' your ass off, an' I couldn't figure out what ya were tryin' to say."

I gave him a smile, but I couldn't remember that part. Why the hell would I be laughing and singing after I'd been shot and poisoned?

I turned back to Dr. Roth. "You should ask Arnie what happened. He's got a photographic memory."

"I'm aware of his powers of recall. I've also watched the surveillance footage from all the cameras." Her blue gaze probed me. "I want to know what *you* remember."

"Nothing after that." I knotted my fists in my hair and tugged. "I... I feel as though I did remember more earlier... when I first woke up..."

Shiny slippery memories, flickering just out of my grasp. I clenched my fists tighter but the thoughts were gone.

"...but now I don't even remember whether I remembered," I finished with frustration. "It's like... like a dream fading away after you wake up. I'm sorry, that's all I've got."

Arnie frowned. "Do ya remember hallucinatin' that I got my head cut off?"

I recoiled. "No! That would be horrible!"

His frown deepened as he turned to Dr. Roth. "She remembered that earlier. She's losin' her memory."

"That would be the effects of the ketamine," the doctor said reassuringly. She returned her attention to me. "Just relax, and let's see if we can dredge up any other memory fragments before they fade. Tell me what you remember about the dart."

"I got jabbed in the shoulder." Fear bubbled up again. "Can you do blood tests to find out whether I got injected with... some kind of disease or something? How long does it take to find out?"

"Just tell us what you remember about the dart," the commander snapped. He sounded pissed off. What the hell did I ever do to him?

"I don't know anything about the damn dart," I retorted. "Did you ever find Grandin's pen? Or any kind of blowgun? Or the dart itself? Did you check the floor? Or maybe the person who shot me picked it up off the floor and threw it away. Did you check the garbage containers?"

Dr. Roth and the commander exchanged an unreadable glance.

What the hell?

Anxious confusion seized me. Had I forgotten something again?

"Never mind the dart for now," Dr. Roth said. "What else can you remember? Did you..." Her gaze flicked warily toward the commander before returning to me. "...did you trip and fall at any point? Or maybe crawl on the floor to stay below the smoke?"

"No." I frowned. What the hell was she getting at? "At least, not that I remember..."

"She fell," Hellhound said firmly. "After he..." He jerked his chin at the commander. "...questioned her. He wouldn't let her put her arms down an' she passed out. I got to her before she hit her head on the floor, though."

"That's right, you did catch her," the commander said in a tone of enlightenment. "You were right there. And Dr. Chow was, too..." He shot a hard-eyed look across the room to where Reggie and Katie stood close together, oblivious to everyone else.

Katie was leaning toward Reggie, and I drew a breath of relief. She must have gotten over the shock of his passionate public declaration. And if I had correctly interpreted her Aussie slang at the party and her current body language, she was interested in reciprocating.

But Reggie's posture was stiff and remote. Dammit, what was wrong with him?

"...collusion," the commander finished, jerking my attention back to him.

Shit, what had I missed? Why wouldn't my brain focus?

"Fuck that!" Hellhound barked. "Ya searched us right afterward, an' ya didn't find fuck-all. So you're sayin' ya fucked up the search, is that it?"

"I'm saying that a clever agent might fake an episode of lightheadedness as a diversion-"

"She got shot up with fuckin' ketamine an' your own doc found it in her blood! She was fuckin' unconscious!" Hellhound glowered at the commander. "She wasn't fuckin' fakin' anythin'!"

The commander's voice was icy. "I didn't say she wasn't injected with ketamine. I'm saying she could have injected herself as a diversion."

Hellhound lunged to his feet, but the commander's weapon snapped up with lethal speed, his finger hovering near the trigger.

"Don't do anything rash," the commander advised softly.

"And don't be so sure she's innocent. She's been putting on a good act to misdirect us, but remember..." He spared a contemptuous glance at me. "She had the dart in her own pocket."

CHAPTER 18

I stared up at the commander's angry face and poised machine gun, feeling horribly vulnerable lying on the gurney with only a sheet for protection.

And shit, I really did only have the sheet for protection. Realization finally penetrated my drugged haze. I wore nothing but a hospital gown.

And I was lying here in a room with thirty other people, and...

...had they stripped me naked in front of everybody?

My mouth opened and closed as I clutched the sheet to my chin, unable to speak.

I was practically naked in public. I *had* been naked in public. With people watching. Doing things to me while I was unconscious and helpless.

And worse, somebody was framing me.

I was going to jail.

Trapped...

My pulse bounded up, the rapid beeping of the heart monitor betraying my terror for all to see.

"Aydan? Aydan, what's happenin'? Say somethin', darlin'!" Arnie's urgent voice penetrated my panic. "Aydan!"

"I'm..." My voice came out a ghostly wisp of itself. I tried to say 'I'm okay' but the lie wouldn't come. I was not okay. Not even close.

And my brain still wasn't working right. I should be standing up and shouting. Doing something. Proving I was innocent...

"Aydan, tell me what's happening." Dr. Roth's firm voice held an edge of concern. "Are you seeing or feeling anything unusual? Pain? Disorientation?"

My throat tightened and sparkles darkened the edges of my vision.

"Aydan, listen to me. You're hyperventilating. Try to slow your breathing. Breathe with me. In... two... three..."

Panic attack. That's all this was. I wasn't dying of some horrible unknown disease.

Probably not, anyway.

Shut up. It's just a panic attack.

I could deal with panic attacks.

I could, dammit.

But my brain wouldn't cooperate...

"Help," I wheezed, the gurney vibrating with my tremors.

Bodies bustled in my peripheral vision and meaningless words buffeted me. "...no apparent cause... blood pressure one-sixty over ninety-four... hallucination...?"

Warmth engulfed my icy hand and Arnie's soft gravelly voice spoke beside my ear. "Don't worry, darlin', I got ya. Whatever you're seein' right now, it ain't real. You're safe here with me, an' you're gonna be okay. I got your back, darlin'; I won't let anythin' get ya..."

His words blurred into a singsong croon as he repeated the reassurances over and over; and I slowly allowed myself to believe them.

Gradually I regained control of my breathing. Long slow belly breaths, like ocean waves rolling in...

"That's better.   You're doin' fine, darlin'," Arnie encouraged. "Nice an' easy. Just take it easy..."

"Can you talk now, Aydan?" Dr. Roth asked. "How are you feeling?"

"I'm... okay." This time I managed the lie.

"Did you feel or perceive anything unusual?" she asked. "Your heart rate and respiration and blood pressure all spiked for no reason that we could see. Was there some precipitating event?"

Yeah, being accused of treason and international terrorism will do that.

"I, um..." I began, but the commander's coldly suspicious gaze dried the words in my mouth.   "I... guess... I was hallucinating," I croaked. "I thought I saw..."

No inspiration occurred to me.

"Um..."

I sighed and closed my eyes. Too hard to think.

"Aydan, try to stay awake." Dr. Roth's cool gloved hand patted my cheek. "The drug should be out of your system soon, but it may cause some memory loss. We need you to answer some more questions now."

Overcoming the urge to just pretend unconsciousness, I opened my eyes again. "Okay. But... will I remember this?"

Her forehead wrinkled behind her face shield. "Maybe. I don't know."

I glanced at the steady red light glowing on the commander's headset. "But you're recording it, right?"

"Yes."

I let out a breath. "Good. It's really creeping me out that I can't remember..."

That I'd been stripped naked in front of thirty people...

"Aydan, your heart rate is climbing again. Slow your breathing. Try to stay calm."

"You're okay, darlin'," Arnie added. "I got your back."

His words calmed me. He always had my back. And his photographic memory would replay everything for me later. I might not remember enough to save myself from incarceration, but he would remember it for me.

"I'm okay," I said with more conviction. "What are your questions?"

"What can you tell us about the dart?" Dr. Roth asked.

"They found it in my pocket? Which pocket?"

"The one you put it in after you injected yourself," the commander growled.

"I *didn't!* I told you..."

My memories wavered precariously. Had I told them? Maybe I hadn't.

"I didn't inject myself," I insisted. "I got shot in the shoulder. I never saw a dart, but I sure as hell felt it. How could it have gotten into my pocket?" I frowned as a thought oozed into my mind. "Did you find it when you searched me?" Another wave of uncertainty shook me. "You did search me, didn't you?"

"Yeah, he searched ya," Hellhound confirmed. "But he didn't find it on ya. The scanner caught it."

Sudden cold fear made me shiver. Maybe the commander himself had framed me. It would have been so easy for him to tuck a dart into my pocket...

"Aydan, stay calm," Dr. Roth warned. "Control your

breathing."

I gulped and did my best to obey but my mind galloped ahead, driving my pulse into rapid drumming.

It was the commander, dammit. He could have picked up his accomplice's dart when he came in and then put it into my pocket while he pretended to search me...

As though reading my mind, Hellhound glared at the commander. "Seems to me you're the one that had his hands in Aydan's pockets," he grated. "Maybe ya put the dart there yourself."

"No, of course not," the commander replied. "There were no fingerprints on the dart, and I'm not wearing gloves. I couldn't have put it in her pocket without getting my own fingerprints on it."

"No fingerprints?" Hellhound demanded. "Then Aydan couldn't'a put it in her own pocket, either. She never had gloves on. So somebody else planted it on her. Remember, she said somebody'd bumped into her in the smoke." He turned to me. "Right, darlin'?"

"Uh... I don't remember saying that, but... yeah, I think... people bumped into me in the smoke, I'm pretty sure."

While I spoke, Dr. Roth had been frowning into space. "Aydan," she said. "Would you please roll onto your left side so we can see the injection site?"

I did as she bade, and her cool fingers gently lifted the sleeve of my gown.

"I really don't think Aydan would have been capable of injecting herself here," Dr. Roth said. "In the first place, she's right-handed, so it would be more natural for her to inject her left arm, not her right. But also... Aydan, would you please point out the injection site to us?"

"Um..." I craned my neck, but I couldn't see behind my shoulder. "Here...?" I reached around, probing cautiously for the sore spot. "No..." I found the spot. "...here."

"You see?" Dr. Roth said triumphantly. "She can barely reach the site with her fingertips. It would have been extremely difficult for her to accomplish the injection herself."

The commander scowled. "But not impossible."

"Not impossible," Dr. Roth agreed. "But she certainly couldn't have accomplished it covertly. And I didn't see anything in the security footage that looked as though she'd wrapped her arm around herself to do it."

The commander looked like a man suffering a severe toothache. "She could have done it under the cover of the smoke," he argued. Then he raised his head as though listening, and his face cleared. "Director Stemp is assuming command," he said with obvious relief. "We're still under quarantine, so we'll videoconference him. I'll get everything set up." He toggled his mike, apparently addressing his entire team. "Stay alert. Watch for... everything." His words came out on a weary breath. "The attacker could be anybody."

He strode off, and I gazed up at Dr. Roth, rubbing the ache in the middle of my forehead. "So, the dart...?" I asked.

"It was in your pocket," she repeated patiently.

A small flare of satisfaction warmed me. "I remembered that this time. But if you have the dart, then you should be able to test it to see whether, um..." My throat went dry, and I cleared it and went on, "...there was... anything in it besides, um..." The name of the drug wouldn't come to my mind. "...whatever it was that knocked me out," I finished.

"Ketamine," Dr. Roth supplied. "Yes, you're right. The dart is in the lab now. The ketamine was easy to identify with a standard drug screening, but they're checking the dart for other possibilities. The last I heard they hadn't found anything, but I'll check again. I don't want to go through the decontamination procedure unnecessarily, so..." She patted her breathing mask. "I'll stay in here as long as my air supply lasts." She rose. "You seem to be stabilizing, but don't be too concerned if you still have a few episodes of memory loss or hallucinations. I'll be in one of the offices if you need me."

When she was out of earshot I clutched Hellhound's hand. "I'm naked. How did I get naked? What happened? Who... saw me?"

He squeezed my hand, gentle reassurance from a grip strong enough to crush my bones. "It's okay, darlin', I held up a sheet so nobody saw anythin' 'cept the medics." He grinned. "An' me; but I've seen it before." He lowered his voice to a sexy growl. "An' I'm hopin' I'll see it again real soon."

I relaxed with a long breath. "Wait 'til we don't have an audience."

He gave me a devilish wink. "Aw, come on, darlin', get your kink on. Don't ya have any audience fantasies?"

"Um, no. Audiences have an extremely high pucker-factor for me. I'd dry up like-"

"A dead dingo's donger?" he inquired, straight-faced.

"*What?*" The word burst out of me on a gust of laughter.

Hellhound chuckled. "It's an Aussie thing. I heard their weapons director say it, an' now it's my new favourite sayin'."

"Okay, now it's mine, too."

We snickered companionably for a few moments, but I sobered fast.

"Tell me exactly what happened, in order," I demanded. "Don't leave anything out. And keep telling me over and over until I can remember it for myself."

"Okay, darlin'." He settled back in his chair and stared straight ahead with the unfocused gaze that told me he was accessing his phenomenal memory banks. "Ya remember right up to where ya got shot, right?"

"Yes. Actually, up to where we got to the door and the smoke cleared. The drug must have taken a little while to kick in."

"Makes sense. Okay, here goes..." He methodically described every detail, finishing with, "...an' after they finished the body cavity search, that was about it. Ya were screamin' an' hallucinatin', but ya didn't blab anythin'."

I drew a breath of relief. "Good..." Then his second-last sentence registered and I bolted upright. "Wait, what?" My voice rose to a squawk. *"They looked up my ass?"*

"Yeah, they looked everywhere." He gave me a sympathetic grimace. "They didn't find anythin', but I thought you'd wanna know."

"Oh, God." I flopped back onto the pillow, fighting the urge to pull the sheet over my head and die of sheer humiliation. "No. I really, really didn't want to know."

Arnie looked stricken. "Sorry, darlin', I thought..." he began.

"No, no, it's okay!" I hurriedly squeezed his hand. "You're right, I'm glad you told me. It's just... oh, God, I just..." I shuddered.

"I'm sorry," he repeated, his brow furrowed with

concern.

"Don't be sorry. It's okay," I said firmly. "You did exactly the right thing by telling me. Thank you. It's just... it really creeps me out knowing that those things happened to me and I don't remember anything at all." I squeezed his hand tighter. "Thank you for staying with me and watching out for me."

"No problem." He patted my hand, but he still looked worried.

I changed the subject. "So let me see if I've got everything straight." I repeated the timeline back to him.

"Good job, darlin', ya got it all," he said when I was finished.

"Good. Would you please ask me to repeat it again in ten minutes? And if I don't remember everything then, tell me again; and keep asking me about it every ten minutes until I can get it right every time?"

"I will. You're gonna be okay. You're already rememberin' better than ya did in the last ten minutes. An' the ten minutes before that."

"Thanks, Arnie."

He raised my hand to his lips and brushed a whiskery kiss across my knuckles. "You're welcome."

Ten minutes later he asked me to repeat the timeline, and I managed it with only minor prompting. Just as I was finishing my recitation, Dr. Roth reappeared along with the other doctor who had been attending me.

"How are you feeling?" Dr. Roth asked.

"Better." I sat up and turned my head from side to side.

"No more hallucinations, and I'm not so dizzy now."

"Good. Director Stemp is waiting for you on video in the conference room. Would you like to get dressed?"

"Oh hell yes!"

When I emerged fully dressed from behind the sheet that Hellhound had held up as a makeshift privacy screen, a smattering of applause greeted me.

Reggie and Katie and Murray and Melinda were clapping, but everyone else cast suspicious glances my way.

As I slowly crossed the bullpen clinging to Hellhound's arm, the group withdrew from my path. Ordinarily I might have cringed from their scrutiny as I navigated the gauntlet of narrowed eyes; but I was too busy watching my feet, which had a disturbing tendency to stray.

"Okay, darlin'?" Hellhound asked as I stumbled again.

"Yeah." I tightened my grip on his arm. "But my feet won't go where I want them to."

"You're doin' fine," he encouraged. "We're almost there."

A few paces later I sank gratefully into a chair at the conference table, but my gratitude was short-lived when I caught sight of the video screen.

Stemp was there. But...

So was Greg Holt.

Shit.

CHAPTER 19

My heart sank at the sight of Holt's craggy features and sardonic grin taking up half the videoconference screen.

"Hey, Kelly," he needled. "How's the international terrorism game these days?"

If my brain had been working at its usual capacity I might have managed a snappy retort or at least some righteous indignation, but I had neither. I stared at Holt in silence while my insides chilled.

Of course Stemp had brought another agent with him. As far as he knew, I was compromised. Holt would be here to replace me, and to arrest me if necessary. Or worse.

The prospect of life imprisonment was terrifying enough, but since I carried Stemp's most critical personal secret in addition to the nation's classified knowledge...

I swallowed hard and searched Stemp's impassive expression on the video screen. If he decided I couldn't be trusted, I wouldn't live to see the end of the day.

"Agent Kelly," he greeted me without inflection.

"Hi," I croaked.

"How are you feeling?"

"Shitty." The truth escaped before I could disguise it

with a lie that would make me sound a little less pathetic.

"I'm sorry to hear that."

He didn't look sorry. He looked scary. His reptilian features were utterly immobile; his unnerving amber eyes as hard as stones.

"I didn't do it!" I burst out. "I was just standing there, and then something jabbed me in the arm and the smoke bomb flew out..."

"Really?" Holt demanded, his action-hero jaw jutting. "Or are you just repeating what Helmand told you to say?"

My stomach clenched. Oh God. It wasn't just my life on the line; it might be Arnie's, too, if Stemp thought we had collaborated.

"I remember that part just fine," I said, holding my voice as steady as I could, which wasn't very steady at all. I cleared my throat and tried again. "My memory's good up to where the smoke thinned out and Dr. Mitchell said his bacteria were gone." A merciful moment of clarity straightened my spine and strengthened my voice. "I want to see the surveillance camera footage. Everybody's seen it but me, and I want to see why everybody's trying to frame me."

"Everyone is not trying to frame you," Stemp countered dispassionately. "We are collecting evidence and we will discover the truth." Before I could respond, he continued, "I have collated the footage of the incident from all available cameras. Would you prefer to see them side by side or in sequence?"

"One at a time, please." I rubbed my aching forehead. "My brain still isn't working right."

"Very well. We'll watch in slow motion between when the smoke bomb appears and when the view is obscured by smoke." Stemp's and Holt's faces disappeared and the screen displayed a surveillance camera view instead.

The footage had been taken from across the room so I couldn't make out much detail, but I was relieved to see that I looked a lot more composed in the video than I had actually been. There was no sign of the claustrophobic terror that had been coursing through my veins. My face was pale and grim, but so was everyone else's.

Beside me in the video, Grandin scribbled furiously in his notebook; just as I'd remembered. I nudged Hellhound. "See, he had a pen there."

Hellhound nodded, frowning at the screen.

"Can we zoom in on his pen?" I asked.

"We can magnify, but the detail is probably insufficient," Stemp replied.

The picture obligingly enlarged, but Stemp was right. The details of the pen blurred as the zoom level increased.

"Damn." I let out a breath and slumped in my chair. "I was sure that pen was a dart gun and he was just pretending to write with it; but there's no way to tell from the footage."

"Agreed," Stemp said. The picture zoomed back out to its original dimensions and the video resumed.

A moment later my arm jerked forward and the smoke bomb tumbled through the air.

"Hang on, play that back!" I snapped. "The smoke bomb might look as though it came from me; but I think Grandin threw it from behind me. At this camera angle you can't see his hands at all. And if it had come from me you'd be able to see it in my hand."

"Not necessarily." Holt's mocking voice spoke as the video wound back and replayed. "You could've had it up the sleeve of your sweatshirt."

"But what about fingerprints?" I protested. "Were my fingerprints on it?"

"No fingerprints were found," Stemp replied.

Holt snorted. "It's a no-brainer to dip your fingertips in clear resin to obscure your prints before you handle something."

I gulped. Shit, there was another piece of spycraft I should have known. My self-confidence drained away and I felt myself reverting to a bungling idiot civilian. Just the way I'd felt when I had been partnered with Holt.

He was still talking, his tone condescending. "...and then you could have easily peeled off the resin caps and chucked them while you were hidden by smoke."

Queasy anxiety twisted my stomach. So much for the defense I'd been counting on to clear me.

"Did they check all the garbage cans for fingerprint caps?" Hellhound demanded.

"Yes," Stemp confirmed. "They found nothing."

"Then Aydan couldn'ta done it," Hellhound persisted. "'Cause our whole team can vouch for her while the cameras were smoked out. If she'd thrown the finger caps in the garbage then, ya woulda found 'em; an' she didn't have time to get rid a' anythin' after the smoke cleared. She's on camera the whole time."

"Nice try," Holt sneered. "She probably swallowed the caps while she was hidden in the smoke. That's what any competent agent would do."

"Whose fuckin' side are ya on?" Hellhound snapped. "You're s'posed to be clearin' her, not railroadin' her!"

"As I said before, we are simply seeking the truth,"

Stemp said coolly. "Agent Kelly, would you like to see the rest of the footage?"

"Yes, please," I whispered, my throat dry.

Maybe Stemp had finally decided I was too much of a liability. Maybe the commander had been acting under Stemp's orders, to frame me so I could be conveniently eliminated without any pushback from the chain of command. And if Stemp gave the order, Holt would kill me without hesitation.

Film after film played.

All of them were inconclusive. Either by coincidence or design, the view of Grandin's hands was blocked by either my body or his in all the camera angles. Nausea swirled in my gut.

"Ya okay, darlin'?" Hellhound inquired anxiously. "Ya look pretty pale an' sweaty."

"I feel like shit," I admitted. "Nauseated. Weak." I swallowed hard. "Has... has Dr. Roth heard anything from the lab yet? Do they know whether...?" I couldn't bring myself to say the words '...I've been poisoned'.

"You're prob'ly just hungry," Hellhound said in reassuring tones. "It's damn near two-thirty, an' ya ain't eaten since breakfast." But the worry in his eyes belied his confident words. "I'll go ask the doc," he added. "An' I'll grab ya some food."

He slipped out the door, as always moving quickly and quietly for a man of his size.

The videos vanished from the screen and the display switched back to Holt and Stemp.

Holt studied me with a skeptical eyebrow raised. "You look like shit. Nice acting. And shooting yourself up with ketamine was a smooth move to make yourself look like a victim."

"I *didn't!*" Anger heated my blood, lending me a moment's strength. "I told you, I got shot! And we still don't even know whether it was only ketamine or whether there was some deadly virus or something in there!"

"Couldn't be anything too deadly," Holt drawled. "You're still kicking. And I don't see why anybody would bother using a dart to inject you with something lethal. There are lots of better and faster ways to off somebody. I bet ketamine was the only thing in there."

The door swung open and Hellhound strode in, smiling. "Hey, darlin', good news! They finished at the lab, an' the only thing in the dart was ketamine. You're all clear, an' they're liftin' the quarantine."

I would have been relieved if not for Holt's cynical snicker.

"Why the hell are you so sure I did it?" I snapped at him. "Like you said, any competent agent would be able to do this; so why aren't you investigating Grandin? I've told you over and over, he was right beside me! He's the only one who could have shot me from that angle; and he's the only one who could have thrown the smoke bomb and made it look as though it came from me! And if he or the commander had dipped their fingertips in resin, either of them could have planted the dart in my pocket!"

"We are exploring all possibilities," Stemp said. He nodded to the plate of crackers and cheese in Hellhound's hand. "Please eat. As soon as the quarantine has been officially lifted, Dr. Travers will be in with the lie detector."

I fell back in my chair with a breath of pure relief.

"Thank God! I'd forgotten about our lie detector. It'll prove I'm telling the truth!"

"I certainly hope so," Stemp said.

"Can we look at all the surveillance footage now?" I asked. "I'd like to see everything from the moment we arrived up until Dr. Roth got here."

"Certainly." Stemp turned to Holt. "Holt, you're cleared to enter the area now that the quarantine is lifted, so please go in and take over Kelly's role safeguarding our Weapons team while the rest of our allies continue their presentations."

Holt rose and strode away, his chest puffed out like Superman flying to the rescue of Smallville.

Asshole.

But at least I knew Reggie and Murray and Melinda would be safe. Holt didn't mess around. He wouldn't get distracted and let somebody shoot him in the back.

I hissed out a breath as the screen switched back to surveillance footage. Let it go. The attack on me had been well-planned. If Grandin hadn't gotten me at that particular moment, he would have found another opportunity.

I munched crackers and cheese, feeling steadily better while we watched multiple views of the same action from different angles. Time dragged on, and my mind gradually cleared until I was able to concentrate fully on the details of the videos.

"It's good to see this," I said, watching the footage of the personal searches from yet another viewpoint. "It helps to see what actually-"

"Wait," Stemp interrupted. "Let's look at that again."

The video froze, then went back frame by frame. I

leaned forward to stare at the screen.

"There," Stemp said. "Dr. Pino's search."

We watched in silence while the video ran forward again in slow motion. The guard palpated Pino's right leg, then his left. Paused. Spoke to Dr. Pino.

Dr. Pino shook his head, looking terrified. Even in the low-resolution video, his brow glistened with sweat. Dark sweat stains streaked his clothes.

The guard spoke again, indicating Dr. Pino's left leg, and Pino reluctantly raised his pant leg to display a grubby bandage stained reddish brown with dried blood.

The guard recoiled, unconsciously wiping his hands on his thighs, and nodded at Dr. Pino. Pino lowered his pant leg again and the guard completed his search, avoiding the bandaged area.

"I'll have Dr. Roth remove that bandage and examine Dr. Pino's injury," Stemp said. "If one wishes to conceal something during a search, hiding it under a soiled bandage is an effective tactic. Agent Kelly, that was the last of the video. Do you have any further questions?"

"No, that's it," I said.

"Very well. You may expect Dr. Travers and the lie detector shortly." The video image blinked out.

"Glad Stemp's got everythin' under control, but that Holt's a real fuckin' prick," Hellhound observed in the ensuing silence.

"He's actually okay sometimes," I explained. "But once he starts playing Holt The Magnificent, he's a total tool."

"Is he any good?"

"I have no idea, and I'm sure as hell not going to sleep with him to find out."

Hellhound guffawed. "Your Freudian slip is showin', darlin'. I meant, is he any good as an agent?"

"Oh." Heat suffused my face. "Um, yeah. He's actually a really good agent. The problem is he never lets anybody forget it."

"Huh." Dismissing the topic of Holt with a grunt, Hellhound rolled his chair closer to mine and slipped an arm around my shoulders. "So how ya doin', darlin'? Feelin' any better?"

"Yeah." I sighed and leaned into him, propping my head against his muscular shoulder. "Thank you. Again."

The door opened, making me twitch guiltily away from Hellhound.

"For Christ's sake, are you two at it again?" Reggie growled, but there was a quirk of humour at the corner of his mouth. "You're worse than Murray and Melinda."

I relaxed back into Hellhound's embrace. "No, if we were Murray and Melinda we'd be banging each other up against the wall right now."

"Hey, there's a thought," Hellhound said with interest. "Ain't ever done ya up against a wall..."

Reggie clapped his hands over his ears. "Jeez! Too much information!"

"So, did you want something?" I inquired, grinning. "Or were you just sneaking in here hoping to get a cheap thrill?"

He snorted. "Anytime I want a cheap thrill, I've got my own right hand. Catching you two in the act would only make me puke." He nodded at Hellhound. "Especially him. The only way he could get uglier would be if he was naked."

Hot anger jerked me upright. "Listen, asshole-"

"Hey, it's okay, darlin'," Hellhound interrupted. "Chow

an' me are cool." He flipped Reggie a casual middle finger and a sideways grin. "He likes havin' me around 'cause I'm the only bastard as fuckin' ugly as him."

"You are not!" I snapped, still seething. "Neither of you is ugly, and it pisses me off when-"

"Easy, now." Hellhound silenced me with a light kiss. "Ya gotta know I ain't ever gonna win any beauty contests. But it's nice to know ya got my back anyway."

"Same here," Reggie agreed with unaccustomed softness. "Thanks, Aydan."

Heat rose in my face. "You're welcome. Both of you." Hurrying past the moment, I began, "So what-" just as Reggie said, "So I just came to tell you-"

The door swung open again.

"...the quarantine bubble is down, all the presentations are done, and Stemp and Dr. Travers should be here any minute," Reggie finished as a voluptuous blue-eyed blonde strode in carrying a metal briefcase. "Hi, Honey," he added.

She gave him a warning frown softened by the twinkle in her eyes. "Watch it, Reggie. If you keep calling me by my given name, I'll be forced to divulge the sordid details of-"

"Jack!" he interrupted, throwing up his hands in a gesture of surrender. "Hi, Jack! Nice to see you again, Jack!"

She gave him a wicked grin, incongruous on her angelic features. "Hello, Reggie."

"Okay, I have to know," I demanded. "What do you have on him that works so well?"

"Jack..." Reggie said warningly.

She smiled. "Sorry, that bit of leverage is mine alone." She raised a perfectly-sculpted eyebrow in Reggie's direction.

"Unless *somebody* suffers another memory lapse."

"I'll be going now," Reggie said, and retreated out the door.

Before the door could close behind him, Stemp and Holt strode in and took seats across from us. "Dr. Travers," Stemp greeted Jack. "Let's get started." He shot a level look at Hellhound. "Helmand, wait outside."

Hellhound stiffened. "No."

A tense silence descended. Stemp sat immobile and unblinking, a deadly snake poised to strike. Holt moved forward in his chair as if eager for a fight.

"I ain't leavin'," Hellhound continued mildly. "If you're only questionin' Aydan about this mornin', ya ain't gonna ask anythin' I ain't cleared to hear."

"True," Stemp agreed without changing expression. "Very well, you may stay."

His acquiescence was issued in the same clinical tone he might use to pronounce a death sentence, and I hid a shiver. If he issued a kill order today, Arnie would die with me.

Holt sat back in his chair again, his arms crossed and his expression impassive; but his hard blue gaze challenged me.

Jack busied herself attaching the familiar crown of electrodes around my forehead and tweaking knobs in the lie-detector case. A few minutes later she stood aside and said, "Go ahead, Director."

My pulse ticked up. This was my one chance to prove my innocence. Don't screw it up...

Stemp fixed me with his flat reptilian gaze. "Please answer yes or no. Is your name Aydan Kelly?"

"Yes." The green light flashed its reassurance.

"Did you throw a smoke bomb during Dr. Mitchell's

presentation today?"

Adrenaline gushed into my veins. Usually he lobbed a few easy questions to test the detector's responses, but he was jumping straight into it today.

"No." My voice came out in a croak, and I eyed the lie detector fearfully.

Green light.

Despite my attempt to hide my emotions, a breath of relief escaped me.

"Did you inject yourself with any substance today?"

"No."

Another green light sent my confidence soaring.

"Do you know who shot you with the ketamine dart?"

"No." I waited until the green light flashed before adding, "But I have a pretty good idea."

"We will explore that later. Did you put the dart in your own pocket?"

"No."

The lie detector flashed yellow, and my heart froze in my chest.

CHAPTER 20

Paralyzed, I stared at the damning yellow light flashing on the lie detector machine.

"What..." My voice came out in a dry whisper, and I cleared my throat and tried again. "What does that mean? I've never seen a yellow light before."

"It means you don't know the true answer," Jack said. "The detector compares the brainwaves generated by your memory of the event with the brainwaves generated by your response to the question. If you don't have a memory of the event, it'll flash yellow to indicate an invalid pairing. If you had remembered the event but lied about it, there would be a mismatch in the brainwave patterns and it would flash red. Director, try the question again; and Aydan, this time just answer 'yes' as a test."

"But I didn't!" I protested. "I know I didn't put the dart in my own pocket because I never even saw the dart until..."

My treacherous memories slithered through my grasp.

Had I seen the dart? Arnie had told me the commander found it in my pocket during the metal scan, so I must have seen it then. But I couldn't remember...

"Did you put the dart in your own pocket?" Stemp asked,

his voice and gaze as cold and impersonal as if we were strangers.

Maybe we were.

Maybe I'd never known him.

"No!" I repeated, and the yellow light flashed again.

"Try it once more," Jack urged. "Just say 'yes' this time, Aydan. It'll turn yellow just the same. You'll see, it's only indicating that you truly don't know."

"No." Fear rose in my throat. This was it. Stemp was going to kill me today; and if I said 'yes' now, my own fake testimony would bury me. "No! I didn't do it! I'm not going to say I did!"

"Aydan..." Jack gave me a helpless look before turning to Stemp. "Director, is paranoia a symptom of ketamine reaction?"

"Paranoia can be a symptom of guilt." Stemp's cold amber gaze drilled through to my soul. "And it's frequently a sign of a top agent," he added with an almost-imperceptible softening of the hard lines around his mouth. "There is no need to alter your response, Agent Kelly. Let's try a different question. Do you know who put the dart in your pocket?"

"No..." The word crept tentatively out of my mouth, but the light flashed solid green nonetheless. Holt looked disappointed, the bastard.

"Do you have any reliable recollection of the events after the smoke cleared?"

"No."

Green light.

"Very well," Stemp said. "Dr. Travers, please transfer the apparatus to Helmand."

After questioning Hellhound thoroughly and receiving a series of green lights, Stemp called in each member of our team and questioned each of them in turn.

After the last question had been asked and answered with green lights all the way, Stemp let out a small breath and leaned back in his chair.

"Thank you for your cooperation," he said to all of us. "It is unfortunate that you were all concentrating on Dr. Mitchell's presentation at the time of the incident; but it is understandable given the drama of the presentation."

"Kelly should have been paying more attention," Holt muttered. "It's unprofessional to get distracted like that."

Stemp gave him a cool look. "Kelly's attention is irrelevant.   Even if she had directly observed and remembered the attack, her testimony wouldn't alter this situation."

Holt grunted but didn't argue.

"I still say they faked that presentation," Reggie said. "And I'm sure it was choreographed to coincide with the attack on Aydan."

"Perhaps; but unfortunately we have no way to ascertain that," Stemp said, weariness edging his voice. "Despite their insistence that we 'get to the bottom of this'..." He said the words with a sour twist to his mouth. "...the U.S. delegates refuse to accept the validity of our lie detector. And they and the U.K. delegates have invoked their diplomatic immunity and refuse to be questioned."

"That's bullshit!" Reggie exclaimed. "We know damn well Grandin shot Kelly and threw that smoke bomb. He was the only other person in the area that matches the trajectory for both the dart and the smoke bomb, and Kelly's already passed the lie detector."

"Yes. Nevertheless, our hands are tied..." A tap on the door interrupted Stemp, and he called, "Come."

Dr. Roth slipped into the room, closing the door behind her.

"Your findings?" Stemp asked.

"I examined Dr. Pino's leg," she said. "The bandage is covering a wound that Dr. Pino claims was caused when he tripped on a curb this morning."

Stemp eyed her levelly. "And do you believe him?"

She exhaled a small breath through her nose. "I would say his story is extremely unlikely. His leg is gashed and the bruising is localized immediately around the wound. He has no other bruises or abrasions on his hands or knees. I would say it's more likely that he was struck by a metal object with a blunt edge."

"Perhaps the open sights of a pistol?" Stemp inquired dryly. "Like the one Agent Grandin carries?"

"Possibly. There were also three other anomalies that aroused my suspicions. Firstly, the blood pattern on the inside of the bandage corresponded to the shape of the wound, but the bandage was not soaked through with blood; and the pattern of dried blood on the outside of the bandage was reversed relative to the wound."

"So they slapped the bandage over it to get some blood on the outside and then turned it over so the blood would show," Holt deduced. "They were deliberately making it look disgusting so nobody would touch it."

"Yes, I believe so," Dr. Roth agreed. "That theory also explains the second anomaly, which was that the outside of the bandage was so dirty. If it had only been applied this morning it would have been protected by his pants, preventing any soil from accumulating on it. I suspect the dirt was deliberately applied."

"And the third anomaly?" Stemp inquired.

"Two edges of the bandage were looser than the other two and the skin beneath the tape on those edges showed signs of irritation, as though the corner of the bandage had been recently peeled up and then reapplied."

"So he hid something under there," Holt said triumphantly. "And then got rid of it. Probably went to the john and flushed it as soon as he had a chance. What do you want to bet it was the metal powder?"

"Prob'ly not," Hellhound disagreed. "Nobody left the room 'til they went through the metal scanner. It woulda showed up there."

"Huh. Okay," Holt allowed. "Maybe Grandin's missing pen? Taken apart into two halves so it would fit under the bandage?"

"A take-down dart pen; made out of plastic so it wouldn't show up on the metal scanner. That would work," I agreed. "But why would they go to so much trouble to frame me? And especially in such a ham-fisted way? They had to know I'd deny the whole thing; and Grandin is the only other person who could have done it."

"That..." Stemp said heavily, "...is the million-dollar question. But framing you was clearly their goal. The United States government has already requested your extradition, and Dirk, the FBI agent, is pressuring us to remand you into his custody."

"*What?*" Sheer terror turned my squawk of outrage into

a squeak.

"Needless to say, we will not surrender you to Dirk," Stemp said. "Particularly since your testimony has been corroborated by the lie detector. And in turn, we have requested Grandin's extradition to Canada for questioning."

"Okay..." I said, but I wasn't reassured. Stemp didn't have the final say in any of this. The chain of command had already ignored his advice and capitulated when the States had requested my presence in the first place. There was no reason to believe they'd grow a collective spine now.

Or maybe the whole chain of command was conspiring against me...

Another panic attack quivered at the edges of my mind, making my heart vibrate inside my rib cage.

I drew a long breath and let it out slowly. I could handle panic attacks. My brain was all better now.

...But I was trapped underground and people wanted to arrest me and throw me in jail *for the rest of my life...*

Shut up.

I breathed some more.

Stemp was still talking, and I focused on his words again. "...Holt, Helmand, and the Weapons team will return to Silverside in the helicopter along with Drs. Roth and Travers. Dr. Chow and Drs. West..." He nodded to Reggie, Melinda, and Murray. "Your luggage has already been transferred to Holt's vehicle, and he will escort you to the helipad. Kelly and I will return in the Hummer. Helmand, I have requisitioned a vehicle from the motor pool so you can return to Calgary to retrieve your own vehicle and go home after completing the weapons chain of custody transfer in Silverside."

"Hang on," Hellhound objected. "Why can't Aydan fly back with us? A Griffon'll take ten troops plus crew so there oughta be lotsa room."

"Ordinarily there would be," Stemp agreed without expression. "However, Dr. Gardner and the Australian weapons director and their agent will be flying with you to Silverside, to assist our team in researching the technology presented by the U.S. That forms the maximum personnel payload."

I shot a sidelong glance at Reggie. Quality time with Katie. This could be good...

His face was as impassive as Stemp's, but his shoulders were bunched and his right thumb tapped compulsively across the tip of his index finger, third finger, ring finger, and pinky; repeating the action over and over as though reassuring himself that his fingers were all there.

Shit. That wasn't good.

"But you're comin' straight back to Silverside, right?" Hellhound persisted, eyeing Stemp suspiciously.

"Not directly," Stemp admitted with a glance at his wristwatch. "I have a short personal errand and we will require a meal, after which we will return to Silverside. Our ETA is twenty-two hundred hours."

I did the math. It was only five-thirty. Unless the roads were still really bad, that meant his 'short personal errand' was going to take around two and a half hours.

He was up to something.

"Are the roads still bad?" I inquired, keeping my tone casual.

"Normal winter driving conditions," Stemp said crisply. "The snow ceased late this morning and the highway has been plowed and sanded." His eyelid flickered almost imperceptibly as he spoke.

My next question froze on my tongue.

Was that a secret signal for me to back off, or an involuntary twitch caused by a lie?

I knew the answer before my mind had even fully formed the question. Stemp had been a top agent before he took over as director. There was no way he'd exhibit such a blatant tell if he was lying.

So he was signalling me to drop it.

But why the secrecy? Whom did he mistrust?

My gaze slid to Holt's steely eyes, heroic posture, and smug expression. He was loving every minute of this. Riding in on his white horse to rescue me from yet another botched mission...

Hellhound interrupted my thoughts by speaking my doubts aloud. "Two an' a half hours ain't a 'short errand'." The icy look he received from Stemp would have quelled a lesser man, but Hellhound continued without flinching. "How do we know ya ain't gonna hand Aydan over to the fuckin' FBI as soon as we're all gone an' there's nobody to stop ya?"

"I give you my word that I will not 'hand over' Agent Kelly," Stemp said. "You have your orders. You are all dismissed." He rose. "Kelly, we'll leave immediately."

Hellhound rose, too, glowering down at Stemp. "Nothin' had better happen to Aydan," he said in a tone like the ominous subsonic rumble before a thunderclap.

"That is my goal," Stemp replied, unruffled. "Kelly, if you please...?" He inclined his head toward the door.

I swallowed hard. This could be an ambush. Once I was

separated from all the people who cared about me, Stemp could eliminate me without any witnesses. And I knew without a doubt that he was capable of killing me no matter how well-armed and well-prepared I was.

But despite my fearful speculations, my body was already standing up and my face was radiating a reassuring smile at Hellhound.

"Thanks, Arnie. Don't worry, I'll be fine. Talk to you soon." My voice sounded calm and confident.

What the hell? Did I really trust Stemp that much? Or had he somehow hypnotized me? Or maybe there had been something else mixed with that ketamine. Some drug that made me gullible and pliant...

My feet were walking me toward the door as if they didn't have a care in the world. I paused in the doorway. "Have a safe trip back."

"You, too..." Hellhound said doubtfully, his fist flexing as though he was debating whether to drag me away from Stemp by main force.

The good side of Reggie's face registered worry, too; but I wasn't sure whether it was for me or himself. "See you later," he said absently.

I gave him a nod and smile and let Stemp usher me out.

Was I nuts?

CHAPTER 21

Stemp wasted no time in hustling me through the bullpen, stopping only long enough to retrieve my personal possessions from the guard who had been supervising them since they'd been confiscated in the morning. My small heap of belongings was the last one remaining, and the guard looked relieved when I checked off the final item on the inventory list.

Grandin hovered nearby, his gaze sharp and acquisitive while I holstered the trank pistol and twitched my pant leg down over it. Behind him, Dirk surveyed us without expression.

As I slid my Glock into the concealed holster at my waist, Grandin spoke to Stemp. "I hope you realize you're procuring weapons for a dangerous criminal."

Dirk frowned at Grandin. "The evidence against her is inconclusive."

Grandin ignored him and jabbed an aggressive finger at Stemp. "When she's convicted of international terrorism, you'll be charged, too, as an accessory."

Stemp gave him a look that would have made an ordinary man suddenly remember an urgent task elsewhere.

"It's a chance I'm willing to take."

"She's a danger to everyone!" Grandin said loudly enough to address the remaining people in the room. "What if she opens fire on us all?"

A warm deep voice spoke from behind me. "Since she hasn't shot you yet in spite of all the aggro you've caused, I suspect we're all quite safe."

I turned to face Ian Rand's smile. Sparks kindled in his striking green eyes as he leaned into my personal space. "I hear you've been cleared," he murmured. "I hope that means you'll be allowed some personal time."

I flicked a glance over at Stemp's deadpan face. If I hadn't known him so well, I might have missed the tiny edge of tension in his posture.

Impatience. He was in a rush to get out of here.

Why?

Should I hurry up?

Or should I refuse to go anywhere with him?

"Um, sorry," I said. "Gotta go."

Ian straightened, frowning. "You can't be serious."

"She is quite serious," Stemp confirmed. "Agent Kelly, let's go."

"Duty is a hard taskmaster," Ian said regretfully. "However... if you should happen to find yourself with a few spare moments..." He scribbled a phone number on a scrap of paper and tucked it into my hand. "I'll be at the Palliser until Saturday. And..." His voice deepened seductively. "...the room service is excellent."

Heat surged into my cheeks. Jeez, did he have to make his play right in front of Stemp?

As Ian arched an inviting eyebrow at me, I caught the

flash of seriousness in his eyes.

Dammit, he wasn't coming onto me; he was trying to tell me something. I suddenly remembered our truncated conversation of the previous evening. He had been saying, 'Nora was the one who...' when Reggie had interrupted us.

The one who what?

Was Nora involved in the attack on me, too? My heart clenched at the sight of her motherly figure hovering behind Ian. She was smiling, but she didn't look relaxed.

And even though her desire to speak with me had apparently been pressing enough for her to bring up with my chain of command, she still hadn't made any effort to pull me aside for a conversation.

What the hell was going on?

I pitched my voice to a provocative tone as I tilted a little closer to Ian. "I'll keep that in mind. 'Bye for now." Pocketing the scrap of paper, I turned back to Stemp and together we headed for the door.

Our trip through security and out to the Hummer was accomplished in silence. As I slung my deflated duffel bag into the cargo bay, Stemp inclined his chin at it.

"What is in there?" A tiny twitch of humour softened the corner of his mouth. "Besides the breathing filters that cast suspicion on you so effectively?"

I gave him a sharp look, but he seemed genuinely interested. Not a gibe. I unzipped the bag and showed him. "I requisitioned a P90 and some ammo in case we were attacked on the road. I had bulletproof vests for everybody, but they wore them into the building this morning so mine's the only one left. I'd brought the breathing filters just in case, but I really didn't know what might happen. I also had field dressings and eyewash kits and protective goggles that never got used; but everybody focused on the incriminating stuff."

"You were well-prepared," Stemp agreed, and the approval in his voice warmed me.

We got into the vehicle and left the parking garage without speaking again.

Once on the street, Stemp drove a complicated pattern through the downtown traffic. I didn't ask why. Standard protocol didn't require evasive precautions when leaving a secured facility; but that facility didn't feel very secure to me anymore. I suspected Stemp felt the same.

Twenty minutes later he drove out of downtown and parked in a convenience store lot. Reaching into his pocket, he activated a bug detector.

It flashed red.

My throat went dry despite the knowledge that the locator beacon on the Hummer would trigger it.

Stemp remained expressionless. When he got out of the driver's seat, I hopped out of the passenger side and hurried around the back of the vehicle to meet him. With the bug detector cupped in his palm, he moved to the rear bumper and reached underneath. A moment later the bug detector flashed green and I released a breath I hadn't realized I'd been holding.

Stemp methodically circled the Hummer again, watching the bug detector. When it registered solid green all the way around, he nodded satisfaction as he halted beside the passenger door and opened it for me.

Drawing a secured phone from his pocket, Stemp punched the speed dial. "Stemp here," he said crisply into the phone. "I have temporarily deactivated the locator beacon on H367B for a bug check. I will reactivate in less than twenty minutes."

Warning bells clamoured in my brain, and I hesitated. Why would he want to conceal our location from the Department?

He punched the disconnect button and tossed the phone into the garbage bin next to us. Then he gave me a small frown and inclined his head toward the open passenger door as though he couldn't believe I wanted to stand around in the freezing cold when I could be warm inside the vehicle.

"Please get in," he said.

I swallowed hard, my fingers itching for my Glock.

This was the part where I got back in the Hummer, and then he killed me and drove to some undisclosed location to secretly dump my body.

"Um... why did you deactivate the locator?" I asked.

Comprehension flared in his gaze and I tensed for his attack. He'd likely snap my neck. My body would topple silently into the vehicle and nobody would notice...

"You have nothing to fear from me," Stemp said softly. "I merely wanted to be sure our conversation couldn't be overheard. However, I understand your vigilance. If you prefer, we can talk right here."

The bitter wind flung a stinging handful of snow into my face and I shivered. Maybe I should just get in the Hummer...

"You need to disappear for a while," Stemp said, as if deciding to limit the amount of time he spent freezing his ass off. "I believe that this attack on you was initiated for the sole purpose of removing you to the jurisdiction of the

United States, and there's a very real possibility that they may succeed regardless of your innocence. Our justice system is notorious for rubber-stamping extradition requests even when they are unreasonable."

"But why would they want me extradited?" I wrapped my arms around myself, fighting a chill that came from both within and without. "What would they stand to gain?"

"My surmise is that they want you to work in their brainwave-driven network." Stemp's jaw muscles rippled, and I guessed he was clenching his teeth to keep them from chattering. "After your work in Georgia and your subsequent miraculous cure of their super-user, they would consider you a valuable asset."

"But they have four super-users already," I argued. "Betty Hooper, plus the three women you repatriated after the Knights of Sirius were destroyed." Which was a much nicer way to say 'after I blew them up'.

"It's the United States." Stemp shrugged. "Bigger is always better. Also, the U.S. administrator who took over after you killed Dr. Cartwright has been increasingly reticent about sharing information for our joint research in the brainwave-driven virtual reality. Without the Knights' influence, Homeland Security's natural xenophobic tendencies are taking over. Perhaps they wish to secure all the super-users for themselves."

I blinked. "You didn't tell them we've also got Tammy?"

"No. Nor have I divulged the fact that both you and Ms. Mellor are capable of infiltrating any network and cracking any encryption algorithm in real-time. The only data I have shared is your ability to enhance processing and modelling within the virtual reality network, the same as their current super-users."

I nodded slowly, comprehension forming a cold hard lump in my stomach. "So they think if they've got me, they'll control the whole program. And even if they can't force me to work for them, they'll lock me up forever just to cripple Canada's research."

"I believe so. And for that reason I will continue to keep Ms. Mellor's existence a secret from them," Stemp agreed. "But it is also imperative to keep you within Canada."

Something about the way he said the words chilled my blood more than the arctic wind that was whistling up my jacket. Stemp wouldn't allow the dangerous knowledge in my brain to go beyond our borders. He could justify it to the chain of command as 'protecting national security', but his true priority would be concealing the existence of his secret family overseas. He'd likely be sorry to kill me, but I knew he wouldn't hesitate if he had to choose between my life or his wife's and daughter's.

Suddenly, disappearing seemed like a mighty fine idea.

"O-Okay..." A violent shiver shook me. "Sh-shit, I'm freezing! Let's g-get in the Hummer."

"I thought you'd never ask," Stemp said dryly, and hurried around to the driver's side.

As soon as he had closed the door behind him, Stemp turned up the heat to maximum, and we both sat shivering for a few moments.

Then he glanced at his wristwatch and buckled his seat belt. "My apologies, but we will have to continue this conversation while I drive. My parents' flight arrives in fifteen minutes."

"Oh!" Happiness warmed me despite my worry, and I

buckled up and relaxed into the seat as he pulled out of the parking lot. "That's great! Will they be staying with you over Christmas?"

"Perhaps. It remains to be seen whether we can tolerate each other for that long." He allowed himself a small grimace. "My first priority is to prevent them from freezing in those ridiculously impractical garments they affect."

I bit my tongue. Moonbeam's caftans and Karma's sarongs might seem impractical to Stemp, but they were remarkably good for concealing the secret arsenal his parents carried at all times.

Dammit, if only I could tell Stemp and his parents that they were all doing the same work for the same cause. Their friction would melt away; and maybe Stemp would even feel safe enough to let them meet their granddaughter...

I pulled my own bug detector out of my waist pouch and consulted it. Still green.

Stemp gave me keen glance. "What is it?"

"Um... how are Katya and Anna?"

He stared out the windshield, betraying no emotion.

"I mean, I know those aren't their names anymore," I added. "But, you know. I hope they're doing okay."

"They are well," he said flatly.

"Anna must be growing fast."

"Yes."

The silence that followed was unremarkable. Of course he wouldn't volunteer any information.

To my surprise he spoke again, his voice softer. "She had her seventh birthday last month. I missed it, of course." My heart twisted at the regret in his tone. "But Katya recorded a short video for me. I had intended to be there for Christmas, but when my parents chose to come..." He trailed off with a resigned lift of his shoulder.

"I'm sorry," I said, my chest aching with sympathy. "Why..."

I hesitated, wondering if I was about to overstep our boundaries.

Screw it. He had more than enough reasons to kill me. Asking an impertinent question wasn't likely to put me in any more danger.

I forged ahead. "Your parents already know Anna exists. Why didn't you just tell them that it wasn't a good time to visit because you were going to be with Katya and Anna for Christmas? I know your mom and dad would have understood."

Stemp's mouth flattened into a grim line, and I suspected he was remembering that it was my fault his biggest secret had been leaked to his parents. Or maybe he was still uncomfortable about referring to Moonbeam and Karma as 'Mom' and 'Dad'. Especially since Karma probably wasn't his biological father.

"I would not risk the lives of my wife and daughter by revealing my intentions to civilians," Stemp said stiffly. "And in any case, this situation with the United States would have forced me to cancel my trip; so perhaps it's better that I didn't raise Anna's hopes unnecessarily." A small breath escaped him. "And mine."

"I'm so sorry," I repeated, wishing I could do something to ease his pain and knowing that even reaching over to squeeze his hand would be violation of his reserve.

He nodded silent acknowledgement, and I changed the subject. "So... that exchange with Ian Rand when we left..."

"Ah, yes. The amorous Agent Rand." The corner of Stemp's mouth quirked up. "I make it a policy to interfere as little as possible with my agents' personal lives, so I will only say that since you spent four months sequestered in the Pacific rainforest with him, you are undoubtedly aware of his... generosity with affection."

I laughed. "You're much more tactful than Reggie. He called Ian a horndog who'd screw anything that moved. Or bleated."

A rare smile warmed Stemp's face. "Dr. Chow is refreshingly forthright." He sobered. "But I presume you are not seeking my blessing for your personal interactions with Agent Rand."

"No. I think something's going on with him and Nora Taylor."

Stemp's eyebrow lifted. "In what way?"

"You said Nora asked for me to be at this c-" I stifled the word 'clusterfuck' and substituted, "...conference, but even though she introduced herself right away, she didn't try to talk to me again. And she lied when Brad Wilson asked her how she knew me. I think Ian was trying to tell me something at the meet-and-greet last night, but we were interrupted. He didn't give me his phone number today because he was interested in me. He's trying to get a message to me."

"Or lure you into an ambush," Stemp countered. "How much do you trust him?"

"I... don't know." I gnawed my lower lip. "I think he's a good agent."

"He has an outstanding record," Stemp agreed. "That in itself is reassuring; however, an exemplary agent would carry out the orders of his or her command without regard to personal loyalty or preference. Do you trust him?"

"I don't trust anybody." The words came instantly and involuntarily from my lips, and I sagged back in my seat with a sigh. "I hate this fucking job."

"Understood." Stemp's word came out on a small sigh of his own. He truly did understand.

Somehow that helped a bit.

I sat up straighter. "But if I'm going to analyze this thing with Ian a little more..."

I pondered. If Ian wasn't lying when he said he'd concealed Moonbeam and Karma and Skidmark's clandestine anti-terrorism operation from his superiors, he was likely trying to help me now.

But that was a damn big 'if'.

I thought back to his flashing eyes and the ring of sincerity in his voice and spoke slowly. "I think... Ian's on my side. For now, anyway..." I trailed off, recalling Nora's incriminating comments at the meet-and-greet. "...although..." I added, "...Nora said Ian had told her about me. But he swore he hadn't; and he was trying to explain when we were interrupted. He told Nora and Brad Wilson that he knew my name from the briefing you had issued about the ultrasound weapon, when we were under the terrorist threat last month."

Stemp's face hardened. "He was lying. I never identify agents by name. Particularly not in a general briefing."

I eyed at his stony profile, my heart sinking. "I figured. I'm not really surprised that Ian lied. It seemed as though he'd been blindsided and he had to come up with something on the spur of the moment. But that means Brad Wilson was lying, too; because he said he got my name from the same report."

CHAPTER 22

Stemp nodded grimly, staring out the windshield. "When the request for your presence arrived from the United States I suspected something like this might happen; so before I left Sirius this morning I informed the chain of command that if I could ascertain your innocence I would assign you to drop off-grid and investigate."

He gave me a wintry sidelong smile and continued, "Since they were suitably chastened by their misjudgement in overriding my initial recommendations, I was also able to secure their approval to provide you with your network access key and the portable network generator."

He reached into his pocket and withdrew the tiny cube containing the chip that turned me into a decryption machine, along with the USB drive to generate the brainwave-driven network that carried me invisibly into any computer connected to the internet. Sam Kraus's life's work; and his shitty legacy to me. Damn him.

But it was a mind-boggling expression of trust from Stemp. Warmth bloomed in my chest as I accepted the two precious items.

The demons of my past trickled doubts into my mind as I

pocketed the technology.

I wasn't good enough.

I would botch the investigation and lose our critical classified items in the process...

"Thank you," I said firmly. "Your confidence in me means..." My throat tightened. I swallowed the emotion as best I could, but my voice shook a bit as I finished, "...more to me than you can know. I won't let you down."

Stemp's face softened. "I know. But..." He shot me a warning glance. "...I must emphasize that you should stay completely dark. If the United States escalates its demands, the chain of command might rescind their decision. As long as you can't be contacted, you can't be considered in violation of orders."

A chill settled around my heart. I'd be completely on my own. Nobody to rescue me.

Stemp continued, "I will assign Holt to the investigation as well, and I will aid you as much as I can within the constraints of the command structure; but if the situation changes, that same command structure may force me to issue a warrant for your capture."

My blood went cold. The whole Department could be turned against me. And I knew damn well who would be first in line to carry out the order: Holt the Magnificent.

And he didn't fail.

Stemp's voice penetrated my fear. "I can drop you anywhere you want to go before I reactivate this vehicle's locator device."

"Thank you," I said slowly, forcing back my dread and booting my trembling brain into planning mode. "I think... I don't want you to take me anywhere. If you don't know where I went off-grid, you can't be tripped up in a lie-detector test."

He nodded approval, and I continued, "Let's go and pick up your parents and have a nice dinner. They'll be able to swear that we arrived at the airport together and left separately, so you won't get into trouble for helping me if things go sideways later." I hesitated, then added, "I think... I'd better go and see Ian tonight. After that little show we put on in the bullpen, anybody who's looking for me will be watching him. Better to talk to him before I disappear."

And I could disappear completely. Despite my anxiety, a small self-satisfied voice muttered deep in my psyche: Thank you, Holt the Magnificent. As a result of our humiliating former partnership, I had created secret caches of weapons and equipment, and multiple identities issued by the Department. And more importantly, I had a couple of identities that the Department didn't know about. I might not be Jane Bond, Superspy just yet; but Aydan Kelly was doing okay.

"Very well. I will reactivate the beacon." Stemp pulled into an office parking lot and stopped. When he returned to the driver's seat, he pulled out a secured phone and hit the speed dial. "H367B should now be back online." He paused, listening, then replied, "Good." He punched the disconnect button, then dialled another number.

There was a lengthy pause before he spoke, his tone formal but softened from his usual crispness. "Good day, Mother. Since my call has gone to your voicemail I deduce that your flight has not yet landed; however, I wish to inform you that I will be approximately ten minutes late arriving at the airport. I will meet you at the baggage carousel." He hesitated as though he wanted to add some warmth or endearment to the message, but instead he finished stiffly, "I will see you soon", and disconnected.

My heart ached for him. From my glimpses of his private exchanges with Katya I knew that a warm-hearted passionate man lived behind Stemp's shield of icy control; and buried even more deeply was the desolate teenager who had felt so betrayed by his parents' adherence to a cover story he couldn't understand or accept. That hidden boy yearned for his parents as much as they yearned for him, but their respective cover stories still wedged them inexorably apart.

If only I could tell them about each other, it could fix everything.

Or it could destroy innocent lives that were depending on absolute confidentiality. And I didn't know which it would be.

I sighed and settled unhappily into my seat for the silent drive to the airport.

Only a few minutes later the vibration of my cell phone jerked me out of my uneasy reverie. The call display showed Nichele's number, along with six voicemails since this morning.

Shit.

I clenched my teeth and accepted the call.

"Aydan! Finally! Where have you been, girl?" Nichele's teasing held an edge of relief. "I was afraid you'd been in a car accident or something!"

"I'm so sorry!" I shot a sidelong glance at Stemp's impassive profile. Awkward. Well, fuck it. "You wouldn't believe how awful this stupid work thing was today," I continued. "It just went on and cn and I didn't even get time for lunch. I'm starving and grouchy, and just this minute I finally got a chance to check my phone. Are all six of those voicemails from you?"

"Yes." I could hear the smile in her voice. "I'm in total Bridezilla mode, I admit it! I'm sorry you had such a crappy day, but come on over to our place and we'll go out and grab a scrumptious dinner and then go shopping. You'll be all better in no time!"

My heart squeezed at her innocent optimism. Aydan The Grinch was about to spoil everything. Why was she even friends with me? And after I dropped off the face of the earth right in the middle of the most important event in her life, she might dump me forever. I couldn't blame her if she did.

"I'd love to, Nichele, but..." I swallowed the lump in my throat. "I'm so sorry, but I'm on my way to the airport right now. I'm getting shipped down to the States..."

My blood chilled at the convenience of that lie. Please don't let it come true...

"...for a big international audit," I went on, hoping my voice wouldn't crack. "I don't know how long I'll be gone, and it's going to be the same shitty all-day-all-night stuff as today, so I likely won't even be able to take your calls."

The forlorn silence at the other end of the line stabbed me in the heart.

"I'm so sorry," I repeated. "I wish I had a choice, but I'll get fired if I don't go."

"Will..." Her voice wavered. "Will you be back by... Saturday?"

I blinked hard against the burning behind my eyes. "I

don't know. I hope so. I'll do everything I can to get back in time for your wedding. Oh, Nichele, I'm so, so sorry! I feel awful about this!"

"Well..." Her voice wobbled again but she pulled it back under control, and when she spoke again her artificially bright tone made me feel even worse. "Don't worry about it, girl. I know you'll be here if you can; and if you can't, I know you'll be here in spirit. I'll go out and buy your dress for you; I know your size and..." She managed a little laugh. "God knows I'll pick out something nicer than what you'd buy for yourself."

I forced a laugh to cover the sound of my heart breaking. "You know it! You've been dressing me up since we were five, and I still don't know how to do it for myself. You're the best friend I could ever ask for, Nichele..." I choked up.

"Hey, girl, you're only going to the States for business, not dying!" Her attempt at teasing trembled with emotion, too. "Go down there, kick some bookkeeping butt, and get your ass back here in time for the wedding, you hear?"

"I hear," I croaked. "I will." Stemp pulled into the airport parking garage, and I added, "I have to go now. Take care, and say hi to Dave. And, Nichele... I love you; you know that, right?"

"I know." A sniffle carried over the line, but I could hear the smile in her voice. "I love you, too, girl. But now you made me all teary and I have to go fix my makeup."

"Sorry..."

"I'm kidding, you goofball! I'm only getting misty 'cause I love you to bits! Go catch your plane, and have a safe trip, and call me as soon as you can!"

"I will. Thanks, Nichele. 'Bye."

I hung up and drew a deep breath, embarrassed by my display of emotion and grateful for Stemp's distant reserve.

He pulled into a parking space and tactfully got out of the vehicle without speaking. After a moment I pulled myself together and joined him at the rear of the vehicle to retrieve my backpacks.

"Will you require the duffel bag?" Stemp asked.

I paused, considering. A P90 machine gun was a hell of a persuader if I ran into difficulties. But it was also heavy, hard to conceal, and highly illegal for a civilian to possess.

What the hell. I could always cache the P90 if I didn't need it. And the bag of burner phones I'd stashed in the duffel would definitely come in handy.

"Yeah, I'll take it," I said. "But I don't want to carry this stuff into the airport. Can we meet for dinner in the Delta Hotel restaurant?"

Stemp nodded. "I'll collect my parents and meet you-" A low hum interrupted him, and he withdrew his phone from his pocket with a glance at the call display before he accepted the call.

"Hello, Mother. I apologize for my tardiness..." He paused, listening, then continued, "Good; I'm glad you received my message." Another pause. "Certainly; though I would be pleased to come and meet you... Very well; if that is your preference. I had planned for us to have a meal in the Delta Hotel restaurant if you would like to meet us there... Yes, I said 'us'. Aydan is with me." A smile softened his face at the response, and he concluded, "Very well, we will see you in a few minutes."

He pressed the disconnect button still smiling, albeit with ruefulness lurking at the corners of his mouth. "Mother is most pleased that you are here. I'm afraid we may have inadvertently revived her hope that the two of us are romantically involved."

"Oh God," I groaned, then hurriedly amended, "Sorry, no offense. But I had really hoped that we'd put that particular misconception to bed."

"An unfortunate turn of phrase under the circumstances," Stemp rejoined dryly. "Shall we?" He inclined his head toward the elevator.

I shouldered my burdens and followed him.

When we arrived at the hotel restaurant, Moonbeam and Karma were already waiting at the entrance. Contrary to Stemp's earlier concern, they both sported parkas. Although Moonbeam wore her usual tie-dyed caftan and Karma his batik sarong, they both wore pants underneath, along with stout hiking boots.

They turned as we approached and their faces lit up.

"My dearest!" Moonbeam enfolded Stemp in her warm embrace, and I was pleased to see that he hugged her back without hesitation. "And Storm Cloud Dancer!" She gathered me into her arms. "It's so wonderful to see you both!"

Stemp offered Karma his hand but Karma ignored it, pulling him into a hug instead. Stemp didn't resist, and I let out a breath of relief.

Then it was my turn to hug Karma, my arms barely reaching around his powerful bulk.

"It's great to see you!" I said. "How have you been?"

"Very well, thank you."

Stemp gently interrupted the pleasantries with a gesture at our respective bags nearly blocking the entrance.

"Perhaps we could continue our reunion over din-" He fell silent, stiffening.

With a jolt of adrenaline, I spun to follow his gaze.

CHAPTER 23

"What are *you* doing here?" Stemp demanded.

Following his gaze, I gaped at the scruffy figure that had just emerged from the men's room beside the restaurant entrance.

"*Skidmark?*" A smile stretched my face. "Hey, it's great to see you!" I stepped forward to hug him and nearly choked on the reek of stale body odour and marijuana emanating from his ancient army-issue parka. "God, you stink, old man!" But I gave him an extra squeeze, knowing it was all part of his cover.

He hugged me briefly before withdrawing, his gold tooth glinting in a grin through his scraggly thicket of gray facial hair. "Hey, girlie, how about a kiss for ol' Skidmark?" He licked his lips and wiggled the tip of his tongue lasciviously. "I got a little something special for you here."

I grinned back at him. "Nope, what you've got is 'way too little for me."

He laughed, a wheezy paroxysm that shook his frame. The wheezing went on for longer than usual and I eyed him in concern. He was thinner and paler than when I'd last seen him eight months ago.

"That's not what Moonbeam said last night," he croaked when he had recovered enough to talk again. "Come on, girlie, let me show you what-"

"She said no." Stemp interposed himself between us, his shoulders rigid as he glared at the older man. "You will respect her decision. And her."

"Hey, be cool, sonny," Skidmark mumbled. "You're gonna hurt yourself with that big stick up your ass."

I hurriedly laid a hand on Stemp's arm and eased myself between them, forcing him to step backward to avoid being pressed full-length against me.

"Thanks, but I'm okay with Skidmark," I said. "He's all talk and no action." I shot a fond glance at the man in question. "He's like an old dog that drools and farts and spends all his time licking his balls. He's so disgusting that he's actually kind of cute."

"I was in full agreement until you reached 'cute'," Stemp said coldly, and turned his back on Skidmark to face Moonbeam and Karma again.

Even I had to admit that it was a much more pleasant view. With Moonbeam's long silver braid and luminous smile and Karma's serene weatherbeaten face and neatly bound iron-gray ponytail, they looked exactly like the hippy pseudo-spiritual leaders they had spent most of their lives impersonating.

"Now, Cosmic River Stone," Moonbeam admonished gently, "Please show tolerance. We are a family, after all." She held out her hand to Skidmark, who went to her side and slipped an arm around her waist to kiss her lingeringly. She raised her face to Karma, who did the same, and all three turned back to Stemp with their arms around each other.

Stemp muttered something that sounded like, "Don't remind me," but his expressionless façade was firmly in place and I might have been wrong.

Probably not, though.

"So you were saying..." Moonbeam prompted. "...shall we go in and eat?"

Stemp looked as though he was reconsidering that suggestion, but he nodded reluctantly and picked up his mother's suitcase.

"Thank you, dear," she said, and squeezed his arm affectionately. They led the way into the restaurant while I brought up the rear with Karma and Skidmark.

"Are you okay?" I asked Skidmark. "You look like hell."

He grinned. "Part of my charm."

"His emphysema is progressing," Karma said. "I've prescribed bronchodilators and corticosteroids..."

"And a pill that makes me piss every ten minutes," Skidmark put in grumpily.

"...but he really should quit smoking," Karma finished with a severe look at Skidmark. "He'll soon need a portable oxygen tank, particularly at Calgary's altitude."

"You know I can't quit the weed," Skidmark growled. "It's my cover." He held up a hand to halt Karma's incipient rejoinder. "And you know I only do it if somebody's watching; and I never mingle with the rest of the commune so it doesn't amount to more than a toke or two a week."

"I know." Karma gripped Skidmark's shoulder in a brief warm gesture. "I just wish you didn't have to smoke at all."

"Maybe you could pretend to get straight," I suggested. "I'm sure none of the commune members care whether you toke up."

"No, they don't give a shit about me," Skidmark agreed matter-of-factly, and my heart squeezed. After decades of putting his life on the line to keep the commune members and the rest of the country safe, everyone thought he was nothing more than a repulsive old stoner. Human garbage, to be avoided and despised.

Skidmark must have read my expression, because he scowled warningly and went on, "And that suits me just fine; but if another batch of wackos shows up I need to be able to do my stoned-old-man routine."

"Do you have any... worrisome tenants... at the moment?" I asked, letting him change the subject.

"No," Karma replied. "That's why we were all able to come. And we... it was important... for us all." The bittersweet smile he gave me spoke volumes. Soon Skidmark might not be capable of travelling outside the humid oxygen-rich air of the west coast.

I swallowed hard, eyeing Stemp's stiff posture ahead of us. If they couldn't reconcile soon, it might be too late.

"I'll talk to him again," I promised. "He's softening up, you know; he's just..." I trailed off with a helpless gesture.

"He's a stubborn pig-headed-" Skidmark began, but Karma interrupted.

"A proud, stiff-necked man," Karma said, with meaningful look at Skidmark. "Like his father."

I swivelled my head to stare at each of them in turn. "Are you saying you, um... found out which of you...?"

"Yeah," Skidmark said. "The last time they were here visiting, Karma sneaked out a DNA sample and we had it tested against ours. I'm his biological father." He shrugged. "But Karma's his real father. I never had much to do with the kid." He shot a scowl at Karma. "And the kid doesn't have any use for me now; and why should he? I told you this was a bad idea."

Karma sighed. "I don't disagree. But Moonbeam..." He trailed off, and both men glanced lovingly at the slim figure ahead of us.

I smiled. Moonbeam would never give up hope. Her gentle smile and delicately fluttering caftan concealed an iron will and a spine of steel.

And probably a garrotte and a knife. My smile widened. Stemp might still be struggling to accept his three parents, but I'd adopt them in a heartbeat.

"I think he already suspected you were his biological father, based on your resemblance," I said. "Have you told him?"

"No, and we're not going to unless he asks," Skidmark said firmly. "I'm just getting my shit in order before I kick off."

This time I knew I hadn't hidden the stab of pain in my heart. He scowled at me again and continued, "No big deal. We just have to figure out some legal shit, since I'm a U.S. citizen but he's registered as Moonbeam and Karma's kid so he's officially Canadian. It'll probably never matter, but..." He shrugged and fell silent as Stemp and Moonbeam stopped at a table and we caught up.

Stemp courteously withdrew a chair and seated his mother, and the rest of us pulled up chairs as well. Skidmark chose the end of the table as if trying to put as much distance between himself and Stemp as possible. That placed the old man at my right hand; and despite my fondness for him I wished he'd sit a little farther away. Like in the next county.

His stench would gag a maggot.

Moonbeam was seated across from me, on Skidmark's other side. She smiled and opened her mouth as if to speak as he sat down, but sudden chagrin twisted her face.

"Skidmark, dear," she said in a slightly choked voice. "Your parka is rather... malodorous. Perhaps you could hang it... over there?" She inclined her head toward the coat hooks on the opposite wall.

"Oh. Sure." He rose and divested himself of the garment.

When he returned a faint aroma of pot smoke still lingered on him, but it was no worse than sitting next to any other smoker.

"That's so much better," I said gratefully. "How long did it take you to get that thing so stinky?"

He let out a noncommittal grunt and studied the menu, and I realized I had come dangerously close to blowing his cover. Dammit, I was too comfortable. I'd better remember that everybody here had secrets.

A tense silence fell over our table while we stared at our menus as though studying for a quiz later. Mind racing, I scanned the card without seeing it.

Stemp had clearly not been expecting Skidmark. Would this jeopardize his visit with Karma and Moonbeam?

I sneaked a glance at Stemp's rigid shoulders and clenched jaw. This was a man who dealt with murderous criminals and catastrophic security breaches without even twitching an eyelid. He must be near his breaking point if I could read his emotional upheaval from across the table.

Shit, what if he wouldn't let Skidmark into his home? Moonbeam and Karma would probably refuse to stay without Skidmark. And Stemp, pushed past his limits, would retreat behind his icy shield and tell them all to leave, shattering the fragile bonds of their nascent reconciliation...

"Hey, I've been thinking," I blurted. "I hate to impose, but... Skidmark, would you be able to stay at my place while you're here? I'm going to be gone for a while and it would be good to have somebody looking after the house. My neighbour watches it for me while I'm away, but he only comes every day or two and it's so cold right now that if the power went off the pipes could freeze pretty fast."

Skidmark shrugged. "Sure."

Postures eased all around the table, and Stemp gave me a grateful look.

"In fact," I babbled on, "You're all welcome to stay there if you want. St-" I bit off 'Stemp' and substituted his first name. "...Charles might end up being pretty busy at work. We're in the middle of a giant audit, so if he has to work late at least the three of you could be together. And you remember how my security system works so it would be easy," I finished, turning to Moonbeam and Karma. "I could just give you my key right now."

"It's kind of you to offer, dear, but we wouldn't want to impose..." Moonbeam began.

"Not at all; you'd be doing me a huge favour." I gave Stemp a fake-worried look. "I mean, I don't want to spoil your visit..."

Real worry seized me. Dammit, had I just given Stemp an excuse to ignore his parents completely while they were here?

"I'm sorry," I said hurriedly. "That was rude of me. Of course you're here to see Charles, not stay out in the middle of nowhere at my place. I shouldn't have asked-"

Stemp and Moonbeam and Karma all interrupted at the same time, strained variations of 'no, no, it's quite all right; we'd be pleased to help; it's no trouble at all'. Skidmark maintained cynical silence.

"Well, that's great then," I said, and unhooked my house and gate key from my key ring. "Thank you so much."

"You're most welcome, dear," Moonbeam said. "When will you be coming home, and how will we contact you in the event of a problem with the house?"

"I don't actually know." I shot Stemp a companionable 'work-sucks' grimace before facing Moonbeam again. "I'll likely be working night and day and I may not be able to return calls promptly, but I'll give you a number where you can leave a voicemail." I scribbled my burner phone number on a napkin and added Tom's number before handing it over. "If anything goes wrong, or if you need anything, just call this second number. That's my neighbour, Tom Rossburn. He's a great guy, and he'll take care of everything."

I passed the napkin and keys over, and steered the conversation to the activities of their commune.

After its shaky start, the meal turned out to be surprisingly pleasant. Stemp unbent enough to participate in the conversation with warmth if not actual enthusiasm, and Skidmark said little but smiled often. After the last bite had been consumed and the bill settled, I excused myself for a trip to the washroom.

"Perhaps I will join you," Moonbeam said, rising with me. "It's a long drive to Silverside."

We strolled to the ladies' room and used the facilities in silence.   While we were washing our hands, Moonbeam glanced around to be sure we were alone and spoke softly.   "I presume your travel for the audit is a cover story?"

I sighed.   "Yeah."   Remembering to protect Stemp's cover in turn, I added, "My end of it is, anyway.   I feel guilty leaving Charles and the rest of his team here to handle the audit by himself, but I don't have a choice.   I would have left earlier; but when I heard you were coming I wanted to see you, at least for a few minutes."

"That's very sweet.   We are so pleased that we got to see you."   She hugged me, then drew back with a significant look.   "Your neighbour, Tom.   When you said he would take care of 'everything'...?"

Catching her meaning, I said hurriedly, "No, he doesn't know anything; he's just a good neighbour."

"Should we be prepared for any... other visitors?"

"Not as far as I know."   We strolled out together, and I added, "I'll give you this just in case, though."   I unfastened the video monitor that masqueraded as my wristwatch and handed it to her.

"Storm Cloud Dancer, you mustn't give me that," she demurred.   "You might need it."

"Not where I'm going."   I blew out a breath.   "I'll be completely off-grid.   I have a regular watch in my backpack because I couldn't wear this one anyway.   In fact..."   I dug into my waist pouch and extracted a burner phone along with my personal cell phone.   "...would you please take these back to my farm with you?   Just leave my cell phone on my dresser.   If I need to get in touch, I'll call you on the burner phone; and if you need to call me, the number I gave you earlier is the burner I'm using right now."

She handed back the burner phone. "You needn't give me one of yours; Karma Wolf Song and Skidmark and I each have a couple."

"Thanks. It's no big deal, though. I have lots."

Her face softened. "Of course, an agent of your calibre would be prepared for anything. But please keep it. You are more likely to need it than I." She reached into the folds of her capacious caftan and withdrew a slip of paper. "Here are our current burner numbers."

"Thank you." I hugged her, my heart swelling with fondness and relief. I wouldn't be completely on my own after all. I had three veteran agents in my corner.

As I drew away, I added, "I won't contact you unless I have absolutely no other choice, but..." I swallowed the lump of gratitude in my throat. "...it's good to know you're here."

Moonbeam smiled. "If it is within our power, we will always be available to help you. You need only ask. Now, we should return to the table before awkward questions arise."

I nodded and followed her back. As we sat down again, Skidmark leaned toward Karma and spoke in a poorly-disguised aside. "Why do chicks always have to go to the can together?"

Moonbeam patted his hand. "So we can gossip about our lovers, of course. Storm Cloud Dancer now knows everything there is to know about your genitalia."

"It was a short conversation," I said straight-faced.

Everyone burst into laughter including Skidmark, who wheezed until he choked. Karma and I sprang up and hurried to him, hovering anxiously until he mastered the spasm and waved us off.

Reaching for his water glass with a trembling hand, he shot me a grin and croaked, "Christ, girlie, you're gonna kill me." He sipped, then wiped his streaming eyes before adding, "And what a way to go."

"Let's try to postpone that for a while, okay?" I asked, my heart still thumping.

"Sure thing," he agreed.

"Well..." I sighed and reached for my bags. "I need to get going. It was great to see all of you..."

After a round of hugs and goodbyes with his parents, I turned to Stemp. "I hope the audit goes okay at your end," I said. "I'm sorry you're stuck with it here."

"No need to apologize; I know you will be working hard on it, too." He inclined his chin. "Safe travels."

"Thanks," I muttered, and turned away before I could blow anybody's cover.

Behind me, Moonbeam's gently reproving voice chided, "Surely you could have spared her a hug, Cosmic River Stone."

I hurried off, abandoning Stemp to his fate.

CHAPTER 24

Out of sight of the restaurant, I sank into a chair in the hotel lobby and pulled out a burner phone. My first call was to Tom, and it went straight to voicemail. I left him a short message letting him know that I'd be gone for an unspecified period of time and that my house would be occupied until further notice.

After hanging up, I drew a bracing breath and dialled the number Ian had given me. When he answered with a brisk, "Rand", I replied in a seductive murmur. "Well, you're all business tonight. Can you spare some time for pleasure?"

His voice warmed and deepened. "I always have time for pleasure. Where are you?"

"At the airport. Stemp had to pick up his parents and then we were all supposed to go back to Silverside, but I begged off. Where are you?"

"In my lonely hotel room at the Palliser." I could hear the teasing smile in his voice. "With stellar room service and a decadent shower and a king-size bed with a cozy duvet..."

"Sold," I interrupted. "I'll be there in half an hour. What room are you in?"

"Eight-twelve. I'll have the champagne chilling."

The taxi ride gave me too much time to think and not enough time to plan.

How long should I stay in Ian's room? Only long enough to get whatever information he had to share? Or should I stay longer to make it look as though we were having a tryst?

The thought sent a tingle of anticipation through me. I had only been alone with him a few short times, and things had heated up fast. If I was in his hotel room for hours with a king-sized bed flaunting itself only a few feet away, what would happen?

If only I'd had enough time to indulge in Arnie's expert lovemaking, I would have been sated and relaxed instead of taut with nerves and pent-up need. And if Ian unleashed the full power of his highly effective seduction routine on me now...

The tingles warmed, and my rationalizations swooped in to encourage the temptation.

Would it be so bad to fall into bed with Ian? It would just be an uncomplicated one-night stand; no strings attached, no consequences. The memory of his soft teasing kisses and hard muscles suffused my body with heat.

Maybe I should seize the opportunity. If I had to drop off-grid, I sure as hell wouldn't be getting laid in the foreseeable future.

Arnie wouldn't mind a bit. Hell, he'd be relieved. Our closeness was comfortable and deeply comforting, but only as long as we both knew we weren't committed to each other.

My thoughts slid to Kane.

He would mind.

But Kane already knew Arnie and I slept together every chance we got; and when Kane had been an agent he hadn't hesitated to use sex as a persuasive tool. He should understand that I might need to do the same.

And anyway, Kane was still living with Alicia and, for all I knew, sharing her bed by now.

...But what if he wasn't? What if he was waiting and hoping to get serious with me?

I hissed out a breath. Dammit, we weren't even together. Why was I worrying about what he would want?

The knee-jerk answer rose fully formed in a gut-kick of memory. Because if I cared about him, his tiniest twinge of emotion should be more important than my very life...

"Fuck *off* with the bullshit programming," I muttered. The cab driver gave me a questioning look in the rear-view mirror, and I plastered on a reassuring smile. Nothing to see here. Just ignore the crazy woman fighting the demons of her shitty first marriage.

He returned my smile and kept driving, and I pulled my thoughts back to the mission at hand.

Hot hunger built in my body while my thoughts circled back to Ian. Staying a few hours was a great idea.

Unless...

My desire trickled away as an unwelcome thought intruded. Ian had already lied to me. What game was he playing, and who was dealing his cards? What if he'd allied himself with the United States to turn me over to Dirk and Grandin?

This might be a setup. And here I was, smiling blindly through my lust-coloured glasses while I bumbled into the trap, bringing classified technology as a bonus.

I spent the rest of the trip hunched in the seat, compulsively tracing the butt of my Glock like an inappropriate worry stone while I considered and discarded plan after plan.

When we pulled up at the hotel, I tipped the driver enough to be generous but not memorable. Then I slipped my network key and network generator into the P90's duffel bag and trudged through the front doors straight to the concierge desk. When the uniformed woman greeted me, I dredged up a smile and hefted the duffel bag and my winter emergency pack up onto the desk.

"May I leave these with you for a while?" I asked. "I'm visiting a friend upstairs and I don't feel like hauling all my sports equipment up to the room with me."

"Of course." She reached for a claim check.

"Um... I'm sorry to trouble you, but may I tag these separately?" I gave her my best smile. "I might need one later but not the other."

"Certainly."

A few minutes later I walked away with my overnight backpack perched on my shoulder, two claim checks in my pocket, and the uneasy conviction that I'd just done something incredibly stupid.

What would Stemp do if he knew I'd just abandoned top-secret technology, along with an automatic weapon and enough ammo to mow down half the hotel guests?

I pressed the elevator call button with a quivering finger, still fighting the urge to run back to the concierge desk and grab my bags.

Dammit, this was the best option. The bag lockup was the most secure area in the hotel. If Ian handed me over to be dragged out of the country, at least our classified technology wouldn't go with me.

On the eighth floor, I checked the directional signs and strode straight to the alcove that held the ice and vending machines. Palming the claim check for the P90, I dug through my change purse for enough coins to buy a bottle of water. While I inserted the coins and pressed the appropriate buttons, I propped my hand containing the claim check against the top of the vending machine.

As the bottle dropped into the access port I tucked the claim check out of sight on top of the machine, then departed with my water.

Only one claim check in my pocket. If they searched me and reclaimed my bag, they'd get nothing but my boots and ski pants and sleeping bag.

Vibrating with tension, I headed for Ian's room, stuffing the water bottle into my parka pocket to leave my hands free.

As I approached I unzipped my parka and hitched my right hand comfortably into the waistband of my jeans, inches from my holster. When I stood close to Ian's door and raised my left hand to knock, the sides of my parka swung forward, blocking the sightline of the security cameras as I drew my Glock.

I smiled at the fisheye peephole, wondering as always whether someone was looking back at me or simply raising a gun to the small aperture to shoot me in the face.

I flinched despite myself when the door latch clicked.

A moment later the door swung open. Stepping forward, I wrapped my left arm around Ian's neck and dragged him into a kiss, jamming my gun into his stomach and pushing him into the room at the same time.

He stiffened but didn't fight back. Still crammed against him, I let the door swing shut behind us and walked him backward into the room, checking the open bathroom and scanning the room beyond.

My heart gave a hard thump when I realized we weren't alone.

"Aydan...?" Ian mumbled cautiously against my lips. "What's going on?"

I surveyed the bottle of champagne chilling in the ice bucket, the fluffy duvet turned down invitingly on the king-sized bed, and Nora Taylor sitting very upright in one of the chairs.

"You first," I growled as I turned him loose and retreated a couple of paces to put my back to the wall. "What the hell's going on?"

"Please put your weapon away," Ian said calmly. "You're safe here. Nora wanted to speak with you privately, and we decided this was the least obtrusive way to accomplish that."

"Nora, is that true?" I asked.

"Y-yes."

I scowled at her and Ian, searching for signs of duress. "You don't sound too sure."

Nora visibly gathered herself, her shoulders squaring and chin lifting just like my mother used to do when she was entrenching herself in an argument.

"I'm quite certain," she said firmly. "Put away that weapon, young lady."

My lips quirked at her tone in spite of my tension. "I feel like I'm thirteen again," I said, and holstered my Glock.

Nora and Ian both relaxed into smiles.

"Sorry about that," I added. "I'm not feeling very

trusting today."

"No bloody wonder," Ian said. "May I offer you a drink?"

"You may." I grinned at him. "In fact, if you hadn't, I would have helped myself."

"Manners," he teased as he expertly popped the cork and poured three flutes of champagne.

"No manners whatsoever," I agreed, and accepted one of the glasses. Left-handed. Just in case I needed to grab my Glock.

The bottle had been unopened when I arrived and the glasses had all looked clean. So my drink probably wasn't drugged.

But who knew?

I waited until Ian took a drink before sipping warily, the bubbles sparkling and dancing on my tongue.

"Won't you sit down?" Ian gestured toward the chair beside Nora.

"I'll stand." I regarded Nora over the rim of my glass. "You had some questions for me?"

"Yes. I understand that you worked with my dear Sam. And that you were..." Her lips quivered but she brought them under control. "...the last person to speak with him." She swallowed.

"I don't know about that," I equivocated. "But I did speak to him on the phone once after he disappeared."

True, but not the truth.

I added, "But go ahead and ask me whatever you want. I'll tell you anything I can."

Also true. But I wouldn't tell her everything I knew.

"What... what did Sam say?" she asked. "What were his last words?"

Was she a grieving widow? Or a cold-blooded criminal fishing for information?

"I don't remember exactly," I lied. "He said he was afraid some former friends were trying to kill him, and I encouraged him to come back here so we could keep him safe. It was a short conversation because he was at a pay phone and he was anxious to keep moving. Do you know who he was running from? Or why?"

"No." She shook her head. "He only said he was afraid for his life and he was going into hiding. I tried to convince him to come home to the U.K., but..." Her lips trembled again. "I never saw him again... until... until they returned his... body."

My heart ached for her even though a small cynical part of me knew she might be faking the whole thing.

"I'm so sorry for your loss," I said. "It must have been difficult for you. He had been living here for several months before that, hadn't he? So you had been apart for quite a while."

She dabbed at the corners of her eyes. "Yes..." She lifted her chin. "And it's been over a year since I lost him. You would think that by now I shouldn't be so..." She drew an unsteady breath and returned to her narrative. "Anyway... he had been called over here last October for an urgent development in his research. I don't know what it was. Of course we never divulged our classified work details to each other."

"Of course not," I murmured.

Was she lying? If so, she was damn good at it.

"But he didn't say anything else to you?" She gazed at me imploringly through brimming eyes. "He never hinted that... anything might be wrong? If he turned to you in... in his final hours of need..." Her voice wavered and she gulped. "He must have trusted you. Were you close?" Before I could formulate a reply she burst out, "Oh, Aydan, please! Tell me anything you can about him! Any tiny little thought or detail..." She pressed her hand to her lips, entreating me silently to bring her beloved Sam to life again, if only through my memories.

My throat tightened as I struggled to scrape together some crumbs of comfort. "He was excited about his research, and I'm sure he must have missed you..."

Though he had never mentioned her. Hmm.

I went on, "...but I know he was absorbed in his work. He never mentioned anything that might be bothering him, and he didn't seem upset or anxious..."

Until we discovered he'd been callously risking my life and sanity in the brainwave-driven network. After that he'd been anxious; and with good reason. We had all wanted to throttle him.

I dragged my mind back to the platitudes I was spouting.

"...until I talked to him on the phone," I went on. "We had gone down to the States for work and he seemed fine; and then he disappeared, and the next time I spoke to him was that last phone call. I never knew him very well, but he was always pleasant to work with."

Until he betrayed us, the bastard.

"Oh." Disappointment trembled in the single word as Nora's face fell. "I... I had so hoped you might have been closer to him..." She sighed. "Well, thank you for indulging me. I suppose I'd best get back to my room."

She rose tiredly and moved toward the door, then paused

in front of me.   Throwing her arms around me, she whispered, "Thank you, Dani-dear."

A deluge of icy recognition froze me to the spot.

She withdrew with a wobbly smile and a glint in her eye that made my heart rattle inside my petrified chest.

"If you remember anything else, even the smallest thing, I'm right next door in eight-fourteen," she said.   "Drop by any time of the day or night.   Or here..."   She withdrew a scrap of paper from her pocket and pressed it into my numb hand.   "This is my private number."   She curled my fingers around the paper and patted my hand.   "Call me anytime."

And then she left.

CHAPTER 25

I stood paralyzed, unable to breathe.

No.

No, it couldn't be...

Despite my steadfast refusal to believe, my brain was already racing through memories, computing possibilities and reassessing information...

My mind reeled.

It couldn't be true.

It just couldn't be.

But my mother was the only one who had ever called me Dani-dear...

"Penny for your thoughts," Ian said lightly, eyeing me with a smile that might have warmed me to my toes only a few short minutes ago.

I eased my deathgrip on the champagne flute and forced a smile. "Just trying to come up with some memory of Sam that might make Nora feel better."

"Ah. It's sad when death parts such a devoted couple."

"Did you know them?" I demanded.

Ian frowned at the sharpness of my tone. "Not at all. Is it important?"

"No." I gulped a mouthful of champagne.

He smiled and pried the glass from my grip to top it up. "I would have thought an agent of your calibre would be a better liar," he teased.

"Guess I suck," I snapped, and reclaimed the flute for another large swallow.

"Please," Ian said reproachfully as he confiscated it again. "One does not guzzle a five-hundred-dollar bottle of Krug."

I imitated his posh British accent. "If one is stupid enough to spend five hundred dollars on fizzy vinegar, one is in no position to criticize another's drinking style."

His mouth dropped open. "Fizzy...? Good Lord, woman, I had no idea you were such a..."

I gave him a glare that made him press his sensuous lips together without finishing the sentence.

"I'm sorry, Storm," he said instead, and handed the champagne glass back to me. "I was joking, but I should have seen that something has upset you. Can I help?" His emerald gaze sparkled with such sincerity I had to remind myself that he might not be on my side.

I frowned. "Don't call me Storm. I don't want to take a chance on it slipping out of your mouth when somebody's listening."

"It won't," he promised. "But it suits you so well." His voice coasted down into a sexy murmur. "Storm Cloud Dancer, all tempest and passion. Let's set aside stuffy old duty for a little while and..."

"Why did you lie to me?"

"Which time?" he countered, straight-faced.

"*Every* time, you..." I bit off the words 'lying bastard'

and glared at him again.

Ian sighed. "Won't you please sit down?"

I let out an ungracious grunt and dropped into the armchair Nora had vacated. Ian sat on the end of the bed, our knees almost touching.

"Hang on," I said as he opened his mouth.

Unzipping my waist pouch, I blocked his view with my hand and flicked on my bug detector for a moment. It glowed solid green, and I closed the waist pouch again wondering whether I should feel reassured.

"What, have you got a lie detector in there?" Ian inquired with a teasing smile.

"No." I frowned at him. "I wish I did, though."

"You can trust m..." he began, then silenced himself with a rueful shake of his head and tried again. "Of course you don't know if you can trust me, but I promise I haven't done anything to endanger you. Nor will I."

"Nice to hear." I eyed him steadily. "So, about those lies...?"

"Yes, of course." He sipped some champagne, savouring it unhurriedly.

Stalling while he made up a plausible story? Or simply being the unabashed hedonist I knew he was?

"I was having you on a bit," he said. "You know I told you plenty of lies at the commune, but I didn't actually lie to you at all yesterday. I lied to Nora and Brad Wilson, about that report. Your name was never mentioned in it."

"I know. And they both should have known, too."

"Yes." He smiled. "I was curious to see what they would do. And they both lied right along with me."

"Which was stupid," I persisted. "We were all standing

there lying to each other and knowing damn well we were all lying."

Ian gave a debonair shrug. "Never let it be said that we live boring lives."

At the end of my tolerance, I pressed the cool champagne flute against my aching forehead and snapped, "Spill it, Rand. Start to finish. No bullshit, or I swear I'll finish the job I started on your balls back at the commune."

He flinched, his knees coming together just a fraction before he collected himself. "That was uncalled-for," he protested. "I haven't tried to hide anything from you."

"And yet you're still dancing around and *not fucking telling me anything*," I growled.

He abandoned his playboy act and sat up straight on the bed. "I divulged nothing to my superiors about you or anyone else at the commune," he said crisply. "My official report states that I singlehandedly eliminated sixteen terrorists. The last one shot me in the leg but I was able to kill him regardless. I applied a field dressing and waited for a medical evacuation while JTF2 dealt with the remaining terrorists."

"And nobody ever questioned the fact that the dead guys were wearing bullets from four different guns?"

Ian shrugged. "I ran out of ammunition and had to use some of their own weapons against them."

I bit my tongue so I wouldn't snarl, "Well, aren't you the big hero?" He *was* a hero; and he'd lied to his chain of command to protect all of us.

"Thank you," I said instead. "So what did Nora tell you?"

"Nora's comment took me by surprise at the party last night." He frowned. "I'll begin at the beginning. She was promoted to Head of Weapons Research a few months ago when Howard Coleman retired. I was rather surprised that she wanted the position..." He hesitated delicately before finishing, "...at her age. However, Coleman was in his late seventies, so it certainly wasn't unprecedented. I had no dealings with her until this conference was announced. When she found out that I would be the agent in charge, she came to me to request that I set up a chance to speak with you." His face hardened. "As you can imagine, I was immediately on the alert when she mentioned your name, since nobody at the Bureau should have known it."

"That's what I thought, too," I agreed. "I wondered if you'd sold us out."

"No, of course not. There is no record of you in any of the files. I checked just to be sure. And I checked Nora Taylor's background, too."

My pulse ticked up. "What did you find?"

"Nothing that set off any alarm bells. She has been employed by MI5 since early 1983, slowly working her way up the administrative ranks. Her records are complete and unremarkable."

My mind seized on the date. Early 1983. Just over a year after my mother died in the fiery car crash that left her body burned beyond recognition.

Or maybe not...

Ian was still talking, and I tuned back in as he finished, "...so when she explained her connection to you through Sirius Dynamics and her deceased husband, I saw no reason to question it."

Her deceased husband. Sam Kraus. A man who had vanished from my life around the same time as my mother supposedly died...

"Right," I agreed absently. "Makes sense."

I attempted another sip of champagne only to realize that my glass was empty again. Ian gently liberated it from my grasp and refilled it before passing it back.

"Thanks," I mumbled, still pondering.

Ian went on, "So I had expected her to simply ask questions of you at the party last night, but she apparently wanted more privacy." He hesitated, his brows coming together. "Her questions seemed rather innocuous to require such exaggerated discretion."

"Mm-hm," I agreed.

Her questions were innocuous because they hadn't been her real reason for speaking to me.

As if reading my mind, Ian's gaze sharpened. "Those weren't her real questions, were they? You'll be visiting her room for a private conversation as soon as you leave here, won't you?"

I gave him a noncommittal, "Mm."

Ian pressed his fingertips to the bridge of his nose, his frown deepening. "Surely you realize that as the agent in charge I can't allow that. Particularly since you're still under suspicion for this morning's little cock-up."

"I'm not," I protested. "I've been completely cleared. And if you and everybody else had let Stemp question you with our lie detector like normal innocent people..." I gave him a significant glare. "...we would already know who was responsible. But obviously none of you are innocent."

He gave me a slow smile. "I'm certainly far from innocent." His provocative intonation warmed me despite my worries. "In fact, I'd love to show you how very sinful I am." He stroked a feather-light fingertip over the back of my hand, bringing all my nerves to shivery attention.

I drew back. "Cut it out. I'm not dumb enough to let you sidetrack me like that. Why didn't you do the lie-detector test?"

"Nora refused, and I agreed with her." He shrugged. "Would you have submitted to it if you were in my position?"

"Of course," I began indignantly, then hesitated. "Well... " I blew out a breath. "Okay; maybe not. But I probably would have. Nobody was going to ask about classified information; and even if they did you could have just refused to answer. We only had simple yes-or-no questions: Did you see anybody shoot me; did you see who threw the smoke bomb; and did you see who stole the metal powder?"

"No; no; and no."

I scowled at his disarming smile. "Fat lot of good that does without a lie detector. You're a professional liar. I can't tell the difference."

"Thank you."

"That wasn't a compliment."

His smile widened. "I beg to differ. It's a high compliment from an agent whose skills I respect very much." The smile sharpened. "Which brings us full circle, despite your worthy attempt at deflecting my attention. I can't allow you to visit Nora unsupervised. And I need the phone number she gave you."

I gave him my nicest smile. "No, I really don't think you do."

Unfazed, he rejoined, "And what did she whisper that set you off?"

"She said 'thank you, dear'." I held my best poker face.

"And now you're lying to me." His smile widened as he reclined on one elbow and raised his champagne glass. "To secrets and lies: the spice of life."

"I'm not lying. That's really what she said."

"But it meant something else to you. Which is why you're now panting for the chance to speak to her privately." His gaze coasted over me in a clinical evaluation of my threat level that was almost perfectly disguised as a seductive invitation. His voice deepened, his green eyes sparking with heat. "I can make you pant in a much more enjoyable fashion."

When I threw out a hand palm-first in a 'stop' gesture, he sighed and added, "Come on, Storm. I can't budge on this. Let's just have a nice little romp and then you can be on your way. I can't let you speak with Nora alone, and you know it."

"I know; and I didn't ask you to," I countered, my mind rocketing through possibilities.

Ian wasn't going to yield. I wouldn't either, if I were in his place.

But I had to speak to Nora, and that conversation absolutely had to be private. And it had to happen before I dropped off-grid.

And I needed to drop off-grid tonight.

Should I tell Ian the truth, or part of it? If I told him my mother had faked her own death, moved to the U.K. for three decades, and was now trying to secretly contact me, maybe he'd bend the rules for me.

Or more likely he'd be insulted that I'd tried to make him believe such an improbable tale. And hell, even if he did believe me, it would likely make him even less inclined to allow me a private conversation.

I let my shoulders drop in defeat and gave him a rueful smile and a truth. "Okay, you're right. If I were in your shoes I'd do exactly the same thing; but I have orders to talk to Nora privately. If I put you in touch with Director Stemp and he relays the order to you, would that work?"

"No," Ian said regretfully. "I'm sorry, but your director has no authority over me. The order would have to come through my superiors. Can you get Stemp to talk to them?"

"Probably not tonight."

And probably not ever; because Stemp wouldn't divulge our reasons for investigating Nora.

I sighed. "Well, screw it, then." I drained my champagne glass and held it out to Ian for a refill. "We'll just have to run it up the chain of command in the morning." I let the corners of my words soften. "Wow, this champagne is hitting me hard tonight. Too tired, I guess. Long day."

"I can only imagine." Ian handed over the refilled glass. His hand lingered on mine as I accepted it, and I gave him an appreciative smile. "If you're tired..." He let the sentence trail off with an inviting gesture at the bed.

I gave him a slow look from under my lashes and relaxed into my chair, tracing the rim of the glass with the tip of my tongue. "I don't think I'm quite tired enough to sleep yet."

Ian sat up as though he had steel in his pants and I'd just become a magnet.

I let my gaze drift unhurriedly down his body. Maybe he did have steel in his pants. Mmm. This time my tongue tipped out to caress the glass involuntarily.

"Storm..." Ian's voice was deeper and huskier now, his eyes darkening. "Have you had too much to drink?"

I shook my hair back and gave him a lazy smile. "Nope.

Just enough."

"How fortunate for both of us." He leaned forward, his knees slipping between mine, and reached for my free hand. "Won't you come a little closer?"

I sat up and moved to the edge of the chair, opening my legs so his knees slid up the insides of my thighs. "How's this?"

"Oh, lovely." His gaze locked on my lips as his fingertips traced sensuous circles on my palm.

I shivered, letting my eyes drift closed to savour the sensation.

"Storm?" His voice was only inches away, his breath warm on my cheek. When I opened my eyes he smiled, and I let myself fall into the depths of his striking green eyes.

He shifted forward again, pressing firmly between my legs as his lips found the sensitive corner of my jaw. Butterfly kisses fluttered across my skin and I let out a breathy moan as every nerve ending in my body woke.

"That is..." Ian's lips bestowed soft kisses along my jaw line. "The sexiest sound..." His lips found mine in a slow kiss. His fingertips traced the side of my neck to bury themselves in my hair and I pressed closer, parting my lips to invite him in.

He gently broke the kiss, lifting the champagne flute out of my hand and placing it on the table beside me.

"Now..." He leaned in again, tasting my lips with light kisses as his hands skimmed up my arms to my shoulders. Then he pulled away again. "This is quite a reach," he murmured, indicating the distance enforced by his knees pressed into my crotch. "Maybe we could get more comfortable...?"

"Mmhm," I agreed. "Like this?" I half rose, sliding forward to straddle his lap.

"Oh... yes..." He pulled me closer, settling a highly sensitive area of my anatomy against the firm bulge in his pants.

I tilted my hips, moving slowly against him while our kisses got steamier. His hands slid down my back to cup my ass, his fingertips transmitting flickers of pleasure through the centre seam of my jeans.

Letting my hands roam the hard lines of his chest and shoulders, I tugged gently at the holster strapped under his arm. "Are we a little overdressed here?"

He chuckled against my lips and his hand coasted around my thigh to draw a line of heat from my crotch to the Glock at my waist. "I believe we are. Shall we initiate a disarmament?"

"That sounds like a fine idea." I stripped off my parka and sweatshirt and dropped them on the floor.

"Oh, good start," he agreed. "If I may...?"

Hot hands slid under my T-shirt, gliding up over my breasts before lifting the T-shirt off over my head. As he pulled me closer to kiss his way across my collarbone toward my cleavage, I fumbled the buttons of his shirt undone.

He reached for the button of my jeans, and I slid off his lap to stand in front of him.

"I'll take mine off if you take yours off," I teased, sliding my zipper slowly down.

Ian grinned and peeled off his holster and shirt, revealing the chiselled body I remembered from eight months ago. I surveyed him hungrily, taking my time and letting him see the heat rising in my eyes.

"I'll take mine off if you take yours off." He echoed my phrase with a wicked smile as he undid the button of his pants.

"Oh, hell yes." I unbuckled my waist holster and laid it on the table, then unzipped my jeans and lowered them to my ankles. "Just let me get this one," I murmured as I reached for the trank pistol.

Just a quick shot and he'd be...

A dart stung my thigh. As a wave of dizziness washed over me, I jerked my blurring gaze up to see Ian lowering a tiny blowgun from his lips.

"Sorry, Storm," he said.

"Bashtard..." I mumbled, my knees already wobbling as numbness raced outward from the injection site.

But his drug didn't work quite fast enough.

As grayness swooped in from the edges of my vision, I heaved the trank pistol up with the last of my strength and pulled the trigger.

CHAPTER 26

I dragged open eyelids that felt as though they weighed ten pounds apiece.

Half-naked.

Sprawled on the floor.

Cold.

Ian's legs dangled from the bed above me, twitching. He was waking up, too.

I fought the drug, forcing back dizziness and focusing all my will on my arms and legs.

Move, dammit!

My limbs wouldn't cooperate.

Ian's feet jerked again.

Come on, come on! Move!

My trank pistol was still in my hand. If I tilted it up a fraction and pulled the trigger, Ian would be down for the count.

It might work. I only had to twitch an uncoordinated finger on the trigger, while Ian had to muster enough fine motor control to use the tiny blowgun, or else manually inject me.

But he had more muscle mass, so he would shake off the

effects of the tranquilizer faster.

Long moments crept by in a ludicrous immobile race. Ian was mumbling unintelligible words, most likely profanities. I was doing the same, my unwieldy tongue blurring my swearing into a nonsensical drone while my heart hammered as though it would break free of my ribs.

Ian struggled up onto one elbow, squinting cross-eyed at me.

My hand still wouldn't move.

The classified trank pistol lay in my useless palm, as though I was offering it to Ian in a blaze of idiocy almost as brilliant as my original plan to seduce him and leave him lying unconscious while I had my private conversation with Nora...

Ian tried to grope for something on the bed and fell back again amid another spate of slightly more distinct swearing.

My fingers twitched.

Almost there...

Ian heaved himself up again, managing to slump into sitting position. He pawed clumsily at the duvet. I glimpsed the blowgun momentarily between his fingers, but it fell back onto the bed as he tried to bring his other hand toward it.

"Bugger!" This time his exclamation was much more intelligible.

He was recovering too fast, dammit.

A dart was gripped between his fingers.

The blowgun was in his other hand.

Scowling with concentration, he made a couple of clumsy attempts and managed to fit the dart into the tiny tube on his third try.

"Shorry, Shtorm," he slurred as he raised the blowgun to

his lips again. "You loosh..."

I finally managed to pull the trigger, the tiny 'pffft' of the propellant like music to my ears.

My dart pierced his leg as he sucked in a breath to fire the blowgun, only to collapse motionless.

Mine's better than yours...

The taunt circled through my brain while I flopped toward the door in an uncoordinated starfish-like crawl, holding my breath.

Still inside the nimbus of aerosolized trank. Keep moving...

Starved for oxygen, I sucked in a breath.

Everything went dark.

When I woke, Ian's legs were still motionless. Dizziness twisted my brain. My body shivered continuously, chilled after lying half naked and motionless for... how long?

I couldn't move yet, so I occupied my mind by doing the math. Our tranquilizer darts caused about twenty minutes of unconsciousness. The fast-acting aerosolized part of the tranquilizer usually lasted around five minutes; but I hadn't gotten the full concentration. I had probably only been down for a couple of minutes.

But thanks to Ian's trank, I'd been lying here in my underwear for nearly half an hour. Bastard. No wonder I was frozen to the fucking bone.

But at least Ian still had a good fifteen minutes to go.

Fifteen minutes for me to get up, get dressed, go next door, and find out what the fucking hell Nora was up to. Or if she even *was* Nora Taylor and not Nola, my mother. Ex-mother. Whatever.

And then I had to get out of the hotel and vanish before

Ian woke up. No problem. Piece of cake.

Now if only I could move my arms and legs...

It felt like hours, but it was actually only a minute or two later when I managed to drag myself to my hands and knees. By the time I had struggled into my clothes my coordination was almost back to normal.

Shrugging on my parka, I glared at Ian's sex-god body and slack handsome face. Asshole. If I wasn't so pressed for time I'd strip him naked, tie him to the bed, and dump the ice bucket on his crotch.

I contented myself with a top-speed search of Ian's limp body and the rest of the room. I found nothing except his Walther PPK and the tiny blowgun, which wasn't exciting enough to bother pilfering. I shoved them under the opposite side of the mattress so he'd have to waste precious time looking for them, and shot a glance at my watch.

Twelve minutes left. Tick-tock.

After a wary surveillance of the deserted hotel corridor through the fisheye lens, I slipped out and knocked on Nora's door.

The door swung open as though she had been waiting beside it.

"Thank you for coming," she began.

I sidestepped into the room and whipped out my Glock as I hip-checked the door shut.

"Talk," I snapped, taking aim at her face.

She went white, her eyes widening. "I... I..." she began, then blinked rapidly and drew a trembling breath. "Please don't point that at me, Dani-dear."

"Don't call me that." My Glock didn't waver. "You've got five minutes. Talk."

"I... I... need to be sure we won't be overheard." She gave me an imploring look. "I have a device. May I get my handbag-"

"No. Tell me where it is."

"On the bureau." Her gaze flicked back toward the room.

"Move slowly into the room and sit on the chair," I growled. "One step at a time. Don't talk, don't reach for anything, and don't make any sudden moves."

She gave a faint nod, her chin moving a millimetre down and then up, and followed my instructions.

As we passed the closet and bathroom I darted glances inside, but it seemed we were alone. The room was similarly unoccupied, and as soon as Nora was seated I crossed to the dresser and upended her handbag into the middle of the bed.

She gave a little cry of distress, quickly stifled when I glared at her over the sights of the Glock.

"Th-that's the device," she stammered. "The little black one with the light on it. You just press the button..."

"I know what it does. Where did you get it?" I demanded. Holding her in my sights one-handed, I dared a glance down into my waist pouch as I momentarily activated my own bug detector.

My bug detector, an exact match to the one Nora carried.

The green light assured me that whatever bullshit she might be pulling, at least we wouldn't be overheard.

"I said, *where did you get it*?" I snapped.

"Oh... I found it in this little spy shop..." she began.

"If you're going to waste my time with lies, we're done here." I sidled toward the door, keeping her in my sights.

"No, no! I'm sorry, I..." She made an entreating gesture,

quickly aborted when I moved my finger onto the trigger. "I'm sorry, Dan- Aydan, I'll tell you everything, I promise. Please don't leave!"

"So talk." I maintained my position in the hallway.

"I have so much to tell you," she began.

"Then you'd better talk fast."

"I will, but five minutes isn't enough. You'll have questions..."

"Four minutes."

She spoke rapidly. "Aydan, this is too important! Call me anytime on the burner phone. Nobody knows the number, not even Ian..."

I glared at her. "Talk now, or I'm out of here."

"I got the bug detector from Sam," she blurted. "I know this will be a terrible shock to you, but I'm your mother. Nola Kelly."

I held my voice completely flat. "My mother died thirty years ago when her car crashed into a ditch and caught fire. I don't know who the hell you are or what you're trying to pull, but you're not my mother."

"But I am! Here..." Grimacing, she yanked a few hairs from her head and held them out to me. "Get a DNA test. It will prove I'm telling the truth."

"Right, because I just happen to have a lab in my back pocket," I snarled.

But I stepped rapidly forward to snatch the hairs from her before retreating to my previous position, Glock levelled.

"Please trust me, Aydan. I had to fake my death to protect you, and leaving you and your father to think I'd died was the hardest thing I've ever done..."

"How did that protect me?" The robotic voice barely

stirred my lips. As cold and unforgiving as my Glock.

"They were going to drag you into their program. If I had stayed, you would have been taken away at eighteen years old and forced to work there for the rest of your life. I had to pretend I was in love with Sam and convince him to move to the U.K. with me just to keep him away from you."

"Is that so."

"Yes! Dani... Aydan, my dearest, it broke my heart but it was the only way." She hesitated, gazing imploringly up at me. "You don't believe me. I don't blame you. I wouldn't believe me either, if I were you. But I'll prove it to you. Ask me something that only I could know. Ask me anything. Anything at all."

Dammit, I wasn't going to let her draw me in. And I sure as hell wasn't going to inadvertently feed her information.

"Who did I take to my Grade Twelve graduation dinner?" I asked.

Confusion clouded her face. "Dani-dear, I was gone by then. I don't know who you took." She smiled. "But I'll bet it was Darrell Raven. You had such a crush on him."

"Wrong."

I hadn't gone to my graduation dinner at all. I had been grieving too hard for my dead mother. My supposedly-dead mother, who had faked her death to run off with another man.

"Well, I did tell you I couldn't know," she said reasonably. "And you used to have a terrible crush on Darrell."

"So you say." My voice came out completely flat. "When did Nichele's mom and dad split up?"

"Heavens, dear, did they finally split? Despite his never-ending infidelities, I wouldn't have believed..." Her brows drew together. "Oh. You're testing me, aren't you? If I hadn't known them, I would have pretended not to be surprised."

"Of course I'm testing you," I growled. "Duh."

But dammit, she was right again. Nichele's parents never had split up. Her mom had just kept waiting and hoping and forgiving while her dad sneaked around with every woman he could find. No wonder poor Nichele had such trust issues with men.

I shot a glance at my watch. Running out of time. One more question; and if she got it right, I'd have to believe...

I swallowed hard and racked my brain. Names of pets and classmates and former addresses were too easy for anyone to discover. Ditto for medical and dental records.

"What did I want for my sixth birthday?" I demanded.

Nora frowned into space. "Oh, dear. Was that the year you wanted the pogo stick...? No," she corrected herself before I could speak. "That was your fifth birthday; I remember because you started kindergarten that fall and you took the pogo stick to your first show-and-tell. And Darrell Raven knocked out his front teeth with it." She smiled. "I always thought you'd marry Darrell, you know."

The words 'I wish I had' hovered on the tip of my tongue. How different my life might have been...

"Nice try," I grated. "But that's not what I asked."

"No, no; I know. Just give me a moment." Nora shot me a reproachful look. "It was over forty years ago, after all... wait! I have it!" Her face lit with the radiant smile I remembered from all those years ago. "You wanted a Lone Ranger mask and costume and six-shooter! And you were heartbroken when we couldn't find the costume in your size; but you wore the mask and the holster with the cap gun everywhere. Even to bed; until you rolled on the gun in your sleep and woke up with a black eye." She chuckled. "At least you still wore the mask everywhere, so nobody knew."

Tremors seized my knees and I locked them to keep from falling to the floor. Rage bubbled up like hot acid burning through the scars her abandonment had left on my soul.

"I'm so sorry, Dani-dear." Her voice trembled. "I never wanted to hurt you."

"And yet, you did." I threw the words at her like weapons. "And you hurt Dad. Losing you nearly killed him. And all the time you were making a new life in a new country with a new lover..."

Something in her expression tipped me off and comprehension rolled over me in a searing wave.

"He wasn't new, was he?" My voice came out quivering with suppressed violence, my finger easing toward the Glock's trigger as if of its own volition. "How long had you been fucking him, *Mom?* All those years when Dad was travelling for work? And don't hand me any bullshit about how lonely it was out on the farm all by yourself!"

"I won't," she said softly. "I don't expect you to understand, Aydan, but your father and I both did what we had to do in order to protect you."

"What? Now you're saying Dad *pimped you out?*" My voice was rising, and I clamped down on the need to bellow at her.

"No, of course not. I..." She let out a breath. "I understand how angry you are and I don't blame you one bit-
"

"So why now?" I interrupted. "Why search me out thirty years later and fuck up every happy memory I ever had of you? Why not just stay fucking dead? Because as far as I'm concerned, you're dead to me anyway."

"I understand. I won't agree that I deserve that, because you don't know the whole story. But to answer your question, I'm telling you now because this is the first chance I've had since I discovered you were working for the Department. Before you worked there, you were safe. Now..."

I glanced at my watch again. Out of time.

"Yeah, so it's a dangerous life, yadda, yadda," I snarled. "Tell me something I don't know. 'Cause your five minutes is up."

Nora leaned forward, her face set and grim. "What you don't know is that you've been programmed. All those 'tests' Sam did when you were young? Those mind exercises? He was planting subliminal suggestions, instructions that you aren't even aware of. And now that you're an agent, those instructions are ripe to be triggered. You could carry them out without even knowing you were doing his bidding. You would think it was all your own idea."

I stared at her, icy terror paralyzing my limbs and crushing my throat.

"I can help you, Aydan," she said forcefully. "Let me help you. Let me tell you what the instructions are and how to overcome them."

I couldn't move or speak. Claustrophobia flooded every corner of my mind. I had been controlled since childhood.

I was still being controlled.

Trapped.

Panic spiralled up.

Fight!

RUN...

Nora must have misinterpreted my silent immobility for skepticism.

"Aydan," she insisted. "Please believe me. Haven't you noticed that you don't react normally to certain things? Most women cry and beg when they're threatened. You get angry and fight. And you need more energy than most people. You can eat anything you want without gaining weight; but you collapse when you run out of calories. You're a high-performance machine..."

"Time's up," I croaked, and backed toward the door.

"Dani... Aydan!"

Nora... no, Nola... my mother... was on her feet, fists clenched by her sides and voice trembling. "I didn't give up my life with you and your father on a foolish whim; and I refuse to let you self-destruct now! Keeping Sam away from you, away from Sirius Dynamics, was the only way to protect you. I love you more than life itself!"

I let the door swing shut on her voice.

CHAPTER 27

With my mind shuttered and every muscle rigid with the need to flee, I marched stiffly down the hotel corridor to the vending machine.

Retrieved the claim check.

Rode the elevator down to the main floor.

Claimed my gear from the concierge, making appropriate mouth-noises and stretching my wooden face into a smile-like grimace.

When I slid into the back seat of a cab from the taxi queue, the driver asked, "Where to?"

"Airport." The word fell from my lips without thought, my mind frozen numb.

Sometime later, the cabbie's voice roused me. "Are you cold? I can turn up the heat."

I came back to myself, realizing I was huddled with my arms wrapped around myself while I shivered in long hard waves.

"Y-Yes. Heat. P-Please." My voice came out in a rusty croak.

He frowned. "You wanta stop for a coffee or something? There's a Timmie's drivethrough on the way."

"H-Hot chocolate. Th-Thanks." I fumbled a five-dollar bill out of my wallet with trembling hands and poked it over the seat at him. "K-Keep the change."

Nora's voice came back to me. "...a high-performance machine... collapse when you run out of calories..."

I blocked it out with a shudder and sat carefully thinking about nothing until the cabbie handed a cardboard cup back to me.

The jolt of hot sweetness kicked my brain into gear again. By some miracle, the hairs Nora had given me were still clutched in my white-knuckled hand. I tucked them carefully into my wallet, hoping they would still be viable by the time I got them to a lab.

But Nora had to know I wouldn't be able to have them tested right away, so she was probably lying about the whole thing.

She couldn't be my mother. My mother had died thirty years ago, and the identity of the corpse had been confirmed by dental records. This was some kind of mindfuck, designed to keep me off-balance for some reason.

Ian and Nora had to be conspiring against me, although I couldn't figure out why.

But how could she have known all those things about me?

I gulped more hot chocolate, my eyes watering as it seared my tongue. How could anyone have researched me that effectively? Or had I somehow given the answers away?

It wouldn't have been difficult to dredge up my old crush on Darrell Raven. Practically everybody in our small school had known about it, much to my teenaged humiliation. And anybody from the school could have told her the story of

Darrell knocking his teeth out with my pogo stick. Hell, Nichele and I still laughed about it sometimes...

Another shivering fit seized me. What if 'Nora' had talked to Nichele? A few hours of so-called reminiscing could have dredged up all kinds of obscure facts that nobody else would know.

What if Nichele was in danger right now? What if she was being stalked by whoever was trying to frame me, to be held as leverage against me later?

But that didn't make sense. If Nichele had talked to someone who was pretending to be from our old home town, she would have mentioned it to me. And anyway, Nora couldn't have known what questions I would ask. I hadn't even known, until I'd asked them.

Unless...

What if I'd been programmed to ask exactly those questions?

Hot-chocolate-flavoured bile rose in my throat, and I gulped it down and hurriedly diverted to a different thought.

Okay, so maybe Nora really was my mother. That didn't mean that anything else she'd said was true. Maybe she was just a pathetic cheating slimeball trying to weasel her way back into my life after all these years by making herself out to be a noble martyr.

Or maybe...

"Which airline?" The cabbie's voice interrupted my thoughts.

"Oh. Um... Westjet. Domestic." I shook myself back to the present. Why the hell had I chosen the airport as a destination? If Ian thought I was fleeing, it would be the first place he'd look.

Or... shit. If I was Ian, I'd wake up, swear a blue streak, and rush straight down the hotel lobby to ask the concierge if she'd seen a tall red-haired woman leaving.

I had gone straight from the concierge desk to the taxi stand, so he'd easily discover which cab company had picked me up. From there it would only take a persuasive call to their dispatcher to figure out where I was going.

He might be in a cab only minutes behind me.

I craned my neck to look out the rear window, but of course we were on Airport Road. I could see at least three other taxis behind us, and there were probably dozens behind them.

Should I tell my driver to keep going? Take me somewhere else?

No, Ian would simply tell his cab to keep following me. And I could hardly instruct my driver to do evasive manoeuvres. Dammit.

I slipped my tranquilizer pistol out of my ankle holster and transferred it to my parka pocket.

We stopped in front of the Westjet entrance and the cabbie twisted to give me a smile. "That'll be thirty-eight fifty, ma'am."

I paid him and disembarked warily. And wearily. God, I felt as though I'd aged twenty years in the last hour.

Another cab pulled to the curb behind me and I shouldered my bags and strode away, keeping the corner of my vision trained backward. The dark-coated man who got out was too short to be Ian, and I let out a small breath of relief.

Okay, I'd just walk straight on up to the taxi queue and vanish for good...

The short man was hurrying up behind me. Pulling a dark *something* from his pocket...

I wheeled and fired.

Fortunately there was a brisk breeze to carry the aerosolized trank away, because I forgot to hold my breath when he toppled to the ground and I got a clear look at his face.

Dirk.

Dammit! I'd completely forgotten about the Nemesis Twins. Where was Grandin?

I flung a wild look around but I couldn't spot him.

Stuffing my pistol back into my pocket, I dropped to my knees beside Dirk and shook him as if trying to rouse him, plucking the dart out of his coat at the same time.

"Help!" I yelled at the handful of people who were hurrying toward us. "He's unconscious! Call 911!" Then I recoiled as though I'd just spotted the pistol lying on the pavement beside Dirk.

I lurched to my feet with a frantic shriek. "OHMIGOD, HE'S GOT A GUN!" Still screaming at the top of my lungs, I fled for the parking garage.

A few people coming out of the parkade gaped at me as I barrelled toward them, but their attention rapidly transferred to the chaos of shouts and screams unfolding behind me.

Inside the shelter of the garage, I shut up and ran. My pounding footfalls echoed off the concrete, but nobody gave me a second glance. Just another idiot late for her flight.

The machine gun inside the duffel bag banged against my back. The weight of my burdens seemed to increase with every step and my breath came in sharp gasps of effort.

I slowed my crazed dash to a more sustainable jog. My dart might not have penetrated Dirk's thick coat, so he could be back on his feet in a few minutes. And there were security cameras everywhere. What if Grandin was simply tracking my progress so he and Dirk could corner me and arrest me?

No, he couldn't have tapped into the airport security cameras that quickly and easily; and he wouldn't be able to watch them while he circled around to head me off. And even if Dirk regained consciousness in minutes, he'd be surrounded by airport security guards by then. He was out of commission, at least temporarily.

I emerged from the far side of the garage and hurried toward the outdoor over-height parking lot. Slipping between two tall trucks, I halted at last, bending over to pant. The arctic air cut my throat like a knife, but at least I was invisible to any passersby or security cameras.

When I finally regained my breath I straightened, shaking with nerves and exhaustion.

Okay, this time I would disappear for good.

Stripping off my outerwear wasn't a hardship. My sweat-damp clothing steamed in the frigid air while I unpacked my heavy parka, ski pants, and giant snowboots from my winter emergency backpack and transferred my trank pistol from my lighter jacket to the pocket of the warmer parka.

I took off my hiking boots, pulled my ski pants on over my jeans, and pushed my feet into the snowboots, then repacked my emergency backpack with my castoff outerwear. I stuffed my overnight backpack inside the larger one, too. No need to take a chance on someone recognizing my luggage.

Slinging a strap of the P90's duffel around each shoulder, I snugged it against the front of my body like a baby in a sling and donned my heavy parka over top. The garment barely closed over the additional bulk, but I managed to work the zipper up to my neck. Shouldering my backpack was an exercise in contortionism since the P90 enforced a stiffly-upright posture, but I managed it.

At last I braided my hair and tucked the braid inside the neck of my sweatshirt, then pulled up my parka hood and plodded out from between the trucks.

Nobody should connect the hysterical redhead of a few minutes ago with this bulky figure in its heavy boots and bulging backpack. Just a labourer heading up north to a remote work camp. Nothing to see here.

Inside the parkade again, I angled in the direction of the taxi queue, emerging halfway between it and the flashing police and ambulance lights that marked where I'd left Dirk.

That whole area was cordoned off, and I gawked for a few moments like any other innocent bystander before turning toward the taxi queue with a glance at my watch.

Ten-thirty. Half an hour before the gym closed.

I might make it...

Safely inside the taxi a few minutes later, I gave the driver my destination and leaned stiffly against the back seat. With the barrel of the P90 jammed between my legs, the butt stayed barely below the neck of my parka. Thank God I was tall. A momentary mental image of petite Nichele attempting the same thing brought on a snort of inappropriate laughter.

Camouflaging the sound as a cough, I asked, "What's going on back there? Bomb threat?"

"I don't think so. I heard there was a gun, and I saw somebody lying on the ground."

"That's scary. I must have just missed it."

"Yeah, it's crazy these days..." The cab driver segued into a monologue about crime and guns, and I made encouraging noises and tuned him out.

At five to eleven we pulled up in front of the large recreation complex I'd chosen to house one of my caches. Thrusting a handful of bills at the driver, I levered myself and the P90 out of the back seat and jogged through the door.

The fresh-faced young employee at the desk frowned as I flashed my membership card at the prox reader. "We're closing in five minutes," she informed me disapprovingly.

"I know; lucky I made it here in time," I panted. "I forgot some important stuff in my locker. I'll only be a minute."

"Oh, that's okay, then." She gave me a smile as I bounded through the security gates and hurried to the executive changing room that had cost me dearly for the privilege of renting a private locker.

I made a beeline for my locker and dialled in the combination with trembling fingers.

When I departed a few minutes later, my backpack was strained by its additional items, but my anxiety was diminishing.

Step one complete. So far, so good.

Striding out of the building, I went straight to the bus stop. The schedule I'd memorized a month ago returned reluctantly to my memory. Thank God I had selected a route that ran all night; but it was going to be a long cold wait for the next bus.

I hunkered down awkwardly on the bench and summoned all my patience.

By the time the bus arrived I was shivering, my hands and feet ice cold despite my heavy winter clothes. My tired legs protested the effort as I dragged myself up the steps of the bus, paid the fare, and fell into the nearest seat.

Getting off the bus was even worse. When I'd chosen the location for my second cache I hadn't considered that I might be trying to get to it at midnight in the dead of winter, carrying twenty pounds of extra gear.

I groaned and trudged toward the storage units a quarter mile away.

At that hour there wasn't another human being in sight. Only an occasional car swished past, and the streetlights were spaced so widely that I could barely see my footing on the dark snow-covered sidewalk. Despite the knowledge that any criminal I met out here would be much less dangerous than the enemies I had left behind, my heart thumped an anxious rhythm and I clutched the trank pistol inside my parka pocket.

At last I slogged up to the locked gate, trembling with cold and nerves. It took me two attempts to push the key into the padlock, and as I slid the gate closed behind me I momentarily considered just leaving it dummy-locked. I'd only be a few minutes.

But what if someone was watching? What if I inadvertently allowed a break-in?

I sighed and snapped the padlock shut. I was such a goody-two-shoes. Badass Jane Bond would have left the gate unlocked without a qualm in case she needed to make a quick escape...

"Hey, you!"

A challenging shout seared adrenaline through my veins as I spun to face the threat.

And I was cornered by the gate I'd just finished locking, *dammit all to hell*!

CHAPTER 28

Hand clenched around the trank pistol in my parka pocket, I raked a glance around me.

Security cameras above me. Trained on the gate; and therefore, on me.

Muffled figure approaching fast through the gloom of the inadequately lit yard.

Something in his hand.

Gun?

I hesitated, my finger slipping onto the tranquilizer pistol's trigger without pulling it out of my pocket.

He was probably just an innocent security guard. I couldn't shoot him.

But if I tranked him, it would be recorded in the security footage. When he recovered he'd call the police; and it would be all over the news that he'd been shot with a tranquilizer instead of a bullet. Ian and Dirk and Grandin would know I'd been here. After that it wouldn't be a stretch for them to discover the fake identity I'd used to rent the unit.

Shit, shit, shit!

"Hey!" the man repeated as he hurried over. "What are you doing here?"

As he stepped into the bright floodlights around the gate I spotted the security logo sewn to his parka. The object in his hand was a heavy flashlight.

No threat. Stay calm.

Giving silent thanks for the scarf that concealed everything but my eyes, I kept my head down so my hood would cast a heavy shadow and pitched my voice down to a male register. "Just picking up my car." I held up my gate key as evidence.

"At this time of night?" The guard eyed me with justifiable suspicion.

"Yeah. Been working up in Resolute Bay and figured I'd be there for the winter so I told the wife to store our second car." I shrugged. "And then they sent me home for Christmas. Just got in."

The guard's posture relaxed. "That far north, eh? So you must be used to the dark and cold."

I grunted. "Feels colder here than in Resolute. I'm freezing my fucking bag off."

"I hear you. Well, no point in standing here getting colder. Merry Christmas." He turned back toward the warm light streaming from the windows of the office.

"Thanks. You, too."

Grateful that the rigid support of the P90 prevented me from slumping in relief, I trudged toward my storage locker.

I unlocked the man-door and slipped through with my trank pistol at the ready. When I flipped on the lights and squinted through the sudden glare, nothing but silent stillness greeted me. A quick check under and inside the car confirmed that I was alone. I locked the storage unit's door and propped myself against it, sucking in a gulp of air that was nearly a sob of relief.

Made it.

Thank God.

The temperature in the storage unit felt almost tropical, but I knew it was actually only a few degrees above freezing. Which was at least thirty degrees warmer than outside.

Unzipping my parka, I gratefully offloaded the P90 and flexed my aching shoulders. Bruises were already forming on my collarbones from the duffel straps, and my sternum felt like a drum after a particularly energetic rock concert.

I groaned and tottered over to fall into the driver's seat of the car. Laying my head back, I closed my eyes and sank into the friendly embrace of a seat that had cradled my butt for well over a decade.

I let out a sigh and opened my eyes. Okay, so this particular seat hadn't; but it was close enough. Dragging myself out of the car again, I allowed myself a moment of fond contemplation.

The shiny 1998 Saturn smiled back at me. It wasn't exactly like my beloved original Saturn that Stemp had heartlessly wrecked. This was an SL2, a nondescript goldish colour instead of pristine white, but everything else was the same. And more to the point, it was cheap to operate, reliable, boring and therefore nearly invisible, and legally registered to Teresa Diaz, the fictitious fifty-five-year-old woman I had been when I'd bought the car and rented this unit.

I patted the car's fender and cooed, "I love you, sweet baby."

Then I loaded the P90 into the trunk and unpacked the goodies from my backpack that would turn me into Teresa

Diaz.

Since I was going to be wearing a parka anyway, I didn't bother putting on the padded chemise that would thicken my waist, but I used the template I'd created to carefully draw an irregular loonie-sized birthmark on my right cheek in dark purple-red lip pencil. Give people something to remember, and they'd forget the rest of my face.

After colouring in the birthmark, I applied foundation several shades darker than my normal skintone, being sure to pat it over the 'birthmark' to make it look as though Teresa Diaz wore makeup in an attempt to conceal it. Black mascara darkened my eyebrows, and I made up my eyes with dark kohl, thankful that I had brown eyes instead of blue or hazel.

Tracing my own wrinkles with an eyebrow pencil slightly darker than the foundation aged me rather horrifyingly, but I persevered. My look was finished with a couple of swipes of purplish-brown matte eyeshadow under my eyes for a hollow, tired look, and a coat of matte lipstick that faded my lips to almost the same colour as my sallow skin.

I tied a kerchief over my hair and consulted the mirror. Teresa Diaz looked as worn out as I felt.

Next I loaded a wad of cash along with Teresa's driver's license and credit cards into my wallet. Aydan Kelly's and Arlene Widdenback's documents went into the pocket of my ski pants, which I rolled into a ball and stowed along with the sleeping bag in my winter emergency backpack. That went into the trunk, too, leaving me with only my backpack of clothing and essentials.

I hesitated for a moment over the parka. Teresa would wear my lighter jacket, not the arctic-hero suit I'd worn here.

But if the guard stopped me on my way out, I would still need to look and sound like Teresa's husband.

I sighed and donned the heavy parka again, pulled up the hood, and drove out of the unit.

There was no sign of the guard. Either he was patrolling on the other side of the yard, or else he was tucked snugly away in the office watching the surveillance cameras.

After relocking my unit I drove back to the main gate, tossing a wave in the direction of the office as I passed in case the guard was watching. He made no appearance, and I padlocked the gate behind me and made my escape.

At the low-budget motel I'd selected, a sleepy desk clerk accepted my registration for the week without a second glance.

At last I staggered into the old but clean motel room and locked the door behind me. Taking time only to remove my boots and draw the faded draperies, I fell onto one of the beds.

I had expected to fall asleep in my clothes as I'd done the night before, but no such luck. With no immediate threats in the offing, I had time to reconsider Nora's terrifying revelations.

Staring wide-eyed at the ceiling, I fought back the urge to hyperventilate. She was lying. She *had* to be lying.

What if she wasn't lying?

No. She had to be lying...

I thumped my forehead with the heels of my hands, breaking the panicky cycle.

Think it through. Nora was the head of weapons research for the United Kingdom's clandestine operations. If the programming in my brain was truly as dangerous as she said, why wouldn't she have reported the threat to MI6, or to Stemp?

My throat constricted as I followed that thought to its logical conclusion. What would happen to me if she did? Instant incarceration, that's what. And she would know that.

What she couldn't know was that if Stemp believed I'd been compromised, he would execute me as soon as he could figure out how to make it look like an accident.

Or... hell. He probably wouldn't even have to make it look like an accident. He could issue a legitimate kill order, fully backed by the chain of command.

So maybe Nora... Nola... really had been trying to protect me all those years ago; and maybe she was still trying to protect me now.

If anybody had asked me to swallow that story two years ago, I'd have laughed in their faces. Or punched them.

But now... it was horribly plausible.

What should I do?

If Nora knew what Sam's embedded instructions had been, I needed to talk to her as soon as possible. But how could she know what evil Sam had buried in my brain all those years ago? And what if he hadn't told her everything?

Or...

What if she knew *exactly* what the instructions were?

My heart chilled.

What if she had been with Sam when he planted them? Or what if they were her idea? That would mean she had been ruthlessly using her own child...

No.

I couldn't believe that. Wouldn't believe it.

Nobody could be that cold.

My mind dredged up all the unwelcome memories of the evil I had encountered in my life; particularly in the past two years. No matter how much I wanted to deny it, I knew it was possible.

But she *had* to be lying...

I didn't sleep well.

At seven A.M. I gave up on tossing and turning, and dragged myself out of bed. My stomach growled ravenously, bringing back Nora's words once again: *"...you collapse when you run out of calories. You're a high-performance machine..."*

I shuddered and pressed both hands over my traitorous belly.

A moment later I straightened.

Hang on.   Surely it wasn't possible for mental programming to control my metabolism.

It might convince me that I was hungry even if I wasn't; or maybe it could convince me that if I got too hungry I'd be felled by low blood sugar... but it couldn't change my fundamental physiology. If I was being manipulated into eating more than I needed, I'd be carrying around a few dozen extra pounds, not the modest ten or so that had nestled around my middle for the past decade.

And that was exactly the kind of pseudo-fact that could be twisted to make Nora's story seem true. If she really was my mother, she'd know I was permanently hungry; and if she was trying to mindfuck me she'd use that knowledge to make it seem as though she knew something I didn't.

I backtracked farther along the memory trail to her

statement about how I reacted to pain and fear with anger and aggression. That could be another unrelated piece of knowledge she was spinning to make her story sound more convincing. God knew I had more than enough legitimate reasons for my fucked-up emotional wiring.

"To hell with it," I muttered, and made for the bathroom to shower and put on Teresa's face.

A quick trip to the grocery store furnished enough food to cram the tiny refrigerator in my motel room. Sipping from a juice box after my breakfast of bread and peanut butter, I contemplated the depressing décor around me. The sooner I started investigating, the sooner I'd get to go home.

I sighed and took my laptop out of my grab-and-go bag. Stemp's comments about extradition had been lurking in the back of my mind like an ominous black cloud, but I knew nothing about the process. Maybe more information would make it seem less scary. After all, this was Canada. I trusted our justice system.

Didn't I?

I sighed. Stay on track. After a bit of research on extradition, I'd sneak into the Department's system and have a look. Stemp would be expecting me to invisibly infiltrate Sirius's servers. If he was trying to help me, he would file an update on the situation.

And then I'd slip into the MI5 and MI6 networks and see whether Ian had lied about Nora's employment record. And whether he had betrayed my identity.

I swallowed a small lump of disappointment. Until last night, I had believed Ian was on my side.

"You know better than to trust a guy like that," I muttered, and plugged the brainwave-driven network generator into my USB port.

Holding the tiny network key clenched in my fist, I stretched out on the bed and eyed the laptop unhappily.

All alone. If I got lost in the internet, I could die of thirst and starvation before the motel cleaning staff came into the room next week.

But at least Dirk and Grandin wouldn't get me.

I closed my eyes and concentrated on stepping into the white void of virtual reality.

When it opened around me, I dissolved into invisibility and slipped into the busy data streams of the internet. As I surfed toward my destination I planted frequent data bits along my path, visible only to me. At least I'd have a hope of finding my own laptop again when I was done.

The Canadian government's public information pages were easy to find, and the extradition process looked reassuring. A request for extradition went to the Justice Minister, who decided whether to authorize it to proceed; and if authorized, the request went through the courts to determine whether there was sufficient evidence.

Due process. I'd be fine.

But Stemp's doubts niggled at me. He undoubtedly knew more than I did.

I surfed away from the government pages, sniffing for clues.

They were easy to find, too. With each newspaper article and law journal essay, my fear built. This wasn't due process. This was a travesty of justice.

Over the last ten years and a thousand or so extradition requests, only five had been successfully appealed.

Stemp was right, it was just a rubber-stamp process.

Oh shit...

Too terrified to consider it any more, I diverted my consciousness back to the mission at hand.

Stay focused. Prove my innocence.

Sirius's servers were well-concealed as usual, but I found them eventually. I planted data markers around myself while I hovered outside their firewall with my consciousness quivering fearfully.

God, I hated this. How many tries would it take? How many times would I be torn to shreds and spewed out in terrifying chaos?

I steeled myself and surged forward, clinging to the image of bodysurfing on a wave of data.

The proxy servers repelled me, tumbling me violently over and over like a weir in a rushing river. Utterly disoriented, I clung to the few sparks of consciousness that remained to me, flailing helplessly until the turbulence lessened and I could drag myself free.

Then came the slow and terrifying process of reassembling myself, my tiny thread of data slowly strengthening.

At last I faced the servers again.

This time I would make it.

Please, God.

To my own shock, I succeeded. Floating in the smooth currents of Sirius's internal data, I gathered my strength. Almost there...

I slipped undetectably into the server that held our internal reports.

Stemp had filed a report at ten-twenty last night, but he hadn't filed anything this morning. That was odd. He was always at work by seven A.M., and it was already a quarter to nine.

But maybe for the first time ever, he'd decided to come in at nine when his job officially started. Maybe he'd taken his parents out for breakfast. My heart warmed with hope.

When I opened his report, an icy deluge of dread obliterated every other thought. Clinging to the last vestiges of my composure, I absorbed the contents in a single searing gulp, then snapped out of the report and rocketed through the rest of the server searching out every document that had been filed since ten-twenty last night.

A warrant for my arrest.

Stemp suspended and ordered to be interrogated under the lie detector.

Fuck, fuck, *fuck!*

They would ask if he knew where I was or how to contact me. He would have to tell them I'd given his parents my burner phone number.

Holt might have already traced the phone to my motel room.

I flung myself out of the Sirius servers and into the internet, frantically seeking my markers.

They were gone.

CHAPTER 29

If I could have managed it in my bodiless form, I would have screamed. Sworn violently. Pounded the living shit out of anything within reach.

But I couldn't do any of it. I was nothing but helpless data bits quivering in a hostile electronic sea...

Suck it up.

With a giant effort I yanked my consciousness together and flung out inquiring tendrils in all directions.

My markers couldn't all have vanished. They must have just shifted while I was in Sirius's network. It was only a normal IP reassignment; nothing to worry about...

I was damn worried.

My tendrils stretched farther, then farther still.

Dammit, this couldn't be happening. Holt or Dirk or Grandin could be kicking down the door of my motel room right this moment.

Or maybe they were already manhandling my helpless body into handcuffs. Grandin could be pocketing the tiny computer chip that was so secret only a handful of people in the world knew about it...

Stop it.

Focus.

Still no markers.

Oh, Jesus, what if they'd shut off my network generator? I'd be trapped forever. Locked in an eternal hell of consciousness without body, unable to feel or move or breathe ever again...

White-hot panic scrambled my data for an instant, but I forced it back under control with all my will.

Find. The. Markers.

Do it.

When the first one pinged I would have wept with relief if I'd been capable of it. Locking onto the beautiful little data bits, I hurtled down the data tunnels.

When the white void of my own virtual reality welcomed me back, I dove through the portal with frantic speed.

And crashed into agony.

Violent colours bombarded me with nausea, my stomach wrenching while red-hot lava seared every vein. Incinerating from the inside out...

Beyond control or even thought, my body thrashed in a desperate attempt to escape. Screams tore my throat, the additional pain lost in the firestorm of torture.

At last the suffering lessened. My screams faded to broken whimpers as the agony receded from my limbs to converge into a monstrous headache that pulsed like a pain-bloated jellyfish with every beat of my heart.

I groaned, and the sound pushed blazing spears through my brain. Shit, I knew better than to jump through the portal like that. The pain I experienced from leaving the network at normal speed was bad enough.

Idiot.

Get up. Escape while you still can...

The thumping of my headache increased and I groaned again, clutching my head with both hands.

After a few seconds I realized the thumping was a sound, not a sensation.

"Mrs. Diaz! Hello! Are you all right?"

Thump, thump, thump. Somebody was pounding on the door.

A male voice shouted, "Should I call 911?"

"Fuck," I moaned, then clenched my eyes shut so they wouldn't explode when I raised my voice. "No, I'm fine. I was watching TV."

The knocking mercifully ceased, but the voice persisted, "Can you come to the door? I want to be sure you're all right."

"I'm fine..."

When he knocked again, I let out a small moan and crept off the bed, holding my head together with both hands. As I stumbled toward the door, caution reasserted itself. Was this a trick?

I squinted out the fisheye lens, blinking in an attempt to clear my blurry vision.

A worried-looking man stared back at me. No sign of official-looking vehicles. No agents. No guns.

I didn't recognize the man, but if he was the day clerk, I wouldn't have seen him last night anyway.

As I stood debating, he knocked again, his face firming into determination. "Mrs. Diaz, I'm going to call 911 now."

Fuck!

Out of options.

I cranked an apologetic smile onto my face and opened

the door. "Hi," I croaked. "I'm sorry, I fell asleep with the TV on and I guess it must have changed to this horrible violent show while I was sleeping." I blinked woozily at him. "All the screaming woke me up, but I was so dozy that I took a while to get up and turn it off. I'm sorry."

"Oh." He surveyed me, his gaze lingering on my birthmark for a moment before snapping behind me to take in the rumpled bed. He returned his attention to me, his shoulders relaxing. "I'm glad you're okay. No need to apologize; there's nobody in either of the units beside you. The maid heard screaming and panicked."

"Oh, I'm glad I didn't wake anybody. Please tell the maid I'm sorry for scaring her. And thanks for checking on me."

"No problem." He nodded and turned away.

Trembling, I locked the door and sprang across to my backpack to grab the burner phone. I ripped the battery out of it and dropped the rest of the phone to the floor, then flung on my hiking boots and crushed the small plastic carcass under my heel. Stomping and grinding, I reduced the phone to small pieces, then fell to my knees and scooped up the bits.

Thank God for good old-fashioned water-wasting plumbing. When I flushed the pieces down the toilet, the cataract of water carried them effortlessly away.

Less than two minutes later my belongings were in my backpack and I was standing at the door fearfully studying the parking lot through the fisheye lens. If Holt had already traced the burner phone to this motel room, he knew I was Teresa Diaz. He might be out there right now, concealed around a corner just waiting for me to emerge.

And the Ministry of Transportation database would have

given him the Saturn's year, model, colour, and license number. He would alert the Calgary police, and every officer in the city would be watching for my car.

If I could escape from the motel on foot, I might still be able to avoid capture...

Swallowing my whimper of fear, I slipped out the door. Nobody seized me so I strode away, my back straight. A bus was pulling up to its stop only a hundred yards down the sidewalk, and I broke into a run and waved wildly at it. The driver mercifully waited, and I pounded up the steps and gave him a breathless 'thank you' while I excavated my change purse for the correct fare.

Heart hammering, I fell into a seat.

After several minutes of anxiously studying the surrounding traffic, I decided that nobody was about to pull us over. Time to figure out a plan.

When the bus pulled into one of the LRT stations, I kept my head down. Too many cameras on the train platforms. My makeup might fool a human eye, but it didn't alter the fundamental data points used by facial recognition software.

After a nerve-wracking five minute wait, the bus left the station and turned off the main roads to wind through a residential area. The passengers slowly dwindled, and I got off while there were still a few people remaining on the bus. No need to attract attention by being the last one.

The sidewalks were deserted and nothing moved behind the blank windows of the houses; but just in case someone was watching, I walked with a business-like stride as though I had a destination and a plan.

Too bad I had neither.

But maybe I could get some advice.

Pulling out a burner phone, I dialled the number Moonbeam had given me. When she answered, I hung up without speaking.

Next, Karma's number. Then Skidmark's. Each time I hung up.

Then I kept walking. They would know it was me, and they'd call back when our conversation couldn't be overheard.

Minutes dragged by.

Lacking any other ideas, I followed the bus route signs. At least I wouldn't get completely lost.

Dammit, what if Stemp's parents hadn't figured out my signal?

But they had to know I was the one calling them. Surely nobody else would have all three of their burner numbers.

Maybe they couldn't talk. Maybe Stemp was there with them, pretending he'd taken a last-minute vacation so he could spend more time with them.

Or maybe that 'suspended from duty' order had been the tip of the iceberg. What if they'd arrested Stemp? And what if Holt was handcuffing Stemp's parents at this very moment?

I groaned aloud. God, I could only imagine the shitstorm in the Department this morning...

The ring of my burner phone made me twitch violently, and I punched the button and snapped, "Hello?"

"Storm Cloud Dancer?"

Moonbeam sounded cautious.

"Can you talk?" I asked.

"Yes. We weren't sure whether your house was secure, so we're walking outside. All three of us are listening in on this call. What's wrong?"

Sheer gratitude for their professionalism nearly closed my throat. "Have you spoken to Charles yet this morning?" I demanded.

"No." Fear knifed into Moonbeam's voice. "Is he in danger?"

Thank God. They hadn't given him the burner number.

"No," I replied, hoping I wasn't lying. "Sorry, I didn't mean to scare you..." Shit, now I needed a reason for my question. I blurted the first half-baked idea that came to mind. "It's just that I... I think he might be in trouble at work... because we were working together."

"Oh, no. What happened? What kind of trouble?"

"I don't know; but that's not actually why I'm calling you. I have a situation..." Stubborn pride made me choke off the words 'and I need help'.

Moonbeam's voice turned crisp. "What is it?"

First I had to uphold Stemp's cover. No need to give him any more reasons to want me dead.

I sighed and delivered a mix of truth and half-truth. "I've got several branches of law enforcement after me at the moment, and I expect that by now they've called Sirius looking for me. Since Charles and I were working together on that big audit, they might investigate him, too; or even suspend him until they're sure he's innocent."

"Law enforcement is seeking you? Why?"

"I... might have been compromised. Or framed. Maybe both. Have you told anybody about the phone number I gave you yesterday?" I held my breath, afraid to hear the reply.

"No, of course not."

My knees weakened with relief. "Thank you," I croaked.

"You were afraid they would trace you via the phone," Moonbeam deduced. "Don't worry. No one has asked us, and we wouldn't divulge the number even if they had."

Thank God. I could keep being Teresa Diaz, and I still had a car and a place to live.

"I destroyed the phone," I said. "But I was worried that if you told them you didn't have my number and then they put you on a lie detector..."

Moonbeam's gentle chuckle interrupted me. "We were all trained long ago to withstand polygraph tests, Storm Cloud Dancer. We've beaten them many times. Please don't concern yourself."

"That's good, but there's a new kind of lie detector. Classified." I suppressed my momentary twinge of guilt over disclosing something I had no business sharing. "It reads brainwaves. It's infallible."

"Oh." Her word came out on a whoosh of breath as though she'd taken a punch to the stomach. "Oh, dear. That... could be problematic, indeed."

Sudden realization made me wince as though I'd just taken a blow, too. Dammit, it wasn't only my ass on the line. If Stemp's parents were taken in for questioning, their cover was at risk, too.

And Holt wouldn't hesitate to drag them in and subject them to the lie detector. He'd love the chance to take a shot at Stemp by harassing his parents. Asshole.

And with Stemp suspended, Holt's best buddy Dermott would be acting director. Dermott, with his casual disregard for protocol and due process. Oh, God.

"If anybody asks for that number, just give it to them," I urged. "If you don't get caught in a lie, nobody will have any reason to suspect anything; and there would be no reason to drag you in for a lie detector test."

"True. Thank you, dear. That could have been... an unfortunate situation; although despite our reluctance to divulge our covers unnecessarily, your chain of command would have communicated with our chain of command. We are working for the same side, after all."

"Right," I muttered. "I'm having a hard time keeping track of all the sides."

Karma's deep voice broke in. "You said you might have been compromised. How?"

I couldn't tell them about Nora. Or that I'd infiltrated the Department's top-secret network using classified technology to read all their reports.

"I found out..." I began. My throat tightened with fear and I fought to hold my voice level as I continued, "...that I might be carrying embedded mental programming from... um... an old mission. Last night after I had met with a contact, that contact was discovered unconscious only a short time later. She had been shot up with ketamine."

I didn't bother to add the part about leaving Ian unconscious in his room. No wonder poor Stemp had gotten suspended for handing me top-secret technology right before I apparently went rogue and attacked our allies.

"Did you do it?" Karma asked.

"N-No... I don't think so..."

I ground the heel of my hand between my eyebrows. Nora had been fine when I left. I hadn't even gone near her. I'd gone straight out the door.

Hadn't I?

"I don't remember doing it," I added. "But earlier in the

day I'd gotten shot with a ketamine dart myself, and the dart that was found on my contact was the same type. According to my latest intel, everybody thinks I injected myself as a ruse and then attacked my contact later, but I think somebody else is framing me. But... I don't know for sure."

"So you are hiding from everyone, including your own chain of command." Moonbeam summed up the situation succinctly. "Don't you trust them? Surely they want to get to the bottom of this as much as you do."

"Um... yeah... maybe..."

No way to explain that Stemp himself might end up gunning for me if he found out that my mind might not be my own.

I went on, "But the U.S. was demanding my extradition yesterday, and this morning I found out the U.K. is now fighting to have me extradited to them instead. So my chain of command is under a lot of pressure and I don't trust them not to just chuck me in prison as soon as I surface."

"Sounds like you've stirred up something big, girlie." Skidmark's thready smoker's rasp floated over the line.

I sighed. "Yeah. I'm not sure whether everybody involved is crooked, or whether there's just so much at stake that they're all playing dirty. I don't even know if they're all conspiring to take me down, or whether I'm just caught in a three-way crossfire. I sure as hell don't trust any of them; and now I don't even know if I can trust myself."

"What makes you think that you might be responding to mental programming?" Karma asked. "Are you having memory problems? Cognitive difficulties?"

"N... No. I don't think so. The ketamine did a number on me yesterday, but I'm okay now."

"Are there any blocks of your time unaccounted for?" he persisted. "Have you found yourself somewhere without any idea why you're there? Any unusual bruises or marks on your body, or stains on your clothing that seem to have appeared for no reason?"

"No." My blood chilled all over again. "But... if somebody had planted some secret command in my brain... could I have injected myself? And my... contact? Without knowing about it?"

"Current medical research and opinion agrees that it's not possible to hypnotize or 'program' an innocent person to commit acts that are contrary to their fundamental beliefs..." I was drawing a breath of profound relief when Karma continued, "But..."

"But *what?*" My voice cracked.

"An unscrupulous expert might be able to instil a set of beliefs that would make it seem as though violent or criminal acts were the only choice remaining to a person in order to avert worse consequences. For example, if a person subconsciously believed a loved one would be harmed unless they acted, they might carry out actions contrary to their basic nature. And..." His voice softened. "It would be easier to convince a person who was already conditioned to committing dangerous or deadly acts."

I bit down on the whimper that tried to escape as Karma went on, "The complexity of the actions makes it unlikely; but it is theoretically possible that you could have procured the drug, prepared the darts, and injected yourself and your contact, all while suppressing the memory of doing so. All those actions are within your skill set as an agent, and if you subconsciously believed they were necessary..." He trailed off, leaving me clenching my phone in a trembling grip.

Sam would have had the skill to program me. And he'd had unlimited access to my mind for years.

I sank my head into my hands. "Oh, God."

CHAPTER 30

"You need somebody to watch you twenty-four-seven," Skidmark said. "Can your boys help you?"

My heart yearned to throw myself into Kane's and Hellhound's arms and let them watch over me.

I clenched my teeth. Not an option. That would be the first place Holt would look.

"No. The agent in charge knows we're friends so he's probably already got them under surveillance. As soon as I try to contact them, I'm toast."

"Not if they're half-decent agents," Skidmark scoffed. "You must have contact protocols you can use."

"Arnie's not an agent, and I don't have any secret way to contact him." I sighed. "I have a code that would work with John, but he isn't an agent anymore, either."

"So what? You don't lose all your skills as soon as you quit."

"But you lose interest in putting yourself in danger when you have a new son," I countered.

"Sunstar Desert Hawk has a new baby?" Moonbeam's voice was filled with delight. "How wonderful! ...oh." She hesitated. "And you are not the mother. I'm sorry, dear;

does that mean you and he are no longer...?"

"His son is six years old. Long story. And we're still... um, friends. But... speaking of that... how long does it take to have a DNA test done?"

"A couple of weeks," Karma replied. "Why, do you have reason to question his son's parentage?"

"No, this is for something else."

I swallowed my disappointment. Two weeks. Nora had probably known that when she offered me her hairs as 'proof'.

"We're wasting time," Skidmark broke in. "Moonbeam and Karma need to stay here so our kid doesn't get suspicious, but he'll be glad if I'm gone. I can come down and help you."

My heart lifted with momentary hope, then plummeted again. Would Skidmark be able to stop me if I started to carry out a command without knowing what I was doing? He was an experienced agent, deadly in hand-to-hand combat... or he used to be. But now, with age and emphysema sapping his strength, could he still overpower me?

Or, hell, could he even defend himself? My blood went cold. What if I was programmed to carry out my instructions at any cost? What if I killed him?

"Thanks, but I don't want to take a chance on involving you," I said. "You're there to visit Charles, not rescue me. And I don't want you to risk your cover."

"So you're just gonna keep wandering around like a loose cannon and hoping for the best? That's a shit strategy."

"But..."

"Tell me where to meet you," he urged.

"Skidmark, no! I'm not going to involve you."

"Then you deserve to be hanged for treason."

A gutpunch of hurt stopped my breath, but my old defensive shields snapped up an instant later.

"Well, thanks." My voice came out cold and level. "Nice talking to you. 'Bye."

As I lowered the phone from my ear their urgent voices crackled through the speaker, the gist of the garbled chorus translating to, "Wait! Don't hang up!"

I hesitated.

Fuck them. I had enough worries without my so-called friends stabbing me in the back.

"We have critical intel! Do not hang up!" Moonbeam's steely voice had so much command in it that I raised the phone to my ear again almost involuntarily.

"I'm here," I said flatly. "What."

Moonbeam's voice softened. "Thank you, dear. Skidmark was being unnecessarily-"

"I didn't mean it that way," Skidmark interrupted. "Sorry, Storm. I've been doing this mean-old-man cover for so long I sometimes forget to turn it off."

Still trembling with reaction, I hid my emotions in a dispassionate tone. "Okay. What's your intel?"

A lengthy pause on the other end of the line sent cold fear skittering down my spine. Had they been attacked?

"Moonbeam? Karma? Skidmark? *Are you okay?*" My voice rose to a near-shout.

"We're fine. Sorry." Skidmark's voice softened, and he repeated, "Sorry, Storm. We lied. We don't have any intel; we were just trying to get you to stay on the line. What I was trying to say was that if you think you might be compromised it's your duty to accept any help and protection you can get, even if it's from a crabby old fart like me. I wouldn't have barked at you if I wasn't so damn worried about you. Let me help, Storm. Please."

The unprecedented gentleness in his wheezy voice made my eyes fill, and I blinked back the moisture and swallowed hard. "Damn you, old man..."

I knew he was right. It was dangerous and irresponsible for me to wander around not knowing what I might do.

But what if I harmed him? I could never forgive myself.

"Is that a yes?" he prompted.

I let out a breath of resignation, my heart aching. "Yes. Take my car, it's got all-wheel drive. It's a blue Subaru Legacy, parked in the Sirius Dynamics lot in Silverside. The spare keys are in the kitchen drawer and the registration is in its glove box. Meet me at the popcorn stand in Market Mall at one o'clock. And..." I swallowed again. "Thank you."

"No problem, girlie." He gave one of his wheezy chuckles. "You're gonna end up kissing me yet."

I let out a shaky laugh. "I could kiss you right now." Then I added teasingly, "But I'm pretty sure the moment will have passed by the time you get here."

"Sure, sure," he groused. "Story of my life."

"Thank you for accepting our help, Storm Cloud Dancer," Moonbeam said softly. "We are very fond of you, and we feel privileged by your trust."

"Thanks. I'm really fond of you, too." My voice wobbled despite my efforts to hold it steady.

Moonbeam mercifully changed topics, her tone becoming brisk. "There is one more thing. Your cell phone has been vibrating frequently. Would you like me to check your messages?"

"Yes, please." Thankful for the return to business, I gave her the security passcode and added, "It's probably just agents hoping I'll pick up so they can trace me; but it might be Nichele. She and Dave are getting married tomorrow, and I'm her matron of honour..."

A giant lump blocked my throat. Holt knew Nichele and I were best friends. There was no way I'd be able to attend the wedding. I'd be lucky to be alive by then; and even if by some miracle I wasn't dead, showing up would probably cost my life, or worse, Nichele's or Dave's.

I was going to miss my best friend's one and only wedding.

"Blaze Featherwind has decided to trust in love after all? What wonderful news!" I could imagine Moonbeam's radiant smile, and it made me feel even worse.

"Yeah," I muttered as I trailed to a halt at the next bus stop and flopped onto the icy bench.

"Oh, Storm Cloud Dancer." The joy had gone out of Moonbeam's voice, and her words vibrated with sympathy. "How very difficult for you."

"I can't even text her because she'll be under surveillance," I mumbled miserably. "I told her I was going to be away on business and I might not be able to answer her messages, but I feel like the shittiest friend ever."

"Oh, my dear. I wish I could offer some comfort..." Moonbeam hesitated. "Perhaps... If she is texting you, would you like me to respond? I could be vague enough that she wouldn't guess it wasn't you, and at least she would feel as though you hadn't..."

She trailed off tactfully without finishing, 'abandoned

her'.

I considered. Moonbeam knew both Nichele and me. And she was such a good agent she could probably fake it even if she didn't know either of us.

"Would you?" I asked. "I hate to lie to her, but..."

The words stuck in my throat. I lied to Nichele every single time we talked.

"I'll be pleased to impersonate you," Moonbeam replied briskly. "And when the agents arrive to find out who is texting Blaze Featherwind from your phone, I'll confess immediately and tell them you asked me to do so when you gave me your cell phone at the airport. Now I see a vehicle approaching, so we must go. May the Earth Spirit guide and protect you, dear."

She hung up.

I removed the battery from my burner phone before dropping both items into the garbage can, then stood jittering beside the bus shelter.

Shit, who was arriving at my farm?

Stemp, with an explanation of his suspension that would conflict with the story I'd just spun?

Holt, who would ruthlessly interrogate them? Dammit, Holt was too good an agent not to question why three seventy-plus people would be wandering around outside in thirty-below weather. And when he checked their phones, he would find call records from the same anonymous number only seconds apart, along with one that had ended only moments ago.

I shot an anxious glance up and down the deserted street. If Holt accessed their call records, the Department could triangulate my location from the cell towers.

No; Stemp's parents were too good to let that happen. They had probably pitched their phones into a snowbank already.

But what if the unknown visitor was neither Stemp nor Holt? What if it was some new enemy? One with an automatic weapon who would slaughter three elderly people without a second thought...

The bus pulled up, and I shoved my gruesome imaginings aside and climbed aboard.

It was a long slow ride through a series of residential neighbourhoods, and I kept my hood up and face tilted down behind my scarf. At last the bus emerged onto a busier thoroughfare, and I slumped with relief as more people got on. Soon the loop would return me to my motel.

About time, too. I was exhausted, and my breakfast was nothing but a fond memory. My stomach growled.

I dug into my parka pockets, hoping I'd stashed a cereal bar in there, but found only the bottle of water I'd bought the previous evening.

God, only a little over twelve hours ago. It felt like a lifetime.

Well, water was better than nothing. I opened the bottle and drank. When I tucked it back into my pocket, my fingers encountered an unfamiliar shape. Smooth but yielding, like a little bag of sand.

Frowning, I drew out the object. It was a small clear plastic bag, but I couldn't identify the contents. The bag was heavy for its size, filled with greyish powder.

What the hell?

I hadn't packed that.

As I stared at the bag, horrible suspicion oozed into my

mind and my hands began to tremble.

That looked a hell of a lot like a little bag of metal powder.

Approximately the amount that would be generated if two short lengths of rebar were reduced to their elements...

My pulse picked up, my heart rattling my ribs.

How long had it been in my pocket? And who had put it there?

My parka had been in the coatroom in the secured facility. Anybody could have tampered with it there.

Including me. What if I had been programmed to steal the bacteria and metal powder? And to inject myself with ketamine as a distraction?

But I had passed our lie detector test. It had confirmed that I hadn't injected myself, dammit. If I'd had no memory of whether or not I'd injected myself, the lie detector should have flashed yellow.

Unless fake memories gave off the same brainwaves as real memories...

I shook my head vigorously, generating a questioning look from the woman beside me. Giving her a feeble excuse for a smile, I put the bag gingerly back in my pocket and switched to worrying about it instead.

Should I throw the bag away? Or keep it as evidence?

But what if the only fingerprints on it were my own? That evidence would just send me to prison faster.

I couldn't have stolen it from the secured facility. I hadn't had time. I had collected my team and pushed them through the smoke toward the door.

Hadn't I?

My memories flickered tauntingly just beyond my grasp.

Surely I hadn't had time to run to the front of the room, bag the powder, run to the coatroom and put the bag in my pocket, and then run back to my team. And wouldn't I have remembered doing at least some of that?

Nausea twisted my guts. Not if I'd been programmed *not* to remember.

But that just didn't make sense. Sam was long dead. He couldn't possibly have foreseen the situation unfolding the way it did, so he couldn't have given me such specific instructions.

But Nora could have.

My heart sank.

Shit.

Had she delivered instructions to me secretly at the meet-and-greet? Was I programmed to obey her no matter what she commanded, and forget our conversation afterward? That would have been an easy instruction for Sam to embed in my brain.

Cold chills chased themselves down my spine and I shivered convulsively.

No, that was too creepy to contemplate. There had to be another explanation.

Somebody else must have planted the bag in my pocket under the cover of the smoke.

But the whole area had been searched with metal detectors while I had been unconscious. Surely they would have searched the coatroom, too. If the metal powder had been in my pocket, they would have found it.

Hell, maybe Nora had planted it on me last night. She could have walked into Ian's room while we were both unconscious and put the bag in my pocket. Was that why Ian had tranked me, the bastard? So they could frame me?

And Nora could have shot herself up with ketamine later... but no; why would she do that?

Or maybe Ian and Grandin were working together.

I ran the scenario through my mind. Maybe Ian had told Grandin I was coming to his room. Grandin could have stationed Dirk in the lobby to follow me as I left; Nora could have dumped the metal powder in my parka pocket...

Struck by a thought, I sat up straight.

Hell, Nora could have planted the metal powder on me while she was hugging me after dropping her 'Dani-dear' bombshell. I had been so paralyzed with shock, she could have stuffed cabbages in my pockets and I'd never have noticed.

And then after I had left, Grandin could have found Ian unconscious and seized the opportunity to shoot Nora with the ketamine dart and accuse me of doing it...

My heart thumped faster.

That had to be it. The reports said Nora swore I hadn't shot her; but since she didn't know who had, I was on the hook for it.

Dammit, Holt had better be investigating Grandin as well as hunting me...

Unable to sit still any longer, I rang the bell and wove to the front of the bus.

I was still at least a mile away from my motel, but I welcomed the cold walk. Incipient panic pushed me almost to a jog, as though I could outrun my own brain.

Could I trust myself? I didn't think I'd had enough time to accomplish anything except what I actually remembered doing...

Oh, God, what if I'd been programmed to steal information when I was in the internet, and deliver it who knew where? Maybe I really was the dangerous criminal the Department had made me out to be.

Dammit, I needed Skidmark *now*.

But even though I trusted him, I couldn't tell him everything. The network generator and key were so secret that even Holt didn't know about them. If I told Skidmark, it could very well be considered treason. Canada had abolished capital punishment so I wouldn't be hanged; but imprisonment would be worse.

Far worse.

Claustrophobia clutched my throat and I cast about frantically for other options.

Kane already knew all about the brainwave-driven network. And no matter how thoroughly programmed I was, he could neutralize me without even breaking a sweat.

But I shouldn't involve him. Fatherhood was his top priority, and rightfully so. Endangering him wasn't fair to him or to Daniel.

And he was technically a civilian, so disclosing any of this to him might end in a treason charge, too...

My boots pounded the pavement, shivery weakness stealing through my limbs. Part fear and part hunger.

...a high-performance machine...

I shook the thought out of my head, but that only left room for one thought that repeated itself over and over.

I needed Kane.

I couldn't involve him.

I was so fucked.

CHAPTER 31

Striding up to my motel, I tried to look relaxed and casual while checking every corner, rooftop, and passing vehicle for concealed enemies.

I saw none, but my back still crawled as I walked to my car and got in. A quick glance at my bug detector reassured me that nobody had stuck a locator device on the car while I was away. Pulling out of the parking lot, I drove a complicated evasive pattern for nearly twenty minutes without spotting any evidence of a tail.

Somehow that wasn't as reassuring as it should have been. Was I safe? Or only foolishly oblivious?

At last I parked the car at a small strip mall a half-block away from the motel. I could still get to it with a short dash, but it wasn't dangerously exposed in front of my motel room if my cover got blown.

Dragging my complaining belly out of the car, I trudged back to the small family restaurant that occupied the same lot as the motel. After a lunch that probably would have tasted better if I hadn't been tensed to flee at the slightest threat, I paid the bill with cash and went into the washroom.

As I had hoped, its plumbing was of the same vintage as

the motel's. I lifted the lid off the toilet tank and dropped the small bag of metal powder inside. It sank like a stone, and I replaced the lid with a breath of relief.

If I needed it I could retrieve it; and judging by the ancient mineral deposits caked inside the tank, nobody else was likely to look inside.

...Unless I'd been programmed to put the bag right here in this toilet tank so someone else could pick it up...

I stifled a whimper and hurried out to wash my hands, as though soap and water could cleanse them of sins I didn't know they'd committed.

By then I had used up enough time to head for Market Mall; and once again I drove a circuitous route. No vehicles seemed to be following me and no helicopters hovered overhead, so at last I made for the mall.

The parking lot was crammed with cars. Even its farthest reaches were fully occupied, and I circled time and again looking for a parking spot. Cursing the idiots who delayed their Christmas shopping until the last minute, I conveniently ignored the fact that if I hadn't been running for my life I'd have been one of them.

But my invective was only half-hearted. At least the crowds would keep me, and my car, safely anonymous.

If only I could find a goddamn parking spot...

At last I spotted an SUV pulling out, and I wheeled into its vacated space at ten minutes to two. Feeling as though I had a target painted on my back, I power-walked across the parking lot and into the mall, then forced my stride slower to match the pace of the throng inside.

My heart thumped harder than necessary as I approached the popcorn stand. Skidmark lounged against the wall nearby, munching handfuls of popcorn from the bag he clutched to his chest. With his ancient parka and the stained rucksack at his feet, he looked exactly like an old vagrant. The fragments of popcorn clinging to his tangle of moustache and beard only heightened the impression.

His head was hanging nearly low enough to touch his popcorn bag, concealing his keen eyes under shaggy brows. The well-dressed crowd detoured squeamishly around him, leaving a bubble of space that made him far too noticeable.

Dammit. If I went over to speak to him, I'd be conspicuous.

I wandered closer, pausing as if to admire an evening gown in one of the store windows. Then I headed for the popcorn stand as though I'd decided on a snack. As I went by Skidmark, I let my step hitch as I shot him a glance, twitching my lip as though I'd just gotten a whiff of something unpleasant.

Hell, I had. The range of his miasma was clearly outlined by the unoccupied space around him.

I moved hurriedly out of olfactory range and stepped up to buy my popcorn. My back crawled. Would he accost me like a panhandler? If he did, should I make a show of offering him some spare change, or blow him off? Either way, we'd attract attention.

He didn't move.

I accepted my bag of caramel-coated deliciousness and wandered away, nibbling.

Hadn't he noticed me? Maybe my disguise was too good.

Tucking my popcorn bag under my arm, I went into the nearest glass-fronted store. I browsed slowly through the displays, gradually accomplishing a U-turn so I could look back through the glass as I lifted a sequined top from the rack and held it up as if to gauge its size.

Skidmark was now leaning against the wall only a few yards away. As I glanced over, he dug a pinkie into his ear and excavated vigorously, then withdrew his finger and studied its burden with interest. When he wiped it on his parka and then delved back into his popcorn bag with the same hand, I had to stifle a snort of laughter in the crook of my elbow.

"Bless you," said a cheery voice behind me.

My heart nearly leaped from my chest as I spun to face a perky saleschild.

Good Lord, were they hiring ten-year-olds now? A glance at her bountiful boobs convinced me that she actually had hit puberty; or maybe she knew a plastic surgeon with an open mind and defective judgement.

"Th-thank you," I stammered.

"Would you like to try that on?" She nodded at the sequins clenched in my fist.

"Um... no, it's... not for me."

The girl looked relieved. Clearly Teresa Diaz was not a good candidate for sequins.

"It's for my daughter," I added. "But..." I held up the garment again, eyeing it critically. "It's too low-cut. Women should be modest." I let my frown coast over her generously-displayed cleavage.

"Oh." She didn't quite twitch, but her smile became fixed. "Maybe a nice crew-neck sweater..."

"No, I don't think so." I handed her the sequined top as though it harboured some particularly sordid contagion. "I think I'm in the wrong store."

She gave me another plastic smile. "Well, if you see anything you'd like, just let me know. My name is Jessica, and I'll be happy to help."

"Thank you," I said, and left, pitying the poor kid. What a shitty job. Even though I might be hunted down and killed at any moment, I still wouldn't want to trade places with her.

I wandered through another couple of stores, tension aching in my shoulders. Surely by now I had wasted enough time 'shopping' and I could leave without arousing suspicion.

After being cornered by yet another overly-helpful salesperson, I gave up. Enough. I was out of here.

My feet tried to dash for the exit, but I schooled them to a leisurely stroll. Once outside I picked up my pace to a brisk stride, but stopped as a thought struck me.

Skidmark wouldn't be able to keep up. His breathing had been laboured just from walking indoors at the restaurant.

I paused at the curb and looked both ways as he emerged from the mall doors behind me, rucksack on his shoulder. After I crossed the busy laneway I walked toward my parking spot, but he lagged farther and farther behind.

Dammit, if I got into my car now, he'd never find me.

I trailed to a halt, gazing around the parking lot as if in confusion. Don't mind me; I'm just a ditzy dame who's forgotten where she parked...

I started back the way I'd come, then turned away again as Skidmark approached.

Using up as much time as I could, I wove back and forth between rows as though looking for my car while he plodded closer. When I was sure he'd be able to see which car I was getting into, I raised my key fob and pressed the horn button, giving thanks that I'd gotten an SL2 instead of the base model SL1 that had power-nothing.

My Saturn obligingly blinked its lights and honked its horn, and I straightened as though in relief and made a beeline for it.

I slid into the driver's seat and waited.

And waited.

Where the hell was Skidmark?

Craning my neck to peer in the rearview mirror, I spotted him standing motionless in the next row: head down, hands in front, and legs widespread while incriminating steam rose from the yellow-stained snow at his feet.

I burst into laughter.

When he opened the passenger's door a few minutes later, I was still chuckling. "Jesus, Skidmark," I sputtered as he leaned over and brushed the popcorn crumbs out of his beard. "You're fucking disgusting. How can I find you utterly repulsive and like you at the same time?"

"You love me for my mind, girlie," he wheezed. "'Cause you know how smart ol' Skidmark is. Nobody's ever gonna figure some filthy old druggie is up to anything besides looking for his next fix." He straightened his parka as though it was a fine tuxedo, his gold tooth glinting in a grin. "I suppose you want me to take this masterpiece off?"

"God, yes." I popped the trunk. "Put it in the trunk and put on my spare parka. It's in the big black backpack."

When he slid into the passenger's seat and closed the door behind him a couple of minutes later, I drew an untainted breath of relief. "Okay, let's get the hell out of here."

"Can't be too soon for me." Skidmark shuddered as I reversed the car out of the spot and made for the exit. "Why would anybody go into a place like that? Crammed in there like sardines. I could hardly breathe, and it was nothing to do with my lungs."

"Same here," I agreed.

He shot me a look. "Nice disguise, by the way. I almost missed you, but I recognized your walk."

"Shit." I slumped. "I should have thought of that."

"Hey, don't beat yourself up. I've been playing this game for a long time. Besides, the whole point was for me to recognize you, right?"

"Yeah, I guess."

"So what's the plan?" he asked as I pulled onto the street.

I sighed. "I don't have one yet. I need to speak to my contact again, but she'll be under heavy guard. Maybe I can use you as a diversion and take her somewhere alone…"

"No, I need to watch you."

"I know, but if you're there she'll probably clam up; and even if she doesn't, I'll be in deep shit if anybody finds out you overheard the classified stuff we need to talk about."

"Well, you can't go in alone. What if you attack her?" He didn't add 'again', but it hovered between us nevertheless.

"If I attack her it'll be because she deserves it," I growled. As Skidmark raised a quizzical eyebrow, I sighed and subsided in the seat. "I think. Maybe." I sighed again. "Shit."

"Do your boys know about the classified stuff?"

"John does. Arnie doesn't."

"Then you need Kane."

I thumped a fist on the steering wheel. "I *know* I need

Kane; but I can't have him, so forget it."

A short pause made me glance over, intercepting Skidmark's too-perceptive gaze. "We still talking about the mission here?" he inquired mildly.

"Yes!" I shot him a scowl before returning my attention to the street. "He's a civilian, and a dad. Off-limits, personally and professionally."

"Well, I don't know about your personal stuff," Skidmark observed. "But professionally, I'd say you've got a duty to call him."

"Fuck that," I snapped. "I'm not going to risk taking Daniel's father away from him."

"So instead you're gonna take a chance on killing hundreds of other innocent men, women, and children?" Skidmark rasped. "What if you set a bomb somewhere? What if you go on a rampage with an automatic weapon?"

The thought of the P90 and all its rounds of ammo clenched my guts. My hands quivered on the wheel.

"Yeah, just think about that for a minute," Skidmark advised. "And while you're thinking about that, think about how Kane would feel if he found out you'd murdered innocent people just because you didn't trust him enough to call him."

"It's nothing to do with trust!" My voice came out too loud, and I drew a short breath and modulated my volume. "He quit the Department. Fatherhood is his top priority. I'm just trying to support that. It's not fair to call him up and drag him into danger every time I can't handle my own shit..." Mortifying memories of my partnership with Holt coiled into a corrosive ball in my stomach. "...which is apparently every fucking time a mission comes my way," I ground out. "And I am fucking sick and tired of screwing up and having to be rescued."

Skidmark's voice softened. "You didn't screw up, and you're not asking to be rescued. A good agent stays focused on the results and asks for help when they need it."

I held my face expressionless and my shoulders square, concealing the way my heart flinched from the blow. Yet another reason why I just wasn't good enough.

"Hey, Storm." I didn't glance over, but I could see Skidmark frowning in my peripheral vision. "I know you're a good agent," he said. "There're only two reasons why a good agent wouldn't ask for help. One's ego; and I don't think that's your problem. The other's that they've been burned so bad they don't dare take another chance. Girlie, if that's your problem you've gotta let it go. If you don't it'll eat you up inside. And if you let it compromise a mission, it'll kill you. Or somebody you care about."

"Right. Thanks for the advice," I said shortly.

"It's your duty to talk to Kane," he persisted. "And he needs to decide for himself whether to get involved. You think you're doing the right thing for him, but how would you feel if he made that kind of decision for you?"

"Shut *up*," I grated.

Much to my surprise, he did.

CHAPTER 32

Skidmark and I drove in silence for several minutes while guilt gnawed a burning hollow in my belly.

"Oh, for Christ's sake!" I barked at last. "Fine!"

I cranked the wheel over and parked in the nearest convenience store lot, then took out a burner phone and sent a text to Kane's number: "Spider web. Vet displacement. Eyes on."

I got out of the car and headed for the garbage bin; but jerked to an abrupt halt as a black half-ton barrelled past, nearly running me over.

"Asshole!" I yelled, and pitched the burner phone into the bed of the pickup.

My lips twisted into a savage smile as the driver gave me the finger and roared onto the street, fishtailing and revving the engine. He couldn't have spotted my license plate as he blew by, so my cover was safe.

And he was going to get a hell of a surprise when Holt traced that burner phone.

Still grinning, I got back into my car and pulled sedately out of the lot to head in the opposite direction.

"You look like the cat that swallowed the canary,"

Skidmark said. "Why?"

"I texted Kane. I'm pretty sure Holt will intercept the message and trace it back to that burner phone. And Dickwad there in the black pickup is now carrying that burner phone away to somewhere we aren't. Holt will put somebody on Kane for sure; but I bet he'll follow that phone himself. He'll want to take all the credit for capturing me." My grin widened. "And he'll be pissed as hell when he finds out he's gone on a wild goose chase."

"Who's Holt?"

"The agent who's in charge of hunting me. He's got an ego problem, but he's good." My smile drooped. "Shit. Probably too good. He'll know I'm not dumb enough to keep a burner phone active after sending a text. He's not going to be fooled. Damn."

"Can Kane outfox him? Outrun him?"

"If it was just him and Holt, probably. But if Holt's got a team..."

Skidmark frowned. "If Kane's as good as you say, he won't lead them to you. When and where is our rendezvous?"

I sighed. "Well, if he figured out my message, he should be at a coffee shop where we met a couple of years ago; at four-twenty-seven this afternoon; and he should know he's being watched so he'll make sure he's not followed."

"Four-twenty-seven?" Skidmark eyed me. "That's a pretty specific time."

"It's the engine displacement of my '66 Corvette. I purposely misspelled 'Vette, so I hope he got it."

"He'll get it if he has a brain," Skidmark muttered, then added, "Nice wheels, girlie. You're lucky it's winter, or I'd have taken a joyride in that 'Vette instead of your Legacy."

I laughed. "Lucky for you it's winter. If you touched my baby, I'd probably have to kill you."

He wheezed laughter. "It'd be worth it."

When I pulled into the parking lot of the strip mall that housed our meeting place, Skidmark jabbed a nicotine-stained finger at the far side of the lot. "Park over there by the garbage dumpsters."

"Like I have a choice," I groused. "It's the only friggin' spot available. What's wrong with these people? Don't they have homes?"

Skidmark grunted. "Yep. Homes crammed full of shit they don't need; and they're busy buying up a bunch more shit for other people who don't need any more shit; and those same people are buying them a big pile of useless shit in return. Merry goddamn Christmas."

I parked and turned to him, widening my eyes as if in wonder. "Wow. Can I call you Santa Claus?"

He snorted, then gripped my arm as I reached for the door handle. "You stay here, girlie. I'll do the rendezvous."

I bit off my instinctive argument and considered for a moment. He was right, of course.

I sighed. "Okay. Thanks. Here..." I pulled out a burner phone and programmed the number of my current burner into its speed dial. "When you get to the coffee shop, phone me and leave the connection open. That way I'll know what's going on."

He gave me a ferocious scowl. "What's going on is just me making contact and getting out. If anything else happens, you drive the hell out of this parking lot without looking back, you hear me? Even if they catch me talking to Kane, they won't connect me with you as long as you don't come charging in there."

"I know. I'll just wait here."

He studied me, eyes shrewd beneath his tangled brows. "Give me your word."

I hissed out a breath. "Okay. Fine. I give you my word."

He scowled. "You've got your fingers crossed inside your mittens, don't you?"

"No." I crossed them harder.

He raised a skeptical eyebrow and got out of the car. I popped the trunk so he could swap parkas again, and a few moments later the trunk slammed and I watched in the rearview mirror while he trudged across the parking lot.

When he arrived at the coffee shop he detoured to the garbage can and spent a few leisurely minutes digging through it. He drew out some unidentifiable piece of garbage, studied it for a moment, and then put it in the same pocket as the burner phone I'd given him. A moment later my phone rang.

I shuddered as I accepted the call and put it on speaker. If he gave me back that phone, I'd bleach it.

The speaker hissed and rumbled as the phone shifted in his pocket. He mooched toward the door and disappeared inside.

A moment later, a muffled version of his slurred voice drifted to my ears. "Pretty lady. The Earth Spirit names you Bellavista Dreamwalker. Your planet is blue Venus." A moment later he spoke again. "Good sir. The Earth Spirit names you Stonemountain Warrior. Your planet is orange Mars." A wheezy chuckle. "Well, hello, little lady. The Earth Spirit names you Meadowsweet Stardancer, and your planet is purple Pluto."

A child's giggle pierced the speaker, followed by a high voice that carried with unfortunate clarity. "Mummy, that man's stinky."

The maternal response was blurred as Skidmark apparently moved away. He anointed a few other people, with responses varying from silence to uncomfortable giggles to 'get lost'. Then he announced, "Good sir. The Earth Spirit names you Sunstar Desert Hawk, and your planet is gold Saturn."

I held my breath. Kane was there.

But had he been able to evade Holt's surveillance?

Kane's unmistakable baritone rumbled through the speaker. "That's interesting, but you're making people uncomfortable in here. How would it be if I buy you a coffee and we go outside?"

Skidmark's wheezy rasp took on a wheedling note. "Good sir, you are gold indeed. It's cold outside for an old man's bones, and a coffee would ease the chill."

"Well, come on then. Let's get you a coffee." Kane's tone was indulgent, and I imagined the rest of the patrons eyeing him with gratitude for handling the awkward situation.

While they waited for the coffee, Skidmark accosted a couple more people. Kane made gentle attempts to quell him, completely believable in his role as self-appointed rescuer.

A few minutes later they emerged together. Kane held the door for Skidmark, who shuffled out with both hands wrapped around his paper cup as though desperate for the warmth.

I realized with a pang that he probably was. He couldn't move fast enough to stay warm. I cranked the heater up higher and watched the performance in my rearview mirror.

"There you go," Kane said kindly. "You know where the homeless shelter is, don't you?"

"Don't need it, good sir. I have a home, but thankee anyway."

"Well, you'd better go home," Kane advised. "It's too cold to be outside."

"That it is, that it is. May the Earth Spirit guide and protect you, good sir." Skidmark nodded and shuffled away.

Kane stood at the doorway for a few moments, watching as though making sure Skidmark didn't double back to harass the coffee shop patrons again. But I was pretty sure he was triangulating the path to a gold Saturn.

When Skidmark was about halfway across the parking lot, Kane went back inside.

I kept an eye on the coffee shop, but Kane hadn't come out again by the time Skidmark opened the passenger door and collapsed gasping into the seat.

Worry chilled my heart as I tried to study him and watch the rearview mirror at the same time. "Are you okay?" I asked as he hunched forward, wheezing frighteningly fast.

"Fine." But his panting didn't slow. "Damn... cold... thin air," he gasped between breaths. "All right... in a... minute..."

It was more than a minute. By the time his respiration finally slowed to its usual slightly accelerated tempo, I was on the verge of taking him to the hospital. In the enclosed space the reek of his parka was nearly overpowering, but I didn't have the heart to send him outside again to change it.

He opened the passenger door, letting in a merciful breath of fresh air while he hawked and spat into the parking lot, then settled back in the seat with a groan. "Forgot to take that damn bronchodilator this afternoon." He extracted a puffer from his pocket and sucked in a dose, then coughed feebly. "Damn."

"Do you need to-" I began, but Skidmark cut me off with a sharp gesture.

"He's on the move," he croaked. "Get ready to drive."

Sure enough, Kane had emerged from the coffee shop and was crossing the parking lot in the opposite direction. When he got into a rusted brown half-ton, I let out a breath of relief.

"That's not his truck," I told Skidmark. "So he got the message about being followed."

"Yeah. Let's hope he shook the tail," he replied grimly. "Let's go."

I pulled out and drove toward the exit, gratified to see the brown half-ton drop in behind me a few vehicles back.

"He's good," I assured Skidmark.

"Better than the guys who are following him?"

"Yeah. I'd stake my life on it."

Skidmark grunted. "You probably are. Where are we headed?"

After a moment of thought I said, "Nose Hill Park. It's usually abandoned when it's this cold; we'll have a good view around us so nobody can sneak up; and it's got good road access if we have to run."

"Sounds good. The only running I'm going to do is in this car." He sounded a little less breathless. The inhaler must have been working.

Skidmark and I both kept a sharp eye out for followers while I drove, but saw none. I knew Kane would be doing the same, and I gave silent thanks for both men. As long as we weren't being tracked electronically, we were probably in the clear. For now.

By the time we approached the park, the sky was already darkening. In the failing light the vehicles around us faded to amorphous gray shapes behind too-bright headlights, and I peered at them until my eyes ached. Would I even be able to recognize a tail in the darkness?

We pulled to a stop in the deserted parking lot, and a moment later a dark half-ton pulled in behind us. It parked a couple of slots away, and I drew a breath of relief when Kane's familiar broad-shouldered form got out and strode over.

I opened the door and pulled out my bug detector, activating it to display the steady green light while Skidmark looked on with interest.

"Good," Kane said. "May I borrow it?"

I handed it over and watched while he hurried back to his truck. As he completed a circuit around it his steps slowed, and I whooshed out a breath I hadn't realized I'd been holding.

He returned at an easier pace, sliding into the back seat with his usual powerful athleticism despite the cramped quarters.

"All clear," he said as he handed the device back to me. "What's happening?"

I swallowed a small twinge of hurt at his brusqueness, but hell, we might only have minutes to spare. No point in wasting time with pleasantries.

Or with a hug or kiss.

Arnie wouldn't consider a hug and kiss a waste of time...

"Take these," I said, matching Kane's impersonal tone as I handed the network key and generator over the seat to him. "Don't let me have them back unless you're sure I need them. And don't let me do anything unless I can convince you that it's the best course of action. Use deadly force to stop me if necessary."

"*What?* Aydan, what's happening?" he demanded. But he pocketed the two small devices without question.

Relieved of my burdens, I sagged in the driver's seat. "Sam might have embedded secret programming in my mind. My mother, who was supposed to have died in a fiery car crash thirty years ago but instead faked her death and ran off with Sam, resurfaced last night to warn me about it; and MI6, the CIA, the FBI, the Department, the RCMP, and the Calgary police are all hunting me because they think I've gone rogue. And..." My voice wobbled despite my attempt to keep it level. "I might have."

CHAPTER 33

A short shocked silence greeted my revelations. Fortunately it gave me a chance to gather my thoughts. Dammit, Kane and Hellhound didn't know Skidmark was an agent. They still thought he was a wasted old stoner.

I added, "Skidmark is helping me but I can't tell him anything about, um... anything."

I added a stern psychic message: Don't mention that Stemp is the Director.

Apparently Kane got the message. "Skidmark, it's nice to see you again," he said cautiously. "Are you here visiting for Christmas?"

"Yeah." Skidmark gave a slow-motion shrug, his words blurring into his stoned-old-man routine. "With Moonbeam and Karma. It's not cool, man. Our kid's got a major stick up his ass." He gave me a heavy-eyed look and added plaintively, "If I'd known Storm wouldn't let me toke up, I'd have stayed in Silverside."

"No marijuana," I said sternly. "No smoking at all."

"Bummer," he mumbled, and poked morosely in his parka pocket as if hoping to find a forgotten doobie.

Kane shot him an appraising look before returning his

attention to me. "How much does he know?"

"I had to tell him I'm an agent. That's all," I lied, trying to hide my discomfort. Dammit, I didn't want to lie to Kane, but Skidmark's cover wasn't mine to divulge.

"And you believed her?" Kane demanded of Skidmark.

Skidmark yawned. "Son, I believe in pink elephants. See 'em all the time. If Storm's a spy, it's cool with me." He let one eyelid droop in a conspiratorial wink and added, "I did a bit of cloak-and-dagger stuff myself back in the day. Used it to dodge out of getting sent to 'Nam."

Kane's lips tightened.

I longed to blurt the truth of Skidmark's dangerous tours of duty in Vietnam and subsequent decades of dedicated service, but my promise to maintain his cover kept me silent.

"All right," Kane said shortly. "Give me the details."

I sighed. "My mother is using the name Nora Taylor. She's staying at the Palliser downtown, and she'll be under constant surveillance. She says she can tell me what the programming is and how to overcome it, so I need to talk to her as soon as possible."

Kane frowned. "We'll come back to that. You said you might have gone rogue. What did you mean?"

"Actually, I think I'm being framed... but... I just... I don't know for sure. I got shot up with ketamine yesterday, and right after that there was, um... a theft. I'm almost positive I didn't do it, but the ketamine knocked me out and caused amnesia, so I can't say for absolutely certain. And later, after I'd talked to Nora the first time, she got shot up with ketamine, too. Everybody thinks I injected myself so I wouldn't get blamed for the theft, and then injected Nora later for reasons unknown. Oh, and they think I knocked out..."

I bit off 'Ian Rand' at the last instant. Kane had never known Ian's real name; and Skidmark knew it all too well. And if I mentioned Orion Moonjava, Kane would realize that Skidmark knew more than he should...

I massaged the headache that had begun to thump between my eyes and substituted, "...another agent... to get to Nora."

"Who exactly is 'everybody'?" Kane inquired.

"Well, everybody except, um, the Director," I said, not looking at Skidmark. "I passed a lie detector test after the theft," I added hurriedly. "So the Director believes I'm innocent; and he's the one who gave me the, um... items I gave you... and told me to go off-grid and investigate. So as far as anybody knows, I'm only following orders."

"Oh." Kane's posture eased. "When you said you might have gone rogue, I wondered..."

I followed his train of thought with rising chagrin. "Oh! No! Shit, no; I'm not asking you to hide me or take sides against the Department. I'm sorry; I should have explained better. I would never put you in that position. I just want you to keep me from doing anything... bad. If I've been programmed."

Kane's face relaxed for the first time. "That's a relief. But if the Director believes you and you're under orders to stay dark, why are half the law enforcement agencies in the western hemisphere hunting you?"

I glanced at Skidmark's sleepy face and alert eyes and told half the truth. "The Director is having some problems with the chain of command. And the, um... theft... involved U.S. property, and they've demanded my extradition. Even though I passed the lie detector, they don't consider the test valid."

Because the Department wouldn't disclose how our classified technology worked. And that technology was my only defense.

The thought of it made my throat constrict.

My voice pitched higher as I went on, "The chain of command has already issued a warrant for me, and..."

Despite my attempts to stay cool, all my bottled-up fear rushed out. "John, our extradition process is a joke! There was this guy, a Canadian citizen, who was accused as a terrorist and the only evidence against him was a couple of hand-printed sentences on a hotel phone pad. Two out of five handwriting experts said it wasn't even his writing; and they extradited him anyway. They rubber-stamp nearly every request! And if I get shipped to the States, they'll never let me go!"

Kane looked as grim as I felt. "Yes, I remember that case."

My heart sank. He hadn't even offered a token reassurance. He knew I was in deep shit.

But he didn't know how deep.

I drew a shaky breath and enlightened him. "And there's another complication. If it looks as though my extradition will be approved, I... likely won't make it out of the country."

Kane's jaw clenched and he gave a short nod. He might not know all of Stemp's reasons for keeping me in Canada; but he knew about all the other classified knowledge in my brain. 'Extradition' would be nothing more than a polite euphemism for 'execution'.

"And you said the Department has already issued a

warrant for you," he said tightly. "Who is the agent in charge?"

"Holt."

Kane considered that, drumming his fingertips on his knee. "He's a good agent, but his weakness is ego. We can use that."

"You know this Holt guy?" Skidmark inquired.

Stirring the pot. He already knew Kane used to be an agent, but he was pressing to see if Kane would admit it.

Kane eyed him, and I wondered whether Skidmark's cover was as secure as he thought. Many people might disregard or underestimate a disgusting old man; but Kane was not one of them.

"Yes," Kane said without elaborating. He turned back to me. "So what identity are you using?"

I suddenly remembered my unflattering makeup. Jeez, no wonder he didn't want to kiss me.

"I'm Teresa Diaz. The car is legally registered to me, and I have a motel room rented for the rest of the week." I hesitated. "It's not a Department identity."

Kane nodded matter-of-factly. "I assumed that. They would have found you already if it had been one of theirs. So Nora says she's your mother. Do you believe her?"

I hesitated, my guts clenching in memory. "I... I think... I might have to. She knew things that... would be hard for anyone to unearth. But... I don't know. After all, Sam was there off and on throughout my whole childhood. What if Nora is just one of his associates and he told her a few things that would sound convincing?"

"Did she volunteer these personal details?" Kane asked.

"No. She said to ask her anything. And I did..." I tried

to tug at a lock of hair, forgetting that I was wearing Teresa's kerchief. I settled for mangling my seatbelt in my fist instead. "...but what if Sam programmed me to ask exactly those questions, and fed his associate the answers so I'd be convinced?"

Kane sighed. "That's the big question. And the next big question is, even if you did manage to meet with her and even if she told you exactly what Sam had programmed into your mind, could you afford to believe her?"

I dropped my forehead onto the steering wheel with a groan. "No. Hell, maybe she programmed me to steal the m-" I bit off 'metal powder' and substituted, "...stolen item and now she's just luring me back so I'll deliver it to her."

Kane sat up abruptly. "You have it?"

"Um... Maybe...?" My voice came out very small.

"What's that supposed to mean?" he demanded.

"I have... had... um, found something... that looked like it. In my parka pocket." At the look on his face, I hurriedly added, "But everybody had access to my parka. That's why I think I'm being framed; and I'm pretty sure I know who's doing it, and why."

"All right," Kane said cautiously. "Who, and why?"

I outlined Grandin's activities and my suspicions while Kane and Skidmark listened in silence. While I talked, Skidmark's chin drooped lower and lower onto his chest and his breathing deepened into soft snoring.

I didn't believe his act for an instant.

Kane shot him a suspicious look, too, but made no comment until I'd finished my narrative. "So let me be sure I understand this," he said at last. "Your original orders were to investigate Nora, and now you have even more reason to do so. But if you resurface to contact her you'll be arrested and probably imprisoned until the extradition is decided, which could take anywhere from several months to two years. If the extradition goes ahead you'll have a fatal accident before you ever enter the United States. If you can't determine whether you've been compromised, you're potentially dangerous to everyone, including yourself; and if you *do* ascertain that you've been compromised..."

He trailed off, and I swallowed hard and finished his sentence. "I'll have to turn myself in."

"And be executed," Kane said flatly.

"Probably." I had intended my tone to be dispassionate, but the word crept quivering from my mouth.

Kane frowned. "So if we can prove Grandin is framing you, the U.S. will drop its extradition request; and then we can put Nora on the lie detector and find out exactly what programming is in your mind, if any."

"Except that Nora has diplomatic immunity," I said. "So she can't be forced to take a lie detector test if she refuses; and she already refused. On Saturday she's going back to the U.K., and then she'll be beyond our reach. If that happens it won't matter whether I'm up for extradition or not, because if the Department thinks I've been compromised I'll be dead long before the Minister of Justice ever gets around to ruling on the request." I crushed my long-suffering seatbelt in my fist. "I have to talk to Nora right away!"

"And say what to her?" Kane demanded. "You have no way of knowing whether she's lying. And anyway, if everyone thinks you attacked her they'll have doubled her security in case you try again. And if she's accessible at all, it's likely because they're using her as bait to trap you.

Talking to Nora is a bad idea."

I clenched the seat belt tighter, making my arthritic thumb ache. "But it's the only option I've got."

Kane studied me, looking troubled. "Or maybe it's the only option you're considering. Maybe you've been programmed to seek out Nora no matter what."

A queasy chill settled in the pit of my stomach. "Maybe." My voice trembled, and I steadied it with an effort before continuing, "But maybe not. I didn't have enough time to talk to her. I only asked a couple of questions; not enough to be sure of anything. And she did give me some hairs for DNA testing. Maybe she really is my mother and truly wants to help..."

Kane was already shaking his head and eyeing me as though debating whether to tie me up and throw me in the trunk before I went completely bonkers.

I gave him a 'calm-down' gesture and went on hurriedly, "I'm not saying I believe that. I'm just saying, what if she only wanted to give me a heads-up before she reported this to the Department? What if she's actually willing to take a lie detector test about this? I can see why she wouldn't have wanted to take one in public earlier. If she's been living under an assumed identity all this time, she wouldn't take a chance on being outed. If I ask her to do a lie detector test now and she refuses, there's a pretty good chance she's lying; which would be good news for me. And if she agrees, it solves the problem."

"If she refuses you'll have put yourself in a dangerous position for no reason, because you still won't know for sure what she's concealing," Kane argued. "And if she agrees, it's still not proof that she's telling the truth; plus you'll have to find some way to arrange the test at the Department without getting arrested. We need to nail Grandin first."

"True; but if she tells me what she knows and agrees to take a lie detector test about it, at least..." I directed a significant glance at the pocket where he'd stowed my network key and generator. "I might feel safer using my, um... skills to investigate Grandin. I'm afraid to do that now because if I've been compromised, and I go in..." I bit off the phrase 'into the network' and substituted, "...investigating... you know there's nothing in the world that can stop me." I swallowed the sick feeling rising in my throat. "I could sell out without even knowing it."

"You're right; I don't think we should take that risk." Kane scrubbed his knuckles through his short dark hair, eyeing me worriedly. "I still think it would be best to concentrate on Grandin."

"But without my..." I nodded at his pocket. "I don't have any way to investigate somebody like him. Do you?"

Kane blew out a breath. "No. I don't have access to those resources anymore."

"So I really have to talk to Nora. She gave me her secret burner number and she's got a bug detector; but she's not an agent and I'm afraid she might be under surveillance without realizing it."

"Agreed. Calling her isn't an option."

I sighed. "So I need to find a way to talk to her in person."

"I don't like it."

I slumped lower in the seat. "I don't either; but if I can't call her, I don't see that I have any other choice."

"Yes, you do," Kane said firmly. "I'll make contact with

Nora while you stay dark with Skidmark supervising you."
He glanced dubiously at the smelly form slumbering in the
passenger seat, then went on, "Dirk and Grandin don't know
me and I haven't had contact with MI6 in years, so Nora's
agent likely won't know me either..."

Despair dampened my voice to a weary monotone. "He
knows you."

Kane's brows snapped together. "Who is he?"

I glanced over at Skidmark's somnolent presence. Hell, I
couldn't help it if he blew his own cover. "Ian Rand. AKA
Orion Moonjava."

Skidmark didn't even twitch.

Kane did.

"Dammit! What are the odds of that?" he snapped.

I sighed. "When I'm involved? Anything that can go
wrong, will go wrong. And even things that *can't* go wrong
will go wrong."

Kane slumped against the seat, crossing his arms over
his chest and frowning at me. "How do I even know you're
telling me the whole truth? Or any of it?"

"I haven't a clue. I think I am, but..." I trailed off, then
burst out, "Look, this is stupid! I can't even trust myself, so I
can't ask you to trust me. At least if I don't have any of my
weapons or gear there's only so much harm I can do; so I'll
just give it all to you and you can go home and pretend this
never happened."

Skidmark jerked upright with such suddenness that
Kane and I both jumped.

"Hell, *no!*" he barked.

CHAPTER 34

"You're not leaving," Skidmark snapped at Kane. "You know too much. If Holt intercepted Storm's text to you, he'll be on you with that fancy new lie detector as soon as you resurface. You'll blow Storm's cover all to hell. You stay with Storm, and I'll get to Nora."

Shit, speaking of blowing covers...

Kane was surveying Skidmark speculatively, but maybe it wasn't too late for the old man to backtrack.

"Skidmark, no. Orion Moonjava knows you," I said. "And the Palliser is the fanciest hotel downtown. The doorman will give you the bum's rush if you even get near the place."

Skidmark snorted. "Rand knows ol' Skidmark. I can make sure he won't recognize me, and the doorman won't give me any grief." His diction was far too crisp, and Kane's gaze sharpened.

"You've been smoking too much weed, old man," I growled warningly. "Go back to sleep."

"Nope. Time to lay my cards on the table." He locked eyes with Kane. "I'm an agent. Started off doing intelligence work in Vietnam; and Moonbeam, Karma, and I have been undercover out at the commune ever since. Those terrorists you tangled with last spring were part of one of our ops."

At Kane's narrow-eyed look, Skidmark went on, "Yeah, we knew you were involved in that. And we know you were an agent and your buddy Hellhound is a Special Forces sniper and weapons specialist."

"Aydan..." Kane began ominously.

Skidmark interrupted him. "Storm didn't tell us anything. We researched you through our own channels. Our cover is so deep that your Department doesn't even know we exist; but we let Rand into the picture when Five Eyes assigned him to round up those terrorists. That's how he knows me; but he's only ever seen this." He made an up-and-down gesture at his scruffy appearance. "He won't recognize me when I'm cleaned up."

"Don't be too sure," Kane said. "I don't know how current your training is; but agents these days are up on the latest facial recognition techniques. I could spot you even in a disguise, as long as I could see your key facial features."

Skidmark grinned, his gold tooth barely visible through his forest of facial hair. "Can you see 'em now?"

We studied him in silence. His face was almost completely obscured by his tangled beard, overgrown moustache, and bushy eyebrows. His long greasy hair straggled every which way, concealing his forehead. His eyes glinted with humour and intelligence, but if he kept them heavy-lidded as he usually did...

"Not well," Kane said reluctantly. "If I was paying attention I could still recognize you unless your next disguise obscured your features in some way; but if Rand was involved in an active op with you as an ally he might not have observed you that closely. And if he sees you in another disguise now, with your presence completely out of context... you might get away with it. Maybe."

"'Course I will," Skidmark said comfortably. "'Cause even if he does recognize me, he'll be recognizing somebody else."

"What's that supposed to mean?" Kane demanded.

"Watch and learn, son."

Skidmark reached into the dirty rucksack at his feet and withdrew a small case. From it, he extracted bottles and jars of grooming products. While Kane and I watched in silence, he went to work with a comb, gel, and moustache wax.

After only a few minutes, Kane's eyes widened, a smile spreading over his face. "You old dog!" he exclaimed.

I frowned at him, then turned to stare at Skidmark, who had tamed his rampant eyebrows and slicked his hair into a ponytail, revealing a noble brow and piercing eyes surrounded by a maze of laugh lines. His sleekly-waxed moustache curled in flamboyant arcs on either side of his mouth; and while I watched he braided his beard into a tidy queue and settled a black beret at a jaunty angle on his head.

"Brenton Carlisle!" Kane laughed out loud, the sound full of delight. "It's an honour to meet you!" He extended his hand, and Skidmark shook it, grinning. No gold tooth.

"What the hell?" I demanded.

Kane turned to me, a smile still lifting the corners of his mouth. "Aydan, I'd like you to meet Brenton Carlisle, a reclusive artist who has been revered for his West Coast landscapes for the last forty years."

"Seriously?" I stared at the transformed Skidmark. "You're a famous artist?"

He shrugged, his eyes twinkling. "When you're out in the backwoods for decades, you gotta do something besides toke up and jerk off or you'll go bugfuck crazy."

"Crazy-er," I corrected with a grin, and he chuckled. I added, "John is a talented artist, too. You should see the beautiful illustrations he's done for his children's book."

"Is that so?" Skidmark raised an interested eyebrow.

"Never mind that," Kane said. "How do you propose to get to Nora?"

"You said she's at a fancy hotel, right? So it has a restaurant?"

"Several," Kane replied. "But if I was the agent in charge of a weapons director who had already been attacked, I'd lock her in her room and get room service."

"You could try," I countered. "But don't forget, Nora *wants* to talk to me. She doesn't believe I attacked her. I bet she'd talk Ian into letting her out."

"If he's a competent agent, she could talk all she wanted without changing his mind," Kane said. "But if he wanted to trap you... he might decide to use her for bait."

"I'd put money on that." Skidmark gave me a sly wink. "If you just got the better of Rand again, he'll be hellbent on catching you. I bet he's still smarting over that fifty bucks I won off him."

"What does your bet with Rand have to do with Aydan?" Kane demanded.

Heat rose in my cheeks. "Never mind. So what's your plan, Skidmark?"

"Well..." He delved into the bulging rucksack again and showed us a sketchpad and a well-used set of pastels. "Portraits were never really my thing, but I can do a recognizable likeness of you. If I'm sitting in the lobby sketching, people automatically come and gawk. When your Nora comes by, I'll make sure she sees the sketch of you. If she wants to talk to you as bad as you think, she'll latch onto me."

"And then what?" Kane asked. "Rand will have a bug on her, and a locator device. You can't take her anywhere without him following."

"I'm counting on it." Skidmark grinned. "I'm going to take the lady out for lunch. And if we get a bit frisky in the cab, she might leave some clothes behind." He turned to me with a lascivious eyebrow raised. "Is she hot?"

"Skidmark, she's my *mother!*"

His grin widened. "So if she looks anything like you, she's hot." He sobered. "If you lend me that handy-dandy little device you used earlier... that was a bug detector, wasn't it?"

"Um..."

I glanced awkwardly at Kane, who showed me his unreadable cop face. Damn. My call.

I sighed. "Yes, it was a bug detector. Classified. If I manage to survive all this shit, I'll end up in prison anyway just for telling you all this."

"Hey, I don't know nothin'." Skidmark let his eyelids droop and his face slacken. "I'm just a stoned old fart."

I smiled in spite of my worries. "Yeah, right."

He snapped back to his alert self. "Anyway, I'll get her in the cab. If she wants to talk to you as bad as you say, she'll help me take any bugs and locators off her, and then we'll do a transfer. You sail up behind the cab, grab her, and take off. Rand should be a few cars back, and if we do it smooth enough he won't be able to catch you."

"I'll do that part," Kane said. "We can't risk Aydan getting captured. When we're clear of Rand, I'll bring Nora to her."

"You can't," I objected. "She doesn't know you, so she won't go with you. And even if they don't catch you when you try to grab Nora, they'll arrest you for it as soon as this is over and you try to go home. You're a civilian now, not an agent. At best, it's obstructing an investigation and kidnapping. At worst..." I swallowed hard. "...if it turns out I'm compromised and selling secrets... it's treason."

"Which changes nothing," Kane said stonily. "If you're compromised, *this* is treason." He waved a hand at the three of us.

My heart plummeted into my suddenly roiling stomach. "Oh, shit! Dammit, Skidmark, I *knew* this was a bad idea..." I sucked in a breath, my brain spinning up to maximum RPM. "Okay, here's what we're going to do. John, you're going to get in your truck and drive straight to the nearest police station. Get them to contact the Department and tell them I tried to involve you in this but you tricked me into giving you the n-" I bit off 'network key' and substituted, "...stuff I just gave you. Tell them everything you know, including my fake identity. I'll use a new one..."

My heart sank even farther. I didn't have another car. And I had used a bunch of my cash to pay for a hotel room I wouldn't be able to use.

"No," Kane said.

"Yes!" I glowered at him. "Daniel needs you. And I'm not going to let you go to prison because of my fuckup. Now get out of the car."

A small grim smile tugged at the corner of his mouth as he leaned back, crossing his arms over his chest. "Make me."

He filled the back seat. Six feet four inches of hard muscle, deadly martial arts skills, and pigheaded stubbornness.

I let my head fall against the headrest in despair. "Oh, for... Fine; you're right. I don't have any way to make you." I eased my hand down toward the trank pistol in my ankle holster as I spoke. "But, John, how are you going to deal with this? In just a few hours..." I consulted my wristwatch to direct his attention away from what my other hand was doing. "...it's going to be Daniel's bedtime. He'll be screaming for you the way he always does..." I twisted in the seat as if to face him for a more convincing argument. "...and you can't even call to tell him-"

Kane's hand shot out and clamped an iron grip on the trank pistol I'd barely raised.

"Did you really think that would work?" he asked.

I sighed and let him take the pistol. "No, but I had to try."

"Well, stop. I'm involved, and it's too late for you to get rid of me." He eyed Skidmark speculatively. "And we're going to need more help to pull this off."

"I can get Moonbeam and Karma to come down..." Skidmark began.

"No," I interrupted. "They're visiting with St-" As usual, I had to bite off 'Stemp' and substitute, "...Charles. If they've travelled all the way here for a visit and then they suddenly take off and leave him, he's going to get suspicious."

Skidmark regarded me in silence for a moment. "Don't think it really matters," he said slowly. "'Cause my kid is your Director, isn't he?"

Completely blindsided, I shot a panicked glance at Kane. His cop face was impenetrable.

But I'd already blown the whole thing.

I sank my head into my hands. "Fuck. How did you figure it out?"

Skidmark shrugged. "You keep calling him 'Stemp' instead of using his first name. You work together and trust each other, but you're not friends or lovers. And he just got suspended; and you just said your Director was having problems with the chain of command. I put two and two together. So if we have to tell him the truth, it's no big deal."

"Except that they might haul him back in for another lie detector test," I pointed out. "And then he'd either have to tell them everything; or else refuse to talk and end up getting charged with treason along with the rest of us." Skidmark paled, and I added, "So let's keep him out of the loop, okay?"

"Okay," he agreed. "Kane, you were about to suggest something?"

"Yes," Kane said. "I can get Hellhound to help."

My objection came out in a half-shout. "NO! I won't take everybody I care about down with me! And anyway, we can't contact him without Holt knowing; and Arnie's not even an agent, so he won't be able to get away from Holt."

"He has more skills than you realize," Kane said shortly. "And I know he would rather go to prison than be prevented from helping you."

"You can't know that!" I snapped. "And I already let Skidmark talk me into contacting you, which was a stupid idea..." I glared at Skidmark even though it wasn't his fault, and plunged on, "...and you came here in good faith and then discovered you couldn't back out and I feel *sick* about doing that to you! I'm not going to do it to Arnie, too!"

Kane inclined his chin in Skidmark's direction. "Thank you, Skidmark. Good call." He returned his level gaze to me. "You don't get a vote in this. Arnie and I are brothers, and I know how he feels about you. This is my duty to him."

"John, no! Please!"

"Sorry, Aydan." His lips twisted in a bittersweet smile. "I know how many times you've put your life on the line for us. You'll just have to accept it when we do the same for you."

"But that's not fair! I'm..."

Sudden sick realization closed my mouth. I had almost blurted 'I'm nothing compared to you'.

I didn't truly believe that, did I?

No, dammit, I didn't. I was plenty fucked up after my disastrous first marriage, but I still believed in my own worth.

...Didn't I?

Kane's voice snapped me back to the present. "Aydan, what's wrong?"

My mouth opened but nothing came out. I tried again, and managed a feeble croak. "I... I think I just found some programming."

Kane and Skidmark both leaned forward, their gazes hard and intent. "What is it?" Kane demanded.

"I... uh... I think Sam might have programmed me for a... a suicide mission."

CHAPTER 35

"What just happened?" Kane snapped.

I swallowed against the thickness in my throat. "I... you... when you said you would put your life on the line for me, I had a gut-deep reaction. That I should sacrifice my life for you; but never allow you to do the same for me. That your life..." I glanced at Skidmark, feeling my way through the echoes of the reaction. "Arnie's life... Skidmark's... hell, *everybody* else's life... is more important than mine."

"But you don't really believe that," Skidmark said. "'Cause if you really believed it, it wouldn't have hit you like a ton of bricks. It would have felt normal."

"Right..." I wrapped my arms around myself, fighting the tremors that rocked me. "But... it was just... *there*. So strong it was like a kick in the gut."

Kane eased back in the seat, frowning. "That might explain a few things," he said slowly.

"Like what?" Skidmark asked.

Kane's level grey gaze evaluated me, seeing deep into the dark places I'd hidden from everyone. I squirmed under the weight of it, familiar panic welling up at the thought of revealing my feelings.

I could open my body to him without hesitation, but to open my heart? The old cold terror lashed through me.

Never.

I clenched my fists. Dammit, I had already dealt with that shit. I had put it behind me and moved on.

Hadn't I?

Maybe I had no control over it at all...

As if reading my mind, Kane's eyes narrowed. "I've worked with Aydan for almost two years now. She's one of the bravest people I've ever met. She won't hesitate to lay down her life to protect others. That's admirable, but..." He hesitated, his face softening. "Sometimes I've wondered if there was more to it."

As though he'd forgotten Skidmark's presence, Kane spoke directly to me, our gazes locking together. "Aydan, I've been willing to sacrifice my life to save others, too. So has every other agent in the Department; so has Hellhound. But... even though we would die if it was necessary... we still want to live. Sometimes I've wondered whether you do."

"Of course..." I began, but a memory rose up and choked me.

Lying on icy pavement, cold searing my skin while bullets ricocheted close; too close. Outnumbered and outgunned. Knowing that horrific torture drew nearer with every bullet spent from my weapon.

Some things are worse than death.

I shook myself back to the present. "I don't think I have a death wish. I've been through a lot of shit, and if I was serious about dying I've had more than enough opportunities."

"That's true," Kane allowed.

The logical conclusion hovered in the silence between us.

I hadn't given up my life yet because I'd been programmed to die for something... or some*one*... else.

"I really need to talk to Nora," I said.

Kane sighed. "Maybe you're right. Skidmark? What do you think?"

"No way to know." Skidmark frowned at me. "Karma said it would be damn hard to program you; and I believe him. You've got some pretty strong principles."

"And some pretty bloodthirsty reflexes," I said gloomily. "And if my kneejerk reaction is to sacrifice everything to save someone else..." I eyed him, fondness aching in my heart. "If I thought somebody was threatening your life, I'd kill them on the spot."

His frown deepened. "I don't think so, girlie. I've known lots of killers; and you're not the type to shoot first. Killing is a last resort for you."

"But it wouldn't be hard to convince me it was a last resort." I kneaded my aching forehead. "I'm too used to life-or-death situations."

"Exactly. You're used to making instant judgement calls. That kind of reflex would be pretty hard to reprogram." He eyed my doubtful expression for a moment before turning back to Kane. "My vote is to call Hellhound and get this show on the road."

Kane nodded. "All right. Aydan, we need to make this count. Can you think of any way to get the lie detector without alerting the Department?"

I hissed out a breath and flopped back in the seat. "No. It'll be in Jack's secured lab and..." I trailed off as a half-formed idea floated into my brain.

"And...?" Kane prompted.

"And... I might... have an idea after all. I have Reggie's private cellphone number; and I know he believes I'm innocent. He and Jack seemed friendly with each other, so he might be able to convince her to let us borrow the lie detector for a little while..." I hesitated, thinking through the consequences. "And Holt wouldn't be monitoring them. But if they got caught, they could be charged with treason, too."

"Are you sure Chow won't report you?"

I sighed. "Pretty sure. But... not positive."

"I'll leave that decision to you, then. I'll text Hellhound."

"But Holt will have his phone tapped for sure," I objected.

"That's why I'm not texting to his personal phone," Kane replied as he extracted a burner phone from his pocket. "We set up this code system long ago." His mouth twisted. "And I should have done it with you, too; but I thought after I quit the Department..." He trailed off with a grimace and thumbed the keys of the phone. A few seconds later he turned the screen toward me with a mischievous smile.

I grinned, too, as I read aloud, "Hey, Sexy! See you tomorrow night?" As Kane pressed 'Send', I added teasingly, "I didn't know you and Arnie had a thing."

He chuckled and began to reply, but his smile vanished as the phone vibrated in his hand.

"He's compromised," Kane snapped.

My heart lurched. "How do you know? You haven't even read the message yet."

"The message is irrelevant. Let's go. Meet me in an hour at Carburn Park." Kane slid out of my car, ripped the battery out of the phone, and hurled both items into the park. As he jogged to his truck, I slapped the car into gear and accelerated for the exit.

My getaway was immediately thwarted by a solid stream of traffic. I thumped the steering wheel. "Dammit, it's rush hour! It's going to take us nearly an hour just to get all the way down to Carburn."

I spotted an opening and goosed the accelerator to slip into the gap, the car spinning and slithering around the corner to fishtail onto the street.

Right. This wasn't my all-wheel-drive Legacy.

Fortunately I hadn't lost my two-wheel-drive reflexes, and after its initial skittishness the Saturn settled comfortably into the traffic. My stomach growled, and I glanced over at Skidmark. "Are you hungry?"

"Yeah. Haven't had anything but popcorn since this morning."

"Oh my God! You must be ready to fall over!"

He gave me a bemused frown. "I'm ready to eat, but I'm fine if I don't."

"Oh."

My stomach growled again and I massaged it, wondering whether the quivering weakness creeping into my limbs was nerves, normal hunger, or some sinister invention of Sam's.

Fuck it. No matter where it came from, I still had to deal with it.

"Well, I need to eat." I spotted a fast-food restaurant and activated my turn signal. "So you get to eat, too."

"Suits me." He grinned, his flamboyantly curled moustache echoing the upward curve of his lips. "And now that I'm all dolled up, I want to borrow your clean parka again, too."

"Can't be too soon for me. Your stink has just about melted my sinuses." I pulled into a parking spot. "I don't want to go into the restaurant, so let's do the switch here and then I'll go through the drive-through."

Several minutes later we were on the road again, the car scented with the mouthwatering aromas of grease and flame-broiled meat. I wolfed down my burger one-handed while I drove, then let out a long sigh and plied a paper napkin.

"Remind me not to reach in front of you while you're eating," Skidmark remarked through a mouthful of burger. "I might lose an arm."

"Couple of fingers for sure," I agreed, and reached for my fries. "I probably couldn't get your whole arm in one bite."

"I wouldn't want to take the chance." He swallowed the last of his burger and pulled out a vanity mirror to fastidiously stroke his moustache back into position and flick a wayward crumb from his braided beard. "So what's the deal with you and Kane?"

I stared out the windshield. "Like he said, we worked together for nearly two years."

"And?"

"And nothing."

"Don't bullshit me, girlie."

I blew out a breath. "And... there's too much attraction and not enough trust. I'd put my physical safety in his hands without hesitation, but..." I trailed off.

"Why don't you trust him?"

I shot Skidmark a glare before returning my attention to the road. "Because I'm fucked up, okay? I'm done talking about this."

In my peripheral vision, I saw him nod sagely. "Right. It's all because you're fucked up."

Stupidly, I took the bait. "What the hell is that supposed to mean?"

"Couldn't have anything to do with Kane at all," Skidmark went on as though I hadn't spoken. "Nope, it's all your fault. Makes perfect sense. A guy like Kane; career army, combat veteran, agent; spent his whole life killing and trying not to get killed in return... nope, a guy like that would never have any issues of his own."

"He hasn't spent his whole life killing," I snapped. "He's risked his life to save innocent people. Over and over."

"Yeah; and what's his body count?"

"How the hell would I know?"

"How many that you know of?" Skidmark persisted. "In the two years you've known him?"

I didn't bother to add it up. It was too damn depressing. "Probably about the same as mine. Maybe more."

"So..."

"So nothing, old man. I was fucked up long before I started killing people, and you can stop with the psychological bullshit."

"Okay," he said mildly. "I'm just saying that if you're programmed to think you deserve to die for everybody else, you might have some weird programming about relationships, too."

"Thank you, Dr. Freud. Now shut up."

He nodded and complied.

Guilt started nagging at me immediately.

I sighed. "Sorry. Thanks for trying to help."

He let out a wheezy chuckle. "Wow. Less than fifteen seconds. You're a tough nut to crack."

"Shut up."

He did, but this time he was grinning.

When we arrived early at Carburn Park, there was no sign of Kane's brown truck. I parked and let the car idle, frowning out the windshield.

"Problem?" Skidmark inquired.

"Not that I know of. I'm just debating whether to try for the lie detector." I scowled at the leaden clouds glowing orange in the streetlights while snow crystals sparkled in the dark air. "Even if Reggie's willing to bring us the lie detector, he can't disappear for five hours or more without somebody asking where he's gone. Especially since the roads are so shitty. Nobody would willingly drive the highway in these conditions." I shivered, remembering how close we had come to disaster. "And I don't want him to take the risk anyway."

"Okay, but if this Reggie is on your side, couldn't he give you some strategic intel?"

"Probably not. He's working on another part of the investigation, and he wouldn't know what was going on with Holt."

"But if you trust him..."

I silenced Skidmark with a glare. "I've already dragged you and John into this clusterfuck, and probably Arnie, too. I'd like to have one friend left who won't go to prison when the shit hits the fan."

"He likely wouldn't get convicted," Skidmark argued. "If

he doesn't know anything about Holt's investigation he wouldn't know there's a warrant out for you, so they couldn't accuse him of collusion."

"I'm pretty sure he'd know about the warrant. By now everybody will know Stemp's been suspended, and they'll know why."

"So don't ask Reggie to help you." Skidmark shrugged. "Just call him and ask if he's heard what's going on. If he says yes, tell him to have a nice day, and hang up. If he says no, ask your questions. It's not his fault if your chain of command doesn't keep him in the loop."

I frowned at him, my brain twisting through the logic. Did that make sense; or did I just *want* it to make sense?

Maybe it made sense.

Or maybe I was just too tired to figure it out.

I sighed and pulled out a burner phone to text, "Hey, you lush. Call me." I was pretty sure he wouldn't have told anybody else about his excesses the other night, so he'd know it was me even though he wouldn't recognize the burner number.

My finger quivered over the Send button. Then I squeezed my eyes shut and pressed the button. When I opened my eyes, Skidmark was watching me with a self-satisfied smirk.

"What are you so happy about?" I growled. "You'll be going to prison along with everybody else if this blows up."

He snorted. "What the hell do I care? A life sentence for me wouldn't amount to more than a few years anyway. When I get sick enough they'll put me in the hospital, and then I'll have a warm bed, pain control, and three square meals a day until I die. Not a bad deal."

My heart clenched at the thought of him gasping his life away alone in a prison hospital bed, and his face softened.

"Hey." He patted my hand. "Don't look so miserable. We all gotta go sometime."

I swallowed hard. "I know, but I just..."

My burner phone vibrated and I accepted the call from Reggie's number, already second-guessing my decision to contact him.

What if Holt had been monitoring Reggie's phone after all? What if he was standing right behind Reggie while we talked, taking notes for evidence while the analysts traced the call right to Carburn Park?

"Hey, bee-yotch," Reggie drawled. "Swiped any classified shit lately?"

"Uh..." Anxiety clamped icy fingers around my throat. "H-Have a nice day," I croaked, and hung up.

As Skidmark gave me a worried frown, my phone vibrated again. Then again.

"Answer it," Skidmark urged.

"This is a bad idea," I muttered, and pressed the 'Talk' button.

Reggie was already in full cry. "...and answer the fucking phone, you fucking moronic-"

"Hello?" I interrupted.

"What the fuck was that? I bust my ass to run out of the building into the fucking freezing cold so nobody can hear us, and all you can say is *'Have a nice fucking day'*?"

"Sorry," I mumbled. "I thought this was a good idea but I've changed my mind. Just tell Holt I called you but didn't tell you anything. 'Bye."

As I lowered the phone, Reggie's frantic yelp floated to

my ears.

"Help! They're going to kill me!"

CHAPTER 36

I jerked the phone back to my ear. "*What? Where are you? Do you have your gun? Who's trying to kill you?*"

"Why did you call me?" Reggie demanded. "And don't worry, this line is secure."

"*Who's trying to kill you?*"

"Nobody. I just didn't want you to hang up."

I fell back in the driver's seat, pressing my hand over my thundering heart. "You asshole! You scared the hell out of me!"

"Sorry," he said, but I could hear the unrepentant grin in his voice. "So why did you call me? And don't give me any bullshit."

I sighed. "I need to use the lie detector but I can't come into the Department. I was originally wondering if you could talk to Jack about it but now I've decided it's too dangerous, so just forget the whole thing. Thanks for running outside. I'm sorry you're freezing your ass off for nothing."

He ignored my apology. "Holt took Jack and the lie detector back to Calgary."

My heart sank like a lump of lead. Somebody was getting questioned.

And Kane hadn't arrived yet.

"*Fuck!*" I dealt the steering wheel a vicious blow, then shot a fearful glance around the deserted parking lot. What if Kane had been forced to divulge our meeting place? I hurriedly added, "Thanks, Reggie. I have to go."

"Call me if you want Jack to meet you somewhere. If she can, she will. We believe in you."

A lump rose in my throat. "Thanks. 'Bye." I disconnected and ripped the battery out of the phone.

"What's wrong?" Skidmark demanded.

"They might have gotten Kane..."

The words strangled in my throat as a brown half-ton turned into the parking lot.

Was Kane leading Holt to us?

My hand hovered over the door lock as the truck parked beside us. Should I run?

But I could never elude Holt and Kane if they had joined forces...

As though reading my mind, Skidmark said, "He wouldn't rat you out. Bet on it."

"He has a son to consider. Daniel is his top priority."

"Maybe, but he still wouldn't rat you out."

Kane slid into the back seat and every muscle in my body went rigid with the need to flee.

"Who wouldn't rat us out?" Kane asked.

"What did you do since you left the park?" Skidmark countered.

Kane frowned. "I drove to a bus stop near the University of Calgary and used a burner phone to call Alicia so I could talk to Daniel and explain that I wouldn't be home tonight. When the bus arrived, I planted the phone on its rear bumper and drove away. I drove an evasive pattern to be sure I hadn't been followed; then went through a drive-through for some food and came here. Why?"

"You didn't see or talk to anybody else?" Skidmark persisted.

"I saw hundreds of people, but nobody I recognized; and I talked to Alicia, Daniel, and the Wendy's drive-through employee." Kane's voice hardened. "Why?"

Some of the tension seeped out of my body. "Because Holt's here in Calgary with the lie detector."

"So they're questioning someone," Kane deduced immediately. "But not me. If they'd been questioning me it would have taken much longer than an hour."

"Right, of course." I gave him and Skidmark a sheepish smile. "Sorry, I'm just being paranoid."

"As you should," Kane said. "But since Holt couldn't catch me, I can guess who he would have picked up for questioning."

Comprehension dawned, and my stomach twisted. "Shit. Arnie. That's why he didn't give the right response to your text."

"Probably." Kane shrugged. "Don't worry; he doesn't know anything. When we last talked, he had just found out from Stemp that you'd been assigned to an off-grid mission. He didn't trust Stemp so he's been moving heaven and earth trying to find you; but he didn't expect to hear from you and he's completely in the dark."

"Except for your mysterious text," I said, my voice as hollow as my chest. "Holt's too good an agent to miss that. He'll ask Arnie who it was from; Arnie will say something like 'an old friend', which will be true; but Holt's next question will be 'Is it Kane'. And there's no way to fool the lie detector."

"True, but that's where the interrogation would end. Hellhound would just stop talking."

"So Holt would know for sure that he was hiding something." My guts wrenched at the memory of Arnie tied to a chair, his wonderful hands mutilated beyond repair, suffering horribly...

"Aydan." Kane's big hand closed on my shoulder shook me back to the present. "Hellhound will be all right. He's with the good guys. Holt won't torture him."

I sucked in a gulp of air, fighting tears of residual horror mixed with relief. "Right. Flashback." My voice wobbled and I swallowed hard to steady it. "Sorry."

"It's all right. Understandable." Kane cupped my cheek in a gentle palm for a moment before leaning back again. "Actually," he went on thoughtfully, "It might be good if Holt is interrogating Hellhound. We know Hellhound will never betray us, but Holt will waste hours trying to break him. And while Holt's doing that, he can't chase us."

"I guess." My voice came out small. "But Arnie will get arrested and charged with obstructing an investigation, and he hasn't even done anything wrong."

Kane gave me a grim smile. "None of us have. Yet."

"And you shouldn't!" I twisted to face him fully. "John, please just go to the police!"

He stiffened and I braced myself for his wrath, but instead he drew a vibrating burner phone out of his pocket and frowned at it.

"It's Hellhound," he said, and turned the screen toward me.

I read aloud, "Hey babe wanna rock n roll 2nite?" I added, "Is that the right code? Does it mean he's... okay now?"

Kane popped the battery out of the phone and rolled down the window to toss both pieces into a nearby trash can, making a perfect two-point shot. "There's no 'right' code. The words could be anything; it's the protocol that matters. We have several burner phones we keep in reserve. We've both memorized the numbers, and the initial text goes to one of them. If a reply comes from the phone that received the text, it's a signal that we're compromised. If we're clear to communicate, we reply from a different phone to a different predesignated number."

I sat up, stowing that little gem in my mental spy manual for future use. "Brilliant. So if somebody was coercing you, they'd either prevent you from replying at all, or else force you to reply as though nothing's wrong. And if you're under surveillance, it looks normal to reply to an incoming text. But any reply is the wrong answer."

Kane nodded and withdrew another burner phone from his pocket. "But this is the last predesignated one I have on me. If we need more, I'll have to raid one of my caches."

"So this had better work," Skidmark said.

"Yes." Kane's thumbs tapped rapidly over the keys. "If he wants to join us we'll implement one of our extraction strategies. Between the three of us we shouldn't have any trouble getting him away from any pursuers."

"I still don't think this is a good idea," I protested.

"You don't get a vote," Skidmark said. "Sorry, girlie."

I hissed out a breath of tense irritation, but since my options had apparently dwindled to throwing a tantrum or not, I decided to save my energy.

After a brief exchange of texts, Kane looked up with a satisfied nod. "All right, we're on. The location is one of those convoluted residential areas composed of concentric circles with only one egress for traffic; but it has several walkways through it to surrounding commercial areas. Hellhound will drive into the neighbourhood expecting to be followed. We'll be in position with our vehicles on the commercial side. He'll leave his vehicle as though he's walking to one of the houses, but instead he'll dive down the footpath. The commercial area has fast access for escape in any direction, so we only have to make sure nobody spots our vehicles. The two of you will drive, and I'll be waiting near the commercial side of the footpath. If anyone pursues him on foot, I'll take them out when he emerges through the choke point."

I gulped. "Um... when you say 'take out'... I hope you mean with my trank pistol...?"

"Of course." Kane frowned. "These are our fellow agents. I don't want to cause bodily harm."

"Okay, just checking." I didn't point out that since he'd quit the Department, they weren't exactly his fellow agents anymore.

They might not be mine much longer, either.

The thought formed a cold lump in my stomach.

When we pulled into the busy parking lot an hour later, my guts knotted at the sight of all the vehicles. Pedestrians everywhere. How could we make a fast escape?

I eased out a slow breath and reined in the frantic

bookkeeper inside my skull.

Settle down. We're not going to make a fast escape; we're going to make an unobtrusive escape. Not the same thing at all. The only tricky part would be making sure Hellhound's pursuer, or pursuers, didn't see him getting into the Saturn. After that we'd be anonymous among all the other cars.

My guts tightened another notch. What if Holt had pulled out all the stops and sent an armed team after Hellhound?

Would they shoot when they realized he was escaping?

My heart flinched from the thought.

The map we'd consulted earlier hovered in my mind, and I steered toward the footpath just as Skidmark pointed in the same direction and said, "That should be it. Far as possible from the entrance to the neighbourhood."

I found a spot a short distance away from the fence and parked. A few rows over, Kane steered the brown half-ton into another parking spot.

When Kane approached, I popped the door locks. As he slid into the back, I asked, "Are you sure Arnie's phone wasn't tapped?"

"Not positive," Kane replied. "But even if it was, Holt has no way of knowing where he's going. Neither of us mentioned the location except with a code reference. Holt will have no choice but to follow."

"I just hope he doesn't have a helicopter up."

Kane's lips tightened. "If Hellhound sees a helicopter he'll abort, but I think that's unlikely. Hellhound wouldn't have contacted us if he had doubts about his ability to get clear. And if Holt was suspicious, Hellhound would still be under interrogation; or else under arrest."

I followed his line of reasoning, hoping it was true. "So Holt must believe he's innocent. So he likely won't pull out all the stops to follow him."

"Let's hope not."

I grimaced. "Or Holt's just letting him go to see if he'll lead the way to us."

Kane gave me a grim smile. "That's what I'd do. Skidmark, here are the truck keys." He handed them over, then gave me a commanding look. "If Hellhound or I can't make it to the vehicles for any reason, drive away and leave us. If you spot anything, and I mean *anything* unusual at all, drive away and leave us. Clear?"

I nodded and told an incomplete truth. "Clear."

'Clear'; but not 'agreed'. There was no damn way I was going to leave them.

Kane turned to Skidmark. "Clear?"

"Yep." Skidmark opened the car door. "Give me time to get to the truck and catch my breath before you move."

"All right." Kane glanced at his watch, looking composed as always, but I read tension in the gesture. As the door closed behind Skidmark, Kane added, "I'm going to get in position. We're early, but not by much. Nice and tight, just the way I like it."

He reached for the door handle but I snagged his sleeve, an involuntary grin pulling at the corners of my mouth. "Really? That's your exit line?"

He stared blankly at me as though mentally replaying his previous sentence. Then a naughty answering smile spread across his face and his voice coasted down into a panty-vibrating rumble as he leaned toward me. "Truer words were never spoken."

I sucked in a breath of Kane-scented air, hot blood rushing to places it had no business going. Dammit, why had I said that?

"Well... I guess, um..." My voice came out breathless despite my best efforts to stay detached. His intense grey gaze sucked me in, and I teetered on the edge of disaster for a long moment before we toppled toward each other.

The kiss melted all thought from my mind. Hard and urgent, softening into a hot and hungry exploration as luscious as dark chocolate...

I jerked back, my head spinning.

"Uh..." I tried again, but words failed me. I licked my lips, savouring the delicious remnants of sensation.

Only inches away, Kane's dilated eyes locked onto my mouth and a growl rumbled from his chest. Or maybe it was a groan.

No, that was me.

"Um..." I swallowed hard. "I... I guess you'd better go. Stay safe."

"You, too." Kane pressed another short, hard kiss to my lips and got out of the car.

He strode away, his gait as easy and confident as always. Just a pedestrian among many others, but his movement in the opposite direction from the mall might as well have come with a spotlight and alarm bells.

Nobody gave him a second glance.

I stared around the parking lot. How could people not notice a man of Kane's stature getting out of a car to walk *away* from a mall during Christmas-shopping season? If I were in their shoes, I would have been instantly on the alert.

Letting out a small breath, I forced myself to lean back in the seat. That was only my guilty conscience. Or maybe I was finally developing some actual spy skills. Hooray.

And anyway, it wasn't as though Kane had any other choice. He would have been even more noticeable if he'd been furtively slinking among the vehicles in the darkness. Even the most oblivious civilian would notice that.

When Kane reached the tall fence that separated the residential neighbourhood from the commercial area, he slowed, then took out his phone and trailed absently to a halt as he stared at it.

Keeping his gaze on the phone, he wandered over to loiter near the walkway as though completely absorbed.

I shot a glance over to the brown truck. Skidmark was behind the wheel, slouched down with his arms crossed over his chest and his head drooping. Just an old man grabbing a nap in his truck while his wife was in the mall.

My heart thudded against my ribs, all my senses keyed up to tingling readiness. I pressed my palm against the butt of my Glock, but it didn't reassure me as much as usual. Kane had my trank pistol. Bullets were my only remaining option.

If Kane's or Hellhound's lives were at stake, would I shoot at my own colleagues?

I didn't know.

CHAPTER 37

I stared out the windshield, my gaze locked on the empty walkway where Hellhound would appear. Afraid to blink, I watched for so long that my vision began to blur white.

I blinked.

No, that wasn't my vision; that was snow, dammit. The fine crystals that had spangled the air earlier were thickening.

Over by the fence, Kane shifted his position and wiped the face of his phone, still staring down at it as though there were nothing more important in the world than a text conversation that kept him standing out in the darkness at thirty below.

At least the heat inside my car melted the snow as it hit the windshield; but it wouldn't for much longer...

Was that a flicker of movement at the far end of the walkway?

I powered down the window and strained my eyes, my pulse pounding.

Hellhound's bulky black-clad figure hurtled into view. My heart lurched as another man appeared behind him, legs pistoning as he skidded around the corner and nearly fell, then righted himself to dash in pursuit.

He was gaining.

A hard lump of fear closed my throat.

Hellhound was nearly at the mouth of the walkway. Kane dropped to a crouch, the trank pistol rising.

Hellhound's pursuer yanked a gun from his pocket and his words carried clearly through my open window. *"Stop or I'll shoot!"*

Hellhound kept running.

His pursuer put on a burst of speed, his gun hand bouncing wildly with every step. I could only watch, my muscles knotted. Surely he wouldn't fire toward a crowded parking lot?

But he was only a few yards behind Hellhound...

Hellhound cleared the walkway, and an instant later Kane's dart found its mark as the pursuer sprinted past his position. The man collapsed, his momentum carrying him forward in a boneless tumble that was probably going to leave some spectacular bruises. I would have winced in sympathy, but there was no time.

I stuck my arm out the window and waved, and Hellhound altered course toward me. Kane sprang to the fallen man, crouching to check his throat for a pulse. A few moments later Hellhound wrenched open the passenger door and dove inside. Kane fled for the half-ton.

I backed out of the parking spot, using all my self-control to maintain a sedate pace while I idled toward the exit. In my rear-view mirror, I spotted Kane vaulting into the passenger seat of his truck. Then the half-ton was on the move, too, winding at a leisurely pace through the parking lot toward a different exit.

The huddled heap on the sidewalk looked very alone. My heart clenched and I fought the urge to turn back.

Waiting at the red light, I glanced in my mirror again in time to see another figure pelt up the walkway to slide to its knees beside the fallen man. After a brief examination the second man stood, head flung up as though scanning the crowded parking lot. A moment later his shoulders slumped and his hand went to his ear. Calling in their failure.

Poor bastards. Holt was going to be livid.

"Who the hell was chasin' me?" Hellhound demanded.

I sighed. "One of the good guys."

"Shit. Think he's okay?" Hellhound inquired anxiously, craning his neck to peer in the rear-view mirror as well.

"Yeah. Kane checked him, and so did the second guy. They didn't start CPR or anything so he's probably fine." I let out a shaky breath. "I'm glad you're all right."

"Glad you are, too." Hellhound leaned over to drop a kiss on my lips. "Hey, darlin', nice disguise. I always wanted to get it on with a babe in a babushka."

The light turned green and I laughed as I drove forward, relaxing into the comfort of our companionship. "You've always wanted to get it on with every woman you've ever seen."

He feigned deep thought, his eyes twinkling. "Nah, not all of 'em."

I gave a start of mock surprise. "What? You mean there's actually something that turns you *off*?"

"Jeez, darlin', you're killin' me here. I got discriminatin' taste, ya know."

"In your mouth, maybe. In women, not so much."

He drew himself up, grinning. "I'll have ya know I

turned down a chick just last week."

"Seriously? Why? Was it a guy in drag?"

"Nah, an actual chick." He hesitated. "'Least, far's I know. Didn't get far enough with her to be positive."

"Do tell. What turned you off? I thought 'female', 'human', and 'over twenty-one' were your only criteria."

He gave me a sheepish grin. "Well, ya got me there, darlin'. She was over twenty-one, but just. Think I'm gonna hafta raise my age limit. She had her tongue down my throat an' her hand down my pants an' everythin' was goin' great; an' then she got a text from her BFF an' stopped the whole show while they texted for five minutes. So I walked her to the door." He shook his head. "Damn kids."

"That poor stupid child," I said. "If she only knew what she'd missed, she'd be kicking herself 'til she was old and grey."

Hellhound snorted. "Doubt it. Saw her the next night wrapped around some other guy. She ain't even gonna remember who she did last night, let alone last week."

"Well, you're probably lucky she got the text, then, or you might have ended up with a gift that keeps on giving."

"Yeah..."

When I glanced over, he was frowning.

"Everything okay?" I asked.

"Yeah."

"...But...?" I prompted.

"Later, darlin'. Tell me what's goin' on. Kane said ya needed help, but he didn't tell me ya were in shit with the good guys."

Guilt squeezed my chest. "I'm sorry. I didn't want to drag you into it, but Kane wouldn't listen and he called you anyway."

"Good. I owe him one. So what's up?"

My mind racing, I hesitated.

Could I protect him? So far he had only gone to meet a friend and then fled from an unidentified gunman. He hadn't committed any crime unless he knowingly chose to help me.

Which he would do without hesitation as soon as I explained everything, dammit.

Could I keep him in the dark?

I needed a plan. Stall.

I sighed. "It's complicated. I'll tell you after you tell me what's bothering you."

"Darlin', I'm more worried about you. What's happenin'?"

"First tell me what's bothering you."

"Nothin' big. We can talk about it later."

"Now," I insisted. "The sooner you give in and tell me, the sooner you'll get to know what's happening."

He groaned. "You're too stubborn for your own good, darlin'."

I shot him my fiercest glare before returning my attention to the traffic. "You know it. So spit it out. When I made that crack about getting an STD you got all quiet. Is there something you need to tell me?"

"Nah, ya don't need to worry about that. You're right, there's somethin' botherin' me a bit. Now ain't really the time, but... since ya won't brief me 'til I give it up..." He hesitated and his hand crept over to rest on my thigh, whether giving comfort or seeking it, I wasn't sure.

"What is it?" I asked.

"Well..." He hesitated again before continuing, "Life's been pretty good since you an' I made our deal. An' ya know I said a while ago that I been feelin' kinda guilty about pickin' up chicks 'cause I don't wanna take a chance on catchin' somethin' an' passin' it on to ya..."

Another pause.

Shit, I didn't like the sound of this.

He finished slowly, "This chick's the only one I've brought home in over a year."

Sudden anxiety seized me, but I managed not to tense. "Well, at least you're still trying," I joked feebly.

"Yeah..." he agreed in the same uncertain tone that had set off my alarm bells in the first place.

My belly knotted as I glanced over at his troubled expression and recalled Kane's words: *I know how he feels about you.*

Oh God, no. Please don't let this go where I think it's going...

"So, um... what..." I cleared my throat and tried again. "What's bothering you?"

"So last week I'm sittin' there with this half-naked chick," Hellhound began obliquely, "...an' I'm hot an' ready, 'cause, hello; half-naked chick, right?" He gave me a lascivious bounce of his eyebrows, but there was no twinkle in his eyes.

I forced a laugh despite my worry. "Right."

A horn blared nearby and I jerked my attention back to the road, but I couldn't help sneaking another glance over in time to see Hellhound sober.

That was enough to make me want to stare out the windshield permanently. If he was getting serious about us...

My throat felt as though demanding hands were slowly

closing around it.

Hellhound went on, "So I'm lookin' at this hot young chick sittin' there topless an' textin', an' I'm thinkin', 'Ya know what, Helmand? This's bullshit'. So I kicked her out. I been tellin' myself it's only 'cause she was more interested in her phone than me, an' that was part of it, but... I dunno if that's all of it."

"What..." My voice came out in a fearful whisper. "What are you trying to say?"

"I'm sayin' I need to get laid real bad." He chuckled, but it wasn't his usual easy laughter.

"And...?" I couldn't look at him.

"An'..." His hand tightened on my thigh. "Don't freak out, darlin', 'cause I been doin' enough a' that for both of us. But... as long's we still got our deal, it kinda looks like... I'm off the one-night stands, at least for a little while." He added hurriedly, "But only if we still got our deal; an' nothin' more than our deal. Not now, not ever."

My taut muscles relaxed and I squeezed his hand, my relief overflowing into a torrent of words meant to reassure myself as much as him. "We've still got our deal. No commitment, no lies. You do whatever makes you feel good, and so will I. I love what we've got and I don't want to change a thing."

Still babbling uncontrollably, I made a face. "Good God, could you imagine us trying to be a couple? Even if we somehow got over our commitment phobias, we'd still drive each other nuts. I'm a morning person; you sleep half the day and stay out half the night. You love the bar scene; I hate crowds. You're all music all the time; and mostly I just want silence. And we both need more personal space than any house could hold. We'd be a total disaster together. But we're perfect the way we are." I finally managed to shut up.

The tension went out of him on a long breath, his face easing into a cautious smile. "Glad ya think so."

"I do." I clutched his hand harder. "You scared the shit out of me. I was afraid you were going to tell me you wanted commitment."

Hellhound laughed, a real laugh this time. "Christ, bite your tongue, darlin'! Never gonna happen. I'm still freakin' out a bit 'cause this's the first time I ever felt like maybe I oughta think about somebody besides myself, but... I think I'm kinda okay with it. So far." He chuckled. "It'll prob'ly go straight out the window the next time some cute chick gives me a smile. But I wanted ya to know up front so ya didn't find out later an' get the wrong idea."

"Thanks, Arnie. I might have, but I'm okay now."

He smiled and lifted my hand to brush a whiskery kiss across my knuckles. "Then we're good, darlin'. Now, tell me what kinda shit you're in."

Dammit, I had been so caught up in our conversation that I hadn't come up with any way to keep him ignorant and innocent.

But I was only postponing the inevitable. Even if I didn't brief him, Kane would.

Shit.

With a sinking feeling, I launched into as much of the sorry tale as I could tell without mentioning Sam by name or including any information about the brainwave-driven network.

By the time I finished, Hellhound wore such a fearsome scowl that if I hadn't known and trusted him I would have bailed out of the car in the middle of traffic without even braking.

"So you're tellin' me..." He ground out the words like a gravel crusher. "...that your fuckin' piss-poor excuse for a mother let some fuckin' *sicko*..." His voice was rising. "...*get into your head*..." He stopped to suck in a hard breath, and I was pretty sure I could hear his teeth grinding. After a couple of slow inhalations, he finished in a deadly quiet voice. "...when ya were just a little innocent kid?"

"It sounds that way, but I don't know for sure yet." I kept my gaze on the street.

"THAT FUCKIN' WHORIN' CUNT!" Hellhound's sudden bellow galvanized my already-tense muscles into a violent twitch, and he instantly gentled his tone. "Sorry, darlin'. Didn't mean to scare ya. I'm just... so fuckin' *pissed off* at her..." He drew another breath. "What the hell kinda sick bitch does that to her own kid?"

"It's not as bad as it sounds," I equivocated. "There's a lot of stuff I can't tell you, and it would all make more sense if you knew the whole story. And, anyway, we don't even know for sure if she's my real mother."

"But ya think she is."

I sighed. "Probably... maybe... shit, I don't know. She was pretty convincing. And the way she told it, she was trying to save me from something even worse."

"What the hell could be worse than rippin' your heart out thinkin' she died when ya were barely more than a kid, an' runnin' off with some asshole with never a fuckin' word to ya for *thirty fuckin' years?* An' then showin' up pretendin' she loves ya? What the hell's worse than that?"

I shivered. "I'm afraid to find out."

CHAPTER 38

Hellhound reached over to give my thigh a comforting squeeze. "It'll be okay, darlin'. We'll figure it out, you an' me an' Kane."

"And Skidmark," I reminded him.

Hellhound laughed. "That ol' shithead. Him an' Moonbeam an' Karma bein' agents; who'd 'a thought? I oughta slap the ol' buzzard upside the head for gettin' under my skin like he did at the commune."

I grinned. "It's what he does best. And wait 'til you see him now, all cleaned up as Brenton Carlisle."

"Where're we gonna meet them?"

I nodded toward the bright lights and congested traffic ahead. "Chinook Centre parking lot. It'll be a total madhouse, so nobody will pay any attention to us. It'll be another hour before the mall closes, and even then the theatre will still be open so we can stay as long as we want without anybody looking twice."

"Sounds good." He leaned back in the seat with a sigh and flexed his legs. "Shit, darlin'; guess I better rev up some runnin' workouts. I'm outta shape again."

I ran an appreciative hand over his muscular thigh. "If

that's 'out of shape', I can't imagine what 'in shape' would look like."

"I dunno. Every year I gotta work harder just to keep from losin' ground." He sighed again. "I'm starin' down the big five-oh next month. Maybe I'm gettin' too old for this."

I glanced at his troubled profile. "Are you thinking about quitting?"

"Dunno. I never wanted to kill people for a livin', but I did anyway for the last thirty-odd years. An' now..." His fist clenched as his words slowed. "I'm afraid... maybe... I need to."

"What do you mean?" I made the turn into the mall parking lot and added, "Keep your eyes peeled for a parking spot somewhere in the southwest corner." He nodded, and I went on, "Do you need the income? Or is it something else?"

Hellhound tensed, averting his face as if fully absorbed in searching for the elusive parking spot. "Don't really need any more money," he said to the window. "I been investin' since I was eighteen, an' I'm gonna have a good pension from the Forces; plus I got my PI business an' a bunch a' music gigs. I could quit tomorrow if I wanted."

"But?" I probed gently.

"But... I..." His voice dropped almost to a whisper. "I dunno... if I can stop. What if..." He glanced over for an instant with anguished eyes before turning to stare out the window again. "I said earlier that life's been good lately, an' it has. I feel... almost... normal, ya know? I got Hooker an' Miz Lacey to look after; an' I got you an' Kane; an' I don't spend so much time worryin' about losin' control an' hurtin' somebody..." He drew a deep breath. "...but... what if I only feel that way 'cause I know there's always gonna be somebody else that needs killin', an' I can let it out on my next job? What if I stop, an' it builds up... an'... I can't control it..."

He fell silent with an audible swallow.

My heart broke.

Ignoring the cars around us, I braked to a halt and reached over to turn his face to me. "Arnie..." I caressed his cheek.

What reassurance could I offer? Maybe he was right.

"I honestly don't think that would happen," I began, groping for the right words. "I know you don't like killing, and I don't believe it's a safety valve for you. But... if you found out you needed it... you could always go back."

His face twisted and he shrank away from my touch. "How can ya even say that? Like it's a fuckin' hobby, like... like... fuckin' stamp collectin' or somethin'? Aydan, I fuckin' *kill* people!"

"You said it yourself: You kill people who need killing," I said gently. "We both have to do that, whether we like it or not." I suddenly realized what was truly bothering him, and added, "If you needed to go back, it wouldn't change the way I feel about you. John would understand, too."

"You're wrong," he said flatly. "If either of ya knew, really knew, what I am inside..." He trailed off without finishing the sentence.

"Arnie." I cupped his face with both hands, willing him to see the truth in my eyes. "I know exactly what you are. I've seen The Killer, remember? And I've seen The Animal, too. It didn't change a thing for me. Nothing will."

"It should."

I sighed. "Maybe if I was normal it would. But

remember, we're so good together because our fucked-up pieces fit, not because we're all rainbows and unicorns inside."

Hellhound barked out a mirthless laugh. "Got that right." He stared out the windshield for a moment, old ghosts haunting his gaze. Then he let out a long breath. "Okay, darlin'. I'm gonna believe ya for now, an' hope like hell you're right. But..." He gripped my hand, his gaze boring into mine. "Will ya keep your promise? That if I ever get outta control, you'll shoot to kill?"

"Yes," I said, because I knew he needed to hear it.

"Swear it?" His tormented gaze demanded the truth.

I stiffened my shoulders against the pain in my heart and met his eyes squarely with a lie.

"Yes."

But maybe it was the truth.

I sent a fervent plea to all the gods that I'd never have to find out.

Arnie squeezed his eyes shut and pressed my hand to his lips. "Thanks, darlin'."

The blare of a car horn catapulted me out of our private bubble. Amazingly, a car had backed out of a space directly in front of us. I turned in, leaving the irate driver behind me to continue his quest for a parking spot.

I shifted into Park and leaned back in the seat, rolling my head in an attempt to ease my aching muscles. Hellhound reached over to massage my neck and I let my head fall forward with a moan.

After a few minutes of gentle kneading, he spoke. "So, how ya doin' with all this?"

"So much better. Don't stop," I mumbled.

He chuckled and kept massaging. "I meant, how ya doin' with all the shit you're dealin' with right now?"

"I'm okay."

"You're lyin'."

I sighed. "Yeah. I'm so terrified I can't even think about it without needing to scream and run and throw up all at the same time. So I'm not thinking about it. I'm just focusing on the next thing I have to do."

"Good plan. Easier'n cleanin' puke off your parka." His fingers stilled on my neck. "There they are."

I sat up in time to see the tail end of the brown half-ton disappearing around the next row of vehicles. "Did they see us?"

"Think so. Give 'em a minute an' see if they park."

"I hope they can get close. Skidmark's having a hard time breathing in the cold. We should walk to the truck."

"Sit tight, darlin'," Hellhound advised. "Four people in this little car are gonna look funny enough. Four of us tryin' to cram into a half-ton cab'd attract too much attention. 'Specially if we hadta drive somewhere. The cops'd pull us over, an' it'd blow the whole thing."

We watched as the half-ton circled the lot, patiently inching along the rows.

At last they found a spot. The two of them trudged over, Kane shortening his strides to accommodate Skidmark's slow progress. When they got into the back seat Skidmark's breathing was rapid, but not the uncontrolled gasping of earlier in the day. His medication must be working. Thank God.

Hellhound twisted in the seat to eyeball him. "Well, ya ol' fuck, ya sure as hell had me fooled."

Skidmark grinned. "Thanks, bro. I felt kind of bad about it at the time." His grin widened. "But not that bad, since you threatened to shove a joint down my throat."

"Shoulda done it, too," Hellhound grumbled, but a smile lurked in his beard.

"Has Aydan brought you up to speed?" Kane asked Hellhound.

"Yeah. So we're gonna snatch the fuckin' bitch of a mother." Hellhound bared his teeth in something that was definitely not a smile. "Lookin' forward to that. I got a few things to say to her."

Skidmark widened his eyes at me. "Christ, you're not going to let Frankendude near her, are you? You'll scare the poor woman to death before she can answer any questions."

"Fuck off with the insults, old man," I snapped.

"Ah." Skidmark smiled and nodded as though I'd uttered something profoundly enlightening. "So you're still sweet on Frankendude, too."

"Skidmark..." I clenched my fists and took a deep calming breath. "You can play nicely with the rest of the team, or you can get out of this car and start walking back to Silverside right now. Your choice."

"I only have to take a cab to where I left your car. After that I can drive myself," he pointed out reasonably.

"Nnngh!" I clenched a handful of my kerchief to prevent myself from reaching between the seats and throttling him.

"Relax, darlin'." Hellhound's palm made gentle circles on my back. "The ol' goat's just stirrin' the pot like he always does."

"He's right," Skidmark agreed, looking repentant. "Sorry, Storm." He inclined his chin at Hellhound. "Sorry, bro. I've been playing this role so damn long I don't even remember anymore where the act ends and the real me starts."

"No problem," Hellhound replied. "So... how are we gonna grab the bitch?"

It was a short discussion with only one logical solution. Despite my efforts to deter my co-conspirators, they developed a plan that left me clutching my head in despair.

"I don't like it," I said for approximately the fifth time. "You're all going to end up in prison."

"I won't," Skidmark replied confidently. "I'm Brenton Carlisle. I'll play innocent. If we get caught, I'll just tell them I was taking a nice lady to lunch when we got carjacked."

"And how will you explain the portrait of me in your sketchbook?" I demanded. "And the bug detector? And the fact that Ian will recognize you as soon as he looks closely at you?"

"I'll bet you fifty bucks Rand won't blow my cover even if he does recognize me. When a guy like that makes a promise, he keeps it." Skidmark raised a significant eyebrow. "The bug detector will probably get lost in the struggle; and as for the portrait, well, I was just coming in the back door of the hotel when I spotted this striking redhead running away. The way she moved..." He cast his gaze heavenwards with a rapturous sigh. "Like a hunting panther. Such power. Such grace. I just had to capture it."

My face went hot. "You're so full of shit, old man."

He grinned. "I'm not kidding. You really do move like that. Just like Moonbeam, sexy as hell. But more importantly, it'll take me off the hot seat while they run around trying to figure out how you managed to hang around the hotel without them seeing you."

"O... kay..." I said slowly. "That might work. Maybe. But John and Arnie are screwed no matter what."

Kane shrugged. "I'm willing to take the chance."

"Me, too," Hellhound agreed.

Lacking the space to wave my arms in the small car, I settled for a loud growl. "Don't you get it?" I demanded. "You're not taking a chance at all! You're absolutely, one-hundred-percent *guaranteed* to get arrested! There is no situation where you come out of this without getting charged with kidnapping at best, and treason at worst!"

"Sure there is," Hellhound argued. "If the plan works, we're golden. We get our answers an' drop the bitch off with a cell phone so she can call Rand to pick her up. If she wants to talk to ya as bad as ya say, she'll be grateful. She won't rat us out."

"I wish you'd stop calling her 'the bitch'," I mumbled. "She might be my mother."

"Sorry, darlin'." Hellhound reached over to squeeze my hand, but he and Kane exchanged a worried look.

"What?" I asked.

They eyed each other in silence for a moment. Then Hellhound nodded as though they'd reached an unspoken agreement.

"We're still concerned that you may be compromised," Kane said. "It's understandable that you want to give her the benefit of the doubt, but it's also worrisome. If you've been programmed to believe her even in the face of logic and evidence to the contrary, then this mission is doomed to failure from the start."

"Exactly my point," I snapped. "It's a dumb idea. Let's call the whole thing off. You guys go to the police and report everything. I'll get to Nora some other way or I'll fail on my own, but at least you won't go down with me."

The three men exchanged another glance. "Good enough for me," Skidmark said.

"Me, too," Hellhound seconded.

Kane blew out a short breath. "All right. It's agreed."

I slumped, my guts hollowing with a mixture of relief and desolation. I held my voice steady. "Thank you. Just give me half an hour's head start, and-"

Hellhound chuckled. "Ya ain't gettin' it, darlin'. We just agreed that we're in, not out."

"What?" I stared at them, consternation fighting hope. "But you said..."

"I said it's good enough for me," Skidmark said. "What I meant was, if you're dead set against it, we know we're not playing into any of your programming." He shrugged. "It still might not work, but I'm in. Give me the bug detector and then you can drop me at the Palliser so I can check in for the night."

"No!" I began, my voice rising.

Kane interrupted before I could get started. "Skidmark, can you do portraits from a description?"

"I can try."

"Good." Kane turned to Hellhound. "Let's trade places. Work with Skidmark to create sketches of Grandin, Dirk, and Nora. Both he and I need to know what they look like."

Skidmark extracted his sketchpad and pastels, and Hellhound got out to take Kane's place in the back seat while

Kane slid in beside me. The resulting blast of arctic air made me turn the heater up to maximum.

Eyeing the frost building up on the insides of the windows, I cranked up the fan to top speed as well.

"Lucky there are so many cars in this parking lot," I said over the roar of rushing air. "The way we're steaming up this car, I'm half-expecting some outraged parent to knock on the glass and tell us to stop making out in public."

"Hell with that," Hellhound retorted. "You an' Kane can get it on if ya want, but I wouldn't touch this ol' goat with a ten-foot pole."

"You only wish you had a ten-foot pole," Skidmark gibed.

Hellhound grinned. "I ain't had any complaints about my pole yet."

After a few more good-natured barbs, they settled down to work. As soon as they were fully absorbed by widths of jaws and lengths of noses, I lowered my voice and went to work on Kane.

"John, I can't let you do this."

He gave me his stony cop face. "We've already had this conversation. You can't stop me." As I opened my mouth to try another gambit, he added, "And it's my duty."

Mouth still open, I gaped at him.

"How do you figure that?" I demanded after I'd gotten my voice working again. "The way I see it, it's your duty to turn me in, not help me create yet another international incident by kidnapping the UK's Director of Weapons Research."

Kane squared his shoulders. "My duty is to my country. If Nora's story is true, then she would be subject to prosecution as a Canadian citizen for falsifying her death and for knowingly allowing you to be programmed. And my last orders before I resigned my commission were to safeguard you at any cost. In my professional opinion, Nora is a threat to the national security of both Canada and the United Kingdom, and the extradition order is a frame job. My duty is clear: To protect you and aid your investigation any way I can."

Jaw dangling, I stared at him. "That..." I had to stop and shake my head before I could continue. "That is... the biggest... steamiest... heap of horseshit I've ever heard."

The sexy laugh lines crinkled around his eyes. "Thank you."

"You're welcome. And you're insane. There's no way that will fly."

"Why wouldn't it?" Kane countered. "It's completely true; and your last orders before you went off-grid were to investigate Nora. We're both just following orders."

"That will hold up for about two seconds under the lie detector."

Kane frowned. "I'm prepared to take a lie detector test right now. I'm fully convinced that I'm doing the right thing."

A loud rap on my window made us all jump.

CHAPTER 39

Kane moved so fast it seemed as though the trank pistol had appeared in his hand by magic. Tucking it down alongside his thigh, he nodded at me.

Heart hammering, I powered down the window.

A middle-aged man leaned down. "Hi." He flicked a curious gaze over the four of us, but didn't waste time with questions. "I just wanted to let you know that your driver's side rear tire looks soft." He eyed Hellhound's bulk in the back seat dubiously. "But maybe it's just the weight making it look that way," he added. "Anyway, I thought you should know."

I summoned my best smile. "Thanks. I'll get it checked at the next service station. Merry Christmas."

"Thanks, same to you." He straightened and strode away.

I powered up the window and fell back in the seat. "Christ, he scared the hell out of me."

"Me, too. We're dangerously blind and deaf with these windows frosted over and the fan blowing." Kane handed over the trank pistol. "You'd better take this. And we should get moving. I don't like attracting that kind of attention."

I holstered the pistol at my ankle and turned to the pair in the back seat. "How's it going?"

"Done." Skidmark held up three sketches.

"Wow." I studied them with awe. "They're amazing. And I can't believe you did them so fast."

"Hellhound's got an excellent eye," Skidmark said. "It was like doing a paint-by-number."

"That's his photographic memory." I gave Hellhound a smile.

"We'd better get out of here," Kane urged.

"I gotta grab some shit from one a' my caches," Hellhound said. "How 'bout if I take the truck an' drop Skidmark at the Palliser? Then I'll pick up my shit an' meet ya at Aydan's motel room."

"Perfect." Kane handed over the truck keys.

After a brief flurry of exchanging burner phones and numbers, Hellhound and Skidmark departed. I reversed the car out of the slot and wended my way to the exit.

When we turned onto Macleod Trail, Kane seemed absorbed in his own thoughts so I drove in silence.

Was he angry at me? He certainly had good reason. He had trusted me and responded to my summons, only to discover that I had betrayed him in the worst possible way. Now he couldn't go home to his son tonight; and worse, he might lose precious years of Daniel's childhood while he rotted in prison.

Dammit, I should never have let Skidmark talk me into calling him. I should have just called Stemp and... shit, no; Stemp wasn't in charge anymore. I should have called Dermott, and turned myself in.

I sighed. Maybe I should just end this right now. I could

pretend I'd never talked to Kane and Hellhound at all; just call Dermott as though I didn't know there was a warrant out for me. He'd send Holt to arrest me instantly.

Well, assuming Dermott bothered to pick up the phone when I called. I grimaced at the memory of his lackadaisical response to check-ins. That kind of carelessness was a danger to all the agents. At least if I turned myself in along with the network key and generator, Stemp would probably be reinstated as Director. I might end up dead, but it would be better for everybody else...

"What's on your mind?" Kane's voice made me start guiltily.

"Um... just thinking."

"Unpleasant thoughts, if I'm reading your expression correctly."

"I haven't had any other kind lately."

He grunted. "Understandable."

"I'm sorry," I blurted. "I know you must be really pissed off at me, and I don't blame you. Calling you was stupid and selfish. I promise I'll do my best to get you out of this so you can go back to the life you deserve."

He jerked around to face me, and I managed to dampen my flinch down to a tiny twitch as I steeled myself for his rage.

It didn't come.

"Of course I'm not angry with you." He sounded surprised. "Contacting me was your only viable option. Why would I be angry?"

"Because I've taken you away from the most important person in your life; and if you go to prison because of this, Daniel could be grown up before you get out. You'll miss his entire childhood. I'm as bad as Alicia, depriving you of your son through my own selfishness."

After a short silence, Kane spoke slowly. "Aydan... there are so many things wrong with what you just said, I don't even know where to start."

"Well, start at the top of the list," I said grimly, my heart shrivelling. God, was I destined to fuck up everything?

Kane let out a long breath. "In the first place, the thought of comparing you to Alicia is so ridiculous it's laughable. Alicia is..." He made a frustrated gesture. "I don't know what to say. She's a good mother. She has poured countless hours into studying the latest parenting techniques; and she will always do what she believes is right for Daniel, no matter the cost to herself or... to others. He truly is the most important person in the world to her."

I shifted my suddenly-sweaty grip on the steering wheel. The thought of being that dedicated; that consumed by another human being...

My heart rattled up near my throat, attempting to leap out and flee from this conversation, from this car, from the terrifying bonds of love and dependence...

"Aydan...? Are you all right?"

"Fine," I croaked. "Sorry; I w-was just... Never mind. Go on, I'm listening."

"Are you sure you're all right?"

When I glanced over, he was studying me and frowning. I forced a feeble chuckle and returned my gaze to the road. "I'm fine. Just a jab of stomach pain. That burger I had for supper wasn't my friend. I'm glad Alicia is such a good mom. Daniel needs that. And I know you're a great dad, too. He's a lucky boy."

"I'm not a great dad." Kane sucked in a short breath as though fighting to suppress words that were being wrenched from him against his will. "I'm... struggling," he said raggedly. "Barely... finding my feet in this new role. It's so important to me; *Daniel* is so important to me; and yet it's all so..." He hesitated, his fists clenching. "So... foreign to my nature."

He sagged in his seat with a sigh. "There, I've finally said it out loud. I've been trying to overcome everything I've been; everything I've done for the past thirty-two years; to become an entirely new person who's worthy of helping a child grow up. And I can't do it, Aydan. Alicia... is still capable of that untainted devotion. Don't get me wrong; she's suffered her share of the pain life throws at everybody, but... she doesn't have this... darkness... inside."

"And that's okay," I said gently. "That's why kids have two parents. You're *supposed* to be different. To offer different strengths. Different perspectives."

Kane let out a half-laugh. "I wish I could believe that. But I don't want to get sidetracked here. The point I was trying to make is that Alicia is a good mother, but that's all she is."

"I thought she was a freelance graphic designer," I argued. "She must have busted her ass to work from home while Daniel was a baby."

"That's not what I meant. She has some good qualities; but she isn't brave. She isn't selfless. She has no discernible sense of humour. She's a couch potato who won't lift a finger to do anything beyond the basics of cleanliness and nutrition. She's just a petty, selfish woman who by some God-given miracle has managed not to pass those qualities on to our son. Yet."

I stopped at a red light and turned to stare at him. "I've never heard you say anything so harsh about anybody, ever."

His flush was visible even in the dimness of the streetlights. "I'm sorry. That was inappropriate and unfair. I truly admire her for managing single parenting so well..."

"While she was hiding Daniel from you," I said flatly.

He let out a short breath. "Yes. But the point I was trying to make was that you are everything that she is not, and she can never hope to be. She is a good mother, but you are a hero. I don't think you're even capable of selfishness."

I swallowed hard, my face on fire. "Th-Thank you, but I'm far too capable of being selfish. And all good mothers are heroes as far as I'm concerned."

My heart twisted as I said the words. I used to think my mother was a hero...

"That's true," Kane allowed. "I don't mean to diminish what Alicia has accomplished; but there is no comparison between her and you. You are a better person in every way. As to the other part of your earlier statement; you're right, Daniel is... should be... the most important person in my life. But it isn't your job to keep my priorities on track. That responsibility is mine. And..."

He sighed. "When you texted me, I left the school and slipped back into my old skin without even thinking twice. Disposed of my phone, abandoned my vehicle, took a circuitous route to my nearest cache..." He gave me a half-smile. "...which I still had despite the fact that I resigned from the Department months ago... and went to our rendezvous point. Completely focused on the objective. Not even considering the potential consequences to Daniel. I wasn't a father anymore; I was an agent."

He swallowed, and when he spoke again, his voice was so quiet I had to strain to hear it. "It felt... good. God help me. I don't deserve to have a child."

"That's not true at all!" I gripped his arm, wishing I could shake some sense into him. "You have so much to offer as a father! Courage, dedication, selflessness, patience, critical thinking, sports and fitness, cooking skills, art, stories; you speak eight friggin' languages, for chrissake! If you're not good enough to parent a child, nobody is! And of course it felt good for you to slip back into being an agent. After getting thrown into fatherhood on a moment's notice, it would be a huge relief for you to do something you're confident about doing well."

Silence filled the car.

When I glanced over at him, he was staring straight ahead.

"John...?" I prompted.

"I..." He shook himself. "I... didn't think of that."

"Then what the hell is your damn psychologist doing?" I demanded, suddenly furious on his behalf. "Don't tell me; let me guess. You spend every session talking about how much Alicia suffered during your marriage because you were never there for her. You're killing yourself trying to atone for what you couldn't do; when the truth is that she was dazzled by your uniform but never grasped the fact that the uniform demands sacrifices from a service member's spouse and family as well. She wasn't prepared to make the sacrifices but she won't admit it, so she's turning it around and making it your fault."

Kane winced. "Ouch. Direct hit."

"I'm sorry..." I began.

"Don't be." He reached over to squeeze my hand. "Thank you. That was a valuable dose of perspective. I need to think that through."

I nodded, and we didn't speak again until I parked behind the motel.

"Be it ever so humble..." I indicated the worn façade with a grand gesture and didn't complete the quote. "I'm in one-fourteen around the other side. That window..." I pointed to the one above us. "... is my bathroom."

"Good. Give me your key and I'll go in first to make sure it's secure. Did you give your only bug detector to Skidmark?"

"No, I have another in the trunk." I got out and rummaged through the duffel bag until I located the small device, then handed it over.

As Kane strode around the building I dove back into the warmth of the car, shivering. A few moments later the bathroom window slid open and Kane beckoned.

Teeth chattering, I unloaded my gear and scurried around to the door. I locked it behind me and sagged against it, fatigue nearly dragging me to my knees in the relative safety of the shabby room.

I tipped my head back against the door, closing my eyes. "God. I just want to fall into that bed and sleep forever."

"Ordinarily I'd say 'go ahead', but we need to talk before Hellhound gets here."

My eyes popped open as anxiety clenched my tired muscles all over again. "Um... okay. But first..." I dropped my gear beside the door and ripped off my kerchief, jamming my fingers through my hair to scrub my prickling scalp.

"God... damn... agh..." I scratched some more. "...Ahhh, that thing was driving me nuts. And I have to get this makeup off before I scratch my own face off, too. I'll just be a minute." I grabbed my overnight backpack and made a beeline for the bathroom.

As I passed, Kane's hand shot out to restrain me. "Are you sure that's a good idea? What if you need to leave the room unexpectedly?"

"It's probably not a good idea at all." I dodged around his outstretched hand. "But I don't care. If Holt shows up at the door, it won't matter whether I'm wearing makeup or not; and if I have to leave in a hurry I'll just wrap my scarf around my face. I can't stand having this stuff on my face for one more second."

I shut myself into the bathroom and barely managed not to recoil. My makeup was definitely serving its purpose, but my vanity pained me at the sight of the dilapidated old bag reflected in the mirror.

By the time I had finished scrubbing, my skin was reddened but invigorated. I hurriedly slapped on some moisturizer before turning back toward the door.

My hand hovered over the knob.

What had Kane meant by 'we need to talk'?

God, my emotions already felt as though they'd been worked over with a tire iron. I couldn't handle a relationship conversation right now...

I turned to glare at my fearful face in the mirror. Who was I kidding? I couldn't handle a relationship conversation, ever. Skidmark was right. Something was seriously wrong in my brain.

I shook off the thought. Why would I assume Kane

wanted to talk about our relationship? Maybe he had only meant we needed to talk about classified details that we couldn't discuss in front of Hellhound and Skidmark.

Yeah, that was it.

For sure.

I blew out a breath, set my teeth, and stepped out of the bathroom.

CHAPTER 40

Kane was reclining on the bed, arms tucked behind his head. I only had a moment to appreciate his muscular glory before he rolled to his feet, but that was all the time it took for my mind to skip down yet another X-rated memory path.

Down, girl.

"I like that look much better on you," Kane said as he approached with a smile.

My breath caught as he extended a hand toward me, but he was only reaching past me for the television remote. He powered on the TV and turned the volume down to a conversational murmur before turning back to me.

"I've already cleared the room for bugs," he said, matching the level of his voice to the TV. "But we don't need to take a chance on being overheard through thin walls." He motioned toward the bed. "Let's get started."

Heat rose in my face and arrowed instantly down to more interesting places.

"Um...?" I began, but Kane had already turned away to sit on the bed again. Facing the other bed.

The other bed, where he expected me to sit. And *talk*, idiot.

Oh.

This time the fire in my cheeks was embarrassment as I took my place opposite him.

"Is there anything new I need to know about the network key and generator?" he asked.

"Um... no. It's still the same old, same old."

"So what exactly happened at the secured facility? And what were your exact orders from Stemp?"

I recounted all the details to him, relieved that I didn't need to filter my story this time.

Although come to think of it, maybe I shouldn't have divulged everything about the metal-eating bacteria...

"What's wrong?" Kane asked. "You're frowning."

"Um. Yeah. I just..." I picked at a loose thread on the bedspread. "I've probably told you more than I should have, but I'm just so used to telling you everything..." I grimaced. "I guess it's okay. If I'm programmed to do something weird, you'll need the whole story so you can react appropriately."

"Yes." His voice softened. "Thank you for your trust. That means a lot to me."

Trust. There was that word again. I squirmed.

Kane mercifully kept talking. "So here's a thought that you may not have considered: Nora said you'd been programmed when, exactly?"

"When I was talking to her in her hotel room."

"No; I meant, when was the programming inserted in your mind?"

"Oh." I frowned, mentally replaying my conversation with Nora. "She said Sam had done it while I was young, when he used to come to the farm several times a year and we did what he called 'mind exercises'. Nobody knew he was actually testing me to see whether I was a candidate for his secret program..." I trailed off.

When I didn't speak again, Kane asked, "What are you thinking?"

"If Nora is my mother, I'm wondering when she found out what Sam was really doing. Were they colluding right from the start? Or did she find out later? Did he confess to her after they started their affair?"

My guts twisted at the thought of my dad trusting his wife all those years, while he'd travelled for work and she was betraying him...

I jerked my mind back to the situation at hand. "Or did mom and dad find out together later? Did Sam confess to both of them?" I yanked the loose thread on the bedspread, snapping it and puckering the fabric. I smoothed the puckers, but my hand stilled as a thought hit me. "My Aunt Minnie said Dad took me everywhere with him. He told her I was 'gifted', and he carried a gun in his briefcase, and he said he was 'making sure I had a future'. And that started around the time he started working for the Department of Agriculture, when I was about twelve or thirteen."

"He knew something," Kane deduced.

"He must have. So... does that mean that he and Mom were working together to protect me? Or was he trying to protect me from Mom and Sam?"

"That's the million-dollar question," Kane agreed. "And I don't see any way to find the answer until we can question Nora. But it does lead me to my next point. If this so-called programming occurred when you were a child, and if Nora says that working for the Department puts you at risk to trigger it..." He frowned. "Then, theoretically, that risk began when you discovered the Department nearly two years ago."

Nausea rose in my throat. "Oh, God. I might have been giving away secrets all this time."

Kane's frown deepened and he crossed his arms as though barricading himself from the possibility. "Or you haven't been; and there's no reason to believe you will. Remember, any programming that's in your mind is decades old. And you were never supposed to know you were capable of infiltrating networks and decrypting data. You were never supposed to enter the network except under Sam's control. Maybe you've already overcome the programming because you've been controlling your own access to the network."

A small fearful hope kindled in my heart. "Maybe..."

Kane went on, "So now you're afraid to use the network key in case you unknowingly give away intel; but if you've been giving away intel all this time, using the key now won't likely make things that much worse. And if you *haven't* been giving away intel, why would you suddenly start?"

I wrapped my arms around myself. "I don't know. And that's what scares the shit out of me. Are you saying I should... go into the internet again to see what I can find out about Grandin?"

"No. I'm only trying to wrap my mind around all the ramifications. But it seems like a positive sign that you gave me the network key and generator of your own volition. If you were programmed to use them against us, theoretically you should have gone to any lengths to keep them."

"Right..." I clutched my head, feeling as though a time bomb was ticking inside my skull. "But what if we're wrong?"

Kane sighed and said nothing.

I shivered. "I don't dare risk going into the network again. If I've been giving away information all this time, what if I give away one critical piece the next time I go into the network? One piece of data could lead to worldwide security breaches." Ice formed in my belly and the shivers intensified. "It could lead to a world war. I can't take the chance."

A sharp rap at the door nearly levitated me off the bed.

Kane sprang to his feet. "Get into the bathroom!"

I dove inside as he finished, "It's probably Hellhound, but..."

I swung the door most of the way closed and drew my Glock. Heart pounding, I eased forward, straining my ears.

The sound of the outside door latch was followed by a rumble of male voices, and a moment later I heard the door close and Kane announced, "All clear."

I let out a shaky breath and holstered my weapon before emerging cautiously. The sight of Hellhound lowering a large rucksack to the floor brought a smile of relief to my lips.

He straightened, his expression brightening into an answering smile at the sight of me. "Hey, darlin'." He opened his arms. "Nice to see your real face this time."

I hurried over to step into his embrace, and he held me close. "You're shakin', darlin'." His arms tightened around me. "What's wrong?"

"N-Nothing. Just chilly." I huddled gratefully into his body heat, shivering. "Keyed up and overtired, I g-guess."

"When did ya eat last?"

"Around five."

He consulted his wristwatch without letting go of me. "That's nearly five hours ago. Ya prob'ly need a snack."

"And some sleep," I agreed.

He turned me loose with a gentle nudge toward the refrigerator. "Better eat. We still gotta do some plannin' tonight."

Stifling a groan, I opened the fridge. He was right, of course; but I was so exhausted I could have dropped to the floor and nodded off right there on the worn and faded carpet.

I managed a cheerful tone with an effort. "You guys want anything? I've got fruit, orange juice, bread, peanut butter, milk, some cold cuts and a raw veggie tray..."

"Vegetables, please," Kane said.

"Cold cuts," Hellhound said at the same time. "Got any pepperoni?"

"Sorry, no." I handed him the small package of deli ham. "I wasn't expecting visitors."

He gave a philosophical shrug and helped himself to the meat while I spread peanut butter on a couple of slices of bread and Kane munched on some vegetables.

"So Skidmark got checked into the Palliser okay," Hellhound said through a mouthful, then swallowed and went on, "He's gonna be down in the lobby tomorrow mornin', an' he'll call us soon's he makes contact. He said ya could get the lie detector?" He directed an inquiring look at me.

"Maybe," I said slowly. "But if we don't know when we'll have Nora, we shouldn't get the lie detector yet. I don't want to get Jack in trouble, and if she gives it to us tonight and then Holt wants it for something tomorrow..."

"No big deal," Hellhound said. "Once we grab the b-...uh, Nora, we can hold her for as long's we need to. We can get the lie detector after."

"You or I can get it," Kane said. "Aydan should lie low."

"But that's not fair," I protested. "I'm the one who should be taking the risks. The two of you shouldn't even be involved."

"And that's exactly why we should be involved," Kane countered. "I don't want to give your death wish a chance to manifest itself."

"I told you, I'm pretty sure I don't have a death wish," I argued at the same time as Hellhound bolted up from his slouch on the bed and demanded, "What the fuck? What death wish?"

"I don't have one," I repeated.

Kane frowned at me. "I'm still not convinced of that."

"What the fuckin' hell!" Hellhound growled. "Somebody better start talkin' here, or I'm gonna start bashin' heads."

Kane launched into the tale of my earlier revelation that my life was less important than everyone else's. The way he told it made me sound alarmingly fucked up. I tried to inject some perspective into his narrative whenever I could, but judging by Hellhound's gathering frown I wasn't doing a very good job.

"...so it wouldn't surprise me if she had been programmed to carry out a suicide mission," Kane finished. "Either as a means of furthering a cause; or else as a simple method of eliminating her when her usefulness comes to an end."

"Hm." Hellhound got up and came over to sit beside me on the bed. Wrapping an arm around my shoulders, he pressed his lips to my temple. "Don't worry, darlin'," he said gently. "It's a shitty feelin' to wonder if ya can trust yourself, but we won't let ya do anythin' bad. We'll stop ya, no matter what it takes."

I collapsed against him, soaking up his reassurance. He understood exactly what I was going through.

Would he shoot to kill if I went out of control?

Would I want him to?

I didn't know; but I knew he would make the best decision he could for me. It was enough.

A warm wave of sleepiness washed over me, but his voice roused me and I reluctantly opened my eyes again.

"I dunno about the suicide thing," he said to Kane. "Like Karma said, it'd be pretty damn hard to program somebody; an' Aydan's got lotsa other reasons for havin' a knee-jerk reaction like that."

"What do you mean?" Kane's voice held a slight edge, and he frowned at the two of us cuddled together.

Shit, I should move away from Arnie.

My muscles tensed as the thought occurred to me, and Hellhound's embrace instantly loosened. Not falling away; but giving me space.

It was enough to bring me to my senses. I eased out a breath and relaxed against him once more. Kane knew about our deal, and he had said he was okay with it. I would believe him until he told me otherwise.

"See that?" Hellhound asked.

"What?" Kane's frown deepened.

"Ya frowned at her an' it was like ya stuck her with a cattle prod. She was all set to jump up an' do whatever she thought ya wanted. Ain't that right, darlin'?"

This time I did sit up and pull away, my heart chilling. "Wh- What do you mean?"

"What were ya thinkin' just now when he frowned at ya?"

"Nothing," I protested slightly louder than I'd intended. "I was just shifting position."

"No lies, darlin'," Hellhound reminded me softly.

Kane watched me in silence, his gaze intent.

Reading my mind.

Only now realizing how much power he had. Finally understanding how he could effortlessly force me to do whatever he wanted...

"...Aydan. Hey, darlin', it's okay. Nobody's gonna make ya do anythin' ya don't wanna do."

Arnie's gentle rasp penetrated my panic, and I realized I had scooted to the head of the bed, my knees pulled up to my chest and my arms locked around them.

I forced a laugh and stood up to stretch. "Thanks, Arnie. Listen, I'm really glad you're both watching out for me, but let's finish up this strategy session tomorrow morning. I'm 'way too tired to think straight tonight."

"Too tired to keep your guard up, ya mean," Arnie corrected. He turned to Kane. "Lemme give a scenario. Pretend ya got captured. You're in a POW camp, an' the enemy makes ya salute whenever ya see 'em. Stand up whenever they snap their fingers. Harmless stuff, but they'll beat the hell outta ya if ya don't do it."

Kane frowned. "I don't see where you're going with this, but I'll play along. What you're describing is a classic mind control technique. Begin by requiring obedience to benign commands. Emphasize how illogical it is to suffer so much for failing to follow such harmless instructions; and as soon as those compliant behaviours have been established, escalate to the next level. And the next."

"Yeah," Hellhound agreed. "So, there ya are. Ya know what they're doin'; but ya gotta do what they say or take a shit-kickin'. So what d'ya do?"

"Well..." Kane said slowly. "My duty is always to escape. If complying with harmless commands would prevent me from sustaining serious injuries, it would be smartest for me to pretend to cooperate. Lull them into a false sense of security so they won't be expecting my escape attempt, and stay in the best possible physical shape so that I'm ready to make my move when the opportunity arises."

"Right," Hellhound agreed. "So. Ya finally get rescued years later, an' by now if somebody snaps their fingers you're on your feet before ya even think about it. Right?"

Kane's eyes narrowed, his gaze alternating between Hellhound and me. "Probably. It would take quite a while to overcome the reflex, and there would be a lot of trauma associated with it."

"But you're free, so it's all good, right?" Hellhound asked.

"Yes..."

Hellhound clapped his palms together, a sudden crack like a gunshot. Kane and I both jumped.

"An' then they capture ya again," Hellhound barked. "How d'ya feel?"

My guts had been slowly tightening during their exchange, and his words unleashed a flood of terror and nausea. Kane looked ill, too.

"But ya see a way out," Hellhound added. "It'll prob'ly kill ya, but there's a tiny chance it might work. D'ya try it?"

"Yes!" Kane and I chorused instantly.

"Yeah," Hellhound said softly. "An' to somebody that didn't know what ya been through, that might look kinda like a death wish."

CHAPTER 41

Our silence filled the room, the inane chatter of the television dissolving into meaningless noise.

Kane was frowning again. Hellhound eyed him expectantly. My stomach churned, on the verge of violently ejecting the bread and peanut butter I'd just eaten.

"Where are you going with this?" Kane asked. "Although a person might risk death to avoid the certainty of a worse alternative, it doesn't mean they *want* death, regardless of how it may look to others. That makes sense, but I don't see how it's relevant to our conversation. We were talking about Aydan's behaviour in the absence of an imminent threat."

"Ya didn't get the second half a' what I said." Hellhound gave him a level look. "Just 'cause ya don't hafta do it anymore an' ya don't wanna do it anymore; it doesn't mean you're ever gonna be able to stop jumpin' when somebody snaps their fingers."

At Kane's puzzled expression, Hellhound went on, "If somebody spent every day for years beatin' it into ya that your life ain't worth shit compared to theirs, an' punishin' ya if ya don't agree whenever they snap their fingers; even if ya don't really believe it you're still gonna automatically think it when somebody snaps their fingers. An' if ya finally get free an' then it looks like you're gonna get recaptured..." He trailed off. "Put it together, Cap. Ya ain't stupid."

Kane blinked at him, then slowly turned to look at me, comprehension dawning in his eyes. "Yes." His voice came out in a croak, and he cleared his throat. "Yes... apparently I am stupid." He shook his head as if recovering from a blow. "I'm sorry." He rose and went to the door as if sleepwalking, stooping to put on his boots and mechanically donning his parka.

I stood paralyzed except for the increasing tremor of my knees.

"Where ya goin'?" Hellhound asked.

"I... Out. For a while." Kane shook himself again and his voice firmed, his gaze focusing. "I have... some thinking to do." He glanced at his wristwatch. "Arnie, if you can take the first shift watching Aydan...?" Hellhound nodded, and Kane went on, "I'll be back at..." He hesitated as though calculating something. "...two A.M. sharp."

"Okay. But where're ya goin'?" Hellhound repeated.

"Just driving. I won't be more than half an hour away at any time, and I'll have my burner phone in case you need me. I just... need to think. See you later."

He turned and left. The click of the door latch sounded like the knell of the apocalypse.

"Oh, God." I sank trembling onto the bed, gulping air in an attempt to keep from throwing up.

"It's okay, darlin'..." Hellhound reached toward me, but I scrambled away to jam my back against the wall.

"How could you tell him?" I demanded, my voice crackling on the edge of hysteria. "*How could you tell him?*"

Hellhound retreated a couple of steps, opening his hands in a pacifying gesture. "He needed to know, Aydan. He needed to get it; really *get* what ya been through, in his guts. He understands now."

"I know! How could you..." Tears and bile were rising fast, blinding and strangling me. "How... could you..." My voice rose to the frantic cry of a trapped animal. "*Now he knows how to break me!*"

I fled for the bathroom and vomited.

Over and over, my stomach heaved as if it would turn me inside-out. I clutched the toilet bowl white-knuckled and sobbing. Tears and snot poured down my face while Hellhound's gentle hands lifted my hair out of the mess and made slow circles on my back. If I could have pulled away from him I would have, but it took all my strength just to cling to the toilet while the violent spasms wracked me.

When nothing was left inside me but dry heaves and whimpers, I propped my forehead on the toilet seat and croaked, "Go away."

The door closed quietly behind him.

I slid to the floor and lay there with my wet cheek pressed to the cold tile, too hopeless to even pray for death.

After an endless time, the ache in my abused muscles subsided, slowly coalescing into a sharper pain at my waist. My Glock grinding into my body. I groaned and flopped onto my back to pull it out.

Its familiar grip comforted my hand. The only friend I could count on.

I cuddled it to my chest.

Blessed escape waited behind the impartial eye of its barrel.

I had only to bring it up to my temple and crook my finger. A simple come-hither to peaceful oblivion...

I shook my head at its dark invitation.

Nope.

The guilt would kill Arnie. And the bathroom would be a hell of a mess. They'd never get my brains out of the grout. And with my luck I'd end up haunting the damn bathroom for all eternity, moaning and gurgling in the pipes like some dismal shit-soaked troglodyte.

Arnie tapped on the door and asked, "Ya okay in there, darlin'?"

I groaned. I couldn't deal with him right now...

The bathroom door opened and Arnie froze, fear contorting his face. "Aydan, don't! Put the gun down, please! I'm sorry, I never meant to hurt ya an' I'll make it right somehow, I promise. Just put the gun down so we can talk, okay?"

"Don't worry, Arnie," I said without moving. "I'd love to just drop dead right here and now; but shooting myself would take far too much effort. I'm only holding it because it was digging into my hip."

"Then how 'bout if I hold it for ya for a little while?" he asked, his casual tone belied by the tremor in his voice.

"Sure."

He eased into the bathroom and knelt beside me. "I'm just gonna take it outta your hand now, darlin'," he soothed. "Just relax."

If I'd had an ounce of energy left I might have smiled at him, but it was too much work. Eyelids drooping, I lay still while he carefully removed the Glock from my grip.

He stuffed it into the back of his jeans and leaned over

me again. "Come on, darlin', let's get ya cleaned up an' into bed."

I closed my eyes, shutting him out.

"Aydan." Gentle fingertips stroked the hair away from my forehead, peeling away the sticky strands that had adhered to my cheek. "It's okay if you're mad an' ya don't wanna talk to me, but I gotta know whether I should take ya to the hospital. Just say somethin' so I know whether you're okay."

"I don't need to go the hospital. I'm not mad. I just... I can't..." Tears leaked from under my closed eyelids and trickled down my temples, and I threw the last of my dignity to the winds. "I'm scared, Arnie." I opened my eyes, desperately searching his beloved ugly face and clutching his wrist in a deathgrip. "I... I'm... *scared.*" My voice broke.

"I know, darlin'." He gathered me into his arms, vomit and all, and rocked me, stroking my hair. "I know. I'm sorry. I thought I was helpin' but I'm just a dumbfuck an' I shoulda known better..."

"No." I wrapped my arms around him. "You're not a dumbfuck, and I shouldn't have blamed you. You didn't tell him anything he didn't already know." I sighed. "What kind of an agent would he be if he hadn't already figured out all my vulnerabilities? I've always been at his mercy. I was just pretending it wasn't true because I was too terrified to think about it."

Arnie's arms tightened around me. "He wouldn't ever do that to ya. I know he wouldn't. But even if he tried, I wouldn't let him, Aydan. I won't ever let anybody hurt ya. I'll always be here to protect ya. Even when ya don't want me an' I'm nothin' but a big fuckin' pain in your ass, I'll still be here."

"I'll always want you." I buried my face in his shoulder. "You're the only one I feel safe with."

He let out a half-laugh, half-sob. "The guy who kills people for a livin'. Christ, you're fucked up, darlin'."

"Never said I wasn't." I pulled back far enough to look him in the face, and did my best to summon a smile. It quivered a bit, but I managed it. "And I'm also gross and stinky and covered with snot and puke, and now you are, too."

He chuckled. "What's a little snot an' puke between friends?"

"Sticky."

"That's true." He hesitated, sobering. "Hey, Aydan... just thinkin'..."

My heart chilled. "What?"

"I know you're scared shitless 'bout what might be in your head, but... what if... the way ya feel about commitment... an' the claustrophobia, an' all that shit... what if it's actually just Nora's programmin'?" As I stared at him without comprehension, he added, "An' when ya find out what it is an' how to kick it..."

The oxygen in the room suddenly seemed inadequate. I sucked in a feeble breath, my head swimming. "You mean... I could... maybe..."

"Ya could be with Kane without panickin'. Ya could... not be scared anymore. Get married. Have a normal life."

"I... I..."

It was too much to take in.

I burrowed back into his arms. "I can't think about it. It's too scary. Just thinking about... the M-word... makes me hyperventilate."

"Don't worry, ya don't have to think about it. I won't let it happen unless ya want it." He dropped a kiss on the top of my head and changed the subject. "Let's get cleaned up. Arms up, darlin'."

I complied, and he pulled my stained sweatshirt over my head and pitched it into the bathtub, followed by my T-shirt.

"Up ya get..." He stood and lifted me to my feet.

As I took off my jeans, which had miraculously survived the puke-storm unstained, Arnie eyed me worriedly.

"You're shakin' like a leaf. Come on, let's get ya into the tub, an' I'll bring ya some orange juice." He turned on the water and adjusted the temperature while I stripped off my underwear, and then he offered a strong arm while I stepped unsteadily into the tub and sat down in the warm water.

I leaned forward to scoop handfuls of water out of the faucet, scrubbing my face clean and rinsing out my mouth. Arnie ducked out the door and returned a few seconds later to hand me a small carton of orange juice. "Here, darlin', this'll do ya more good than water. Drink up."

"Thanks." I sagged back against the hard cold tub and sipped. Still watching me anxiously, Hellhound sank down to sit on the floor, his back propped against the wall.

After a few minutes the orange juice was gone and the ancient steel tub was digging into my back. I squirmed, searching for a more comfortable position, but it was no use.

Sitting up with a sigh, I held out a hand. "Give me your shirt. I'll wash it here in the tub with mine, and then I need a shower." I shuddered as the crusty ends of my hair scraped my skin. "God, do I ever need a shower."

Hellhound peeled off his shirt, and together we attacked

the soiled garments with shampoo. I lurched awkwardly to a crouch to drain the tub and wring out the clothes, and Hellhound eyed me dubiously.

"Careful, darlin'," he warned. "Ya ain't lookin' very steady on your feet there. Ya want help?"

I took his proffered hand and rose cautiously as the last of the bathwater gurgled down the drain. "Thanks. I'm still feeling pretty shaky. Will you shower with me? I might need a hand."

And I might need him to hold me until I could pretend that everything was going to be all right.

I didn't say that part out loud.

"'Course." He stripped off his jeans and socks.

I eyed his crotch with a smile. "Somebody's happy to see me."

Arnie flushed. "Don't mind him; he's just bein' a dick. I ain't askin' ya for anythin' tonight, darlin'."

I gave him a smile and turned on the water, concentrating on adjusting the temperature. Thank God for his understanding. Athletic shower sex just wasn't on my radar tonight.

I pulled the curtain closed and turned on the shower, avoiding the first cold needles of spray. As soon as it was warm, I poked my head around the curtain. "All ready for you now."

As he stepped forward, my gaze dipped for another rewarding peek.

Hot damn, he was a fine upstanding citizen. I was too tired to do anything about it, but... mmmm. Very nice indeed.

Arnie stepped into the tub and took me in his arms,

backing me under the hot spray of the shower. I sighed and wrapped my arms around him in turn, resting my head on his shoulder and letting my battered soul relax into the moment of warmth and safety.

We stood locked together for long minutes, his hands gently massaging my back in the warm water. At last I tipped my head back to let the water run through my hair, then pressed close to him to accomplish a pivot that swapped our places under the shower.

I lathered up with shampoo while he scrubbed himself under the spray, and we switched places again. The warm water coursing over my head felt as though it was cleansing my very soul. I ran my fingers through my hair over and over again, eyes closed.

Rough chest hair grazed my nipples, making me shiver as Arnie moved closer. His fingers joined mine, running through my hair and massaging my scalp while the water poured down. I pressed closer to him, wet skin sliding against wet skin. His erection stiffened between us and he sucked in a breath, but when he spoke there was no trace of urgency in his voice. "How ya doin', darlin'?"

"Ready for conditioner." I wrapped my arms around him again and swivelled him into my place under the shower.

As I stepped away my breath caught at the sight of him, eyes closed against the spray while the hot water sluiced over his bulging tattooed muscles. His erection jutted hard and ready but he stood motionless, a statue of lust personified.

My body tightened, heat coiling down between my legs despite my exhaustion.

Droplets of water trickled along his length, hot and juicy and lickable...

Arnie opened his eyes, catching me staring slack-jawed with the tube of conditioner clutched forgotten in my hand.

"Hey, darlin'," he rasped softly.

I shivered at the sexy voice that stroked my eardrums the way his knowing hands would stroke my body...

"Are ya cold?" he asked, and held me against his heat to pivot me under the shower again.

Pressed full-length against him, I went up on tiptoe to trap his erection between my thighs. Sliding back and forth, I whispered, "No, I'm hot. And so are you."

He groaned. "You're so hot I'm gonna lose it right here if ya keep doin' that." He stepped away and extracted the conditioner from my hand. "Turn around an' I'll do ya."

My heart dipped with a twinge of disappointment. "I... If it's okay with you, I'd rather be face to face tonight."

"Aw, darlin'." He stepped forward again to hug and kiss me softly. "That ain't what I meant. I meant, turn around an' I'll do your conditioner for ya. You're so bagged ya can barely even stand up. If you're still int'rested later when you're lyin' in a nice soft bed, then we can see how it goes."

Thankful for the water that concealed my tears of gratitude, I turned around and gave myself to his gentle ministrations.

CHAPTER 42

Arnie slowly worked the conditioner through the ends of my hair, running his fingers through it over and over. The tiny tugs sent pleasant tingles to my scalp and I sighed with bliss.

Far too soon, he finished; but as I began to turn he stopped me with light hands on my shoulders. "Hang on, darlin'. Lemme do this for ya."

Washcloth in hand, he made soothing circles across my shoulders and back, working unhurriedly down my arms, then down to my thighs and lower legs. His completely non-sexual touch was somehow intensely arousing, every nerve flaring into awareness under the light friction of the cloth.

By the time he finished at my ankles and turned me to face him I was hot with desire, my nipples hardening under the teasing spray.

Arnie surveyed me up and down, smiling, and his cloth went into action again, making delicate circles across my upper chest. Still circling lightly, he detoured around my breasts without touching them.

I let out a small sound of protest as the cloth moved down my ribcage, but he didn't falter. Circling lower still, he traced my waist and hips.

Sinking into a crouch, he worked the cloth slowly lower.

Lower.

Please...

His face was so close, that magic tongue almost within range...

The perfidious cloth moved down to my thighs, leaving my body blazing with need.

"Arnie..." I quavered.

"Shhh, darlin'." He worked the cloth steadily down my legs to my feet, then stood.

"Come here," I whispered, and used a gratifying handhold to tug him closer.

He groaned, his eyes half-closing as I stroked him, then reached past me to turn off the water. "Let's get outta here, darlin'."

We stepped out of the shower together and I pressed close to slide against him while he towelled my back. "Easy, now," he murmured, scattering light kisses down my neck along with his words. "I promised ya a soft bed, remember?"

I grabbed another towel to speed up the drying process, but he refused to be rushed despite the obvious evidence of his readiness.

At last we emerged from the bathroom and I hurried to the bed and flung myself onto it, my earlier exhaustion forgotten. Spreading my arms and legs wide, I gave him a grin. "Come and check out this soft bed."

He chuckled. "Pretty nice lookin' bed, darlin'. I'm likin' it already."

I let my gaze dip to his crotch. "I can see that. Come on over here and you can try it on for size."

"Sounds good to me. But first, this." He held up the small bottle of body lotion that represented the motel's only amenity.

"Later."

"Nope." He grinned as he advanced on the bed. "This's the Helmand Spa Special Deal. Flip over."

"Arnie! Are you purposely trying to drive me nuts?"

"Hell, yeah." His grin widened. "Come on, darlin'. Roll over an' lemme get my hands on ya."

I complied, being sure to spread my legs wide in case he could be distracted from his appointed mission.

"Jesus, Aydan, you're makin' it hard to concentrate," he said hoarsely as he sat on the bed beside me.

I reached over to fondle him again. "It's been hard for too long already. You'd better let me help you with that pretty soon or you're going to have a serious problem."

"Hands off the spa workers, ma'am," he teased as he pulled away. "Now settle down an' relax for your massage."

The first strokes of his palms over my back drew a moan from me and I sank into the pillow. As he worked slowly down my body, my muscles melted into warm pudding and my eyelids drifted closed.

Firm but gentle hands kneaded my back, my legs and calves... my feet. Oh, God yes. A foot massage. Bliss...

His touch eased to feather-light strokes, then ceased. A blanket settled over me.

"Hey," I protested sleepily as I turned over onto my back. "You missed a side here."

"Thought ya were sleepin', darlin'."

"And miss a massage like that? Are you kidding? Besides, I still have evil designs on my spa worker." I ran a teasing hand up his thigh. "My secret admirer isn't quite as wide awake as before, but I know how to fix that." The admirer in question twitched and began to rise again as I tickled.

"Hell, darlin', I just got him settled down," Hellhound groused, but he was grinning. Then he sobered. "Seriously; ya don't hafta do this tonight. If ya just wanna sleep..."

"You know me better than that."

He lay down beside me, his smile returning. "I was hopin' I did."

"Well..." I threw off the blanket and stretched languorously. "You'd better start massaging, or I'll complain to the spa owner."

"Damn customers, always complainin'," he rumbled, and sat up. "Now, let's see. Where should I start with this stuff?" He brandished the half-empty bottle.

"Forget that stuff," I began, but he had already stroked it onto my belly, his hands sliding up my ribs to graze the undersides of my breasts.

I sighed, nipples tightening in anticipation of his caress.

It didn't come.

"Close your eyes, darlin'," he growled.

I obeyed, my skin awakening under his touch in the absence of vision.

Slow sensuous strokes glided down my body. Ribs... waist... hips...

The tiniest brush of sensation between my legs made me suck in a breath, but his hands continued down my thighs, bypassing the place that was begging for his touch.

Knees, ankles...

His hands slid upward again, then stopped.

"No peekin'," he warned.

I lay still, skin tingling with anticipation.

Touch me.

Oh, God, touch me...

A warm current of air ghosted over my belly, moving upward.

Higher.

I clenched the bedspread in both fists. The warmth intensified, hovering over my breast. My body arched off the bed in supplication, to be rewarded by a moustache-tickle that shot sparks through my body.

Light fingertips traced the inside of my thigh, then upward to brush the lightest of touches between my legs, sending molten heat spiralling inward.

"Arnie... please..." My voice came out in a choked whisper. "I... I need..."

The bed dipped under his weight.

"What d'ya need, darlin'?" he rasped. "D'ya need... this?"

Hot hands cupped my breasts while a hot mouth unerringly found its mark lower down. The sudden deluge of stimulation wrenched a cry from my throat, my body straining up to his touch.

Every nerve ignited under his dexterous fingertips and magic tongue. Sensation flooded my body, filling it to capacity, intensifying and expanding.

The fiery updraft of pleasure whirled me up toward heaven.

Then beyond...

"*Arnie...*" His name wrenched out of me in a choked gasp. "Oh... *God!*"

Tipping into freefall, I lost myself in long spasms of

ecstasy until my mind rejoined my body at last, panting in Arnie's arms.

"Okay, darlin'?" He stroked the damp hair back from my forehead. "Ya went off like a rocket."

"Not done," I gasped. "Need you... fuck me... please..."

"Just a sec, darlin'..."

He sat up and rolled on a condom with practiced speed before poising himself above me. "Now?"

"Now-oh-God-Arnie-now-*please!*" I clamped both hands on his ass and drove up to meet him.

He gasped and rocked into his usual perfect rhythm. Mindless, I urged him on with my body, tightening around him and matching him stroke for stroke.

Already my vision was hazing, all thought fading until nothing mattered but heat and friction and the breathless coiling of tension in every muscle.

He shifted against me, riding higher to deliver explosions of pleasure with every thrust. My nerves lit like firecrackers, chain reactions crackling over every inch of sensitized skin.

The firestorm of orgasm flared up to consume me, my body bucking out of control, my mind shattering.

I blazed with glorious sensation for long brilliant moments, only dimly aware of Arnie's deep-throated groan as he reached his own climax.

Together we floated down from the pinnacle, locked in each other's arms, our spasms slowing. At last I went limp, my rubbery muscles releasing the last of their strength.

Arnie's lips found mine in a soft kiss.

"Damn, that was quick," he murmured. "Sorry, darlin'. Guess I needed to get laid worse'n I thought."

"S'perfect," I mumbled, my eyelids sinking shut.

"Couldna done more. Too tired.' With an effort, I dragged my eyes open again to focus on his face. "Thanks, Arnie." I kissed him, my eyes closing again.

Tapping roused me. My hand shot instinctively under my pillow, and I bolted upright when I found only bed linen instead of my Glock.

"It's on the nightstand," Arnie whispered as he hurried toward the door.

I had already spotted the weapon and snatched it up. Arnie peeked out the fisheye lens, his shoulders relaxing. "It's Kane."

I fell back with an outrush of breath and tucked the gun back under my pillow where it belonged. Kane sidled in accompanied by a blast of icy air, and I snuggled lower in my cozy nest.

Feigning sleep, I lay listening. The only sounds were the rustle of clothing as they moved around for a few minutes; the soft closing of the bathroom door; the toilet flushing. More quiet movements; then silence.

I jolted awake, jerking upright with my Glock already in my hand.

"It's all right," Kane said softly. "It was just the door slamming in the unit beside us."

"Oh." I snapped a glance around the room. The clock radio read 6:23. No light seeped around the edges of the tightly-drawn draperies, but a glow from beneath the closed bathroom door provided dim illumination. In the other bed,

Hellhound snored quietly.

Kane sat in the sole chair, an ancient butt-breaking wicker contraption. Even in the murky twilight of the room his face looked pale with fatigue, and my heart smote me. He must have traded vigils with Hellhound at two A.M., which meant he'd been up all night.

"Come and lie down," I murmured, hoping not to wake Hellhound. "You look exhausted."

Kane shifted in the chair, his shoulders stiffening. "That would defeat the purpose of having one of us supervise you at all times," he said without looking at me.

"Oh, right..." I puzzled for a moment over his avoidance of eye contact before realizing that my bare boobs were on full display, the blanket crumpled around my waist.

I tucked my gun under the pillow and lay back, trying to look casual while I pulled the blanket up around my neck. "You're a light sleeper. If you put your arm over me, you'll wake up if I try to move."

He rose slowly and stretched his arms above his head, only to wince as a percussive symphony of pops and crackles announced his body's displeasure. Padding silently over to sit on the edge of the bed, he murmured, "That chair should be banned by the Geneva Convention."

"Yeah," I agreed. "I sat on it for about five minutes and that was enough for me. I'm amazed you aren't permanently crippled after nearly five hours in it."

His lips quirked up. "I think I might be."

"Well, lie down." I indicated the expanse of bed beside me.

"I don't think that's a good idea. It would leave me too vulnerable to attack."

"I'm not going to attack you," I whispered indignantly.

"So you say." His gaze measured me. "What does your programming say?"

My guts clenched. "I... I don't know."

He gave me a resigned nod. "Neither do I. Besides..." He hesitated. "Would you... be able to bear it? If I held you?"

My heart gave a kick of instinctive fear. "I... don't know that, either." The spasm of pain that flickered across his face made me reach for him. I ran my hand up the hard curves of his bicep, across a mountainous shoulder and down the rippling muscle of his back. "I love touching you, and being touched. I'd probably be fine..."

"As long it was only a short time in bed together and nothing more." Sadness shadowed his words.

"I..."

What could I say? He was right.

I sighed and sat up, tucking the sheet around me so I could sit beside him without offering a peep show. I leaned against his shoulder and his arm came around me automatically.

I couldn't relax into him, but I didn't panic, either. Much.

I could deal with this. Last night's meltdown had only been because I was overtired and freaked out about Sam's programming. I was okay now...

I swallowed my thumping heart and spoke my thoughts aloud. "Maybe all my issues are part of what Sam programmed into my mind. Maybe if Nora tells me what it is and how to overcome it, I could..."

Could what?

Commit to a husband?

A child...?

A deluge of renewed terror choked me to silence. Kane turned to study me and I had to fight the urge to jump up and flee.

"Maybe," Kane said. "But maybe it's nothing to do with Sam. Now that Arnie has explained it, I can see that you show symptoms of post-traumatic stress if I do or say anything that even hints at commitment. With time and an enormous amount of effort you can probably mitigate that reaction, but..." He took my hand, stroking his thumb over the back of it in slow gentle circles. "...some things change you forever, no matter how hard you try to overcome them." His lips twisted in a bitter smile. "Believe me, I know."

CHAPTER 43

"I'm sorry," I murmured. "You deserve better."

"Don't apologize," Kane whispered fiercely. "Aydan, it isn't your fault." He took both of my hands in his. "It doesn't matter why you feel the way you do. Your emotions are as valid and important as mine. And I promise that you are safe with me..." He gave me a twisted smile and added, "... and from me." He nodded at the slumbering form in the other bed. "And Arnie will never let me overstep your boundaries. Even if you can't trust me, trust him."

I eased out a slow breath. "I do."

I knew I had hurt him again, but Kane squeezed my clammy hand and said, "Yes. I finally understand why you have that with him but not with me. And for the first time..." He let out a breath and faced me with a smile. "I'm not taking it personally."

"Oh, thank God!" The relief was so intense that I flung my arms around him and buried my face in his chest.

Kane's arms came cautiously around me, his touch light on my skin, and we stayed that way for long moments.

"I just realized something," he said, his lips moving softly against my hair. "This is the first time since I said I loved you that you've actually relaxed in my arms."

"This is the first time that I haven't felt like you're mad or hurt or disappointed," I mumbled into his shirt.

"Oh, Aydan." His arms tightened around me, then loosened again to a safe pressure. "How could two well-meaning people go so wrong?"

I sighed and sat up, readjusting the sheet around me. "Like I told you: With me, anything that can go wrong..." I didn't bother to complete the quote.

"Ha."

We sat side by side in silence for a few moments.

"I'm sorry it took me so long to understand all this," Kane said. "I hope you'll..." He broke off, making a frustrated gesture. "Dammit. I didn't realize how often I lay my expectations on you. No wonder you felt trapped." He let out a breath. "Just know that whatever you choose to do or not do, it won't change the way I feel about you. Your wellbeing is far more important to me than my own."

"Th-Thank you."

Even though I wanted with all my heart to believe him, the old ugly suspicions whispered darkly in the back of my mind. It was just another ploy to lull me into a false sense of security...

I shook my head violently to dislodge the demons. No, dammit; John wasn't like that. He wouldn't manipulate or force me. And Arnie would protect me no matter what.

Kane gave me a questioning look.

"Headache," I muttered.

"Why don't you go back to sleep? It's only seven A.M., and until Skidmark calls we're stuck here doing nothing anyway."

"Good idea," I said gratefully. "You should wake Arnie up and get some sleep yourself."

"I will. Sleep well." He hesitated, then leaned over and kissed me lightly.

"You, too." I returned the kiss and then pulled away to burrow into the pillow.

Maybe Nora's information could fix me.

What would it be like to welcome my attraction to Kane? To easily love a man who had proved over and over that he loved me? Who wanted to spend his life with me in spite of everything I'd put him through?

My heart fluttered between terrified hope and sick panic.

What if it was only Sam's programming?

What if it wasn't?

Shut up.

I lay still, keeping my eyes closed while Kane and Hellhound switched places. After a few minutes of quiet movement and bathroom activity everything fell silent again. Kane's breathing gradually slowed and deepened into sleep, but I lay keyed up and alert.

I could feel Arnie watching me.

Dammit, I hated it when people watched me sleep.

Was this another piece of my fucked-up programming? Afraid to be vulnerable, even for an instant?

I hissed out a breath and reared up to punch the inoffensive pillow.

Arnie crossed the room to sit on the bed. "Can't get back to sleep, darlin'?" he whispered.

I flopped facedown into the pillow, then rolled over and sat up with a sigh. I matched his quiet volume, hoping we weren't disturbing Kane. "No. I'm going to get dressed and put Teresa's face on."

"Then I'm gonna sit on your bed 'stead a' that fuckin' chair. Christ, I only sat there a few minutes an' already my ass feels like I spent the night with a chick with a whip fetish."

"And you would know that feeling, how...?" I teased sotto voce.

He waggled his eyebrows at me. "A gentleman never tells, darlin'."

"And you're such a gentleman."

"Fuckin' A." He grinned. "I'd rip off a fart to prove it, but I already cleared out my system in the can earlier."

"For which I am truly thankful." I kissed him and headed for the bathroom.

Putting on Teresa's face and clothing used up twenty minutes.

Breakfast took a whole fifteen.

Then Hellhound and I reclined on the bed with our backs propped against the headboard, staring at the dingy walls. Anemic dawn eased listless fingers around the edges of the draperies. Around us, doors opened and closed and plumbing gurgled. Kane slept on.

I glanced at the glowing red numbers of the clock radio and sighed. Eight-ten. Three minutes since I'd last looked.

Tension wound up in my guts.

Dammit, Skidmark wasn't due to check in with us until noon. Four long hours of our lives, slowly ticking away in the gloom.

What if Ian had already recognized Skidmark, and he'd

been arrested?

They could be coming for us right now...

No. Skidmark wouldn't tell them anything.

But there had to be something I could do besides wait. My skin itched with the need for action.

With a sigh, I rolled off the bed and retrieved my laptop. As I settled back beside him, Hellhound leaned over to whisper, "Whatcha doin'?"

"Just..." I made an impatient gesture. "Surfing the web. I can't check my email; Holt's probably tracing it. I can't do any research because they might have Spider and the rest of the analysts watching for relevant search engine keywords..."

"So you're pretty much stuck with LOLCats," Hellhound summed up the situation.

"Yeah."

He shrugged philosophically and snuggled closer to watch over my shoulder while I browsed to the site.

The comical memes didn't hold my attention. I skimmed some news sites, then closed the laptop with sigh. "Now I'm really fucking depressed."

"Yeah, the news is best in small doses," Hellhound agreed. "Now what?"

"Argh!" I clutched the kerchief that was already making my scalp itch. "This is driving me nuts. There has to be something we can do besides hiding like rats in a hole. The longer we sit here, the more chance Holt's going to show up outside."

"Or Grandin an' Dirk," Hellhound offered helpfully.

"Or Ian." I punched the long-suffering pillow. "Dammit!"

Kane's eyes flicked open. "Status?" he snapped.

"Everything's fine. I'm sorry, I didn't mean to wake you. Go back to sleep."

He nodded and closed his eyes, and within minutes his breathing softened again.

They were long minutes.

Long, *long* fucking minutes.

My legs twitched and I sprang out of bed to pace. Back and forth along the narrow walkway between the beds and the TV. Six paces. Turn. Six more paces. Turn.

I had to do something. Maybe I should use my network key to sneak into Sirius's network. Find out what was happening there.

What were the chances that I was compromised? Karma had said it was unlikely.

And Nora was probably lying. She wasn't my real mother; she was only one of Sam's minions. She was probably hoping to convince me to work with her, to take up Sam's treasonous mantle again and sell intel to the highest bidder.

That had to be it.

All these other reactions were only my usual fucked-up-ness. So I could just go ahead and sneak a peek into the network...

"What, darlin'?" Hellhound whispered.

I peered at him in the dimness, realizing I had been standing stock-still staring into space. "Uh?"

"Ya look like ya got an idea."

"I was thinking I might try... something John and I talked about last night."

"Better wait'll he wakes up an' talk it over," Hellhound advised.

"We talked it over last night."

"An' since ya didn't do anythin' about it last night, I'm thinkin' ya prob'ly decided it wasn't a good idea. Somethin' change between now an' then?"

"N-Not really..."

His expression firmed. "Then you're gonna hafta wait'll he wakes up before ya go ahead."

"He's the one who suggested it," I argued. "I was too scared to try it at the time, but now I'm thinking it might be a good idea."

"Okay, so what changed?" Hellhound repeated patiently.

"I've just had more time to think about it."

"Or somethin' clicked in your brain an' now you're doin' what somebody else wants instead a' what ya know is right."

A flood of icy claustrophobia made me shudder. I had to get out of this room. Out of my own skin.

Run.

"Thank you very much, damn it!" I hissed, raking my fingernails up and down my arms in an attempt to overcome the creepy sensation.

"Sorry, darlin'." Hellhound got up to hug me, but the confinement of his embrace set my teeth on edge.

"Sorry. I can't..." I backed away, still scrubbing at my arms.

"It's okay." He eyed me worriedly. "D'ya wanna go for a walk or somethin'?"

"Yes!" I scurried for the door and shoved my feet into my boots. I was straightening to reach for my parka when my burner phone vibrated.

A deluge of adrenaline made me fumble the phone. I juggled it frantically for an instant before it escaped my grasp, bouncing off the TV stand with a nerve-shattering crack before thudding to the thin carpet.

CHAPTER 44

Kane jerked upright in the bed as I pounced on the phone.

"Please, please don't be broken," I implored, and pressed the Talk button.

My anxious 'hello' was greeted by Moonbeam's gentle voice.

"Good morning, Storm Cloud Dancer."

I collapsed onto the bed, my knees weakening half in relief and half in disappointment.

"Hi, Moonbeam Meadow Sky," I replied, remembering for once to address her by the full name she preferred.

Kane let out a breath and lay down again, and I made an apologetic face in his direction and headed for the bathroom.

"Is anything wrong?" Moonbeam asked as I swung the door shut behind me. "You sound breathless."

"Everything's fine; I just dropped the phone. Is everything all right there?"

"Yes." I could hear the smile in her voice as she added, "Karma Wolf Song and I are still coming to terms with the news of Cosmic River Stone's true occupation." Her voice warmed. "We are bursting with pride. What a blessing that all our years of training and preparation were not wasted after all."

My pulse ticked up. "Have you... said anything to him yet?"

"No, of course not. Skidmark made your situation clear to us. Despite our eagerness, we will wait as long as necessary for the correct time to bring it up." Ruefulness coloured her voice. "After all, we have waited over twenty years. Another day or two won't make a difference."

I let out a quiet breath of relief. "Thanks. I'm sorry you have to wait."

"It's quite all right, Storm Cloud Dancer. But that is not why I called. Do you have time to talk about Blaze Featherwind?"

My heart sank. Poor Nichele. She must be going crazy.

I sighed. "I have time. What's wrong?"

"Nothing is wrong, exactly, but she is pressuring you for a firm answer as to whether you will attend their wedding this evening."

Sickening guilt clenched my stomach. "I... I..." I had to swallow hard to hold my voice level. "I don't see any way that I can."

"I assumed as much." Moonbeam's voice softened. "I will try to let her down gently. I'll tell her that the chances are slim, but that you are doing your best to catch the last flight out of..." She paused. "Did you tell her where you were ostensibly working?"

"No. Just..." I cleared the thickness from the throat. "Just tell her I'm trying. And then later in the day..."

"I will break the news to her that you missed the flight," Moonbeam said. "I'm sorry this is such a difficult situation for you, Storm Cloud Dancer. Just know that Blaze Featherwind would be proud of you if she knew what you were truly doing."

I swallowed the growing lump in the throat and whispered, "Thanks."

"May the Earth Spirit guide and protect you, dear. Goodbye."

I disconnected and slumped down onto the toilet seat, head in hands. I hated this stupid job; this stupid life. I'd never asked for it. Never had a choice. The course of my life had been steered by the needs and greeds of others since childhood.

The walls of the bathroom seemed to press closer.

Trapped...

I shuddered and sprang up, using all my self-control to step calmly out of the bathroom instead of fleeing pell-mell.

Out. I had to get out...

I had only taken a few steps toward the door when the phone vibrated again.

My already-thumping heart picked up the pace. Moonbeam must have forgotten something. I scurried back into the bathroom and hit the Talk button.

"Hello?"

Skidmark's wheezy voice spoke three words: "Lunch at eleven-thirty." The connection went dead.

"*YES!*" I burst out of the bathroom, meeting Kane's and Hellhound's wide-eyed expressions with a grin. I gave a savage fist-pump. "That was Skidmark. He did it! Lunch at eleven-thirty. I'll call Reggie and see if we can get the lie detector." I pulled out my burner phone and texted him. Only moments after I sent the message, my phone vibrated.

When I answered, Reggie said, "Make it quick. I'm just going into Sirius."

"Any chance we can get the lie detector around noon?"

"I'll call Jack and see. Where do you want it?"

"I don't know yet. Hellhound will call you around eleven-thirty if we need it."

"Okay. Good luck." He hung up.

"Done!" I said to Kane and Hellhound.

"So far, so good," Kane observed. "Why are you wearing your boots?"

The walls closed in again and I hurried for the door. "I was going for a walk."

"Alone?" Kane shot a frown at Hellhound.

"Nah, I was gonna go with her," Hellhound assured him.

Kane's eyes narrowed as he studied me. "Why do you want to go for a walk?"

"I just need to get out of these four walls. I'm getting antsy."

"Ya oughta ask Kane about your idea now, too," Hellhound prompted.

"I was thinking I could check... into things," I said with a significant look at the pocket where Kane had stowed my network key.

Kane's frown deepened. "What happened to the objections you voiced last night?"

"I've had more time to think it over now."

He shook his head. "I'm sorry, Aydan, but I don't trust that kind of about-face. And I'm concerned that you're so anxious to leave for no apparent reason. I think you'd better stay in the room; and I definitely don't agree with your..." He shot a glance at Hellhound and obviously decided not to go into details. "...idea."

My pulse ticked up. "I just need a breath of fresh air," I argued. "I'm feeling claustrophobic."

"All right," Kane said slowly. He rolled to his feet and nodded to Hellhound. "We'll both come with you. We'll stand outside the door for a few minutes so you can get some fresh air."

Like prison guards.

The creepy feeling returned with a vengeance, and I scrubbed at my arms again.

"Ya keep doin' that," Hellhound said worriedly. "I've never seen ya do that before."

"It's..." I squirmed and scratched my scalp again through the kerchief. "I don't know whether it's because I'm so freaked out at the thought of having somebody else's programming inside my brain, or whether it's this damn kerchief and makeup giving me the heebie-jeebies, or whether it's just plain old garden-variety claustrophobia; but I want to climb right out of my own skin."

"It's prob'ly all those things together," Hellhound said with a sympathetic grimace.

"Or none of them," Kane countered grimly. "Maybe you're having a physical reaction to having your programming thwarted."

"*Not helping!*" I scratched some more.

"Come on, let's go outside," Hellhound said, and stepped into his boots to lead the way.

When the door opened, we all groaned. Several inches of fresh snow adorned the parking lot, and a bitter wind whipped sharp flakes into our faces.

I drew a couple of breaths that nearly freeze-dried my

lungs, and shivered. "Well, my claustrophobia's all better now. Let's go back inside."

"Thought you'd never ask," Hellhound said, and we retreated to the warmth of the room again.

After we had divested ourselves of our outerwear, Kane studied me. "How are you feeling now?"

"Better. It was just that... sitting here in the dark, it was like being in a dungeon."

"All right." He sank back onto the bed. "Traffic will be slower than usual with this weather, so we'd better allow an hour to get into position. That gives us half an hour to kill. I'm going to sleep some more, and you should, too."

"I already tried. I can't." I flopped down on the bed. "But at least it's only half an hour."

"You should take off your disguise," Kane said. "Nora will need to recognize your face; and if Holt catches us it won't matter whether you're wearing makeup or not."

"Right. Thank God!" I popped up from the bed. "That will help. Go back to sleep, then. I'll manage not to scream for the next thirty minutes."

He smiled and lay down again, and I hurried to the bathroom.

I spent the remaining time staring at the clock and imagining all the ways our plan could go wrong. Lost in his own thoughts, Hellhound hadn't spoken; and every tired cell in my body envied Kane's ability to sleep under any conditions.

When the glowing red digits finally showed ten-thirty, I sat up. "Showtime."

Kane rolled off the bed and onto his feet, looking so wide awake that I wondered whether he'd actually been sleeping after all.

"How ya doin', darlin'?" Hellhound asked.

"Okay," I lied. "I've been running over everything in my mind. At least this snow will make our little traffic jam more plausible when we grab Nora. It's a good thing we don't have any deadlines after we get her." I picked up my gear and headed for the door, still babbling. "And if this works; and if we can get the lie detector this afternoon; and if Nora talks; and if it turns out that she was lying about the programming; or even if there *is* programming but it's not an immediate threat; you could both go home tonight; and then I could investigate Grandin..."

I ran down. I had no idea how to prove that Grandin was framing me. And even if everything went exactly as planned with Nora this afternoon, there was still no way I'd get to Nichele and Dave's wedding tonight.

I sighed and slung on my parka with a heavy heart.

At eleven-twenty-five I jittered in the back seat of the Saturn while Kane sat calmly behind the wheel. His brown truck idled ahead of us in the alley, the cloud of exhaust in the icy air nearly obscuring it.

"Got them." The phone on the seat beside us spoke in Hellhound's voice, and the truck pulled out onto the street.

Kane followed at a leisurely pace, and I attempted to look relaxed while scanning for the taxi that contained Skidmark and Nora.

"I see them, too," I said, and pointed at the yellow cab wallowing along the snowy street ahead of us.

The brown truck appeared to be having difficulties. The

rear tires spun frequently, making the tail end of the vehicle bobble uneasily. So far, so good.

Kane eased into the other lane to pass Hellhound on the left. The Saturn's front-wheel drive chewed ungracefully through the ridges of snow between the lanes, but it slithered into its assigned position tractably enough. The vehicles around us moved slowly. A timid driver ahead of us seemed to be obstructing traffic, and the taxi extended its lead.

"Is that Rand?" Kane snapped.

"In the blue car that's holding everything up?" I strained my eyes. "Nope. Not Holt, either; or anybody else I recognize."

"Good." Kane changed lanes again, speeding up enough to pass the dawdler without looking unduly rushed.

Behind us, Hellhound fell back a car-length, still apparently struggling to maintain traction in the truck.

"He's going to burn out my transmission," Kane muttered. "Let's hope it doesn't go before we get this done."

We were approaching the taxi. In the back seat Skidmark and Nora sat close, their heads together as though enthralled with each other.

My heart hammered my ribs and I tried to look in all directions at once. Any bugs or locator devices on Nora should now be lying on the floor of the cab; but Ian wouldn't be far away. Like us, he would be cruising a few car-lengths ahead or behind and watching the taxi like a hawk.

"Where the hell is he?" I muttered.

"I don't know. Hellhound, can you see Rand?" Kane asked.

"Nope."

"Dammit." Kane let out a short breath. "Well, it can't be

helped. Let's set this up."

He changed lanes again, easing up on the right side of the taxi. Nora's side.

I held my breath.

Any minute now...

The light ahead of us turned yellow, but the cab went straight through.

"Dammit!" Kane stepped on the gas.

A roar behind us indicated that Hellhound had run the light, too. With typical Calgarian disregard for traffic signals, three other vehicles followed Hellhound through the intersection on a dead red light.

I snapped a glance at each of the drivers. "I don't recognize any of them."

"Good." Kane shifted his grip on the wheel. "We should catch the taxi at the next light."

We did.

This time the cab slithered to a stop. As we pulled up beside it, Kane yanked a black balaclava over his head, concealing his face.

"NOW!" Hellhound's shout through the phone was accompanied by a chorus of honking horns.

I was already out the door and into the street, yanking open the taxi's back door as the brown half-ton slid sideways toward us.

Nora scrambled out, wide-eyed, and I shoved her into the back seat and half-fell on top of her. Jerking the door shut behind us, I yelled, "GO!"

Kane accelerated into a hard right turn. More horns blared.

I popped up to see the brown half-ton stopped sideways

across three lanes of traffic, but I didn't see any dented fenders. Both rear doors of the taxi hung open and Skidmark was clambering into the passenger side of the half-ton.

Just before we turned a corner that hid the scene from view, the light changed and Hellhound drove smoothly away. The cabbie stood beside his abandoned car amid renewed honking, wearing a shell-shocked expression and clutching a fistful of cash.

"We're clear," Hellhound said a few moments later.

"Same," Kane replied, and disconnected.

"Aydan?" Nora sounded strained. "Could you please get off me now?"

"Sorry." I squirmed over to the other side of the seat and activated the bug detector as she righted herself, wincing.

"Green," I reported, and Kane's shoulders relaxed.

"Wh-Who...?" Nora began, leaning forward to peer at Kane.

"A friend," I said. "Tell me more about this programming in my mind."

"I... ah... where are we going?"

"That depends on you." I gave her my best steely glare. "I want everything you know. And I want you to tell me under a lie detector."

Her mouth dropped open. "Oh... Dani-dear, I... I couldn't." She blinked and sat up straighter, her jaw firming. "You know I can't consent to a polygraph test. I have far too much classified knowledge that I'm not at liberty to divulge, to you or..." She glanced at Kane's silent figure in the driver's seat. "Anyone."

My heart plummeted. Despite my conviction that she was nothing more than a fraud and a liar, some small idiotic part of me had been hoping she would pat my hand and reveal everything in a burst of maternal love.

What a moron.

But I still had to try.

"You can say anything you want in front of him," I said without much hope. "He won't tell anybody. And I'm not asking you to take a truth serum or anything; just a simple lie detector test. Yes or no questions. And you wouldn't have to answer any questions that weren't directly related to me and the programming Sam left in my brain."

"I... I don't think..." she began.

I turned to Kane with a sigh. "Okay, she's been lying right from the start. Pull over and we'll dump her."

"No! No, wait!" Nora clutched my sleeve as Kane slowed. "Dani-dear, please, this has been such a shock. And there's so much that you need to know, I barely know where to start. Just... give me a moment..."

I nodded at Kane and he resumed speed.

Nora sagged back in the seat. "Thank you. You were always such a quick-tempered child. I was hoping you might have grown more patient."

"I have *no* patience," I growled. "Especially not for you and your lies."

Her chin jerked up in a familiar gesture that wrenched my heart. "Don't you take that tone with me, missy! I had enough of your backtalk when you were a teenager."

"Obviously," I snarled. "Since you faked your own death to get away from me."

Her frown smoothed into sympathy. "Oh, Dani-dear, I'm so sorry. I can't blame you for being angry, but I hope you'll be able to forgive me when you know the whole story."

"You're stalling," I snapped. "Will you answer my questions under a lie detector or not?"

Her chin rose again. "Yes. I'll take a polygraph test."

CHAPTER 45

As I stared at Nora's determined expression my stomach clenched with fierce hope and queasy fear.

Nora had to know that my first question would be 'are you my mother'. And if she was prepared to answer that question under a lie detector, she had to be telling the truth.

She was my mother.

And Sam had programmed me.

I suppressed a shudder and diverted my mind to the less terrifying part of that combination.

Mom. Alive, after all these years. After sacrificing her home and family and the life she had known, to protect me...

I jerked my thoughts back from the beguiling fantasy. Just because I wanted it to be true didn't make it so; it only made it dangerously seductive.

And snatching Nora had been too easy.

I reactivated the bug detector. Green light again. Unbelieving, I waved it around the interior of the car.

Kane didn't speak, but I read his concerned gaze in the rearview mirror.

"It's still green," I said, and pocketed the device before leaning toward Nora. "Is this is a setup?"

She blanched. "No, of course not. Your friend Brenton searched me... very thoroughly..." Colour rose in her cheeks as she went on, "...and he removed a bug and a locator, which I left in the taxi. I wanted this, Dani-dear. I wanted to speak with you."

"What did you tell Ian?"

"Nothing."

"Bullshit."

We glared at each other for a moment before she sighed and capitulated. "I told him that you had come to visit me two nights ago to discuss Sam, and that you had left without harming me. I don't know who drugged me after that, but I told Ian I was certain it hadn't been you. The agent from your Department... Holt, is it?"

I nodded, and she sniffed and went on, "What a rude man. But he unwittingly helped my cause by pressuring Ian to use me as bait to lure you back to the hotel. I was at my wits' end worrying that you'd come back and fall into their trap."

"So how did you get away?" I demanded. "If you had the locator on you when you left the hotel, then Ian and Holt knew exactly where you were. At least one of them would have followed you."

"Not Holt. I am Ian's responsibility, and he certainly wouldn't entrust my safety to another agent."

"You're avoiding my questions again," I ground out. "How did you get away from Ian? And don't hand me any bullshit about how you slipped away without him noticing. If you got away, it was because he let you go."

Her chin rose. "Of course he did. I'm sure he had been listening to the bug he had planted on me, and Brenton is very charming."

I managed not to snicker at the combination of 'Skidmark' and 'charming' in the same sentence while Nora went on, "Brenton showed me your portrait so I knew he was my contact, but we didn't say anything out loud that would make Ian suspicious. We chatted for quite a while and Brenton asked me to pose for a portrait, so it was completely believable when I told Ian I had met an interesting man and was going out for lunch with him. After all, I am on vacation so it would be reasonable for me to want to enjoy myself a bit."

"Vacation?"

"Yes. I requested two weeks' vacation after the official part of our trip here." Her eyes softened. "I was hoping to spend the time with you."

I fought the rush of warmth to my heart and kept my voice cold and level. "You still haven't told me how you got away from Ian. What are you hiding?"

She looked hurt. "I'm not hiding anything, Dani-dear. I knew Ian would have to follow me, so I simply asked him to respect my privacy by hanging back. He agreed, although not without some arguing. He must have been too far behind the taxi to react in time when you made your move."

Ian wouldn't screw up like that.

Heart thumping, I scanned the vehicles around us but saw nothing out of the ordinary. Where was the trap, dammit?

Or had we actually gotten away clean? It was remotely possible. Ian wouldn't be accustomed to driving in heavy snow; and particularly not on what he would consider the wrong side of the road. Maybe he had miscalculated and let us slip away.

"Where was Holt during all this?" I asked.

Nora waved a dismissive hand. "I have no idea. He and Ian didn't see eye to eye; and Ian made it clear to Holt that he didn't want or need assistance."

I eyed her with suspicion. "There's no way Holt would have just backed off because Ian told him to. If Holt thought there was a chance I'd show up, he'd have been there."

"I really don't..." Nora began, but the vibration of Kane's phone interrupted her.

Kane passed it back to me. When I answered, Hellhound's voice crackled through the speaker. "We're on. Rendezvous at twelve-thirty." He disconnected.

"Did you get that?" I asked Kane.

A silent nod was my only reply, and I breathed a sigh of relief. With Kane's face obscured by the balaclava and no voice to recognize, Nora wouldn't be able to positively identify him even if she did decide to rat us out.

I returned to questioning Nora. "What did Sam program into my mind?"

She glanced at Kane, her lips tightening. "That is for your ears only."

"That's not going to happen," I countered. "As long as I don't know what programming is in my mind, I'm not going anywhere or doing anything without supervision; and that includes talking to you. So spill it."

Nora crossed her arms and leaned back in the seat. "I'm sorry, Dani-dear, but that's the way it has to be. I can't tell anyone but you."

I tried a different tack. "When did you find out about Sam's programming? How much did he tell you?"

"I'm sorry, but I must insist on privacy."

I persisted with my questions for most of the half-hour ride, but she remained obdurate. Finally I abandoned the effort and we lapsed into silence.

A few minutes later Kane slowed and turned into the small parking lot under the bridge at Heritage and Glenmore. The brown half-ton was already there, and I was pleased to see that the continuing snow had deterred everyone else and we were alone. The Saturn wallowed valiantly across the rutted lot to park beside the half-ton.

As we slithered to a halt, Hellhound and Skidmark got out of the truck. The familiar lie detector case dangled from Hellhound's hand, and hope lifted my heart.

Finally, I could get all my answers...

"*Dammit!*"

Kane's sudden epithet made me snap my head around looking for the threat, but the Saturn was already in motion. Engine screaming under Kane's heavy foot, we churned across the parking lot.

Too late.

A car had already stopped sideways across the driveway. A moment later a second car blocked the other exit.

Kane slammed on the brakes and barked, "Run, Aydan!"

I hesitated, gripping the door handle. Ian was already crossing the parking lot, gun in hand. Nobody had gotten out of the second car yet, but it was probably Holt behind that tinted glass.

I wouldn't shoot either of them; and if I ran I wouldn't get far. Even in frigid weather the Bow River rarely froze, so escape was impossible in that direction unless I wanted to die a quick death in its icy water. And if Ian and Holt had cornered us so easily, it meant they'd been monitoring us all along. They undoubtedly had teams in place to nab me if I fled down one of the walking paths.

"AYDAN, GO!" Kane roared.

I sighed. "No point. It's over. Stay here while I go and talk to Ian. Maybe I can still get you out of this."

I climbed out of the car, keeping my hands where Ian could see them. Behind me, Hellhound and Skidmark stood uncertainly.

"I'm disappointed, Storm," Ian said as he ambled over, looking deceptively friendly and relaxed. "I thought I'd been clear that you weren't to speak with Nora unless I was present."

Hoping to hide the pounding of my heart, I emulated his casual tone with a shrug and a smile. "Sorry about that. Orders. You know how it goes. How did you find us?"

"Satellite tracking." He smiled in return. "I recognized Skidmark this morning, so I expected you to act soon. I picked up a live satellite feed through MI6 to watch the hotel and surrounding streets. Since I didn't know what vehicle you'd be driving, I had to wait until you made your move."

"You recognized me?" Skidmark demanded. "Well, shit."

"You owe me fifty bucks, old man," I told him without turning.

Ian laughed. "Thank you for betting on my powers of observation. I'm flattered."

I sighed. "Satellite tracking. Damn. I wasn't actually expecting you to screw up and lose Nora, but I was hoping."

"That was a lovely little vehicular dance you did in the middle of the street." Ian tipped his chin in a deferential gesture. "I'm sure I would have lost you there if I had actually been following Nora's cab. Now, I'm sorry; but I must break up this little party. Will Kane give me a problem if I open his car door?"

Nausea twisted my guts. Ian had barely glanced at Kane wearing the balaclava and he still recognized him. Granted, Kane's height and the breadth of his shoulders were difficult to miss in the small car; but I had been clinging to the foolish hope that he might remain anonymous.

And now he and Arnie and Skidmark would be arrested.

And so would I.

All my worst fears were coming true...

I must have made some small desperate sound.

Ian frowned. "Don't cause any more trouble for yourself than you've already done, Storm. Be a good sport, now."

As I stood frozen with indecision, Skidmark advised quietly, "Do what he says, Storm. We're all on the same side here. We can figure everything out as long as nobody does anything stupid."

I swallowed hard. Skidmark trusted Ian. I should, too.

But why had he shot me earlier?

"Come on, Storm," Skidmark urged. "Just do what Ian says."

Skidmark was right. Even though I wasn't sure I could trust Ian, my only other option was to shoot him.

And I couldn't.

I finally managed to unlock my stiff neck muscles with a nod. "We'll cooperate. I'll tell John."

Tottering forward, I opened the driver's door and leaned down. Kane stared rigidly ahead, both hands on the wheel.

"Ian wants..." I began, but Ian's hand flashed past me and jabbed a small dart into Kane's neck.

Kane reacted instantly, his hand clamping around Ian's wrist.

"John, no!" The words had barely left my mouth when Kane's hand slid nervelessly off Ian's wrist to dangle limply by his side. His body slumped, lolling sideways in the seat.

"That's how it's supposed to work," Ian said with satisfaction. "Straight into the bloodstream instead of messing about with an intramuscular shot and giving someone..." He shot me a disapproving look. "...the opportunity to shoot me in return."

My heart hammered in my chest, my words ghosting out on the tiny breath of air still available from my rigid diaphragm. "That's... just... a tranquilizer, I hope...?"

"Of course." Ian frowned. "We're all friends here. Now, Skidmark? Hellhound? Into the car, please. I don't want you to freeze to death in the twenty minutes you'll be asleep."

"What d'ya want me to do, Aydan?" Hellhound asked. His voice was calm, but his knuckles glowed white on the handle of the lie detector case.

"Just do as he says." The words burned like acid in my throat.

All my fault.

The two men I loved, plus a man who had sacrificed most of his life to uphold the law; all of them would rot in prison because of me.

Hellhound nodded and moved closer, his weight on the balls of his feet and his gaze locked on mine. My slightest flinch or blink would send him into a murderous rampage if he misunderstood my intentions.

I drew as deep a breath as I could manage around my aching heart. I didn't deserve his loyalty, much less his love.

"I don't want any trouble, Arnie," I said firmly. "You haven't done anything wrong, and I want to keep it that way. Just get in the car. Skidmark; you, too."

They both shuffled over and climbed into the vehicle. As soon as they were settled, Ian tranquilized them.

"You, too, Nora," Ian said as he rounded the car and opened her door.

"How dare you..." she began, but slumped into unconsciousness as Ian's dart found its mark.

"So that's sorted," Ian said jauntily as he closed the door. "There's plenty of petrol so the heater will keep them warm until they wake up. And..." He gave me one of his sparkling smiles. "...perhaps we can conceal this little escapade from your authorities so nobody has to go to prison. Now, Storm, I'm sorry to have to ask; but I'll need your weapons."

Fearful hope made my hands tremble as I handed over my pistols butt-first. Maybe Ian would let us go. Maybe he only wanted to question me about Nora.

Ian eyed me with a half-smile as he stowed my weapons in his parka pockets. "I've been dying to get my hands on that tranquilizer pistol. I do hope that's all of your weapons. It would be a disappointing breach of professional courtesy if you were holding out on me. Do I need to search you?"

Couldn't hurt to flirt a bit.

I turned around, widening my legs and placing my hands on the car while I shot a smile over my shoulder. "You don't need to, but you can if you want."

He laughed. "That didn't end well for me last time. I'll take you at your word."

I straightened and turned again, and Ian leaned against the Saturn beside me, looking perfectly comfortable despite the frigid wind that was making my teeth rattle and my knees knock.

Or maybe that was only fear.

"Why are you investigating Nora?" Ian asked. "And give me the whole story this time. If you don't..." He nodded toward the drooping occupants of the car, his beautiful eyes as hard as emeralds. "...I'll make sure all three of them go to prison for kidnapping. But if you tell me everything, maybe we can work something out."

Dammit, what could I tell him? I couldn't betray my country's classified information, not even to save my friends.

But Ian was an MI6 agent. An ally. Maybe it would be okay.

Or maybe he was an enemy.

How could I know?

Stall.

"Well, it's a long story and a lot of it's classified," I began.

"*Wait there!*"

Ian's sudden shout made me twitch violently, but then I realized he was looking past me toward the road.

I spun to follow his gaze and my stomach plunged at the sight of the occupants of the other car approaching fast.

It wasn't Holt after all.

It was Grandin and Dirk.

Shit, shit, shit!

CHAPTER 46

Grandin and Dirk momentarily slowed at Ian's shout, but then hurried forward again.

"Bollocks!" Ian muttered without moving his lips. "Play along, Storm. Trust me."

"What...?" I began, but Ian had already moved several paces forward, all his attention on the other two.

As they strode past him toward me, Ian said, "I told you I needed a few minutes. I'm not finished."

"Time's up," Grandin snapped. His hand arced upward.

I hesitated an instant too long. Pain stung the side of my neck, and I jerked away to see Grandin smirking as he pocketed a spent dart.

"That was uncalled-for," Ian objected, frowning. "She wasn't going to cause any trouble."

I pressed my hand to the stinging spot on my neck and my fingertips came away bearing a small smear of blood.

Tranked.

Any second now the world would turn black...

It didn't.

"Was that...?" Ian began as the first waves of vertigo rippled through my vision.

"Just a little Vitamin K," Grandin said. "She'll be fine. Thanks, Rand." He and Dirk each grabbed one of my arms and dragged me toward their car.

I lashed out with frantic kicks, but already my legs were turning to rubber. Dammit, the dart must have hit a vein. The drug was working much faster than it had before.

"Ian! Help!" My unwieldy tongue barely managed the words.

"Grandin!" Ian shouted as they dragged me away.

Thank God. He had weapons. He would save me...

"Remember, you owe me!" Ian yelled behind us.

What?

Ian's words looped through my fuzzy brain, echoes fading into horror. Grandin owed him. Ian had set me up...

"Here's what I owe you!" Grandin yelled back. He let go of me and spun.

Gun.

No...

I tried to strike his hand, but my arm flailed uselessly through empty space. Depth perception gone...

The explosion of the gunshot was like a physical blow.

Ian's body jerked backward, slamming into the Saturn before dropping to the snow with the boneless finality of death. A streak of fresh crimson marred the Saturn's gold side.

Time tumbled into chaos. Impossibly slow, yet too fast for me to comprehend.

I was screaming. Wordless cries, my mouth sundered from my brain. Already the drug was taking over, my extremities tingling and burning.

"What the *hell*?" Dirk let go of me and snatched his own

gun from his holster, the weapon swinging toward Grandin.

My knees buckled and I fell.

Barely able to feel my fingers, I dug into my pocket. Poor treacherous Ian hadn't searched me. I still had a secured phone...

Grandin's pistol spoke the only explanation Dirk would ever get.

The first shot spun him around and slapped him to the ground. The second blew off the top of his head, blood spraying across the white snow. Scarlet droplets danced in my blurring vision.

I couldn't stop screaming.

My fingers wouldn't work.

I mashed my hand on the phone's keypad over and over.

Please hit the speed dial button, please, please...

Grandin swooped down on me. His nose was an eagle's beak slicing the air, ready to tear me to ribbons...

Ridiculously loud in the slow silence swelling between my ears, I heard the phone's first ring.

Saved.

Stemp would know something was wrong. He would trace the phone and send a team...

Ring.

Ring.

Grandin yanked the phone out of my limp hand and disconnected, glaring down at me. "Nice try," he snapped, then grabbed my hand and pressed my useless fingers around the butt of his gun and onto the trigger. Carefully retrieving one of the ejected brasses from the snow with his gloved hand, he pressed my finger onto one of them, too.

"You're such a dangerous criminal, murdering these

good agents," he said conversationally. "It's going to look even worse for you when you injure me and escape my custody, but at least I'll get to come home a hero." He tossed a contemptuous nod at the two bodies leaking red into the snow. "Not like these poor schmucks. Walk."

"Wha..." I mumbled as he yanked me to my feet. I toppled helplessly toward him and he slung my arm over his shoulders and dragged me toward his car. "Esktrdite?" I slurred. "Why...?"

He laughed. "Forget extradition. I found a better market for you, Arlene Widdenback."

Suddenly we were only a few feet from the car.

I must be walking.

Maybe flying. I couldn't feel my arms or legs.

My head floated, a helpless balloon filled with only one thought.

Stemp wasn't there.

Only Dermott.

Dermott, who never answered until the fourth or fifth ring.

The car opened its gaping maw and swallowed me.

They had me.

Even as I struggled up through choking blackness, I knew it. Words buffeted me but I couldn't make them stick together. When I opened my eyes, nightmare figures jousted above me. Spears plunged through my body to emerge dripping with gore.

Unable to move, unable to feel, I could only scream in imagined agony. Beside me, Kane and Hellhound sat chained to chairs. Their lips moved in incomprehensible words of anger or fear.

A glittering blade sliced down, beheading them both. Their bodies twitched and jerked, blood drenching their clothes and filling the room ankle deep, then knee deep, then higher. A tidal wave of blood lapped around me, submerging my body, running into my nose and mouth until I choked and drowned in the metallic taste of my own screams.

Then the blood was gone. Kane and Hellhound stood on either side of my bed, smiling and stroking my face. Their hands slid down my body to plunge into my belly. Grinning, they raised slippery loops of my intestines above their heads in a gruesome tug-of-war...

At last the words began to make sense and my eyelids responded to my desperate attempts to shut out the horrible sights that surrounded me.

"It's okay, darlin', everythin's okay. You're safe. Kane an' me, we got your back. Nobody's gonna hurt ya. It's okay..."

Arnie couldn't be here. I had been captured. It was just another hallucination. I squeezed my eyelids more tightly, clinging to my last merciful moments of delirium before I had to face the horrible reality.

Where was I?

Had Grandin already turned me over to his buyer?

What barbaric torture would I suffer when they realized I was conscious?

I lay still, pretending with all my might that the steady reassurance of Arnie's voice was real.

When his screams of agony began, I didn't open my eyes.

"Hey, Aydan." A gentle hand stroked my hair. "Talk to me, darlin'. How ya doin'?"

Afraid to think, afraid to move, I kept my eyes closed.

"Come on, darlin', talk to me," Arnie persisted. "It's okay, you're safe here at the Silverside hospital. Ya got shot up with ketamine again but you're gonna be okay. It oughta be mostly outta your system by now. Are ya feelin' better?"

I knew how this would end.

I lay still, waiting for his screams to start.

"Thought ya said she oughta be comin' around," Arnie said, sounding worried.

Cool fingers closed on my wrist. "She should soon."

"She hasn't screamed for nearly half an hour," Arnie persisted. "Why ain't she wakin' up? Last time she was awake even while she was goin' through the last of the hallucinatin'."

"She has been conscious for at least an hour." The voice belonging to the cool fingers sounded like Dr. Roth. "She may be reacting to trauma by withdrawing. Keep talking to her. I'm sure she can hear you."

Kane's strong baritone joined the conversation. "Do you think she might have lasting problems?"

"From the drug? It's unlikely. From the emotional trauma..." Dr. Roth didn't finish the sentence. "Just keep reassuring her," she said instead. "I'll be back to check on her again soon."

Warm hands closed around mine, Arnie's strong fingers on my right and Kane's broad palm on my left.

"Hey, darlin', don't worry, you're safe," Arnie began again. "Kane an' me, we're both here watchin' your back."

"Everything's all right," Kane joined in. "You're here at the Silverside Hospital and you're safe..."

There were no more screams. John's and Arnie's voices alternated reassurances, my hands warm in theirs. The squeak of passing rubber-soled shoes, the steady beeping of monitors, and announcements on a public address system created a soundscape of familiar hospital noises in the background.

Was I safe?

Or was this only a cruel hallucination?

At last my aching bladder left me no choice. I had to admit I was conscious, or wet the bed.

I opened my eyes.

"Hey, darlin'," Arnie said softly. "D'ya know where ya are?" He and Kane both leaned forward, their gazes locked on my face.

I surveyed my surroundings. It looked exactly like the secured wing of the Silverside Hospital, right down to two burly black-clad armed guards standing in the corner of my cubicle.

But I could be wrong...

"I... I'm hallucinating," I croaked. "I'm not really here. Grandin took me..."

"Holt arrested Grandin and retrieved you," Kane said. "This really is the Silverside Hospital. You're not hallucinating."

"Really...?" I studied their faces, waiting for them to rip

my guts out all over again.

They just smiled and squeezed my hands, one on each side.

"Really, darlin'," Arnie said. "You're really here. You're really safe."

Necessity took over. "I *really* need to pee," I squeaked, afraid to take a full breath in case my bladder overflowed.

Hellhound laughed. "C'mon then, darlin'. The can's right across the hall. Ya need a hand?" He helped me sit up and swing my legs over the edge of the bed.

Dr. Roth hurried in, then stopped with a smile. "That's better. How are you feeling?"

"Need to *pee...*" I gritted.

She laughed and stepped aside as I stood up. With the aid of Arnie's strong shoulder I staggered into the bathroom. He withdrew, closing the door behind him, and I dropped onto the toilet practically keening with relief.

At last I dragged myself to my feet and propped myself against the sink to wash my hands, then emerged cautiously.

One of the guards was stationed in the hallway beside the bathroom door, eyeing Hellhound and me with equal intensity. Clutching the inadequate hospital gown closed over my ass, I accepted Hellhound's arm and wobbled back to my bed.

"Better?" he inquired as I lay back with a sigh.

"So much better," I assured him. "Good God, I thought I was going to keep peeing until I shrivelled up and fell in..." Suddenly remembering Kane's presence, I muttered, "Sorry, too much information" as heat climbed my cheeks.

Kane chuckled. "You don't need to apologize. I've known you for a long time. I would only be shocked if you actually managed to shock me."

I grinned. "Damn, I'll have to try harder."

One of the guards pressed his fingertips to his earpiece, listening intently, and my smile slipped away.

Grandin's unknown buyer might not have me, but I still wasn't free; or even safe. The programming in my brain could still decree my death sentence. And Kane and Hellhound were still guilty of kidnapping, and maybe treason.

"What happened?" I asked.

Hellhound began, "They cleaned up the site an' flew us all here in the Griffon-" but the second guard snapped, "No talking!"

"I ain't givin' away anythin'," Hellhound protested. "Everybody's done their statements already, an'-"

"You were only allowed to sit with Agent Kelly as long as you didn't discuss the case." The guard gave him a flat stare. "Until she completes her report under the lie detector and Command decides what charges will be laid, you are all detainees. Will I need to separate you?"

Hellhound gave him a look that would have made any sane man fall to his knees and beg for mercy. "No," he grated.

The first guard said, "Yes, sir" into the handset clipped to his chest, then fixed us with a hard gaze as his hand dipped casually to rest on his machine gun. "Command wants to see you now," he said.

CHAPTER 47

Kane turned to face the armed guard, his posture stiffening. "Tell Command they'll just have to wait until the doctor clears Aydan," he said.

"She's cleared. Command just got word," the guard replied impassively, but his calm tone was belied by the tension in his posture.

Hellhound turned, too, to stand shoulder to shoulder with Kane. The guards were big men, but they seemed to shrink by comparison.

"Who the hell cleared her?" Hellhound growled. "'Cause I ain't seen the doc-" He broke off as Dr. Roth slipped into the cubicle. "Hey, Doc," he said. "Did ya clear Aydan to go to a briefin' with Command?"

She took in the strained atmosphere with a glance, and laid a calming hand on Hellhound's arm. "Yes, I did. The drug should be almost completely out of her system by now. She may still have a few minor visual disturbances or memory problems, and if she's feeling shaky she can use a wheelchair; but there's no reason to keep her here. She has been conscious for quite some time. Physically, she's just as healthy as any other patient who has recently recovered from anaesthesia."

She stepped sideways to make eye contact with me. "Aydan, you should be fine. Technically you're considered to be impaired for the next twenty-four hours, so no driving, no operating heavy equipment, no signing contracts or making major decisions; the usual. And of course, if you have any unexpected reactions, come straight to Emergency."

I nodded, my heart sinking. Trying to convince Command of my innocence didn't seem like something I should attempt while legally impaired; but apparently I wasn't going to be offered a choice.

How the hell could I prove I hadn't killed Dirk and Ian? I was pretty sure I hadn't, but the drug had already been in my system.

My memories flickered, flaring into horrible clarity as Dirk and Ian fell; but sideslipping and fading before and after. Grandin had shot them both, I knew it... but somehow I couldn't quite remember him pulling the trigger.

There had been a gun in my hand. But I hadn't fired it, I was certain. Almost certain...

The sensation of slick snow-chilled brass lingered vividly on my fingertips. A spent cartridge. I had been holding a spent cartridge. I shuddered. What if I *had* killed them, under the influence of the drug?

And if I didn't even know myself, what would the lie detector indicate? Grandin had almost certainly accused me by now; and with no witnesses...

I swallowed hard and tried not to think about it.

By the time I had quivered into my clothes and signed all the necessary paperwork under Kane's supervision, Hellhound had commandeered a snack and a wheelchair for me. Flanked by the two guards, he wheeled me toward the door with Kane pacing beside us while I gobbled a hospital-issue egg salad sandwich and orange juice.

A windowless black van waited at the hospital entrance, and I reluctantly parted with the wheelchair to clamber unsteadily into the back. The guards shackled us to the benches, and one of them took a seat in the back with us while the other slammed and locked the doors.

Fighting claustrophobia, I breathed slowly and deeply.

Please don't let me go to prison.

Kane and Hellhound watched me worriedly, and I closed my eyes to shut them out. Guilt burned in my chest.

I shouldn't have listened to Skidmark. I should have told him to stay in Silverside, and I should never have called Kane. If he went to prison now, Alicia would make sure he never saw Daniel again.

"Ya okay, darlin'?" Hellhound asked softly.

Unable to trust my voice, I nodded without opening my eyes.

The short trip to Sirius felt interminable.

At last we disembarked, to be herded through the deserted lobby and into the secured area's time-delayed entry.

Four big men and me.

The heavy door thumped closed behind us and my breath accelerated to shallow panting. No air.

No space.

No freedom, ever again...

"Would you mind stepping back against the walls?" Kane asked politely. "Aydan needs some space."

The guards eyed me with suspicion.

"Space for what?" one demanded.

"Just space," Hellhound growled.

The first man shrugged and stepped back a pace while the other turned away to place his eye at the level of the retinal scanner. The cramped chamber didn't allow anything more, but even those few inches were better than nothing. I gave Kane a grateful look but kept silent, afraid my voice would betray me if I spoke.

When the second door opened thirty seconds later to reveal the featureless concrete stairway that always made me feel as though I was being buried alive, I tucked my hand into the crook of Kane's elbow and squeezed my eyes shut.

His hand closed over mine and he guided me down the stairs while I pretended with all my might that I was somewhere else. Walking down my own basement stairs, retreating to the safety of my secret room...

The clang of the final door behind us was accompanied by the movement of cool air across my face. I opened my eyes again and tried to reassure myself.

Lots of space down here. Constant circulation of fresh air. Nice big white corridors and lots of glass in the labs.

And beyond them, high-security prison cells that had never seen the light of day...

My breath hitched and I stumbled.

"Okay, darlin'?" Hellhound's arm came around me, warm with affection I didn't deserve.

"Yeah," I lied faintly. "My legs are just a bit shaky."

"This way." The guards ushered us down the corridor toward the conference room. When the door swung open my trembling knees nearly dropped me to the floor.

Far too many uniforms with far too much gold braid.

Good God, the whole chain of command was here. Dermott and Stemp and Holt, too.

Fuck, I couldn't do this...

Stop panicking. Focus.

I drew an unsteady breath and tried to let it out slowly as we moved into the room. Among the impassive faces around the conference table, I spotted a few friendly ones. Skidmark offered me an ironic salute and Spider gave me a feeble smile, his face drawn with worry.

Farther down the table, Jack's ivory complexion was paler than usual and her beautiful blue eyes had dark smudges under them. Oh, God, I'd forgotten that I'd dragged her into this. And Reggie, too; although he wasn't here at the moment. Had I destroyed their lives as well?

My guilty gaze flitted away from Jack to the other end of the table.

I stopped short.

Hellhound walked into me and I stumbled forward a couple of paces, my jaw dropping.

"*Ian?*" My voice pitched into an incredulous squawk.

He winced and whispered, "Not so loud, please. Terrible headache."

"I thought you were dead!" My volume made him wince again, and I lowered my voice and added, "Sorry. But what happened? The way you hit the ground I was sure you were dead..."

"I almost wish I had been," he murmured, cradling his temples. "I was wearing a bulletproof vest. The bullet threw me back and I cracked my nut on the car. Knocked me out and came damned close to scalping me." He rotated his chair cautiously to exhibit a large shaved patch on the back of his head decorated with dozens of stitches.

"Well, that explains all the blood..." Hope rose in my chest, only to subside immediately. "But you were unconscious. So you didn't see what happened with Grandin and Dirk."

"Out cold, I'm afraid," Ian agreed ruefully.

Dark suspicion whispered in my ear. Ian had said Grandin owed him. And Grandin had double-tapped Dirk, but not Ian.

My heart froze. Ian and Grandin were working together to frame me.

Omigod.

I was completely fucked.

"Enough jawing," Dermott snapped. "Sit."

I stumbled to the nearest chair and fell into it. Kane and Hellhound took seats on either side of me, and the two guards stepped away to form an ominous backdrop against the wall.

"Travers, hook her up," Dermott said. As Jack stood and made her way around the table, lie detector case in hand, Dermott added, "Everybody else gave their statements while you were in the hospital, so this is just a formality."

My heart plummeted.

It was over before it started. With Ian and Grandin both testifying against me, I didn't have a chance.

Jack's icy fingers trembled against my forehead while she fastened the headdress of electrodes.

When I was hooked up, Dermott waved an impatient hand. "Holt, go ahead."

Holt rose and stalked toward me, his steely gaze pinning me mercilessly to my chair. "Is your name Aydan Kelly?" he snapped.

"Y-Yes."

Green light. I took small comfort from that, at least.

"Tell us what happened," he said.

I froze. That wasn't a yes or no question. Had they modified the lie detector?

"Come on, Kelly," Holt prompted. Or maybe he was taunting me.

"I, um..." My voice came out in a feeble croak and I cleared my throat. "Where do you want me to start?"

"Start when you left the secured facility in Calgary with Stemp."

I darted a glance at Stemp's expressionless face. Oh, God, was I going to ruin him, too?

"We, um... we left. Stemp gave me..." I scanned the room. Not enough security clearances here. "Some, um... classified items... and told me that the chain of command had told him to give them to me. He said my orders were to drop off-grid and investigate Nora Taylor. Then we went to the airport to meet his parents for supper. I gave his mom my cell phone to take back to my place, and we went our separate ways."

The lie detector didn't blink and Holt didn't interrupt with any questions, so I went on with my story, leaving nothing out. When I got to the part about meeting Nora and Ian in his room I dared a frown at Ian. "Why did you shoot me?"

He gave me a sheepish smile. "Sorry, Storm."

A flicker of alarm must have shown on my face at his use of the nickname. He added, "Don't worry, I'm not giving away secrets. Your chain of command has always known about my involvement at the commune, and now they know about Skidmark and Moonbeam and Karma, too." I eyed Stemp, trying to gauge his reaction, but he remained impassive while Ian went on, "And as per our agreement, your names..." He included Skidmark with a flick of his gaze. "...will be redacted from my reports to my superiors."

"Thanks," I said. "So why did you shoot me?"

He gave one of his debonair shrugs, followed by a wince as the movement jarred his head. "I wanted the phone number that Nora had given you."

"So you *shot* me?" I couldn't keep the outrage out of my voice.

"You were going to do the same to me so you could talk to Nora alone," he said reasonably.

I deflated. "Right. Sorry."

"Get on with it," Dermott snapped.

Nobody interrupted while I described Nora's revelations about our relationship and Sam's mental programming; my discovery of the metal powder in my pocket; and my conscription of Skidmark, Kane, and Hellhound. Keeping the varying security clearances of my audience in mind, I filtered out the classified information while still telling the whole story as best I could.

"...And then I woke up in the hospital," I finished at last, and slumped with exhaustion.

Holt stood staring down at me, arms crossed over his chest and jaw jutting. This was the part where he pronounced my guilt without even cross-examining me...

A small defiant part of my mind reared up and pushed a question out of my mouth. "Ian, what did you mean when you told Grandin he owed you? Were you working together to frame me?"

Holt snorted. "No, he was working with me to sting Grandin. Supposedly." He shot a glare at Ian.

Ian remained unperturbed. "I *was* working with you," he told Holt calmly. "But I had my own interests to protect, too. I had promised Skidmark that I wouldn't reveal his identity so I couldn't tell you about him; and I wanted a private conversation with Storm. But I made sure I activated the audio and video feed when it mattered, didn't I?"

"Huh," Holt said, clearly irritated at being left out of the loop. "It was just damn lucky you did."

My stomach lurched. Audio and video feed? Oh God, had Holt been watching while I was making out with Ian?

"Wait," I said, my face flaming. "What audio and video feed?"

"The one that recorded Grandin shooting Dirk and me, and trying to frame you," Ian said cheerfully.

CHAPTER 48

"*What?*" The word leaped from my mouth with all the force of my suddenly-surging hope behind it. "You recorded that?"

Ian smiled. "Of course. I activated the recorder as soon as I saw Grandin and Dirk coming over."

"I saw you reach up to your throat when you stepped away from me. I thought you were zipping up your parka because it was so damn cold out."

Ian's smile widened. "So did they."

"But... But..." Words failed me. "Explain," I demanded.

"Not so fast," Holt snapped. "You're the one answering questions here."

"Right," I said faintly. "Sorry."

My heart rattled in my throat. Did this mean they believed me? Or were they only offering me a flash of false hope before the axe fell?

"Was that a complete account of everything you've done since you left the secured facility on Thursday?" Holt asked.

"Yes," I said absently, my mind still reeling over the ramifications of Ian's recording.

The green light blinked on the lie detector and I caught

my breath. Shit, that had been a real question.

But I had passed.

Easing out a careful breath, I sat up straight and focused all my attention on Holt.

"Was everything you told us true?" he asked.

"Y-Yes..."

The instant between my answer and the flash of the green light seemed like an eternity.

Passed again. I dared one more breath.

"Are you aware of any crime you have committed that might be the result of outside programming embedded in your mind?"

I struggled to unravel the question. Dammit, my brain still wasn't up to normal speed. Was he asking if I'd knowingly committed any crimes? What would that really mean? As an agent I sometimes did things that would be considered a crime if a civilian had done them...

I gave up. "I'm sorry, I don't know how to answer that question. Could you simplify it?"

Holt glowered at me. "To your knowledge, have you done anything that would compromise national security?"

Guilt swamped me. I had revealed classified technology to Skidmark. And I'd told Kane, a civilian, about the U.S.'s top-secret weapons presentation.

But did that count as compromising national security? Skidmark was an agent, and Kane was an ex-agent...

"I... don't know," I stammered.

Holt hissed out an irritable breath. "That's why I said 'to your knowledge'. It's not a hard question, Kelly! Yes or no?"

"Well, I told Skidmark and Kane..." I began.

"Never mind that," Holt interrupted. He scowled at me

and put sarcastic emphasis on his words. *"To your knowledge*, have you told anybody *except our trusted allies...* anything that might compromise national security or violate your oath as an agent?"

Asshole.

"No," I snapped.

The green light flashed, and Holt fired the next question at me. "To your knowledge, and assuming you can trust our allies, have you *done* anything that might compromise national security or violate your oath as an agent?"

"No."

Green light.

"At any time, did you *intend* to do anything that might compromise national security or violate your oath as an agent?"

"No."

The green light flashed again and Holt shrugged and turned to the roomful of people. "Those are the only questions I have. Her conscious actions and intentions are innocent; and if she's been programmed there's no point in asking her about it. We'll have to question Nora Taylor for that. Anybody else have questions for Kelly?"

Nobody spoke, and Holt jerked his chin at Jack. "Okay, you can unhook her." As Jack moved to obey, he added, "Kelly, any questions for us?"

I stared at him. So many questions. "What... what the hell *happened*?"

Holt smirked. "After you passed the lie detector test at the secured facility we knew Grandin was trying to frame you but we couldn't prove it, and with his diplomatic immunity as an agent-"

The door crashed open and everyone jerked, whipping around to face the threat with weapons at the ready.

Reggie bounded into the room, apparently oblivious to the small arsenal pointed at him. "We *nailed* them!" he shouted. "Nailed the fucking bastards! We know how they did it!"

"Thanks for knocking," Holt snapped, holstering his pistol. Everyone else stood down, too.

Reggie blinked as though barely registering the fact that he'd nearly taken a volley of bullets approximately equal to his body weight. "Whatever," he said with an impatient wave of his hand. "I'm telling you, we solved it!"

"Well, don't wait to enlighten us," Holt said sarcastically.

Reggie launched into his explanation as though Holt hadn't spoken. "It was a setup right from the start. Mitchell and Pino faked the whole thing, and they admitted everything when I confronted them with it on the phone a few minutes ago. The rebar was fake. It was plastic microbeads cast in a loose matrix of organic resin so it looked like steel rebar from a distance. The glass vial held a miniscule amount of fuming nitric acid. When the vial broke, the released vapour was concentrated enough to destroy the organic bonds within the small containment vessel, but it dispersed harmlessly into the air and got sucked out by the ventilation fans when the vessel was opened."

He hesitated. "Well, it was mostly harmless. Mitchell and Pino had some respiratory and mucous membrane irritation, but they passed it off as a reaction to the smoke."

"What did...?" I began, but Reggie was already hurrying on with his explanation.

"So as soon as the smoke obscured everything, Pino

opened the containment vessel, blew the plastic microbeads onto the floor where they'd look like ordinary dirt, and threw a pinch of metal powder into the bottom of the containment vessel to make it look as though metal powder had been stolen." Reggie cast a triumphant look around the table. "And get this: We found traces of metal powder in the storage bag where Grandin had stored his so-called diplomatic archival material."

"So that's how he did it!" I exclaimed. "The bastard had the bag of metal powder on him right from the start. He put it in the archival storage bag to avoid the metal detector search, and then while I was unconscious he planted it in my parka pocket."

"You have the metal powder?" Reggie demanded.

"Yes... well, no; not exactly. It's inside a toilet tank in a restaurant on Macleod Trail."

"Excellent." Reggie grinned, the good side of his mouth turning up despite the immobility of his prosthetic face mask. "We'll be able to match its chemical composition and nail Grandin for sure. And when I told Pino that Grandin had been arrested, he broke down and told the whole story. Mitchell was in on faking the demo, but he thought the order had come down from his higher-ups to feed us disinformation instead of revealing actual classified technology. He didn't know about the rest of the plot."

He shot me an 'I-told-you-so' look. "Remember I said Pino had been caught stealing research?"

When I nodded, Reggie went on, "Grandin knew about that, so he leaned on Pino. Threatened to have his security clearance pulled, create another big shitstorm unless Pino cooperated with him. So Grandin gashed Pino's leg that morning and put the dirty bandage on it; and as soon the room filled with smoke, Grandin handed Pino the plastic blowgun he'd used to shoot the ketamine dart. Pino hid it under his bandage, and then flushed it down the toilet as soon as he had the chance."

"Nice sleuthing," Holt drawled. "Not really relevant since we already knew Kelly didn't have anything to do with the theft of the metal powder; but at least it kept you out of trouble. More or less."

"Bite me," Reggie retorted. "There never was a theft; and Mitchell and Pino were dicking with all of us, not just Kelly. Five Eyes needs to know that." He turned and marched out.

"Where was I?" Holt asked, as though Reggie's brilliant deductions had been nothing more than an irksome appropriation of his spotlight.

"You were telling me what happened after I went off-grid," I reminded him.

"I knew your orders were to investigate Nora Taylor," Holt said. "So all I had to do was wait for you to contact her." He scowled at Ian. "And MI6 here was supposed to cooperate."

"And I did," Ian said mildly. "I played up to Grandin and pretended I wanted to capture Storm as badly as he did. I built a rapport with him while you investigated behind the scenes; and I made sure you were in place to capture him when he made his move."

I eyed Holt. "So you were right around the corner the whole time?"

Holt gave me a self-satisfied smirk. "Of course. With a full tactical team; and a helicopter on alert; and the Calgary police were diverting traffic from blocks away." His tone turned patronizing. "You should have noticed there was no traffic."

Shit, and I'd been thinking we were alone because of the bad weather.

I didn't admit that.

"I'm glad you recorded the whole thing," I said to Ian instead. "I called in with a secured phone but nobody answered. If not for you..." My throat went dry at the thought and I didn't finish the sentence.

"When did you call?" Holt demanded.

"When Grandin shot Dirk."

All eyes turned to Dermott, who flushed. "I didn't get any call."

"I called," I repeated. "It rang at least three times."

Stemp turned an icy gaze on Dermott and spoke for the first time. "*Three times?*"

Dermott went redder. "So what? It didn't change anything. I don't see why the Director should answer secured phones anyway. That's an analyst's job."

"I answer secured phones because my agents' safety is my top priority," Stemp said in a voice that could have frozen nitrogen. "If you choose not to do so, then it is your duty to hand off the task to an analyst who *will* make it their top priority."

"You can't talk to me like that," Dermott blustered. "I'm the Director of Operations and-"

A throat-clearing interrupted him as General Briggs rose, exuding his usual air of effortless authority. "Thank you for your service, Dermott," he said. "But Stemp's suspension was only a concession to Five Eyes in the first place. Now that Agent Kelly has completed her lie detector test, the chain of command agrees..." He swept the rest of the gold-braided crowd with a gaze that challenged anyone to argue. They all nodded, and Briggs went on, "Director Stemp has been cleared of any wrongdoing and is reinstated, effective immediately."

"Well, *fine!*" Dermott snapped, and sprang to his feet. He strode out and slammed the door behind him.

In the momentary silence, Ian turned to me. "I'm sorry this sting turned out to be so dangerous for you." He sighed. "And lethal to Dirk. As far as we know, he wasn't involved in the plot against you."

"So why was he even there?" I asked. "Why would Grandin bring him along only to shoot him?"

Holt spoke up. "Grandin's not talking yet, but we guess he wanted to make it look as though he was following the extradition procedure. Only FBI has the authority to arrest, so he needed Dirk to keep up the pretense. Plus Dirk's murder would have been another serious charge against you so even if you managed to escape, Grandin would have the law on his side while he continued to push for your extradition."

I swallowed to wet my suddenly dry throat. "Um... about those extradition requests...?"

"Withdrawn," General Briggs said. "The United States is cooperating fully with our investigation of Grandin, and the United Kingdom has also withdrawn their extradition request now that they know it was Grandin who drugged Nora Taylor."

Thank God. One more hurdle cleared.

But not the most important one.

"So that means John and Arnie and Skidmark and

Reggie and Jack won't be facing any charges," I said, and held my breath.

If I said it as though it was a foregone conclusion, maybe everybody else would agree...

"Correct," Stemp said.

I sagged with relief.

"That concludes our business here," Briggs said. "Stemp, we'll leave the questioning of Nora Taylor and the decision regarding Kelly's status to you." He shot a commanding look around the table. "Dismissed." He rose and strode out.

In his wake, Stemp added, "Kelly, Travers, and Holt; stay."

Everyone else rose and moved toward the door. The gold-braided crowd left first. Spider came over to hug me on the way out, but his face was strained and I could feel him trembling.

"Good luck," he whispered, squeezing me fiercely. "I... I hope..." He gulped and hurried away without completing the sentence.

Skidmark lingered, helping Ian into a wheelchair that I hadn't noticed behind the crowd in the conference room. When Ian was settled, Skidmark wheeled him over.

"No hard feelings, I hope," Ian murmured.

I lowered my voice in deference to his headache. "No, of course not. Thank you for everything you did. Will you forgive me for tranquilizing you, too?"

"Of course." He smiled with a ghost of his usual joie de vivre. "All part of the game."

My heart clenched at his pallor and the lines of pain etched on his face. "I hope you feel better soon," I added. "You must have a hell of a concussion."

"Yes," he whispered. "My only remaining goal is to go to bed for a very long time."

"I'll get you back upstairs and into the ambulance," Skidmark said cheerfully before turning to me with a grin. "And I don't owe you fifty bucks after all. He recognized me, but that wasn't our bet. I bet you that he wouldn't rat me out, and he didn't."

I made a face of mock disgust. "Fine. I'll let you weasel out of it this time, old man." I stood and hugged him. "Thanks," I whispered.

He squeezed me in return. "No problem." He drew back, his hands on my shoulders as he eyed me steadily. "No matter what happens... it's been an honour to serve with you."

I swallowed the lump in my throat and croaked, "Thanks. You, too."

Skidmark nodded and pushed the wheelchair away, his rapid breathing loud in the silence.

Kane and Hellhound were hovering behind me, and I turned to look up at them. "You'd better help him. He won't even make it to the elevator before he runs out of breath."

"Guess we don't have a choice," Hellhound said reluctantly. "Good luck, darlin'. Love ya." He gathered me into a hug, his lips pressed to my hair.

"I love you, too," I whispered.

We held each other for a long moment before he released me. Kane stood uncertainly, and I went to him without hesitation and wrapped him in a hug, too. His arms came gently around me and I pressed my face into his muscular chest.

If Sam had twisted my mind to fear Kane's love, could I

overcome the programming?

But if Nora said I'd been programmed, I wouldn't live long enough to try...

I pulled away. "You'd better go after Skidmark."

They nodded and each squeezed my hand before they left. Their grip should have been comforting, but the warmth of their hands couldn't dispel the chill at my heart.

This was it.

Nora would be questioned.

And her answers would determine whether I lived or died.

CHAPTER 49

When only Stemp, Holt, Jack, and the two guards remained with me in the conference room, Stemp rose and nodded to the two guards.

"Please escort us to Nora Taylor," he said. His gaze coasted over me, his face devoid of expression.

The guards took their place behind and ahead of me, and we marched out of the room. Too afraid to think about what lay ahead, I studied Stemp's back as he strode in front.

What was he feeling right now?

Anger at me for concealing that his parents were agents? Or for not turning myself in as soon as I found out I might be programmed?

Fear that I might have revealed the existence of his wife and daughter?

Regret that he might have to kill me?

Or relief and triumph at the knowledge that if he killed me I would cease to be a threat?

Or maybe he felt nothing. Maybe he turned off all his emotions while at work.

I wished I could do that.

Too soon, we rounded the last corner and stopped in

front of a closed conference room door. The guard beside it eyed us impassively as Stemp nodded to our two escorts, who took places on the other side and across from the door.

Three guards. Not for Nora.

For me. In case I had been programmed...

I sucked in an unsteady breath as Stemp opened the door and gestured me inside. I crept through, locking eyes with Nora.

She sat in a comfortable chair with a teacup on the table beside her. Like a guest. Not like a prisoner.

Not like me.

"Hello, Dani-dear," she said gently.

I gave her a nod, unable to trust my voice.

Holt took up a position beside me, just out of arm's reach. I wasn't fooled by his apparently casual posture. Stemp stood on my other side, just as dangerous as Holt and even more frightening with his cold control.

"Dr. Travers," he said, motioning Jack forward. "Please set up the lie detector."

Jack moved forward to secure the electrodes around Nora's forehead. After she had finished calibrating the instruments, she looked up. "Ready for your questions now, Director."

"Very well," Stemp said. "I'm activating the video recording..." He keyed the appropriate commands into a small remote before continuing, "Dr. Travers, you're dismissed. I'll let you know when we're finished."

She wordlessly clasped my hands with cold fingers before hurrying out and closing the door behind her.

Stemp turned back to me. "Kelly, you may begin questioning."

"Me?" Shock popped the word out of my mouth before I could stop it.

"If you wish." Stemp eyed me, his expression giving away nothing. "If not, Holt or I will do so."

Was he testing me?

Or was he only trying to make this easier on me? He of all people would understand how I was feeling right now.

But did I really want to ask the questions?

I glanced at Holt, and Stemp added, "Holt has been briefed regarding all your activities with the Department, and his security clearance has been upgraded accordingly."

My heart wavered between relief and dismay. I wouldn't have to watch what I said around Holt now; but his upgraded security clearance probably meant I'd be working with him more in the future.

Shit.

But I wouldn't be working with anybody ever again if Nora didn't give the right answers...

I turned to face her, but she was already speaking to Stemp. "I'll have to ask you to leave now. As I told you earlier, what I have to say is for Aydan's ears only. I won't answer questions if I'm being observed or recorded."

"Understandable," Stemp replied smoothly. "I apologize for the inconvenience, and we don't expect you to divulge any classified information. But we are aware that you told Agent Kelly you are her mother; and also that you said Sam Kraus had embedded secret commands in Agent Kelly's mind. For your own legal protection and also for ours, you must confirm or deny only those two questions under the lie detector with witnesses."

I studied him, searching for a clue in that unreadable

façade. Was he lying?

"Only those two questions?" Nora asked.

"Yes," Stemp confirmed.

"Oh." She relaxed. "All right, then. Go ahead and ask."

Stemp gestured for me to proceed.

Suddenly I couldn't speak.

What if she was really my mother?

What if she wasn't?

Holt shifted impatiently but Stemp stood motionless, watching me with that disturbing reptilian gaze.

"Are..." My voice came out in a croak, and I cleared my throat. "Are you... my m-mother?"

Nora lifted her chin in that wrenchingly familiar gesture and smiled at me. "Yes."

The green light flashed.

My heart stopped.

My knees wobbled and Stemp's strong hand closed around my upper arm, steadying me. "Do you need to sit?" he asked quietly.

"N-No." I sucked in a breath and locked my knees, aware that my entire body was vibrating but unable to stop it. My head floated dizzyingly and I realized I was breathing too fast, shallow ineffectual panting.

I forced a long, slow belly breath. In... two... three... four...

Out... two... three... four.

Holt frowned. "Come on, Kelly, spit out the second question. I'd like to get out of here in time for supper."

Supper.

Nichele and Dave's wedding was in a couple of hours.

I wouldn't make it.

I would never see the light of day again, because Nora had been telling the truth.

She was my mother.

And that meant Sam had programmed me.

Despair drained the last of my emotions and my voice came out completely flat. "So is your real name Nola Kelly, and was your maiden name Nola Smithers?"

She smiled again, as though she wasn't ripping my world apart. "Yes."

Green light.

"Formerly married to Gordon Kelly, my father?"

"Yes."

Green light again.

There was no other way to ask the question.

I moved on, feeling nothing but leaden exhaustion. "And did Sam Kraus plant secret mental programming in my brain?"

"Yes," Nora said without hesitation.

The light blinked red.

Red.

My knees buckled and I staggered. Only Stemp's grip on my arm kept me from falling.

Nora frowned. "There's something wrong with your polygraph. I'm telling the truth. Ask the question again."

I couldn't speak.

After a moment of silence, Stemp rephrased the question. "Are you aware of any subliminal programming in Aydan's mind?"

"Yes!" Nora crossed her arms and frowned at the blinking red light. "Your polygraph is defective."

I found my voice at last, a papery whisper that hurt my

throat. "It's not a polygraph. You're a good enough liar that you can probably beat a polygraph, but this is a new kind of lie detector." I summoned the strength for the last two words, my heart burning with bitter betrayal. "It's infallible."

"Wha...?" Nora blanched and swayed in her chair, but a moment later her spine stiffened and her chin came up. "That's ridiculous."

"But it is the truth," Stemp said in clinical tones. "Would you care to explain why you lied about the programming?"

"I didn't lie!" She glared at us, but she must have read the reality in our faces. The starch went out of her and she reached a trembling hand toward me. "Dani-dear... Aydan... I'm sorry. I'm so sorry, but I had to be sure you'd talk to me. I was so afraid you wouldn't want to have anything to do with me..." Her lips trembled.

Frozen in an icy coffin, my heart didn't even quiver. A dead voice fell from my lips.

"You were right. I don't." I turned and tottered toward the door.

"Aydan, *please!*"

I didn't stop.

Nora's voice rose. "Wait! Don't let her go!"

"Kelly, wait." Stemp's flat voice halted me but I didn't turn.

Far beyond the ability to think, I stood there as though transformed to a pillar of salt in retribution for my mother's sins.

"Oh, thank you!" Nora quavered. "Aydan..."

"Nola Kelly." Stemp's iron-hard voice cut across hers. "Or Nora Taylor, if you prefer. Under the terms of your diplomatic immunity, you are officially free to go. Please complete the necessary paperwork with Agent Holt, after which he will escort you out."

Nora's voice rose. "No, I need to speak with Aydan, now!"

"Why?" Stemp snapped. "If you are withholding information pertinent to this case-"

"No, of course not! I just want to speak with my daughter. I'm her *mother*, for God's sake, I haven't seen her in *thirty years...*"

I tuned out her voice, letting her pleas blur into gibberish.

Stemp came up beside me. "Let's go," he said quietly. As we went out the door, he spoke to the guard on our left. "Notify Dr. Travers that she can pick up the lie detector now."

"Yes, sir."

I plodded down the corridor, concentrating only on placing one foot in front of the other. Stemp strode beside me in silence.

When we reached the stairwell to the exit chamber I stopped. Unable to face him, I stared straight ahead. "Is... is it... over?"

He let out a small breath that might have been a sigh. "Yes and no. Your status as an agent is unchanged with the Department."

"And..." I didn't dare glance at him. "My status with you... personally?"

"Unchanged. As usual, you are beyond reproach both personally and professionally, and you are free to go." He hesitated, and when he spoke again his tone was wry. "Or as free as any of us are."

To my own surprise, that drew a bitter half-laugh from my throat.

He went on, "As yet, we haven't identified Grandin's buyer. Holt will continue questioning Grandin in the hope of uncovering more information. We discovered that your mother is legally a British citizen, and as a member of their intelligence agency she is fully protected by diplomatic immunity; so we may never be able to investigate her to our satisfaction. I suspect that reconnecting with you on a personal level was not her primary motive. Although..." Dry humour crept into his voice. "Parents have been known to go to unreasonable lengths for their offspring."

I did turn to him then, finding him smiling. In spite of my own turmoil, my lips quirked up in return.

"Were you surprised?" I asked.

Stemp startled me with a belly laugh. "'Surprised' does not even begin to describe my feelings."

"But... you're okay with it?"

"More than okay." He sobered, but the softness didn't leave his eyes. "Thank you, Aydan. Thank you for believing in my parents when I could not; and for not allowing me to turn my back on them. I am grateful beyond words."

I blinked away the sudden moisture in my eyes. "I'm so glad you've reconciled. With... with Skidmark, too?"

"With Skidmark especially," Stemp replied, smiling. "I have immense respect for anyone who can fool me that completely for that long."

I swallowed the lump in my throat. "That's great. Well, you'd better get going. Don't waste any more time that you could be spending with them."

He started forward, but stopped when I didn't come with

him. He turned, frowning. "I thought you would be eager to escape the secured area."

"I..." The lump in my throat swelled. "I... can't face anybody just yet," I whispered. "Please tell John and Arnie I've gone to the bathroom and I'll be up in a few minutes."

"Very well." He hesitated, his gaze compassionate. "I'm sorry about... your mother."

I squared my shoulders to prevent myself from collapsing. "That woman may be my biological parent, but she's not my mother."

CHAPTER 50

Inside the washroom, I crept into a stall and locked the door. Curling down onto the toilet seat, I rested my forehead on my knees and wrapped my arms over my head. For once, I was comforted by the knowledge that I was interred in a subterranean vault.

Maybe the earth would close around me, burying me forever in blessed silence and solitude. No more fear. No more pain. No more fucked-up knee-jerk beliefs that had turned out to be my own after all.

If Sam had programmed my mind, Stemp might have killed me; but instead I'd been handed a life sentence without parole, trapped in the torment between my ears.

I hugged myself tighter and a whimper escaped. I had almost dared to hope that I might finally be free...

Stop it.

I sat up and shook myself.

No.

No, goddamn it, I *would* be free.

I shoved myself to my feet, straightening my spine. This new self-awareness was a gut-punch, but it was also a beneficial kick in the ass. I didn't have to keep reacting the same way forever. Kane was probably right; I'd never get back to 'normal'. But with enough time and work, maybe I could change.

Dammit, I *would*.

When I emerged from the washroom, the sound of approaching voices made me spin to retreat inside again.

Too late.

Reggie, Jack, and Katie rounded the corner and spotted me.

"Kelly!" Reggie exclaimed. "I don't see any guards. Does that mean you're in the clear?"

I pushed a smile onto my face. "Yep. Thanks for all you did. And Jack, Katie... thank you."

"Oh, Aydan." Jack hurried forward to wrap me in a hug. "Thank God. We were so worried about you."

"Thanks, Jack." I hugged her in return. "And Reggie and Katie... you guys were brilliant! I can't believe you figured that stuff out."

Katie grinned. "We're scientists. It's what we do." She nudged Reggie with a suggestive hip. "Maybe now we can let our hair down and have a bit of fun."

Reggie stiffened and my heart sank.

"Katie..." he said in a gentler tone than I'd ever heard him use. "There's something I need to tell you."

Her smile faded. "I'm not going to like it, am I?"

He sighed. "Probably not. Working with you has been a blast. You're brilliant and beautiful and funny, and-"

"And you don't fancy me," she said flatly. "Got it. So why did you blow all that bull dust in front of everybody?"

I caught Jack's eye and backed away, hoping to give them some privacy.

"Oh, not so fast now." Katie snagged my sleeve. "I want witnesses. Make sure the ratbag tells me the truth this time."

Reggie reddened, but looked her in the eye. "I honestly didn't think you felt that way about me. I thought you'd slap me down in public the way I did to you. That's what I deserved."

"Oh." She made a face. "It's no big deal; I just thought we could have a bit of fun."

"I'm sorry I wasn't honest with you," Reggie said. "But the truth is..." His gaze flicked to Jack, then focused on me. "I'm... in love with somebody else."

Oh, shit.

My heart plummeted to my toes. "Reggie, um... don't be too hasty..."

He frowned. Then his face cleared in comprehension and he let out a whoop of laughter. "Shit, Kelly, stop panicking. I wasn't talking about you. I wouldn't fuck up a perfectly good friendship. I meant..." He reached out, and Jack tucked her hand into his. "Honey and I are... together."

She smiled and leaned over to kiss him. "And he'll finally let me tell everybody."

I stood gaping like an idiot.

"Hey." Katie nudged me. "You're catching flies, love."

I closed my mouth, then opened it again. "Wh... When did... Well, shit. You sneaky bastards. So that was the big secret Jack was holding over you!"

"Congratulations to you both," Katie said sincerely. "Reggie, it's been fun. Next time you have a bit of a mystery, give me a call." She headed for the stairs. "Cheers, all!"

As soon as the door closed behind her, Reggie let out a breath. "Thank God. I can finally take off this stupid goddamn face and hand!"

Jack patted his arm. "Just hold onto your disguise for a few more minutes. Wait until she's out of the building."

I stared at the two of them for a few more moments while a grin slowly stretched my face. "Well, shit. I had no idea. Congratulations! I'm happy for you both!"

"Thank you," Jack said complacently. "I've been working on him a long time, you know. He's been very slow to respond."

Reggie snorted. "When I realized you were interested I responded so fucking fast I damn near tore a hole in my pants. But... I didn't want to rush into a relationship. It wasn't fair to you or the kids until I'd dealt with some of my shit. I've been working on cleaning up my language..."

"And mostly failing," Jack teased. "But you do very well around the children."

He grinned and kissed her again. "I'm not trying when I'm at work." His smile faded as he faced me. "But my main worry was my alcoholism. I was stalling, afraid to tell Honey about it; but after I tested myself at the meet-and-greet and failed, I knew I had to." He turned back to Jack. "And I still don't think this is a good idea. Alcoholics wreck families."

Jack frowned. "I won't deny that I've had a couple of sleepless nights pondering it." She waved a rueful hand at the dark circles under her eyes. "But as I pointed out earlier, it wasn't a realistic test for you to dive into a difficult social situation after an immensely stressful day and expect to be able to drink in moderation. I believe you're sincere about not relapsing again, and I'm willing to take a chance on you.

But I will unhesitatingly cut you out of my life if it becomes necessary."

Reggie looked into her eyes, his jaw firm with resolve. "That's the only reason I'm willing to try this. I'll try not to let you down."

Jack smiled. "I know you won't." She turned to me. "We shouldn't keep you, Aydan. You must be eager to get above ground."

Suddenly I was.

When I hurried out of the time delay chamber into the lobby, it was filled with people. Katie and her team occupied one corner along with their luggage; Moonbeam, Karma, Skidmark, and Stemp formed a smiling knot near the door; and Kane and Hellhound stood at parade rest near the reception chairs, frowning.

As I emerged, their expressions lightened. I hurried over to hug each of them in turn.

"How did it go?" Hellhound demanded. "Stemp said everythin' was okay, but he didn't tell us what happened."

Resisting the urge to burrow into his arms and stay there forever, I squared my shoulders and held my voice level. "Nora Taylor is actually my mother, Nola Kelly."

"And...?" Kane studied me worriedly.

"And she was lying about the programming."

I found myself engulfed in a three-way hug while they murmured relief and commiseration. I clutched them both, their love and concern feeling for the first time like a bastion of safety instead of smothering bonds.

When I pulled away at last, Moonbeam was approaching with her usual luminous smile. "Oh, my dear. You have certainly borne the burdens of the universe lately." She hugged me, a motherly embrace that filled my heart with bittersweet memories.

Banishing them, I hugged her tightly. At least I had one mother figure I could love and respect.

She greeted Arnie and John with hugs as well, then turned back to me with her smile fading as she held out my phone. "I texted Blaze Featherwind when it became obvious that you wouldn't be able to get to Calgary in time. She knows you won't be there for the wedding, but I'm sure she would appreciate a call from you."

Accepting the phone with a heavy heart, I checked my watch. Five-thirty.

A two-hour drive to Calgary...

"Maybe they can delay it a bit," I said with rising hope. "It's scheduled for seven o'clock with a cocktail reception afterward. If they just had a few cocktails first, I could get there in time for a ceremony at seven-thirty..."

Moonbeam's expression made me trail off.

"Oh, dear," she said. "You haven't been above-ground since noon, have you?" She took my hand in a sympathetic clasp. "I'm so sorry, Storm Cloud Dancer, but it's been snowing all day and the highway is closed. You couldn't make it even if you tried."

"Oh."

The single syllable fell out of my mouth and plummeted into silence. I flopped into the nearest chair and closed my eyes to hide the stinging of tears.

I had tried so hard.

Not good enough.

CHAPTER 51

Fortunately nobody touched me or offered sympathy, and I managed to cram my emotions back into their usual box. Dragging myself upright in the chair, I held my voice level.

"Thanks, Moonbeam Meadow Sky. I really appreciate all you've done. I'll read through the text conversation before I phone her." I slumped back on the cushions and started scrolling through texts.

The earliest ones were Bridezilla moments, written with Nichele's usual impish humour. Reading them and Moonbeam's deceptively realistic replies, I smiled in spite of myself.

My smile faded as I read the more recent texts. Even though Nichele's comments were upbeat and she poked fun at the ongoing disasters, I knew how much she had needed someone there to help her with the myriad details, to laugh with her and commiserate over fuckups like the florist who didn't seem to know an orchid from a lily.

When I read Nichele's response to the 'I'm so sorry but I won't be able to make it' text, my eyes filled all over again.

"*Hey, girl, it's okay. We know how hard you tried. When you're back, we'll get dressed up and re-enact the whole thing just for you. Luv U 4ever!"*

Moonbeam had responded, "Luv U 4ever 2!"

I sank my head into my hands and took some deep breaths. Dammit, as soon as I heard Nichele's voice on the other end of the line I was going to bawl like an idiot; I just knew it.

When I felt a gentle touch on my shoulder I straightened, expecting Moonbeam; but instead Stemp stood beside my chair.

"The Australian team is leaving now," he said formally. "They will be flying by Griffon directly to the Calgary airport. I understand you have a pressing personal engagement in Calgary, and there are seats available in the helicopter."

For a moment I sat blinking with dull incomprehension. Then hope rose, a slow warm tide swelling into my chest.

"Are you... offering me a ride to Calgary...?" I hardly dared to say the words in case I'd somehow misinterpreted his offer.

"Yes." Stemp smiled and glanced at Kane and Hellhound. "And there would be sufficient seats for you to bring two guests."

His words sank in, and I rocketed out of the chair and seized him in a bear hug, pinning his arms to his sides. "Thank you, thank you! Omigod, I have to call Nichele right away..." Half laughing and half crying, I released him self-consciously.

He gave me a stiff nod and straightened his suit jacket, but he was smiling as he said "Be ready in five minutes," and turned away.

My shaking fingers barely managed to punch in Nichele's number.

When she answered with a falsely-bright, "Hey, girl!",

my throat constricted.

"I'm coming!" I babbled. "I hope you have that dress ready for me because my luggage is gone and I've got nothing but jeans and boots and I'm on this crazy flight that doesn't get in until six-thirty, but I'm coming! I'll be there! Don't start without me!"

"Omigod, *omigod* ... DAVE!" Nichele's shout was filled with joy. "SHE'S COMING! AYDAN'S GOING TO MAKE IT AFTER ALL!" She returned to the phone at her normal volume, laughing and sniffling at the same time. "Omigod, girl, this is the best news I've had all day! You wouldn't *believe* everything that's gone wrong; the caterer slipped on the ice and dropped the wedding cake, and the string quartet we hired is stuck in Banff so we don't have any music, but *omigod* I'm so glad you're coming!"

"I'll be there! I'm leaving right now..." Inspiration seized me. "I'll see if Arnie can bring his guitar to do your music. He can play beautiful classical music, or whatever you want..."

In the background, Hellhound nodded acquiescence, looking pleased.

"And..." I questioned Kane with my eyes. "...Is it still okay if I bring a guest...?"

He nodded, smiling.

Nichele pounced. "Hell yes, girl! Please tell me you're bringing Hot John!"

"All right." I winked at Kane. "I'm bringing Hot John."

Kane's smile widened to a wicked grin.

"Omigod, *seriously?* Or are you just messing with me?"

"Seriously," I confirmed.

"Omigod, girl, *finally!* It's about time you came to your senses!" Nichele switched to planning mode. "Dave will pick you up at the airport and then-"

"No, it's okay, I'll grab a cab," I demurred. "You and Dave stay at your party and enjoy your guests, and I'll call John and Arnie and we'll be there as soon as we can. I have to get on my plane now. See you soon!"

A little after seven o'clock the taxi deposited me outside the upscale hotel where Nichele and Dave had rented a ballroom. Feeling self-conscious, I hurried through the elegant lobby in my jeans and boots and parka. When I got to the ballroom I poked my head in the door, remembering as I did that I hadn't even brushed my hair since... shit, since before Grandin had attacked me.

Raking my fingers through the tangles, I was about to retreat to the nearest bathroom for a date with my hairbrush when Nichele's squeal cut across the murmur of voices.

"THERE SHE IS!"

She and Dave descended on me and we staged an embarrassingly emotional hugfest. At last we pulled apart and Nichele wiped her eyes, smearing her makeup beyond repair.

"Oh-em-gee!" She giggled, surveying the black smudges on her fingertips. "I must look like a raccoon. And you look like..."

"Absolute shit," I completed her sentence, and we all laughed.

Dave took charge of the situation. "Okay, you two go and do your girl stuff. I'll hold the fort here."

"Thanks, Sweetie!" Nichele kissed him, then seized my arm and hurried me to the elevator. "I have your dress and shoes and everything up in our room. And we have to do something about your *hair,* omi*god...*"

Half an hour under Nichele's expert hands transformed me from a bag lady to a tired-looking woman who could at least enter a nice restaurant without getting kicked out.

"Hold still," she commanded. "I'm just going to fix those dark circles under your eyes."

I obeyed, and several minutes later she pronounced me finished.

As we emerged from the elevator into the lobby, I said, "Lucky you bought matching shoes. Hiking boots would have been quite a look with this." I indicated the dark green gown that hugged my body in all the right places while concealing the not-so-right bulges and jiggles.

"You look awesome," she said with satisfaction. "I knew that dress would be perfect on you."

"Thanks, Nichele. I mean... really." I halted, looking down at her. "Thanks for being my best friend. I'm so glad I can be here to watch you and Dave get married."

She dabbed at her brimming eyes. "Stop it, or I'll have to go back and fix my makeup again." She flung her arms around me. "Thanks for being *my* best friend. I'm so glad you're here. It just wouldn't have been the same without you."

As I hugged her in return, a warm baritone voice said, "I hope you're saving a hug for me."

"An' me," added a familiar rasp.

"John and Arnie!" I straightened and turned, my jaw dropping. "Wow, you look... wow. Just... wow!"

Both men smiled at me. John's perfectly-tailored dark suit and crisp white shirt showed off his short dark hair and breathtaking physique to perfection. Arnie was casually sexy in a tan suede blazer over an open-necked black dress shirt and dark blue jeans, his beard neatly shorn.

"Well, come on!" Nichele tugged us toward the ballroom, a tiny dynamo in a designer silk wedding dress. "Let's get this party started!"

As we stepped into the room, I leaned over to whisper to Arnie, "How's your wedding phobia?"

He chuckled. "Alive an' screamin'. I'm tellin' myself this ain't a weddin'; it's just another gig with everybody dressed up a bit better'n usual."

"Hold that thought." I gave him a quick kiss before Nichele whisked him away to the front of the room with his guitar.

Taking a much-needed moment, I faded back against a wall and took in the scene. Despite the absence of the ill-fated wedding cake, the rest of the ballroom reflected Nichele's impeccable taste. The linens on the cocktail tables glowed in rich jewel-toned colours accented with floral centrepieces that managed to be festive without actually screaming 'Christmas'. Banks of fresh flowers surrounded a bower decorated with a fairyland of tiny white lights and misty tulle. Tuxedoed waitstaff circulated with silver trays of gourmet canapés and flutes of champagne.

As the first notes of Arnie's guitar began, Kane dropped back to stand beside me, and I reached over to lace my fingers in his. He smiled and leaned down to place his lips next to my ear. "I like this new easiness between us," he murmured.

I cuddled a little closer. "Me, too."

My old demons stirred, whispering poison. What if Kane started expecting me to be like this all the time? He would be hurt and disappointed later...

I couldn't help easing away a fraction.

Kane's grip loosened instantly. "It's all right; I don't have any expectations," he said gently. "Let's just take it as it comes."

I let out a breath and relaxed. "Thanks."

Nichele hurried over. "Hey, girl, I need my matron of honour!"

"I'm all yours."

We retreated to the small alcove at the ballroom entrance, and Nichele clutched my hand. "This is it." She drew a deep breath. "The point of no return."

"Are you okay?" I asked.

"I..." Her grip on my hand tightened and she let out an unsteady breath. "I'm scared."

My heart clenched. "Oh, Nichele, I know. Believe me, I get it. But-"

"But I'm okay," she said firmly. She peeked around the corner, where Dave and his best man had taken their places in front of the bower. Dave glanced back, and when their eyes met I glimpsed the radiant bond of love between them.

Nichele drew back to face me, her smile glowing. "I'm more than okay. I'm sure. I'm scared spitless, but I'm *sure*."

I threw my arms around her, barely able to speak around the lump in my throat. "I'm so glad. I'm so happy for you."

Then the wedding march sounded, and I led Nichele down the aisle.

Soon my best friend was saying 'I do' to the steadfast man she'd waited her whole life to find. Dave and Nichele were pronounced man and wife at last, and our joy overflowed in toasts and dancing; laughter and happy tears.

Much later, I stood at the edge of the room with aching feet and a full heart, watching Dave and Nichele bid fond goodbyes to their guests. The two of them orbited each other comfortably, coming together with kisses and touches, their brief partings bridged by the love shining in their eyes.

An intricate classical melody floated to my ears, and I stood watching in awe as Arnie's beautiful hands drew magic from the guitar strings.

"What a gift," Kane said quietly behind me.

I eased backward to lean against his chest, and his arm tucked lightly around my waist.

Arnie's talent. Nichele and Dave's long-awaited love. And this one perfect moment.

Gifts beyond price.

I smiled. "Yes."

The first book in the series, NEVER SAY SPY, has had over 450,000 downloads to date, and stayed on Kindle's 'Women Sleuths' Top 100 list for 60 consecutive months.

Diane enjoys target shooting, gardening, auto mechanics, painting (art, not walls), music, and martial arts; and loves food and drink almost as much as she loves her husband. They live in the wilds of British Columbia, Canada, where they get all the adrenaline rush they could ever want by growing fruit trees in bear country.

Want to know what else is roiling around in the cesspit of my mind? Drop by my blog and website at dianehenders.com, check out the extras, and don't forget to leave a comment in the guest book to say hi – I love hearing from you! Or you can connect with me on Facebook at:

https://www.facebook.com/authordianehenders.

See you there!

About Me

Before I started writing fiction, I had a checkered career: technical writer, computer geek, and interior designer. I'm good at two out of three of those. Fortunately, I had the sense to quit the one I sucked at (interior design).

When my mid-life crisis hit, I took up muay thai and started writing thrillers featuring a middle-aged female protagonist. ('Walter Mitty', you say? Nope, never heard of him.)

Writing and kicking the hell out of stuff seemed more productive than more typical mid-life-crisis activities like getting a divorce, buying a Harley Crossbones, and cruising across the country picking up men in sleazy bars; especially since it's winter most months of the year here in Canada.

It's much more comfortable to sit at my computer. And Harleys are expensive. Come to think of it, so are beer and gasoline.

Oh, and I still love my husband. There's that. So I stuck with the writing.

Diane Henders

And here's my "professional" bio, in case you need something more suitable for mixed company:

Diane Henders is the Kindle best-selling author of the NEVER SAY SPY series: Sexy thrillers packed with tension, laughs, profanity, and sometimes warm fuzzies.

A Request

Thanks for reading!

If you enjoyed this book, I'd really appreciate it if you'd take a moment to review it online.

Here are some suggestions for the "star" ratings:
Five stars: Loved the book and can hardly wait for the next one.
Four stars: Liked the book and plan to read the next one.
Three stars: The book was okay. Might read the next one.
Two stars: Didn't like the book. Probably won't read the next one.
One star: Hated the book. Would never read another in the series.

You can help prospective readers by writing a few sentences about what you liked or disliked about the book.

Thanks for taking the time to do a review!

Book 14 is available!

Visit my Books page at dianehenders.com/books for progress updates and announcements.